SARAH'S GAZE
FELL TO HIS MOUTH

His lower lip was somewhat fuller than the upper. Both were firm and strong. Unconsciously the top of her tongue darted out to moisten her own lips, which had suddenly gone dry.

"Don't," Philip murmured. His hands touched her shoulders. His mouth was warm and coaxing on hers, easing Sarah through the first shock of such intimacy until she began to relax. Only then did his arms go around her, drawing her into his embrace. Through the fine linen of his shirt, she felt for the first time the hardness of a male body so different from her own. Fascination robbed her of the will to resist. With a soft moan, she melted against him.

Sarah

Sarah

MAURA SEGER

WORLDWIDE

TORONTO · NEW YORK · LONDON · PARIS
AMSTERDAM · STOCKHOLM · HAMBURG
ATHENS · MILAN · TOKYO · SYDNEY

SARAH

Worldwide Library/August 1987

ISBN 0-373-97041-2

*For my parents in love and gratitude
for teaching me to love books and history.*

Part One

1848-1852

Chapter One

Lowell, Massachusetts

THE SCREAMS STOPPED in late afternoon. Seated in the shadows at the top of the stairs, Sarah Mackenzie listened to the silence. It pressed down on her narrow shoulders and further tightened the sharp features strained in agonized concentration.

When the screams had begun the previous afternoon, she had hidden in her room, her hands over her ears, trying without success to muffle the sounds. Mrs. Hobson, the cook, had found her there eventually and taken her down to the kitchen.

There had been murmurings among the servants about sending the children away, but they were powerless to do so and their relationship with their employer was not such that any would approach him to suggest it. Josiah Mackenzie was a stern man who believed in an implacable God. He saw no reason to spare his children the harshness of His hand.

Throughout the night Sarah had drifted in and out of sleep. By then the screams had been fainter and she had become less afraid of them. At least they told her that her mother was still nearby, fighting the terrible thing that was happening to her. Now the silence made her wonder.

There were dark shadows under her pale gray eyes. Her straight, thin nose was pinched at the nostrils. Above the curve of her chin, her lips were swollen where she had bitten them. Strands of wispy brown hair clung to her wide forehead. The sleeves of her dress were a little too short, revealing knobby wrists. She had grown three inches since early spring, along with other changes in her body that frightened her. Never plump, she had become so thin that her collarbones stuck out sharply above the modest collar of her dress.

"She's dying, you know." Sarah looked up. Her elder brother, Gideon, stood beside her, hands on his hips, his narrow face impassive. They were alike in features, but not expression. In Sarah's eyes there was a wistful yearning to always believe the best. In Gideon's was the fully formed conviction that the worst was always far more likely.

She turned away, staring into the shadows that hid the curve of the staircase. Despite the heat of the summer day, her hands were cold. "She's not."

"You don't know anything. Dr. Carter told her not to have any more babies. Nathan should have been the last."

Nathan was seven, Sarah twelve, Gideon thirteen. In between them, and since the birth of her youngest, Catherine Mackenzie had suffered innumerable miscarriages and two stillbirths in her attempts to be a dutiful wife.

The doctor came out of the room. He was a middle-aged man with a florid face, handlebar mustache and a prominent belly. He looked tired as he put on his jacket and refastened his collar. Behind him, Sarah caught a glimpse of Grandmother Mackenzie, her hands folded neatly at her waist. She was dressed in black, which she had worn for the last quarter century, since the death of her husband. Upon arriving at the house, she had removed her gloves but not her hat. It threw her features into shadow, hiding her thoughts.

"I'll be going down to tell Mr. Mackenzie now," the doctor said, "unless you'd rather..."

He looked hopeful for a moment, only to have that fade when she shook her head. "It would be best for him to hear it from you. Tell my son we will be here when he is ready to come up."

Behind her, Aunt Caroline nodded. She was a younger version of her mother, strong-boned with blunt features, pale eyes and a small mouth that reflected only two emotions, disapproval or self righteousness. It was a source of great bewilderment to her that despite her family's standing in Lowell, no man had ever asked for her hand. Her bitterness had grown over the years, as she saw so many other less deserving women marry, until it had become as much a part of her being as her untouched breasts and unfilled womb.

For as long as Sarah could remember, Aunt Caroline had smelled of lavender lozenges, carbolic soap and barley water. It was a smell the little girl somehow associated with illness, even though Aunt Caroline was quite proud of her rude good health. Unlike Sarah's mother, who was said not to come from strong stock.

Sarah had stood up when the door opened. As the doctor headed for the stairs, she pressed herself back against the wall. Her plain brown dress that brushed the tops of her high-buttoned boots blended almost perfectly with the wood paneling, but perhaps he would not have noticed her in any event. Certainly he gave no sign of seeing Gideon as he passed, wiping his forehead with a wilted handkerchief.

Her brother slipped after him, going soundlessly down the stairs. Holding her breath, Sarah crept to the door of her parents' room. Her grandmother was talking, but she couldn't make out what was being said. Her hand fumbled for the knob, turning it inch by inch until the door slid open a crack.

At first everything looked as it should. Heavy velvet curtains were pulled back from the windows, admitting late-afternoon light. Her mother's paisley sewing basket lay on the floor beside a large, overstuffed chair with needlepoint footstool. Sarah had sat there many times, when she wasn't stretched out on her stomach on the Chinese rug, tracing the intricate patterns of flowers and vines. A book lay open on the round pedestal table. Catherine Mackenzie had been reading Cooper's *The Deerslayer* before she became too weak to continue it.

Only gradually did Sarah realize that things were not as they should be. Piles of linens stained rust-brown were heaped on the floor. On a nearby dresser she could see a basin of reddish-brown water. A small bundle swathed in a sheet lay next to it. As she watched, Grandmother Mackenzie picked the bundle up. "We'll have to get this out of here before Josiah comes in."

"Put it in the dressing room," Aunt Caroline suggested.

Sarah barely heard her. She was staring at her mother stretched out on the four-poster bed. Catherine Mackenzie's face was waxy white. Her hair was covered by a white lace cap. She wore a white nightgown and lay beneath a white sheet. All the color seemed to have left her as though drained away along with the bulge in her belly, which was also gone.

There were footsteps on the stairs. Sarah pulled away from the door and shut it carefully. She stood with her hands clasped behind her back, staring at the floor.

Her father appeared first, closely followed by the doctor who seemed to have shed much of his self-importance and become somehow smaller. Sarah wasn't surprised; her father had that effect on people.

Josiah Mackenzie was a big man with broad shoulders and a barrel chest. At forty, he had the solid constitution of a farm boy, which he had once been. He wore a black wool suit and highly polished black boots. His hair, parted on the side and slicked back from the forehead, was as black as his sideburns and mustache.

In keeping with his overall size, he had a large head with prominent features. His black eyes were set deeply beneath thick brows. His nose had been broken years before and had never fully recovered; there was a slight bump in the center that he rubbed whenever he was preoccupied. His mouth under the black mustache was full and red.

He had a ruddy complexion with a smattering of broken blood vessels across the bridge of his nose and on his slightly pendulous cheeks. He shaved those cheeks each morning with a straight razor stropped on a leather strap that hung beside the porcelain basin in the room he shared with Sarah's mother. After shaving he always splashed on a few drops of bay rum.

Sarah smelled that as he went into the room without acknowledging her and left the door ajar. Gideon had trailed behind him but did not dare go inside. Sarah caught the flash of fear in his eyes.

"It's all right," she said. "Momma's asleep."

"Don't be stupid. The doctor came to tell Father that she's almost gone."

"Gone?"

"Dead. I told you, she's dying, because of the baby."

The thing wrapped in the sheet. Sarah had seen babies, but they weren't still like that or had their faces covered, and they weren't called "it." People were happy around babies, they didn't look angry like Father or impatient like the doctor.

"Be strong, Josiah," Grandmother Mackenzie was saying. "We've always known this would happen eventually."

"It's the lot of women," Aunt Caroline added, and Sarah tensed against the words. Barely understanding them, yet she felt a wave of resentment and rejection so strong that she trembled.

"I told you," Gideon rasped. "You never want to listen to me."

There was a good reason for that; Sarah didn't like her elder brother. She knew this was wrong and prayed each Sunday that her heart would change, but it did not. The older she got the more uncomfortable she was made by the boy who looked like her on the outside but in whom she could sense no resemblance.

"Where's Nathan?" she whispered, not wanting to remind the adults of their presence and risk being sent away.

"Downstairs, go get him."

Sarah shook her head. "No, he's too little."

Gideon looked scornful. "You're always coddling him. Why shouldn't he know?"

"He will, soon enough, but not this way." She was determined about that even if she wasn't exactly sure of why. Some instinct warned her to keep Nathan away. It was bad enough that she should be there, and Gideon.

The door knocker sounded downstairs. Sarah jumped slightly. Gideon grabbed her hand. "We'd better go."

"No, I don't want to." He was bigger than her and stronger, and usually she could not withstand him. But this time she sensed that he would back down rather than risk her making a fuss.

"Oh, all right," he said when he saw she was determined to stay. "Just don't blame me when you're sorry."

She already was, but could not bring herself to leave. It would be worse in her room, not knowing what was happening.

The Reverend Foster Betler was a young man only recently graduated from the seminary. He was fortunate in his family connections, which had secured for him his first congregation when most recent seminarians could expect assistantships at best. Thin and pale, he was plagued by a high-pitched voice still liable to crack, particularly during the sermons he regarded as an ordeal. Sarah and Gideon were united in their dislike of him, if only because they had to spend hours in church each Sunday listening to him.

"The ch-children," Reverend Betler stammered when he caught sight of them. "S-surely they shouldn't be here."

"Mr. Mackenzie has given no instructions to the contrary," Mrs. Hobson told him. She had shown him upstairs, but had no desire to linger. Not when nothing further could be done. Still, he was right about the children.

"Come along then," she said to Gideon and Sarah. "Nathan's in the kitchen and you should be, too."

Gideon did not bother to answer her, preferring to press his eye to the crack left in the door when Reverend Betler entered. It fell to Sarah to respond. "We'd rather stay here," she said softly. "In case Momma wants us."

Mrs. Hobson's apron twisted between her hands. "Child, that won't be."

"Of course it won't," Gideon said, turning back to them. "She's dying. I keep telling Sarah that, but she won't listen."

The housekeeper's mouth tightened. Beside her Sarah looked stricken, her shoulders trembling and her face averted. Mrs. Hobson put an arm around her. "You stay if you wish, Mister Gideon, but Miss Sarah should come with me."

Sarah was tempted to agree. In the cook's ample form, she found a measure of comfort. Unlike Aunt Caroline, Mrs. Hobson smelled of good things—ginger, butter, caro syrup. Her big hands, raw from a lifetime of hard work, held a world of gentleness. The voice that could flay the skin off a tardy delivery man or a laggard kitchen maid could sing with the softness of a spring breeze.

But Mrs. Hobson was not her mother. Sarah did not want to be any farther than she could help from the pale figure in the bed. "I'll stay," she murmured.

Living under their father's heavy hand, all the children had developed a deep streak of stubbornness. They might never show it to Josiah, but it was still there. Mrs. Hobson understood and accepted that. "Come downstairs if you change your mind," she said.

When she was gone, Gideon again pressed his eye to the crack in the door. "Reverend's praying."

Sarah could hear his high voice rising and falling. "Holy Father, in Your perfect wisdom You choose to call this woman to You. We humbly accept the righteousness of Your will and ask that You forgive her her sins and allow her to dwell with You in eternity. So, too, do we ask that You look with favor upon her husband, Josiah, Your servant, and upon their children. Amen."

"Amen." Josiah's response was firm, his mother and sister's equally so. In the silence that followed, Sarah stared at Gideon. For all his earlier bravado, the knowledge that their mother was dying had not truly sunk in. Now it had, and it left him pale and shaken.

Instinctively she reached out a hand to him. "At least she won't hurt anymore."

He jerked away from her touch. "Yes, she will, if she goes to hell."

"How could she? She never did anything wrong."

"Father says we're all sinners. We must guard against evil every day of our lives."

Sarah had heard that often enough but didn't understand it, at least not where people such as her mother were concerned. Catherine had been the source of all love and comfort. What sins could she possibly have committed?

But then there were so many, and they were so easy to stumble into. The slightest slip—a single thought of greed or pride or jealousy—could undo a lifetime of purity.

Bile rose in the back of Sarah's mouth. She swallowed and wiped her damp hands on her skirt. "What do you think will happen to us?"

Gideon shrugged. He had regained control of himself and looked once again impassive. Gray eyes, like hers yet not, narrowed as he considered Sarah. "Father will expect more of you now. You'll have to take over much of what mother used to do."

"I couldn't." She wouldn't have any idea where to begin. Catherine had run the large house so well as to make the task appear effortless. Only Sarah, who alone among her children spent any appreciable time with her, understood all that had gone into that.

From early morning until late at night, Catherine had overseen every aspect of domestic life. Though in keeping with her husband's position as mill owner, she had a good-sized staff, she was personally responsible for all the preparations of food and clothing, as well as the care of the house itself.

Always the watchwords were prudence and humility. "Nothing displeases God more than a prideful display," Josiah Mackenzie was fond of saying. He required a prompt accounting of every penny spent for the household and had not hesitated to punish his wife for anything he viewed as extravagance.

"I can't do it," Sarah repeated.

"Mother always had you with her, teaching you. Didn't you learn anything?"

"Of course I did, but not enough for that. In a few years, perhaps..."

"In a few years Father will have remarried and you can stop worrying about it." Gideon spoke so expressionlessly, as though stating a fact beyond dispute, that Sarah did not at first understand him. When she did, her gray eyes widened.

"Remarry? But he can't. No one could ever take mother's place."

Her brother looked at her pityingly. "Father is a very important man. It is only proper that he have a wife, particularly because he wants more children."

His thin body tensed as he thought of that. The spring before he had seen a stallion mate with a mare, and the image had remained imprinted on his mind. Often he thought of it at night when the strange new urgings of his body kept him awake. Once he had risen in the darkness and gone out to the hallway. Standing near the closed door to his parents' room, he had heard odd sounds, low animal gruntings that he realized only afterward must have come from his father.

His mother's pregnancy had embarrassed him; he had found it impossible to look at her directly once the evidence of what had been done to her began to show. It was easier to think about how relieved he was to have that over with than to admit how frightened he was by her impending death.

The thought of a second wife enduring what her mother had was too much for Sarah. She closed her eyes tightly against the tears that threatened to fall. "I won't think about it. I won't."

Gideon shrugged. "Then don't, but don't pretend to be surprised when it happens."

"You're hateful," Sarah said, unable any longer to check her tears. They streamed down her pale cheeks. "You don't care at all about Mother, and you're only saying these things to hurt me."

Before he could respond, she ran from him. He tried to stop her but she was too quick. Instead of grabbing hold of her, he was left holding only air and a vague sense of regret. Vague because he knew her anger would not last. She would only refuse to forgive him if he hurt Nathan, and that he grudgingly tried not to do.

Sarah did not go to her room. She remembered how she had cowered there the day before and what little good that had done. Instead she fled outside to the field behind the house.

The afternoon light was beginning to fade. A meadowlark sang in the tall grass near where a fox had its den. The vixen had borne young earlier in the year; Sarah had learned to lie absolutely still some little distance away to watch them. She had collected the wild strawberries that grew in the field and picked bouquets of Shasta daisies and Queen Anne's lace for her mother. Nathan had found a wasp's nest, fortunately empty, which he brought home to put in his treasure box. He had also tried to rescue a sparrow that had fallen from a tree. The tiny bird had died despite his efforts and was buried nearby.

The field sloped downward to a stream where frogs and turtles lived. Sarah went there sometimes to sit with her feet in the cool water and daydream, but that was not the place for her now. She preferred the top of the hill where she could lie unobserved and watch the town on the other side of the river.

The sound of the evening whistle drifted up to her as she stared at the neat rows of long red buildings beside the river. She watched as the mill girls in their calico dresses and bonnets began to emerge. In the morning they arrived for work painstakingly clean and tidy, walking with dignity and chatting quietly among themselves. By the time they returned to the company-run boardinghouses where they lived, they were covered with lint, their hair hung limply and they seemed barely able to put one foot in front of the other. The din of the looms temporarily left them all but deaf, so that speech, even if they had had the strength for it, was impossible.

Sarah had met some of the girls when she went with her mother to visit the sick. Lung ailments were particularly common, and it wasn't unusual to see robust farm girls transformed into pale wraiths after a year or so in Lowell. Most victims were sent home quickly, before their condition could demoralize the others. But in a few cases that wasn't possible, and these were housed in a clinic provided by the mill owners.

Catherine Mackenzie had been a regular caller there, bringing baskets of nourishing food and perhaps more importantly, genuine kindness. The girls would miss her.

Sarah thought of the Reverend Betler asking forgiveness for her mother's sins, and anger welled up in her again. With it came the pain she had managed to hold off until now. While there had still been hope, however faint, she had been able to deny herself the truth of what was happening. That was no longer possible.

Over the past few months she had watched her mother's stomach grow larger and her eyes bleaker. Her father had brushed aside his wife's tentative expressions of concern, but Mrs. Hobson had continually cautioned her to take better care of herself.

Catherine Mackenzie had tried to obey but nothing she did seemed to help. In the final weeks of pregnancy, her feet and ankles had swelled to twice their normal size, her head throbbed incessantly and she had difficulty rising from her bed for even brief periods.

Sarah had last seen her two days before when she had been summoned to her mother's room by a flustered housemaid. She had stood beside the bed, holding her mother's hand, and trying not to show her bewilderment. The bloated woman before her with her stringy hair, yellowed skin and red-rimmed eyes did not look like her mother. Catherine Mackenzie had always looked younger than her age, which was just short of thirty-five. Suddenly she appeared decades older. Sarah wanted to run away from her but knew that she couldn't.

Her mother lay back against the pillows, struggling to breathe. It was hot even for August, and the air in the room was motionless. Catherine's palm was damp against her daughter's. "There's so much I wanted to do for you," she said through cracked lips.

The deep regret in her mother's voice troubled Sarah. She felt as though she was personally responsible for something she could not understand. "Momma...?" She pressed her mother's hand.

Catherine returned the pressure slightly, all she could manage, and closed her eyes wearily. "Maybe you shouldn't be here."

A bee buzzed on the windowsill nearest the four-poster bed. Gideon and Nathan were playing outside, near the pond where the ducks lived. Sarah wanted to be with them, not trapped in the stifling room with the strangely sweet smell of death and decay. She tugged at her mother's hand, trying to pull loose.

Catherine held her a moment longer, then let her go. Her voice rose slightly but still sounded as though it came from a faraway room. "Tell Mrs. Hobson to give you some of that gingerbread she was going to bake this morning."

A brief pang of conscience kept Sarah in place. "I'll come back later?" she offered even though she didn't want to.

Her mother shook her head. "No, this was enough." As her daughter turned toward the door, she called after her softly, "Sarah, remember I love you."

Lying facedown on the ground, Sarah remembered. Her tears ran down blades of grass dry from the almost rainless summer and vanished into the parched earth.

_____ *Chapter Two*

TWO DAYS LATER, Sarah stood beside her mother's grave as the first shovelfuls of dirt struck the plain wood coffin. The sound rang sharply in the stillness otherwise disturbed only by the rustlings of the small group in attendance.

There had been no letup in the heat, not even after a violent thunderstorm had racked the town the previous night. A bolt of lightning had struck an ancient oak tree on the edge of the cemetery. Sarah focused on its gnarled trunk, cleaved down the center to expose stark white wood.

She hurt, as much from crying as from the beating her father had given her after discovering she was absent from the house when her mother died. In Catherine Mackenzie's last moments, her husband had summoned their children to her side. Gideon and Nathan had dutifully come, though the younger boy had wept and tried to get away. Of Sarah there had been no sign. She had returned to the house an hour later, to face the reality of her mother's death and her father's fury.

Sarah had been beaten before; always, as her father said, for the good of her soul, but never with as little effect as he had managed this time. She had made no sound, which caused him to bring the switch down even harder than he had intended. When he was finished, she had rearranged her skirt and quietly asked if she could go to bed. Since then they had not spoken.

Grandmother Mackenzie and Aunt Caroline had laid the body out at home. It had rested in the front parlor on a table provided for that purpose by the undertaker. Catherine had been simply dressed, her hair neatly combed and her hands folded on her chest, the baby's swaddled remains beside her.

Because of the heat, it had not been possible to delay the funeral long enough for Catherine's family from New York to attend. The Vandenheuvels had sent their condolences, stiffly worded in acknowledgment of the breach that had developed as a result of Catherine's marriage. The rift had not been of her making, but had come about through the natural antipathy between her family and Josiah. Though they had initially approved of the match, doubts had arisen after the fact. Gradually over the years, contact had diminished until nothing was left except formality.

Sarah closed her eyes briefly, blocking out the sight of the shattered oak tree. Her black serge dress was uncomfortably heavy. Sweat trickled down her thin back, making her itch. She clenched her hands with the effort not to scratch.

Beside her Nathan shifted restlessly. He had been sick the night before, throwing up his dinner and crying fretfully. Sarah had bathed his forehead with cool water and stayed with him until he finally fell asleep. Now she reached out and quieted him with a gentle touch. His small, round body, still with a young child's softness, responded. He relaxed slightly and gave her a wan smile.

"Ashes to ashes," the Reverend Betler was saying, "dust to dust. In the sure and certain knowledge of the resurrection to come..."

Sarah blocked out the words. She forced herself to concentrate on everything that would have to be done once they returned home. A cold dinner had to be laid on for those who had attended the funeral. There were about two dozen of them, mostly business associates of her father's and their wives. Two representatives chosen by the mill girls stood off to one side. They, of course, would not be returning to the house.

Though she knew Mrs. Hobson could be trusted to make sure everything went smoothly, she ran down in her mind the list of dishes that would be served, the numbers of plates and forks that would be needed, the availability of seating in the parlor now cleared of the undertaker's table.

Before she had finished, the last prayers were over. There was a ripple of movement among the mourners. One by one they walked past Josiah to murmur a few words of comfort. He inclined his head to each with proper solemnness. On either side of him, Grandmother Mackenzie and Aunt Caroline did the same. Gideon copied them, holding himself very straight in an effort to seem more adult than he was. He was wearing a grown-up suit, unlike Nathan who was still in short pants. Bewildered, the little boy put his hand in Sarah's. She continued to hold it as they started down the hillside toward where the carriages were waiting.

"It went very well," Grandmother Mackenzie said as she settled herself for the ride home.

"A good turnout," Aunt Caroline pronounced.

Josiah wiped his forehead and signaled to the driver. "They shouldn't plan to stay too long," he said as the horses started up. "I must go to the mill this afternoon."

Squeezed in between her grandmother and Nathan, Sarah half listened to the exchange. She was thinking of how polite they were being to each other, unlike the conversation she had overheard the night before.

Unable to sleep because of Nathan, she had tiptoed downstairs to chip a few pieces of ice for him from the block in the kitchen. Her father and grandmother had been in the library. She hadn't meant to eavesdrop, but their raised voices had been inescapable.

"I have never understood why you insisted on Caroline and myself maintaining a separate establishment," Grandmother Mackenzie had said. "And now it's more unnecessary than ever. How do you expect to run this house without a woman's help?"

"Sarah is old enough to accept more responsibility. What she does not yet know, Mrs. Hobson can teach her."

"A child and a servant. Do you think it so easy?"

Josiah's voice took on a note of strained patience. "We've discussed this before, Mother. I have provided a very comfortable home for you and Caroline within walking distance of my own. If you think about it, I'm sure you'll decide that you don't really want to give that up."

"What you mean is, you don't want us living with you."

"No," Josiah said flatly, "I don't. It isn't fit for a man to live with his mother and sister, not when he can provide for them elsewhere. Besides, I intend to remarry someday and a bride will expect to run her own house.''

So Gideon had been right. Sarah leaned her head back against the carriage seat. Through half-closed eyes she observed her father. He looked hot, as they all did, and ill at ease, but she saw no evidence of grief. Her resentment of him redoubled, helping her to hold her own anguish at bay.

When they reached the house she took Nathan upstairs and turned him over to one of the maids with instructions that he be put to bed for a nap. He protested, wanting to stay with her, but she insisted. The blue shadows under his eyes and the weary droop of his shoulders told her how tired he was.

''Go on now,'' she said gently. ''You'll feel better after a rest, and I'll come up to check on you.''

He nodded trustingly and went with the girl, leaving Sarah to return to the parlor. This she did reluctantly. Voices reached her up the stairwell. The somberness imposed by the funeral was falling away. She heard a man's deep laughter and the higher-pitched tones of women in cheerful conversation.

Her hand tightened on the banister. She smoothed the black skirt of her dress. Its bodice was snug, forcing her to take shallow breaths. Her feet in the too small boots felt damp and sore. The braids Aunt Caroline had made of her waist-length brown hair were too tight. She longed to undo them, to change into one of her loose smocks and run barefoot through the grass. Instead she straightened her shoulders and entered the parlor.

Catherine Mackenzie had furnished it in the Classical style introduced a few years before and still very popular. The high ceiling boasted ornate plaster moldings and a crystal chandelier that required forty small white candles to fill. The walls were painted a soft shade of green that complemented the darker shade of the long velvet drapes. A prized Aubusson rug covered the wood parquet floor. The room was filled with large, impressive furniture: marble-topped tables with scrolled pedestals, tufted chairs with lion's paw feet, low-backed couches with curving arms, bronze and glass lamps and candelabras.

So heavily furnished was the parlor that there was little room for people to move around. Once having found places for themselves, they stayed put. Sarah's father was deep in conversation with several of the other mill owners. They were gathered near the bay windows, sipping whiskey, while the women sat on the horsehair and velvet couches, fanning themselves and chatting desultorily. Sarah glanced at the women and decided she did not want to join them. Their tight corsets and heavy, cumbersome clothes made her even more uncomfortable. She could not explain it, even to herself, but those feminine bodies locked in harsh confinement repelled her. Instead she found an unoccupied corner where there was a slight breeze and did her best to remain inconspicuous.

Gideon had drifted over by the men. He hovered at the outskirts of their group, listening attentively to everything that was being said and occasionally nodding as though he belonged with them.

"I have nothing against the Southerners," Josiah was saying. "Some of them are very pleasant people. But they are also undeniably backward. They have no appreciation for where the world is heading. On the contrary, they do their damnedest to keep progress at bay."

"Because they don't view it as progress," Daniel Holstein said. He was among the most prosperous of the mill owners, a man who decades before had sensed a great change coming and had not hesitated to make himself part of it. From a wealthy Boston family, he had been a personal friend of Francis Cabot Lowell, whose ingenious theft of England's secret design for water-driven power looms had brought the Industrial Revolution across the ocean.

"The Southerners," Holstein went on, "see all change as a threat to them, and they really are not far wrong. Their way of life is obsolete yet they refuse to give it up because they find it so congenial."

"Congenial only for a very few," Matthew Withers pointed out. A tall, stately man, he ran a law practice serving the mill owners and had excellent contacts in the capital. "The average Southerner is a small farmer working a piece of land with only his family and perhaps a few hired hands. He has no slaves, yet fiercely defends the peculiar institution. Why?"

Josiah shrugged his broad shoulders. "Ambition, of course. The South is riding a wave of expansion. New lands are opening up, new fortunes being made. Every small farmer scraping a living from the exhausted soil can dream of owning a magnificent plantation complete with slaves to mix his mint juleps and empty his slop pail."

"And so long as he can," Holstein added, "he will defy anyone to take that dream from him."

"Which is where North and South come to odds," Withers said, "for slavery cannot be permitted to continue."

"Besides the moral offensiveness so many feel," Holstein said with a nod to the lawyer, "there are the simple economic facts. Slavery is an inefficient system. Having to feed, clothe and shelter people from cradle to grave means less profit to invest in new development.''

"And less profit to spend on the products of our factories,'' Josiah added. "Worse yet, whether buying or selling, Southerners seem to prefer dealing with Britain or France. We must compete for their cotton and their coin, as though we were not their countrymen.''

"They don't recognize us as such,'' Withers said. "For all their courage in the two wars of independence we have fought together, they have no real sense of nation. The Southerner is rooted to his own particular piece of land; he does not see beyond.''

"Yet,'' Josiah murmured, "as you said, they have fought well and bravely. I for one would not be eager to take arms against the South.''

The other men nodded somberly. For all their pride, they were realists. They knew that what Josiah had said was true. The South was a place of mystery, of fiery arrogance and cold honor. A place where men still settled differences in an empty field at dawn, where roots ran so deep beneath the red soil that they became part of the very bedrock of existence.

Moreover, it was a place whose values they could not understand. By comparison theirs were simple and easy to grasp. Life flowed in the neat columns of a ledger; success or failure was there to be read in copperplated numbers. In the South everything was far more complicated. Land counted for more than money, though land was limited and vulnerable, whereas money properly husbanded was immortal. The Southerner didn't seem to understand that, any more than he understood why change had to occur. He clung to his love of the land that was his heritage and turned his back on the great tremors shaking the earth to the north.

But the tremors were reaching southward, following fault lines that ran from the textile mills of New England to the cotton fields of Georgia. North and South were yoked together, unwilling companions on a journey growing more dangerous by the day.

The men, made uneasy by talk of war, began to speak of other things. Sarah's attention drifted away. She was relieved when whether out of simple courtesy or from awareness of their hosts' disinclination, the guests did not stay long. By midafternoon the last of them was gone. Nathan was soundly asleep, Gideon had wandered off somewhere and the servants were finishing clearing up when her father summoned Sarah to the library.

She went reluctantly, the memory of the beating still fresh in her mind. However, there was no sign of the switch. Josiah sat in his high-backed chair behind the mahogany desk. He had removed his jacket and the collar of his shirt. His sleeves were rolled up, revealing powerful forearms sprinkled with black hair.

"Come here," he said when she hesitated at the door.

Sarah obeyed as slowly as she dared. Standing before him, her eyes lowered, she waited to hear what he had to say.

"This has been very difficult," he began, the weariness of his tone surprising her. "Your mother's death . . . so unexpected."

"She shouldn't have had any more babies." The words, spoken without thought, rang in the quiet between them.

Josiah froze. His features were rigid, his fists clenched. For a moment Sarah thought she had gone too far. She had almost reconciled herself to another beating when he shrugged. "You are a child, and a girl. We will not discuss this. What matters is that with your mother's death, more will be expected of you."

She swallowed against the resentment that threatened to choke her. "I will do whatever I can." Anything not to give her grandmother and aunt an excuse to move into the house.

"Good. Mrs. Hobson tells me that you have been well instructed, so I will begin by trusting you with the next month's housekeeping funds. You will spend them as you believe necessary. Each week, you will provide me with a full accounting. Is that clear?"

Sarah nodded, though she felt some concern. "What about school?"

Her father looked surprised. "You will continue as before."

"I had thought, next year, to board at Mrs. Davies's academy."

He frowned. "Your mother spoke of that. I told her there was no need."

Catherine had kept that from her daughter, not wanting to shatter so dearly held a dream. Josiah had no such scruples. "You will stay at home to look after your brothers and myself. That is the best preparation for your future life."

Sarah started to speak again but thought better of it. She knew only too well what her father's response would be were she to disagree with him.

Someday, she promised herself, her life would be different. But in the meantime, the need to accept and obey was galling. Her mother's death had brought home to her where such helplessness led. She was afraid and angry, and did not know what to do about either.

Chapter Three

Calvert Oaks, Virginia

THE HOUSE BEGAN to wake well before dawn while ribbons of mist still wreathed the ancient oaks from which the great plantation took its name. Calvert Oaks stood on a hill overlooking the James River, at the end of a winding tree-lined road. It was a large and stately residence, in keeping with the stature of the family who had lived in it for almost half a century.

The main house was a three-story building in the Greek Revival tradition with graceful white columns fronting on the portico protected by an overhanging roof. High windows were hung with lace curtains and framed by dark blue shutters. Twin brick chimneys, one on either side of the house, were set against a clear sky growing rapidly light as dawn approached. On either side of the front entrance, roses bloomed in profusion. They were the legacy of the late Elizabeth Calvert, who had brought them as a young bride from her home in North Carolina. Though Elizabeth had been dead some ten years, her memory lingered in the scent of the roses and their gentle beauty.

A lamp flickered on in the window directly below the eaves. Augusta would be rising from her bed, her old body stiff in the predawn air. Her husband, Rameses, who had been butler at Calvert Oaks longer than anyone could remember, would be complaining about the early hour even though he had gotten up at the same time all his life. In the attic rooms around them, the other slaves permitted to sleep in the house would be stirring. There would be fires to be started, water to be boiled, vegetables to be peeled, clothes to be washed and mended. All part of the unending round of work that nurtured the great house.

Philip Calvert leaned forward in his saddle, his hands crossed over the pommel, the reins held loosely. He was a tall, well-built young man of twenty, dressed for traveling in boots, breeches, a loose shirt and a jacket stained with the dust of the road. His long, somewhat narrow face was shielded by a broad-brimmed hat. When he removed it to wipe the perspiration from his high forehead, his thick hair gleamed golden in the early sunlight. He had ridden hard all night and, despite his excitement, was tired. The nostrils of his long, Roman nose quivered slightly, and his usually generous mouth was thinned with fatigue.

Yet he had no regrets for having pushed himself as hard as he had. From the hillside, he could see all of Calvert Oaks spread out before him. His blue eyes glowed as they swept from the house itself to the outbuildings. The smokehouse, laundry shed, storehouses and kitchen with its adjacent vegetable garden were located within easy walking distance of the main house. Farther away but still within his sight were the barns, stables, warehouses, workshops and slaughtering pens so essential to a community that in many ways was self-sufficient. Surrounding all of this, indeed giving it meaning, were the vast stretches of fields where tufted bolls of cotton ripened in the warm southern sun.

The roan shied beneath him. He soothed him softly and went on watching. In their quarters a short distance from the big house but separated from it by a high stone wall, the field slaves were also awake. They stumbled sleepily from their cabins, paused at the water trough to splash their faces and joined together around the communal fire. Breakfast mush simmered in a large cast-iron pot. They dipped bowls in it and ate with their fingers. The fluid rhythms of their voices reached Philip on the motionless air.

By half-past six, the work teams had formed up and were marching out to the fields to the cadence set by the drivers. Last to come was the overseer on horseback. Philip did not recognize him; the man had been hired since his last visit home.

A plump black woman in a calico skirt with a cotton turban covering her head came out the back door of the house carrying a hamper full of clothes and walked toward the laundry shed. Soon freshly pounded sheets would be fluttering in the sun. It promised to be a warm day. Philip thought of cold lemonade in the shade of the portico and pressed his heels into the horse's sides.

Augusta saw him first. She was looking out the window of the cookhouse, wondering where the two girls she had sent for turnips had got to, when she caught sight of the rider. Visitors were common at Calvert Oaks, but not at such an early hour. Besides, something about the man looked familiar.

She dropped the towel she had been holding. "It's not...Rameses, git yo'self over here an' take a look. Don' da' look lahk Massa Philip?"

Her husband paused before taking another bite of a warm seeded roll but did not rise from the worn oak table in the center of the room. "Wha' yo talkin' 'bout? Yo knows he up north."

"Not no more he ain't. He right here. Massa Philip," she called as she ran from the kitchen, "yo done come home."

She reached him as he dismounted and flung wide her arms. Philip scooped her up, lifting her generous form clear off the ground, making her laugh all the harder.

"I have indeed, Mammy. Come home from the North and damn glad of it." Setting her on her feet, he grinned. "Haven't had a decent meal since I left."

"Ah believes it," she declared, standing back to get a better look at him. He had grown up some, this white boy she had suckled. When he had left four years before, he had been all gangly limbs and youthful uncertainty. She had sensed the changes happening when he returned for rare visits, but now she was sure. The lankiness was gone, replaced by broad shoulders and a strong chest. He stood proudly, his golden hair gleaming in the sun. There was a new look in his eyes, too, that she liked.

"Massa Charles 'bout burst t'have yo home," she told him, shooing away the cluster of curious slave children who had run up to see what was happening. Other slaves were emerging from all parts of the house, murmuring among themselves when they saw who had arrived.

"Welcome home, Massa Philip," Rameses said, inclining his graying head with courteous formality. "We shor didn' expect yo yet. Tha' last letter ob yos said might be a month or more fo' yo git here."

"I couldn't stay away any longer, Rameses," Philip said with a smile for the older man. He turned his horse over to an eager young boy and unfastened his saddle-bags, preparing without thinking to hoist them over his shoulder.

Immediately Augusta bristled. "Yo shouldn't be doin' da', Massa Philip. Samson, yo gits yo'self ober here an' carry dem bags fo' young massa."

A slender black boy of about fifteen sprang to obey. He took the bags carefully, surprised by their weight. "They're filled with books," Philip explained. "My clothes and everything else will be coming with Jacob. He ought to be here in a day or two."

Jacob was a house slave, the same age as Philip, who had been given to him when they were both children. When Philip went north to school, so did Jacob, to serve as manservant and companion. They had been traveling home together by coach until Philip, overcome by impatience, had decided to ride on ahead.

That same impatience continued to propel him as he strode into the house. The spacious receiving hall was cool and shadowy in the early morning light. He could make out the doorways leading to the dining room, parlor, music room, ballroom and library, but otherwise he could see little. "Isn't anyone up yet?" he demanded of Augusta.

"As though anyone could still be asleep with the racket you've been making," a deep voice replied from the second floor landing. Philip looked up to see his father coming down the curved marble and mahogany staircase. Charles Calvert had risen hurriedly at the sound of his son's arrival and was still tucking his shirt into his trousers. Yet he looked completely in command, as always.

Philip met him halfway up the stairs. They eyed each other cautiously for a moment before the older man embraced his son. "By God," he murmured as he pounded the younger's back, "it's good to have you home."

Philip nodded, too overcome for the moment to speak. He had envisioned his reunion with his father many times but had not quite expected the depth of emotion he was experiencing. His feelings for his father were complex, combining as they did love, respect, even a measure of awe mingling uneasily with a fundamental disagreement of principle that had grown steadily more profound over the years.

No one looking at the two men could mistake them for anything but father and son. Both were tall and well built with strong features set off by powerful blue eyes. The older man's once golden hair was streaked with silver and deep lines were etched into skin weathered by some forty years of sun, but he still looked remarkably fit for a man of any age.

His settled air of authority was as much a part of him as any physical characteristic, and this Philip could not yet match. But looking at him closely, Charles saw what Augusta already had; his son still possessed the open countenance of a young man, yet there was a seriousness about him that boded well for the future. Charles nodded with satisfaction. "It looks as though Princeton didn't do you any harm."

"On the contrary," Philip said as they walked down the stairs, his father's arm around his shoulders. "I liked it fine there, but nothing is better than home."

The words were simple, yet they marked an important concession on the part of both men. Charles had resisted sending Philip to Princeton; though it was

aptly known as the northernmost of the Southern
schools, there had been a chance that his son's heretical tendencies would be exacerbated by too much contact with Yankees. The decision had been made only
because Charles Calvert was something of a gambler,
never with money but with a far more important stake:
the future.

He had been determined that Philip should learn
more of the world. Only in that way could he assume
his rightful place in it. Though it was too early yet to
be certain, hearing his son express such deep happiness at being home greatly reassured the elder Calvert.
Whatever their differences, at least they agreed on what
was most important, the land and all that it represented.

"You must tell me everything," Philip was saying.
"I appreciate all your letters, but there's still so much
I want to know. How many acres are planted? Cotton
looks strong, but do you think the price will hold? How
are Aunt Louise and Kitty...?"

"So you remembered us at last," a laughing voice
called. He turned in time to see a slender blond girl hurl
herself down the stairs in a welter of skirts. He met her
at the bottom where his sister threw herself into his
arms and hugged him tightly.

She laughed up into his face. "I shouldn't be so nice,
since you didn't even think to ask about me until after
the land and the cotton."

"Brat, you haven't changed at all. Nor you, Aunt
Louise," he added, holding out an arm to a small
dumpling of a woman who had come down the stairs
at a more sedate pace. Short and plump in her simple
navy blue day dress, Louise was a dearly longed for
sight. His mother's older sister, she had come to live at

Calvert Oaks ten years before, after Elizabeth's sudden death. For both children, she had rapidly become a second mother they could not imagine doing without. As she studied them both, her softly lined features were gentle with love, despite her best efforts to look stern.

"Kitty, you know perfectly well you aren't to go throwing yourself about like a hoyden," she said, "and as for you, Philip, what do you mean coming home at such an hour and all covered with dust? Look at you, don't they take baths up north?"

"They do and I will," he said, squeezing her until she broke down and laughed. "But first you must feed me and tell me all the news." With his arms around both women and his father leading the way, he entered the dining room where Augusta was hurriedly laying out breakfast.

The room was set in a corner of the house, its floor-to-ceiling windows open to catch whatever breeze might happen by. Like the rest of the house, it was furnished with Heppelwhite and Chippendale pieces brought over at the turn of the century when the present structure was built. Before then there had been a smaller residence on the same site, which had in its turn replaced the simple two-room cabin built by the first Calvert to settle on the banks of the James 150 years before.

Several house slaves hurried to get breakfast on the table under Rameses's critical eye. Two others took up their positions on either side of the ropes controlling the ceiling fans. The warm air stirred languidly as Charles Calvert took his place at the head of the table, with Aunt Louise on his right and Kitty on his left. Philip sat at the other end in the place traditionally belonging to the eldest son and which had remained empty in his absence.

"You have to tell me all about what the ladies up north are wearing," Kitty exclaimed as soon as they were seated. "Not," she added, "that I expect it's anything exciting."

"On the contrary," Philip teased. "A woman of the north never ventures out without first attiring herself in silks and satins. Why even the simplest serving girl could put a duchess to shame."

"I don't believe you," Kitty scoffed. "Everyone knows that Yankee women are dull and have no fashion sense. Besides, they would never be so wasteful with their servants."

Philip surrendered good-naturedly. "This sister of mine cannot be fooled. She's too quick-witted for me."

"Don't say such a thing," Kitty protested, only half-amused. "Men don't like witty women."

"They certainly don't," Aunt Louise agreed. "Why think how you would feel, Philip, if you had to come home each day to the bon mots of a witty wife."

"I'd be exhausted, I'm sure, just trying to match her. But seriously, a bit of intelligence doesn't go amiss in a woman."

Both ladies were skeptical. It was left to Charles to settle the matter. "A woman must have a capable brain so that she can properly manage her household and look after her family. However, it isn't attractive for her to make a display of it." He leaned over and patted his daughter's hand. "Don't worry, Kitty. I've seen you with young Hudson. He doesn't have a clue that you can so much as write your own name."

She tossed her blond curls and cast them all a flirtatious glance. "Jeremy is sweet, but he's never been one for book learning." More seriously, she added, "He admires you tremendously, Philip, for doing so well at Princeton."

"Which reminds me," Charles said, "I suppose the Hudsons will be coming to the party?"

"What party?" Philip asked.

His father laughed and eyed the women. "Why the one these lovely ladies are planning, of course, for your welcome home. I'm right, aren't I? You do have a celebration in the works."

"I did consider the possibility," Aunt Louise acknowledged. "However, I would never be so bold as to plan an entertainment without your prior knowledge."

"Heaven forbid. Which day have you selected?"

Kitty put a hand to her mouth to stifle a giggle. "What about the Saturday after next?"

Charles considered for a moment, then nodded. "Yes, that will be fine. But no more than fifty guests. I can't abide a bigger crowd than that."

"Fifty?" Aunt Louise protested. "But we'd have to leave out so many. Why every one of our neighbors has houseguests and there are plenty more people who will want to come down from Richmond."

"Fifty," Charles repeated. "You'll manage somehow."

"Oh, dear, I just don't know..."

"That's my final word."

Aunt Louise sent Philip a pleading look, but he merely shrugged and began to tell them of his experiences up north. An hour later, pleasantly sated with smoked ham, shirred eggs, hominy cakes and grits, he leaned back in his chair and sighed deeply. His sister and aunt exchanged an indulgent smile that faded as Charles Calvert lit a cigar.

"If you're going to smoke that horrible thing," Aunt Louise said, "Kitty and I will take ourselves off." Knowing perfectly well that her brother-in-law wanted to talk with his son alone, she rose and moved gracefully toward the door.

Kitty followed, but not before pausing to give Philip a quick hug and kiss. "Now don't you dare disappear for the day. I want some time with you, too."

"You'll have it," Philip promised. The little sister who had once been such a thorn in his side had grown up to be a very pretty young girl. At sixteen, she was in the full bloom of her beauty, a fact which made him feel quite indulgent.

When she had gone he met his father's eyes and laughed. "She must be quite a handful. I suppose there's a whole gaggle of besotted beaux?"

"A few. The Hudson boy looks like the best of them."

"Jeremy Hudson? I remember him as a thin rail of a boy with more than his share of pimples."

"He's changed. So, for that matter, have you." Charles leaned across the table and pushed the cigar case toward his son. "Help yourself. I take it they taught you to enjoy a good smoke at Princeton?"

"And one or two other things." Philip selected a plump cigar, rolling it between his fingers to hear the leaves. "Actually, Marcus and I were both smoking for years before I left."

"I did notice whenever a handful of my best Cubanos vanished." Charles tilted his head back and blew a smoke ring toward the ceiling.

Casually, Philip did the same. "By the way, how is Marcus?"

"Quite well. He's a driver now."

"Isn't he young for that?"

Charles shrugged. "Twenty-two is hardly a child. Besides, the darkies respect him."

They would, Philip thought. There had always been something compelling about Marcus. When they had both been children running freely over the plantation, it had more often than not been Marcus who led and Philip who followed. The two-year difference in their ages had accounted for some of that, but not all. It was reassuring to believe that would also have changed.

"I want to check on the new acreage we put under plow this season," Charles said. "Care to come along?"

"You couldn't keep me away."

Chapter Four

TOGETHER THE TWO MEN walked out toward the stables. The day was already warm with the promise of higher temperatures to come. Philip loosened his stock from around his neck. He had left his jacket in the dining room where a house slave would recover it and return it to his room after cleaning. Like his father, he was attired in a cotton shirt, broadcloth trousers, boots and a wide-brimmed hat. Both men had their cigars firmly between their teeth.

Stablehands nodded respectfully as they approached. For almost a century the Calverts had been known for their breeding of fine horses. Charles took special pride in his racers, which routinely won first place in sporting events as far afield as New Orleans. Unlike his grooms, his trainers and jockeys were white, being mostly young men from Scotland and Ireland. They had comfortable accommodations above the stables and were well paid. A few horsebreeders were experimenting with black jockeys, but Charles did not trust slaves to coax the best from his proud stallions and he had an aversion to hiring free men of color whom he felt set a bad example for the slaves.

"We've a good crop of colts this year," he was saying as they entered the stables, "and a stallion you may want to try. I bought him in Richmond a few months ago."

Philip nodded as he rubbed the soft nose of his roan. The horse had been well cared for but was bound to be tired from the fast pace he had set to get home.

"You're still riding Satan?" he asked as he noticed the large black stallion in the last stall. He stood several hands higher than the rest of the horses and, even in the confined space, moved with powerful grace, his nostrils flaring and his eyes rolling.

"We're growing old together," his father said, stroking the horse affectionately. "He's calmed down a bit."

"Which means he's only twice as dangerous as any other horse. Has he savaged any grooms lately?"

"No, they've learned to be more careful. But even if he had, I wouldn't put him down. Every colt he's sired has magnificent spirit."

Philip gave up the argument, knowing by long experience that his father's special fondness for the horse would never end. He was not at all displeased, however, to see that his own mount was made of calmer stuff. The chestnut looked strong enough to give him a good ride, but not so temperamental as to require special handling.

They rode out toward the east, following the path the slaves took each morning to the fields. "We've planted five hundred acres of tobacco," Charles said, "and the same of grain, mostly for our own use. Half the rest is cotton, the remainder lying fallow."

Philip nodded. With the mills of both New England and Britain so hungry for cotton, it made sense to put more than a thousand acres into a single crop. On the other hand, the temptation to leave none to rest must have been great. Undoubtedly many planters had succumbed to it. He gave silent thanks that his father was more prudent about caring for the land that could all too rapidly become exhausted.

As it was, the rains had been good and the cotton was high. Small groups of slaves moved among the rows, picking the soft tufts and dropping them into burlap sacks slung across their chests. They sang as they worked to the cadence set by the driver.

"The new overseer," Philip said, "how's he working out?"

His father shrugged. "Johnson's no better or worse than usual. I made it clear when he was hired that I expect the whip to be used sparingly and so far he's managed that. He also appears to be honest, though I'm sure he wouldn't hesitate to steal if he thought he could get away with it." On an afterthought, he added, "And he has a wife with a sharp tongue, so he doesn't bother the women."

That was important, as Philip well knew. Few things were as guaranteed to cause trouble in the quarters as white men imposing themselves on the female slaves. Besides the unrest it created, it led to the awkwardness of half-breed children, about which Calvert Oaks already knew quite enough.

"There's Marcus," Charles said, rising in his saddle to beckon him. The man who came toward them was tall and strongly built. His café au lait skin glowed with a sheen of sweat. He was bare chested, dressed in cutoffs and a straw hat that shaded his blue eyes. Except for the lighter shade of his skin and proud bearing, he looked like any of the other slaves. Only when he spoke did the difference become starkly apparent. Marcus had lived for years in the big house, sharing the same room and even the same tutor with Philip. Perhaps it was no surprise that even their voices were alike.

"Massa Charles," he said, inclining his head slightly. "Massa Philip, welcome home."

"Thank you, Marcus," Philip said. "It's good to be back. How is everything?"

"Just fine. Good crop this year."

"Any problems with the workers?" Charles asked.

"No sir. They're all fine."

"Mister Johnson mentioned something about one of the new bucks being unruly," Charles said.

"Just a misunderstanding, sir. He's settling down now."

Charles looked doubtful but didn't press the point. If Marcus had had a word with the new slave, so much the better. "Anything else I ought to know about?" he asked.

Marcus hesitated a moment, looking up at the men on the horses. He weighed his words carefully. "Missus Johnson, sir, she whipped one of the girls this morning."

"What for?" Charles asked.

"Said she'd gotten uppity."

"Had she?"

"Doesn't seem likely. Sally's a smart girl."

"I'll have a word with Johnson."

Marcus touched the brim of his hat lightly. "Thank you, sir."

The two men rode off in silence. They had gone some little distance when Philip asked, "Does he do that often?"

"Do what?"

"Intercede on behalf of the slaves."

"He didn't; the girl was whipped."

"But you'll speak to Johnson and presumably it won't happen again."

"Marcus serves a purpose," Charles said. "He helps to keep the peace."

"I suppose..."

"Why are you so doubtful?"

"I don't know exactly." Philip shifted in his saddle. He was uncomfortable talking about Marcus. Once he would not have been, but since coming to manhood and learning to understand the implications of the other man's presence at Calvert Oaks, his attitude had changed. He could no longer simply accept much that he had once taken for granted. "Perhaps because I wonder why he does it."

"I've given him responsibility; he doesn't want to let me down. Hell, if he'd let me, I'd give him more. There's no reason for him to be working in the fields except that he says he prefers it."

Philip supposed his father was right, but a feeling of unease lingered. The Marcus he remembered had been proud and spirited; the man he had just met seemed little changed. More controlled, certainly, but that would only make him stronger. Silently he resolved to seek out Marcus again and try to put an end to the vague sense of disquiet he could neither resolve nor dismiss.

The remainder of the morning was spent riding over the estate. Charles pointed out the improvements that had been made in the time his son had been away. Several dozen acres near the river had been drained, new drying barns had been built for tobacco, and a larger dock erected. Philip noted each with pride, yet a continuing sense of discontent.

There was no sign of the mechanization he continued to hope for despite his father's opposition. In the north, more and more of the labor once done by people was being turned over to machines that could do it faster and cheaper. Philip believed that the same could be done in the south; he saw the solution to slavery in the technology that would make it obsolete. But he was also aware that his opinion was unpopular.

Many of the planters were deeply suspicious of anything new and different. His father wasn't like that; he was always willing to at least consider an innovation he believed might prove effective. But about slavery he was adamant. The blacks were an inferior race who left to their own devices would sink back into the godless savagery from which the whites had rescued them.

Philip had tried and failed to convince his father that wasn't the case. He believed the shuffling, downcast pose adapted by most blacks was simply a mask behind which a full measure of human pride and anger seethed.

There had been proof of that often enough, in the slave rebellions that were the greatest nightmare of every plantation owner. But the lesson failed to be learned. Rebellion inevitably brought increased suppression, which in turn fed the rage that seemed almost like a living thing slowly eating away at the roots of a mighty tree.

Someday the tree would topple and then not all the frantic efforts of men would be able to save it. Increasingly he believed that the only way to prevent such a disaster was to do away with slavery, yet he found it very difficult to voice that conviction even to himself since to do so would make him an outcast among his own people.

In the heat of midafternoon, the men returned to the house. Philip withdrew to bathe, then dozed briefly in the shadows of the mosquito netting. Half-asleep, he listened to the drone of cicadas outside his window and the muted voices of slaves going about their duties.

In Jacob's absence, a young black boy brought him a cold glass of lemonade when he arose and helped him dress. Greatly refreshed, he returned downstairs and joined the family on the portico. They remained there until Rameses called them in to supper, then lingered over the meal. It was well past twilight when Kitty and Aunt Louise went up to bed and Charles adjourned to the library to take care of some paperwork. Left to his own devices, Philip wandered outside.

The heat had abated somewhat, and there was a light breeze off the river. He could hear the murmured voices of the house slaves as they prepared to retire. A few lamps could still be seen burning in the quarters, but most of the cabins were dark.

He walked on, skirting the edge of the quarters and coming at last to a wooden gate that led to the horse pasture. He leaned against it, looking up at the full moon. A "runaways' moon" some called it because by its light fugitive slaves could hope to find the way north. Why should he think of that now? It had been years since the slave hunters had had to be called out to catch a fugitive from Calvert Oaks.

The gate creaked under his weight and he smiled, remembering how he and Marcus used to swing on it until one day it had broken. His father had paddled them both so thoroughly that it was a week before either could sit down comfortably.

A sound made him turn. He tensed slightly as a shadow moved out of trees, only to relax when he recognized who it was. "You're up late, Marcus. Can't sleep?"

"Guess not. How about you?"

"I must be too excited about getting home. It's good to see everyone again." He spoke warmly, making it clear that Marcus was included.

The other man nodded. "You've been missed. Massa Charles especially will be glad to have your help."

"Perhaps I can make things a bit easier for him," Philip allowed.

Marcus leaned against the fence, staring out across the pasture. They shared a companionable silence before he asked, "What did you think of it up north?"

"It was all right. I got along better than I thought I would." He reached into his pocket and pulled out a couple of cigars, handing one to Marcus. As he did, he chuckled. "Father told me today that he always knew who was stealing these."

"Probably did." Marcus leaned forward to accept a light. The match illuminated two sets of similar features: high foreheads, deep-set eyes, straight noses, firmly drawn mouths, square chins.

It flickered out as Marcus inhaled appreciatively. "Remember the first time we tried these, how sick we were?"

"Do I ever. I thought we were going to die."

"If it hadn't been for Augusta, we might have."

"She looks good," Philip said. "So does Rameses."

"They missed you, too."

"Well, I'm home to stay now."

"Miss Louise know that?" Marcus asked.

"I suppose, why?"

"Cause if she does, she won't be wasting any time getting you married."

"Oh, no," Philip said with a laugh. "Not me. I intend to stay footloose and fancy free for a while yet."

"Nothing wrong with being married. I like it."

"Say that's right, Father did let me know you'd taken a wife. What's her name again...Ginny?" When Marcus nodded, Philip asked, "Is she from around here?"

"She was on Beauterre."

Philip frowned. Beauterre was owned by the Danvers family, who had a reputation for mistreating their slaves. "How did you meet?"

"Ginny was Missus Danvers's maid. She came with her one day a few months back when she was visiting Miss Louise."

Philip didn't have to be told the rest. His father would have been delighted to learn that Marcus wanted to marry and wouldn't have hesitated to buy the girl for him. "Well, I hope you'll be very happy. Is there a baby on the way yet?"

Marcus's smile faded. "No, not yet. Maybe someday."

There was a vague hint of sadness about the way he said that, but it was at once too faint and too complex for Philip to pursue. "Anyway, I'm glad to know you're happy."

"And if I want to stay that way, I guess I'd better be getting back. Thanks for the cigar."

"Sure, and Marcus..."

"Yes?"

"I'm also glad you're still here."

_____ *Chapter Five*

THE PARTY TO WELCOME Philip home was held as planned the following week, despite Aunt Louise's protests that she had underestimated what needed to be done and couldn't be ready by then. As it turned out, by the time all the invitations had been issued, the list had grown to seventy-five. Charles bore up tolerantly, having only intended to hold the number to under a hundred.

"Left to themselves," he advised his son as they sat in the library before the first guests arrived, "women will invite every living soul for miles around. A man has to set limits."

"I don't even remember some of these people," Philip said, his eye running down the list Aunt Louise had given him. Both men were formally dressed in frock coats, snugly fitting evening trousers, embroidered waistcoats and pleated shirts.

Charles took out a handkerchief and wiped his forehead. The night air was heavy with scents from the river. "There are several new families in the neighborhood. Some of the older ones couldn't hold on after the Panic."

The financial upheaval of 1837 had wreaked havoc throughout the South. The price of cotton had fallen drastically, as had the value of slaves and all other property. They were only just recovering, too late to help those with heavy mortgages, many of whom had lost everything. Much as he sympathized with them, their plight had reaffirmed Charles's determination to keep Calvert Oaks free from debt.

"It's a damn shame," his son said, "when the skulduggery of Yankees can bring good Southern families down."

"I'll drink to that. Care for a quick one before we're surrounded?"

"None of that now," Aunt Louise said, sweeping into the room. She looked regal in dark violet silk trimmed with alençon lace, her gray hair swept up in a becoming coronet and a smattering of powder on cheeks flushed with excitement. "They'll be arriving any minute, and the ladies won't want to smell liquor on your breaths when you greet them."

Charles gave in gracefully, with a wry glance at his son.

"You look lovely, Aunt Louise," Philip said, bending over her hand. "As pretty as a girl."

"Don't waste your soft words on me," she chided even as she smiled. "There are plenty of belles coming tonight. You'll be kept busy paying attention to all of them."

"I'll do my best," he promised gallantly, then looked toward the door and smiled. "Speaking of belles . . ."

"Do you like it?" Kitty asked as she glided toward the door, a vision in white lace and dimity. She twirled around, giving them the full benefit of her wide skirt. Soft blond ringlets cascaded over her bare shoulders. She fluttered her fan and gazed at them over it.

"Absolutely ravishing," Philip declared. "I'll go strap on my sword and be right back. You're going to need protecting."

"Silly," she said, tapping his chest lightly with the fan.

He had to bite his tongue to keep from laughing. She had obviously worked hard to learn the proper behavior of a belle and couldn't resist showing off how successful she had been.

"Never mind, Philip," their father said with a smile. "Rather than resort to swordplay, the two of us will simply keep Kitty so busy that no love-struck swain will have a chance to get near her."

"Don't you dare," she exclaimed. "I'm going to have a wonderful time tonight."

"I'm sure you will," Charles said. The sound of creaking carriage wheels and the accompanying hoofbeats coming up the gravel drive interrupted them. He held out his arm to Aunt Louise as Philip gallantly offered his to his sister.

They greeted the guests in the reception hall. The women teased Philip about how handsome he had become; the young girls weren't so bold but their glances told him they agreed. The men were hearty and jovial, making him feel truly one of them. He was slapped on the back, his hand was wrung and he was invited to join them in a hunt planned for the following week.

About half the guests had arrived and drifted into the ballroom when Philip's attention was drawn to the party coming through the door. He recognized his Uncle James and Aunt Caroline; they had changed little in the years he had been away. But the girl with them brought him up short.

"Daphne, is that really you?"

The lovely, dark-haired creature smiled enchantingly and nodded. In a voice that reminded him irresistibly of a warm, still night pregnant with promise, she said, "I guess I have changed some, Philip."

"Some? You're—" He broke off, abruptly aware of the interested looks he was getting from his father and aunt. Daphne lowered her eyes becomingly, allowed him to hold her hand a moment longer than was proper, then followed her parents.

When she was gone, Philip cleared his throat. He avoided looking at his family but was not so successful in keeping his gaze from drifting toward the ballroom. From time to time he caught a glimpse of Daphne. It seemed that she was continually surrounded by admiring men, all vying for her attention. Philip gritted his teeth, impatient to join them.

As soon as the last guests had arrived, he hurried into the ballroom. There was no dancing yet—that would wait until after supper—but people were standing around in clusters, chatting amiably. Jeremy Hudson was hanging over Kitty as though afraid that she might vanish at any moment. Philip frowned, making a mental note to get to know the younger man better and continued on his way. He was stopped often as he tried to cross the room, but at length he had almost reached Daphne's side, only to be halted by a peremptory hand on his arm.

"Tell us what you thought of the north, Philip," a large, florid-faced man with a stentorian voice directed. Judge Beauregard Rider was in his sixties, the owner of a plantation a dozen miles downriver from Calvert Oaks. He had served on the circuit court several decades before and retained the honorarium of his title.

Before Philip could reply the judge went on. "Never understood why you had to go up there. Plenty of fine schools right here. William and Mary, for instance, or the Military Institute. Course you could have gone to the Point. That would have been all right." The judge's youngest son was in his last year at West Point and wrote back glowing letters of the fine education he was getting there.

Philip, long accustomed to the older man's outspokenness, was not offended. He merely smiled and accepted a bourbon from a house slave in knee breeches and tail coat. "Princeton's not a bad place, Judge. Plenty of Southern men go there."

"I suppose there's something to be said for learning to know your enemy," the judge allowed.

"Enemy?" Charles repeated. "Surely that's going a bit far?"

Rider shook his white head. "What else would you call them? They want to tell us how to live, how to manage our property, how to decide what's right and wrong. When a man attempts to interfere with me in that way, he is my enemy."

Several of the men listening nodded, but Charles remained unconvinced. "Such a term dignifies them unnecessarily. The Yankee is merely a businessman, a merchant who cares only for his profit. He has no other values, little sense of honor and no commitment to anything beyond himself. If we understand that, we will handle him correctly."

"We will handle him best with the brunt of our swords," Frederick Danvers insisted. He had joined the group as Charles spoke, despite the fact that none of them were pleased to see him. A small, slump-shouldered man with a weasel's face, he was disliked as much for the unreliability of his business dealings as for the mistreatment of his slaves. He, his wife, Hortense, and their son, Paul had been invited only because they were neighbors and courtesy demanded that they not be overlooked.

The judge took another swallow of his mint julep and frowned at Danvers. "You have a point, Charles," he conceded, as much to irk the other man as because he believed it. "But isn't such a man extremely dangerous?"

"He can be, if we let him. My only concern is that we of the South are peace-loving men, and as such we seek to promote accord, not dissension. While I disagree with Mr. Danvers," he inclined his head toward his neighbor who glared back, "I do think it important that the Yankees understand we are not weak."

"What do you think of that, Philip?" James Calvert asked. "You've lived among Northerners for several years. Are they counting on us not standing up for ourselves?"

"There is something to that," Philip said slowly. He really didn't want to involve himself in a political discussion, not when he would so much rather be basking in Daphne's smile. But the topic interested him, and he was flattered that his father had asked his views.

"It is true that Yankees don't think the same way we do. They don't have the same reverence for the land, for instance, or the same feeling for tradition and the importance of continuity. But they are smart enough to realize that we have something they lack. That makes them suspicious of us and even, I believe, afraid."

"Let them fear," Judge Rider said. "They have reason. New states will shortly be added to the Union.

Many of them will vote for slavery. The day will come when we outnumber our opponents."

"The North will do everything possible to prevent that," Philip said. "They wish to remake this country in their own image, to build factories in every field and turn every village into a teeming city. To do that, they must retain the majority in Congress."

Four years of talking with the sons of Northern businessmen had convinced him that was true. But there was an additional element that also worried him, not the least because it contradicted what his father had said.

"There is the question of religion," he reminded them. "As coldly unemotional as the Yankees can be, they are prone to evangelical fervor. They enjoy nothing so much as righteous indignation."

"Their religious belief is simply a smoke screen," Charles insisted. "They use it as an excuse to promote their business aims."

"Some may," Philip acknowledged. Carefully he added, "But others genuinely believe that the nigra has all the same attributes as the white man, and as such should not be held in slavery. They can work themselves into quite a frenzy over this issue."

"Ridiculous," James Calvert said. "Why if we were to free our nigras tomorrow, how long would it be before they were back, knocking on our doors and pleading to return? They are no more capable of caring for themselves than children are. It would be extraordinarily cruel to abandon them to their own resources, such as they are." He shot a glance at Frederick Danvers. "And, of course, none of us can countenance cruelty."

"The Northerners don't understand that," Philip said. He had caught sight of Daphne again, laughing gaily in the midst of a crowd of young men. This discussion really had gone on long enough. "If you'll excuse me, I shouldn't neglect my duties."

The other men, who had followed the direction of his gaze, smiled tolerantly. They let him go before returning to the subject. Others had joined the group and the talk was growing increasingly heated. Not that there was any real disagreement, only that each man vied with the next in his defiance of the Yankees.

Philip left them with relief. Had he stayed longer, he would have felt driven to express his own views, which at the very least would have put a pall on the evening. How much more pleasant to put aside such uneasy thoughts and concentrate on more congenial matters. Standing off on the side, he watched Daphne. She was aware of his presence, going so far as to cast him a warm glance from beneath her thick dark lashes. But she did not break off her conversation with the several young men. Despite his fascination, he couldn't help but notice that she seemed to say and do many of the same things as Kitty. Yet what he had found so amusing in a younger sister he took much more seriously in Daphne.

Philip finished his bourbon, put the empty glass down and went to join the group. They made room for him reluctantly. Louis Devereaux was there; heir to properties along the James and in Richmond, he was considered an excellent catch. But then so were John Carlisle, William Morgan and Paul Danvers. The latter looked nothing at all like his father, being as tall and well built as Philip himself. But rumor had it that beneath the skin he resembled his sire in every way. The number of mulatto children at Beauterre seemed to prove that, since not even as randy an old rooster as Frederick Danvers could have spawned them all.

Philip took a deep breath and smiled. "It's been so long since I've had any time with my cousin, I'm sure you gentlemen won't mind if I borrow her for a few minutes."

They all did mind, very much, but good manners prevented them from saying so. That and the fact that when a man went to such lengths to cut a woman out from the pack, he was announcing a very high degree of interest. They had to respect that even as they wondered if Philip wasn't being a bit precipitate.

He wondered the same thing himself as he steered Daphne toward a quiet corner. Never had he behaved so forwardly with a woman, at least not a lady. His actions surprised him, yet he didn't care to question them too deeply.

Daphne, however, felt no such qualms. "Really, Philip," she murmured as she allowed him to lead her away. "Don't you think you're being awfully forceful?

"Am I?" He looked down at her and smiled reassuringly. In her satin dancing slippers, she came no higher than his shoulders. Her ebony hair, caught back in ringlets, glowed with a silver sheen. Wide green eyes returned his gaze innocently. She had a small nose that turned up slightly at the tip, a full mouth and a chin framed on either side by enchanting dimples that deepened when she smiled.

He remembered that she was Kitty's age and noted approvingly that she wore the same sort of simple but appealing white gown. Her smooth shoulders were left bare. He could see the slight swell of her breasts and the enticing narrowness of her waist.

"Did you really want to keep talking to all of them?" he asked as he leaned against the wall and smiled at her.

"Perhaps," she murmured, without much certainty. He nodded politely, though he barely heard her. It was enough that she was beautiful and agreeable. For the remainder of the evening, he stayed close by her side, escorting her into supper, sitting next to her and dancing with her often enough to draw attention without completely neglecting the other ladies. When she danced with others, he did the same, but not once did he lose sight of her.

By so concentrating his attention on Daphne, he missed the pleased glances that passed between her family and his. Charles Calvert felt particularly vindicated by what he saw. Daphne was one more tie that would bind Philip to his proper place and help put an end to his fanciful views. He took another swallow of his bourbon and basked in the sense that everything was working out just as he wished.

_____ *Chapter Six*

FROM HIS OFFICE on Merrimack Street, Josiah could faintly hear the constant creaking of the waterwheels, the clacking of the mills and the clatter of horses on the cobblestones in front. He savored those sounds. They were to him the clink of coins piling one on top of another, which was in turn protection from so much that he remembered but prayed never to experience again.

Much had changed since Josiah had first come north as a boy of thirteen in 1821 shortly after his father's death. That was the year the textile merchants founded Lowell. With the fast-running Merrimack River to provide power, the once quiet countryside was rapidly transformed into an industrial center.

As the eldest child and only son, Josiah had been charged with the care of his mother and sister. He had left them temporarily in Virginia, where the family had settled after immigrating from Scotland shortly before his birth, and had journeyed north where opportunities were said to be better.

His business career had begun on the barges serving Lowell. Large for his age, he toted hundred-weight bales, took his turns at the poles and generally made himself useful. He slept on deck, ate whatever he could and saved virtually every penny he did not send back to Virginia. When he was sixteen he bought his own barge and offered cut-rate prices to the mill owners if they would guarantee him freight. The arrangement drove more than one competitor out of business, with Josiah buying up more barges at distressed prices.

In 1826, when he turned eighteen and sent for his mother and sister, he bought a piece of land and promptly offered it as security against a loan for the amount needed to build a mill. Lowell was becoming a boomtown, and the bankers were more willing than usual to take a risk. Within three years their faith was rewarded when Josiah not only paid off the loan but also bought the bank.

The nation's appetite for cloth was insatiable and Josiah prospered. By the time he married Catherine Vandenheuval in 1833, he owned half a dozen mills outright, as well as shares in many others. His business interests had spread as far as Boston and New York. It was in the latter that he had met Sarah's mother, the daughter of a prosperous merchant.

Catherine had been twenty, not beautiful but with an innate dignity that appealed to him greatly and a pleasant manner that made him feel at once soothed and excited by her presence. In the early months of their acquaintance, as business called him more and more frequently to New York, she had seemed the epitome of all his dreams. If he could acquire her, he would feel that the final seal had been put on his success.

She had been hesitant at first, but he had worn her down gradually, wearing away at her reluctance, which he was convinced stemmed from simple shyness rather than any dislike of him. That there was no love between them did not worry Josiah. He had never known love in his life and did not expect to ever experience it.

If some men wanted to believe it existed and to seek after it, that was fine for them. He had more realistic aspirations.

He wanted, first and foremost, money and position. Without those things, a man was helpless. With them, he could be master of his own fate. Added to that, he wanted children. Without them he would be too keenly aware of his own mortality. So long as he could think of passing along everything he built to a future generation, he could endure the inevitability of death. Endure it, but never accept it.

Death was the ultimate affront to Josiah. It bespoke a wastefulness in the universe that made him seriously question the wisdom of God. That was extremely unsettling, since he genuinely considered himself to be a religious man. But ever since Catherine's death six months before, he had been plagued by doubts.

Looking up from the letter he had been trying to write, Josiah glanced out the window. It was beginning to snow. In Virginia, where the letter was going, it would be cool but pleasant. He thought of Charles Calvert, wondering what the planter was doing at that moment. He might be in his library, attending to business even as Josiah was. Or perhaps he was riding over his lands on that devil of a stallion he kept, pride of possession in every inch of his being. Against his will, Josiah sighed. Though he had never thought of himself as a Southerner even when he was living there, he sometimes couldn't help but wonder what his life would have been like if he hadn't come north.

Such speculation was futile. Had he stayed where fate had placed him, he would have been like thousands of other tenant farmers vainly trying to scratch a living from the remorseless soil, seeing his youth, his manhood, his very substance drip away year by year until there was nothing left except the withered husk his father had been at the end.

Men like Charles Calvert grew rich on the labor of others. That was fine with Josiah, so long as he wasn't one of those providing the labor. Early on it had occurred to him that there were really only two kinds of men in the world, those who served and those who ruled. The realization had come to him while standing knee-deep in muddy clay, trying to push free a stuck wagon wheel. Not the wagon nor the bales of cotton loaded on it had belonged to him any more than had the dirt in which he sank. At that instant, his body straining, his mind crying out, he had looked up at the indifferent sky and vowed that such would not be the sum of his life.

He had been eleven years old at the time. It had taken him two more years to make his escape and many more years after that to assure that he would never be pulled back down into the mud. In the process, he had become hard, but he didn't regret that. The meek might inherit the earth but it was men like Josiah who would enjoy it in the meantime.

Not that there was much enjoyment in his life since Catherine's death. It was only after she was gone that he had begun to realize how much he had needed her. Not simply for the children she had provided, though that was his primary concern, and certainly not for her presence in his bed, to which she had brought the proper reticence of a lady. She had, he realized belatedly, given him a sense of his own importance that he sorely missed.

The solution was simple enough: he would marry again. But something in him held back from doing that as quickly as he had intended. He put his pen down, the ink on the nub having dried, and absently fingered the black mourning band around his arm. He had thought to wait a year, a respectable length of time, before beginning to consider potential brides. Now he thought he might not be so hasty. He wanted a woman with all of Catherine's attributes, but he also wanted something more. Until he was sure what that might be, he thought it prudent to withhold any decision.

The snow was becoming heavier. It was growing cold in his office. Daugherty had undoubtedly let the fire in the coal stove go out again. The old man who served as his assistant was chronically forgetful about such mundane matters, despite his continual promises to reform. Josiah kept him only because of his ability to find the last dime—never mind dollar—in any deal. That and his knowledge of the other mill owners, most of whom he had worked for in one capacity or another before coming to Josiah. Daugherty knew how the minds of those men worked, what did and did not matter to them. He passed that knowledge on to Josiah, who used it well.

He went to the door, intending to call Daugherty from his perch in the outside office and reprimand him. Only then did he remember that he had sent the old man home before the storm began. Such a magnanimous gesture was so unlike him that he had momentarily forgotten it.

It was rapidly growing dark. If he wanted to get home himself, he would be wise to leave soon. With a final glance at the half-finished letter on his desk, he decided it could wait until tomorrow. His greatcoat hung on a hook near the door. He put it on and took the beaver-skin hat from the shelf above it. With a scarf wrapped around his throat and his gloves in place, he was ready to venture out.

His carriage was brought round quickly from the stables behind the office. He stepped into the snug enclosure and signaled to the driver outside. The horses started up, their hoofbeats muted by the snow already several inches deep on the cobblestones. If he had delayed much longer, he would have had to use a sleigh.

Josiah sat back against the tufted leather upholstery. As was his habit, he began to methodically review everything he had done that day to see if anything might have been omitted. This practice, begun in boyhood, was characteristic of him. He took nothing for granted and left nothing to chance. More than once, he had benefited from such scrupulousness.

His stern features were creased with thought when his concentration was abruptly interrupted. The horses shied nervously as the carriage suddenly veered. He heard the driver curse and thought for a moment that the wheels had slipped. Only when he made out what the man was saying did he realize the cause of their distress.

"You damn stupid bitch," the driver hollered. "What're you thinking of lying out in the road like that? You could have killed us."

"What's the problem here?" Josiah demanded. He had released the leather catch on the window and shoved it down. Snow blew into the carriage and collected rapidly on his hat when he stuck his head outside.

"Someone in the road, sir," the driver said. "A girl, I reckon."

Josiah narrowed his eyes, peering through the swirling snow. He could vaguely make out a shapeless bundle lying beside the carriage. His mouth thinned as he pushed the door open and got out.

"No need to bother yourself, sir," the driver called. "I'll move her out of the way."

"Be quiet, fool. You might have hit her."

"I did not, sir," the man protested at once. "She was trying to cross the road and fell. It was all I could do to keep the horses under control."

Josiah supposed the man was telling the truth. At least when he turned the girl over, he could see no evidence that the carriage had struck her. She was conscious, though only partially, and seemed to be suffering from the cold and weariness more than anything else.

Her thin calico dress and cotton cloak were scant protection from the elements. She was painfully thin, her collarbones sticking like knobs through her ashen skin. The wide dark eyes that stared at him unblinkingly reminded him of a bewildered animal's, facing death without understanding how it had come to be.

He had gotten out of the coach not because of any humanitarian impulse but rather from a proprietary concern with the condition of both the road and whatever was on it. As one of the leading citizens of Lowell, it was his duty and his right to assure that the town ran smoothly. Roads could not be blocked, especially not in such weather, and people could not be allowed to lie about on them.

"Get up," he said firmly, grasping the girl's thin arm.

She continued to stare at him but did not move. Snow clung to her pale hair, uncovered even by a kerchief.

"I don't think she hears you, sir," the driver ventured. He stood some little distance away, swinging his arms in an effort to keep warm and wondering how much longer Mr. Mackenzie intended to tarry. The girl was clearly one of the mill workers. She belonged in the boardinghouses kept for their use. "Maybe we could find out where she rooms, sir, and take her there."

"Where do you live, girl?" Josiah demanded, shaking her slightly. When she still didn't respond, he pulled her to her feet, only to discover that her legs could not hold even her slight weight. They buckled as she collapsed against him. "Damnation," he muttered. Now what was he to do? He could take her to any one of the boardinghouses and insist that she be looked after. His position and authority were such that he would not be questioned. However, afterward, when he was gone, there was bound to be speculation about how he had come to be with the girl and what had happened to her. He did not care to have his name brunted about in such a way.

"We'll take her with us," he directed the driver as he lifted the girl and carried her to the coach.

Whatever the driver thought of that, he was wise enough to keep it to himself. With difficulty he got the coach back on the road and on its way.

Josiah had laid the girl on the seat opposite him. She was so slight and small that she took up little of it. He frowned at her, trying to puzzle out some explanation for her circumstances.

The mill owners were very proud of how well they looked after their employees. While it was true that there were problems—the incessant lung complaints, for one—Lowell was considered a model of the new industrial community. The girls arriving from farms that they were most often leaving for the first time in their lives were rapidly absorbed into a carefully structured and disciplined existence.

The boardinghouses they lived in were overseen by formidable matrons charged with protecting the girls' virtue. Living four and five to a room, they had little excuse for loneliness. In their rare off-hours, they were encouraged to attend cultural lectures, join choral groups, even publish a booklet of their own writings, which came out regularly.

The work was certainly hard; every girl who came to Lowell understood that in advance. But there was no excuse for the pitiful creature opposite him who, Josiah noted, had gone to sleep.

She was still sleeping when they arrived at the house. He lifted her out of the coach and carried her up the walk. Behind him the driver murmured in relief and spurred the horses on toward the stable. Before Josiah reached the door, it had been opened and the warm light from the interior spilled out over the snow-covered path.

Mrs. Hobson gasped when she saw what her employer was carrying. "Why, sir, what . . . who is that?"

"I've no idea," he told the housekeeper as he strode into the hallway. "Is there an empty bed in the servants' quarters?"

"Yes, sir. . ." She stood uncertainly for a moment before remembering to close the door. In response to her employer's impatient frown, she hurried up the stairs. He followed until they reached the third floor. The ceiling was lower there and Josiah had to stoop slightly. His greatcoat dripped water on the floor, and droplets from his hat ran down his face into his sideburns and mustache. He was eager to be rid of his burden, whoever she might be, so that he might go downstairs and warm himself by the fire.

"In here, sir," Mrs. Hobson said, indicating a small, dark room. She fumbled on the table for a match and tinder with which to light the tin lamp kept there. Its light revealed an iron bedstead with a thin mattress rolled up on it and blankets folded over the foot. A dresser was opposite along with a washing bowl and pitcher. There was a braided rug on the floor but otherwise the room was empty of amenities.

It was also very cold. "You'll have to get more blankets for her," Josiah said as Mrs. Hobson quickly straightened the mattress and laid out the covers. The moment she was done, he laid the girl down and turned to go. "I'll leave you to do what's needed. If she wakes up and tells you who she is, let me know."

"As you wish, sir," the housekeeper said, but he was already gone.

For several minutes after he had left, Mrs. Hobson stared at the girl on the bed. She had not stirred since being brought into the house. Her thin body lay on its side, the knees pulled up toward her chin. Her pinched face was ashen and her pale hair lay in damp strands down her back.

With a deep sigh Mrs. Hobson resigned herself to taking care of the stray.

_____ *Chapter Seven*

SARAH SCRATCHED her fingernail across the pane of glass, then peered through the hole she had made in the frost. She could see very little; even the hill behind the house was all but invisible beneath its covering of snow. The blizzard that had begun the previous evening had continued throughout the night. Now, at midmorning, it was as dark as at twilight.

Behind her, on the round table that had once been in her mother's room, a lamp burned. She had been trying to read, without much success. There was no school that day because of the storm. She should have been downstairs in the kitchen helping Mrs. Hobson, but she had needed some time alone.

Time by herself had become increasingly rare in the months since her mother's death. She had been kept continually busy with her inherited responsibilities. In a few days, she would be thirteen years old. She viewed her approaching birthday regretfully, seeing it as one more signpost of her rapidly vanishing childhood.

She left the window seat and glanced again at the book left open on the table. The words blurred slightly. She made a sound deep in her throat and pressed her hands against her abdomen. Since early morning, she had been hurting there. At first, the pain had been so slight that she had barely noticed. Slowly it had increased, and changed from dull to sharp. In the past few minutes it had grown so bad that she could no longer ignore it.

She went over to the bed and laid down on top of the comforter. Lying on her back with her hands still pressing, she felt a little better, though not for long. Too soon the pain returned. Sarah closed her eyes tightly. She was more bewildered than frightened. Nothing had happened to hurt her; there was no reason for the pain. Yet her skin was clammy, and she felt as though she needed to relieve herself.

Shakily, she got up and went behind the screen, where the chamber pot was kept. After long moments, when nothing happened, she gave up and returned to the bed. The pressure in her lower body continued to build. She could neither understand nor ignore it.

A knock on the door made her stiffen. "Who is it?"

"Me, Nathan. May I come in?"

Despite her discomfort, Sarah smiled. Only with great difficulty had she persuaded her brothers not to come barging into her room whenever they felt like it. Gideon still frequently forgot or claimed that he did. Nathan, however, was scrupulously considerate.

"Yes," she said, sitting up. She grimaced as she did so but managed to hide her discomfort as Nathan demanded, "What's the matter?"

"Nothing, I'm just feeling lazy."

He frowned, not quite believing that. Since his mother's death, he had been extremely sensitive to any suggestion of illness. At the slightest hint that someone in the household might be sick, he became withdrawn and fearful. He was particularly liable to be upset if anything seemed wrong with Sarah.

Managing a reassuring smile, she swung her legs off the bed and stood up. "I shouldn't be lying around anyway. Let's go downstairs and see if Mrs. Hobson needs any help."

Still watching her closely, Nathan shook his head. "Father sent me to get you. He wants you to come down to the library."

Sarah managed with some difficulty to hide her dismay. Interviews with her father were always unwelcome, but particularly when she was feeling so poorly. "All right. You go ahead, I'll be right behind you." She needed a few moments to comb her hair, splash some water on her face and otherwise try to make herself look presentable.

When she did enter the library a short time later, she found her father seated at his desk. To her surprise, he was not alone. A girl stood facing him. She was small and fraily built, with delicate features and feathery blond hair that fell about her shoulders. Her clothes were poorly made, showing evidence of repeated patchings. The hands she held clasped in front of her were red and badly chapped. Sarah eyed her with puzzlement as she said, "You wanted to see me?"

Josiah nodded. He looked from one girl to the other as though confirming something to himself. Marilee, as he had learned was the waif's name, stood with her gaze modestly lowered. Mrs. Hobson had dried and pressed the bedraggled dress she had been found in, and she was wearing it again. It hung from her thin frame and did nothing to complement her pale coloring.

Sarah's dress, though of better quality, was no more attractive, but Josiah didn't notice that. He was interested in the difference in the two girls' mannerisms.

While Marilee exuded humility, Sarah faced him with a flicker of defiance she could not quite conceal.

In the months since her mother's death, their relationship had become increasingly strained. Though she never presumed to defy him outright, neither did she extend to him the respect he believed to be his due. In his presence, she was quiet almost to the point of sullenness. At the first possible opportunity, she absented herself. If he insisted that she stay and tried to talk to her, she retreated behind a wall of resistance he could not breach.

Deep in his heart, Josiah knew the cause. His daughter blamed him for her mother's death. The more he struggled to believe in his own innocence, the more her condemnation angered him. He was determined that Sarah would change, and now he thought he had the means at hand to bring her round.

"This is Marilee Jamison," he said. "Marilee, this is my daughter, Sarah."

The two girls nodded at each other in silent curiosity.

"Marilee has been telling me how she happened to come to Lowell," Josiah went on. "Her father was a schoolmaster in Boston. When he died a year ago, the family fell on hard times. Her mother was already dead, so Marilee was left with only an older brother. William, you said his name is?" When she nodded, he went on. "Her brother has gone to sea to try to earn a living and Marilee must fend for herself. She hired on in one of my mills, but the work has proved too strenuous for her."

That Sarah could believe since it was hard enough on robust farm girls, which Marilee had clearly never been.

"You are what, Marilee, fifteen?"

"Yes, sir," she answered without looking up. Her voice was soft to the point of being all but inaudible.

Josiah had remembered her age perfectly well but had wanted to exhibit again for Sarah's enlightenment the other girl's respectfulness. "Ordinarily," he went on, "I would not consider bringing any mill girl into my house except as a servant. But Marilee's background is unusual. Therefore, I have suggested that she stay on here as your companion."

Sarah stared at him in surprise. She had no idea that he had ever considered finding a companion for her, nor was she at all sure that she wanted one. Not that it mattered. Her father, having made up his mind, would not be swayed.

"She will have the room next to yours," Josiah went on when it was clear that Sarah was not going to be so foolish as to protest. "Mrs. Hobson will help to prepare a suitable wardrobe for her. I hope you will settle in quickly, Marilee."

"Thank you, sir," the girl murmured. "I'll do my best."

"I'm sure you will." He smiled expansively and waved his hand to dismiss them.

Once they were both outside in the corridor, silence fell between the girls. Neither had any idea of what to do or say next. Finally Sarah said, "I'll show you to your room, if you'd like."

Marilee nodded hesitantly. "I would appreciate that."

They went up the stairs without speaking further. As they walked along the corridor, Sarah recollected her manners. Puzzled though she was by Marilee's sudden advent into her life, she had no reason to be rude to her. Besides, she couldn't help but feel sorry for so bedraggled a creature.

"That's Gideon's room," she offered. "He's my eldest brother. Have you met him yet?"

Marilee shook her head. "No, but Mr. Mackenzie said he had two sons."

"Nathan is the other. He's younger than me. Here's where he sleeps." She gestured to the room they were passing, then moved on toward her own. "This one is mine and you'll be next door."

The room they entered was very much like Sarah's own, pleasant despite somber furnishings. A four-poster bed faced tall windows that overlooked the gardens. A matching dresser and tables completed the set. Several botanical prints hung on the walls covered by a dark damask paper.

"It's lovely," Marilee said reverently. "I've never had a room so beautiful."

Sarah shot her a curious glance. Having grown up in the house, she saw nothing particularly noteworthy about it. For the first time it occurred to her that not everyone would feel that way.

"I hope you'll be comfortable here," she said, and rather to her surprise found that she meant it. Marilee's plight stirred hitherto unexperienced emotions within her. She wanted to help the other girl even though she remained suspicious of her father's motives for extending such uncharacteristic charity.

"If you're hungry," she said, "we can go down to the kitchen and get something to eat." By way of encouragement, she added, "Mrs. Hobson makes wonderful gingerbread."

"That would be nice," Marilee acknowledged diffidently. "If you're sure it wouldn't be any trouble."

Sarah was not accustomed to people deferring to her. She would have been less than human if she hadn't responded to it. "Of course not, and afterward I'll show you around the house and we'll get started on your clothes. All right?"

Marilee allowed as to how that was quite agreeable. Her somewhat dazed acceptance further spurred Sarah's protective instincts. It was clear that the older girl had been through a terrible ordeal. Even as Sarah's natural curiosity made her want to know all about it, she resolved not to pry. Virtuously she told herself that her new-found companion must have time to rest and recover.

Mrs. Hobson felt much the same way, even though she was clearly suspicious of the household's newest member. As she set a cup of milk and a plate of gingerbread in front of each of the girls, she asked, "Whatever were you doing out on the road last night, lass?"

Marilee swallowed, her eyes on the gingerbread, and said, "I . . . uh . . . was walking, ma'am. I lost track of the time and didn't notice that the weather was worsening."

The housekeeper looked plainly doubtful but before she could ask anything further, Sarah intervened. "Go ahead and eat, Marilee. It's best warm."

After a moment the other girl did as she said. Marilee's light blue eyes closed as she savored the gingerbread. She chewed it slowly and with such obvious enjoyment that even Mrs. Hobson softened toward her. "Oh, this is good," she said when she had finished the bite. "I haven't had anything like that in so long."

"You go ahead and enjoy it, dear," Mrs. Hobson murmured. She turned around quickly to hide the look of pity in her eyes. For a brief moment she had forgotten how terribly thin and ill-used the girl was. Whoever she was, and whatever reason she'd had for being out in the storm, simple Christian charity demanded that she be looked after.

While she concentrated on Marilee, Sarah felt better. She was able to hold the pain in her abdomen at bay and even, for brief snatches, to ignore it altogether. "I've always wanted to go to Boston," she said as she picked up the earthenware pitcher on the table and refilled their cups. "Did you like it there?"

"I suppose," Marilee said. "It's the only other place I've known and the circumstances were ... very different."

"Since your father was a schoolmaster, did he teach you himself?"

The other girl smiled and shook her head. "No, my mother did at first, then I went to an academy for young ladies." She didn't mention that it had been the cost of her education, and her brother's, which had eaten up her parent's small nest egg and left them destitute at his death.

"I wanted to go to a school like that," Sarah murmured. "My mother said she would try to win Father's approval, but she wasn't able."

"Your mother ... she's dead?"

Sarah nodded. "Last year."

"How old were you then?"

When Sarah told her, Marilee sighed deeply, her blue eyes filled with sympathy. "I was also twelve when my mother died." The way she said it, matter-of-factly but with an underlying note of enduring sorrow, touched a chord in Sarah. She felt as though finally another human being truly understood her grief.

That feeling of no longer being completely alone drove her to say, "There are some clothes upstairs that should fit you with alterations. We can get started on them today."

Marilee was suitably grateful. After a quick tour to familiarize her with the house, the two girls settled in Sarah's room. One of the housemaids had helped them carry down two large boxes from the attic. Packed in them were clothes Catherine Mackenzie had worn as a young woman, before time and childbearing had altered her figure.

Though her mother had once been slender, the clothes still hung on Marilee. They chose a soft wool dress in a shade of blue that matched her eyes and worked on it throughout the afternoon. As they sewed, they talked.

At Sarah's prodding, Marilee told Sarah about life in the mills. She was careful of exactly what she said, censuring any comment that might have sounded critical. But she managed to make clear all the same that she was infinitely glad to be free of the relentless toil.

"I really couldn't do the work," she admitted as they began to piece the dress together after taking it apart for recutting. "I thought I would be able to, but that didn't turn out to be the case. I got so tired after eight or ten hours on the looms that I began to make mistakes." She looked down at her sewing, a frown creasing her high forehead. "The foreman kept giving me different jobs to try to find something I could do, but nothing seemed to work. Truthfully, I'm surprised they waited as long as they did to fire me."

"Is that what happened, you were fired?"

Marilee nodded. "I was ashamed to admit it in front of Mrs. Hobson. She seems so capable."

"She is," Sarah agreed, "but she's also very nice. She wouldn't blame you for not being able to do such difficult work."

"I don't know what I would have done if your father hadn't found me when he did," Marilee said softly. "After I was fired I couldn't stay in the boardinghouse any longer since they're only for mill girls. I had to leave and try to find work elsewhere, as well as a room. For days I walked up and down every street, asking for any sort of job."

"You weren't offered anything?" Sarah asked.

"Well...I..." Marilee flushed, remembering the offers she had had. "Nothing I could take. Anyway, I was out of money and had no place to go when the snow started. I was trying to find a church where I might be given shelter when I fell in the road."

"How terrible. You might have died."

"Yes," Marilee said somberly, "I believe I might have if Mr. Mackenzie hadn't come along. I owe him my life."

The idea of her father having rescued someone from such a fate was so odd to Sarah that she had to ponder it at length. Marilee clearly saw him as some sort of shining knight such as were portrayed in the books on the shelf above Sarah's bed. The image was so out of keeping with the way Sarah herself had always thought of him that she couldn't help but giggle.

Marilee looked at her doubtfully, wondering if she was being mocked. "I'm sorry," Sarah said hastily. "It's nothing. I'm just feeling a little strange today."

"I did notice," Marilee said softly, "that you seemed uncomfortable from time to time. You aren't ill, are you?"

"I don't think so..." She broke off, too embarrassed by the strange sensations to speak of them.

Marilee accepted that, for the moment, though she continued to glance at Sarah from time to time as they sewed. The younger girl had to concentrate fiercely to keep her stitches even. She sat hunched on the floor where they had spread out their work, her lower lip stuck out and her brown bangs flopping in her eyes.

Watching her, Marilee felt a rush of affection she had not experienced since being separated from her family. She had never had a younger sister, but now she felt almost as though she did. That was presumptuous, she reminded herself. By the grace of God and Mr. Mackenzie's charity, she was being allowed to remain in the house. But it would never do to mistake her status. Though she was apparently going to be treated almost as a cousin might be, she was only a few steps above a servant.

Her task, so far as she had been able to define it, was to be a friend to Sarah. That her father should go to such lengths to provide her with one only convinced Marilee all the more of his intrinsic goodness. Clearly he worried about his young daughter and wanted her to have congenial company.

In the warmth of the cozy bedroom, as the snow continued to fall, Marilee silently promised herself that she would be worthy of his trust. She would be Sarah's true friend and do everything possible to help her.

At that moment, Sarah needed help. She had begun to feel a strange wetness between her legs and thought for a moment that she might somehow have soiled herself. Only after the first shock passed did she realize that she hadn't done anything. Something was happening to her over which she had no control.

"Would you...uh...excuse me for a moment?" she asked as she rose hastily, casting a quick glance at the rug to make sure it wasn't stained. Hurriedly she ducked behind the screen, lifted her skirts and pulled down her pantaloons. What she saw made her cry out in fear before she could even think to stop herself.

"Sarah, what's wrong?" Marilee called. She had jumped to her feet and run to the screen, where decorum forced her to stop.

"Uh...nothing. I'm sorry I..." Her voice gave way to a terrified sob. With no idea of what was causing her to bleed or to feel such pain, her only thought was that she was going to die.

Banishing restraint, Marilee stepped around the screen. At first she could only see Sarah hunched by the chamber pot, her thin shoulders shaking. Only then did she notice the pantaloons around her ankles, the white linen stained bright red with blood.

"Oh...it's that..." She paused, uncertain. "Sarah...is this your first time?"

"F-first...?"

"For the curse. It hasn't happened to you before?"

Sarah shook her head. "Nothing like this has ever happened to me. I don't understand what it is."

Marilee took a deep breath and went to her. She put her arm around her shoulders and gently urged her down on the stool. "It happens to all women. Did your mother never say anything?" Sarah shook her head. "There's no reason to be afraid. It's perfectly natural."

As unfortunate as she had been in her recent life, Marilee had been blessed by a mother who saw no reason to make a mystery of a completely normal function. She had prepared her daughter to cope with it matter-of-factly.

"I'll go down and see Mrs. Hobson," Marilee said. "You'll need cloths to catch the flow."

"I'm so embarrassed," Sarah murmured, her head in her hands. She was shaking all over and felt nauseous.

"There's no reason to be," Marilee insisted firmly. "It's always a shock the first time, but you'll get used to it." She helped her stand and drew her from behind the screen. "The first thing to do is get you into bed. Then you should have some hot tea and a brick to warm your feet. That will make you feel better."

Under the older girl's calm ministrations, Sarah began to relax a little. By the time Marilee returned, with Mrs. Hobson on her heels, she had slipped off her clothes and put on a night rail. The stained pantaloons were bundled out of sight behind the chamber pot. She couldn't bear to have anyone else wash them and couldn't stand to do it herself, at least not right then.

"Poor little lass," Mrs. Hobson said, her heavy bosom rising and falling. "I'd hoped you'd have a bit more time before this started." She continued to cluck as she slipped the hot brick wrapped in a towel under the covers at the foot of the bed. With a slight blush, she drew from her pocket a long, rectangular piece of linen folded several times over.

Quietly Marilee explained what to do with it. Sarah was many shades redder than Mrs. Hobson by the time she had complied. With a sense of relief she lay back against the pillows and closed her eyes. The tea Mrs. Hobson had also brought was beginning to have some effect. Sarah suspected the housekeeper of putting a few drops of laudanum in it and was grateful for anything that eased the pain.

"I'll stay with her," Marilee whispered, sitting down on the edge of the bed. She took the younger girl's hand in hers and held it gently.

Sarah's eyelids flickered. She wanted to stay awake, to talk with Marilee and find out more about the strange thing happening to her body. But she was overwhelmingly tired and could no longer fight off sleep. She drifted off feeling curiously content for all the upheaval of the day, knowing only that for the first time since her mother's death she was no longer quite so alone.

Chapter Eight

IN THE MONTHS after his return home, Philip's relationship with his father took a turn that pleased them both. Though they continued to disagree on the issue of slavery, they found many other areas where they were in full accord. Philip was beginning to emerge from his father's shadow to stand as a man in his own right. Charles tacitly acknowledged his son's new status by leaving to him such important tasks as negotiating the purchase of some additional land and the sale of a part of the cotton crop.

In this, Philip knew they were unusual. The young men of his acquaintance—men such as Louis Devereaux, John Carlisle, William Morgan, Jeremy Hudson—all complained of the same problem: their fathers would not give them any responsibility, much less authority. They zealously guarded their privileges, while nonetheless expecting their sons to be able to assume their places when the time came.

"Without practical experience," Louis said one early spring afternoon when they had all ridden out to hunt, "how can we hope to manage our lands properly?" It was noontime, and they had paused beside a stream. House slaves had gone ahead of them to prepare the spot. White cloths covered the ground and fine china gleamed in the sunlight. For Philip the day was a rare break from his duties. For the other men it was simply a way to stave off tedium.

After several bottles of claret, cooled in the stream, words flowed freely. "Our education is purely theoretical," Louis expounded as he reclined on the grass, his jacket off and his stock undone. "We study Latin, religion, mathematics, the arts, all excellent training for the mind but hardly of practical use. We need to learn how to care for the land and everything on it, but we also need to understand finance, law, politics."

"An ambitious curriculum," John Carlisle said with a yawn. "I'd settle for having my sire recognize that I am no longer in the nursery."

"This is the way it's always been," Jeremy Hudson said. At nineteen, he was the youngest in the group by a year or two as well as the least perturbed by the problem. "We'll be no more anxious to make room for our sons. While we wait for our fathers to do so, we might as well enjoy ourselves."

"Easy for you to say, Jeremy," William Morgan insisted with a grin. "We all know why you're so tolerant these days."

To their amusement, Jeremy flushed. He was two months away from his wedding to Kitty and was so besotted with her that she had pleaded with Philip to get him out of her hair for a few hours. "I'm very fond of Jeremy," she had told her brother, "but I can't have him underfoot all the time. Not when there's so much to do."

They had ridden well all morning, bringing down a brace of deer, which the slaves accompanying them looked after while the young men rested. Philip and his friends from the old planter class disdained the ritual of fox hunting gaining in popularity among the newer aristocracy who sought to ape their British cousins. They preferred to pursue more substantial game and had even ventured into the western territories to hunt boar and wolf.

The more hotheaded among them, principally Louis Devereaux and William Morgan, expressed interest in seeing the Far West. Vast stretches of land had been acquired from Mexico in the war concluded the year before. That conflict had opened up untold opportunities for men determined—or desperate—enough to take advantage of them.

"That was the perfect war," Louis said. "Plenty of glory and a rich prize at the end. Wouldn't I like to have been there."

"Then why weren't you?" John drawled. He had become somewhat tired of hearing his friend endlessly beat the same dog of a subject.

"For the same reason none of us was," Louis said. He emptied his wineglass and added, "Our fathers wouldn't have permitted it. We are, after all, their precious heirs." A slave hurried forward to refill the glass, after which Louis raised it in mocking toast. "To us, the lads in waiting. May we live long enough to enjoy our just deserts."

The others joined him, somewhat hesitantly since such cynicism unsettled them. It wasn't that they disagreed, not even Philip who understood how fortunate he was, but to even hint that they might be in a hurry to supplant their fathers seemed to be tempting fate.

Certainly Philip felt no such urgency. Whenever he tried to imagine Calvert Oaks without his father, he ran up against a stone wall his mind could not breach. The older man was so intrinsically a part of the natural order that the mere thought of his departure from it seemed to signify some great upheaval. Even as he grew more confident of his own abilities, Philip also became more grateful for his father's guiding hand.

Particularly when it came to the complex matter of plantation finances. Shortly before Kitty's marriage to Jeremy, her family paid a visit to Richmond. Kitty and Aunt Louise came to shop for her trousseau; the men had other intentions both serious and frivolous. Arriving in the city, they put up with second cousins who maintained a comfortable town house.

The women went out with much excitement to examine the shops while the men paid a visit to their bank. Calvert Oaks's finances were in excellent condition, so the meeting passed pleasantly with the banker—one Hiram Bercher formerly of New York—agreeing that prospects for the coming year looked very promising.

"I swear," the man said after he had expansively provided them with cigars and bourbon, "we should consider making Lowell, Massachusetts, an honorary part of the South. Its millers are so eager for our cotton that they line our purses with every breath they take."

Philip and his father exchanged a tolerant glance. Bercher might try his utmost to identify himself with the South, but he would always be considered a Yankee. His speech, mannerisms, even his very thoughts betrayed him as such. To even suggest that the honor of being Southern could be given by something other than the hand of God was to expose how far he was from what he presumed to be.

"I suppose you've seen this most recent letter from Josiah Mackenzie," Bercher said, indicating his copy. "He's offered five cents more on the bale for next year."

"Generous of him," Charles said, "since the price may well rise above that."

"Or it may not," Bercher said. "And at any rate, Mackenzie offers to pay a large deposit immediately, before the next crop is even in."

"I take it," Philip asked, "that you advise accepting his offer?"

The banker shrugged. "I am a prudent man; I make no apology for that. It seems to me that money in the hand is better than money in the future." He smiled at his own cleverness in a way that invited them to join him.

Philip and his father exchanged another glance, then the older man said, "Were we in need of capital to bring in next year's crop, I might consider accepting Mackenzie's terms. However, since we are not, I prefer to wait and see what the intervening months may bring."

"It might not be anything good," Bercher said. "We've seen the price of cotton go down, sometimes precipitously."

"But the conditions for such a fall are not present now," Charles countered.

"Still, I advise you to be cautious."

Charles took a draw on his cigar, found it inferior to his usual brand and snuffed it out. He rose to go. "That," he said cordially, "is why you are the banker and I am the planter." He might have added, but did not need to, that was also why he was the Southerner.

"What a bantam cock," Philip said, laughingly, as soon as they were out of earshot. "How does he presume to tell us our business?" He was too amused to be offended, but a slight feeling of irritation lingered.

Charles shrugged and set a brisk pace down the cobblestone street. "He dares because so many planters are inept at business. They may know well enough when to put the seed in the ground and when to harvest, but beyond that they are woefully ignorant."

Philip nodded, recalling the recent conversation with his friends. "Surely more could be done to educate the coming generation."

"Certainly," his father agreed, "but part of our great strength is our adherence to tradition, and that decrees that little thought be given to practical matters."

"A costly philosophy."

"For some," the older man said as they turned into a marble-fronted building. It housed a private club popular among planters and those who wished to be taken for such. "For us," he went on, "the weakness of others breeds opportunities, provided we are swift enough to seize them."

He and Philip nodded to several men of their acquaintance as they made their way to a quiet room in the back. There they enjoyed a simple dinner and a bottle of better-than-average claret. Afterward they paid a visit to the tailor they both favored, then returned to their cousins' house where they patiently listened to Kitty exclaim about all the wonderful things she and Aunt Louise had seen, and bought.

Supper was a small but enjoyable affair with some half-dozen couples invited in to meet the visitors. Basking in her status as a soon-to-be-married woman,

Kitty proved particularly charming. She won indulgent smiles from every man present before eventually retiring with the other ladies.

Several hours later, after the guests had departed and the family was preparing for bed, Charles drew Philip aside. "What do you say to slipping away for a few hours?"

Not at all surprised, Philip readily agreed. With the women in bed, the men left the house and took a carriage to a part of Richmond near the docks. There they gave the driver instructions to return for them around dawn and made their way to a large, three-story building from which the sound of piano music could be heard.

Philip had visited such places more than a few times in the past, the first visit being at his father's suggestion when he was fifteen. He had found that the experience, as initially pleasant as it had been, improved with repetition. During his years at Princeton, he had done his manful best to uphold the reputation of Southern virility. Since returning home, he had been so busy that there was little opportunity for such dalliance. But lately he had begun to notice certain female slaves more than he wished to, a sure signal that other arrangements had to be made.

More frequent visits to Richmond might be the best solution. Certainly the red velvet parlor into which he was ushered along with his father and cousins was a pleasant room, if a bit garish. The champagne they were served was excellent, if undoubtedly overpriced. The young women who arrived to keep them company were lovely, if rather informally dressed. In their frothy petticoats, their nearly transparent gowns, their wispy negligees, they presented a delightful picture of dishabille guaranteed to clarify the intentions of any man worthy of the name.

Philip found himself hard-pressed to make a selection. He was torn between a lovely little blonde with breasts the size of ripe melons and a graceful mulatto whose long legs seen through her gauzy skirt frankly enchanted him. In the end, he chose the mulatto and went off with her to her room.

The girl was skillful and eager to please. She undressed him, folding his clothes carefully, then as he watched her, seductively removed her own garments. When she was naked, she crawled onto the bed beside him and pressed her high, firm breasts against his chest. Softly she asked, "Is der anythin' special yo'd like, suh?"

Philip was already fully aroused and in no mood to wait. He shook his head, took the girl by the shoulders and turned her onto her back. She opened her legs obediently and a moment later he was deep inside her, thrusting hard and fast to his climax.

Afterward he lay back against the pillows and smiled at her. "What's your name, girl?"

"Lur'aine, suh. Yo lahk to stay awhile?" After his hasty performance she judged that the young man's ardor was not yet completely spent.

He thought about staying with her or returning downstairs to give a different girl a try, and decided to remain where he was. Variety was fine but he had yet to taste all of Lurraine's charms. "I'll stay. Get us some wine."

She went to do as he bid, walking across the room naked to ring the bell for a servant. He studied the long, slender line of her back appreciatively. Her waist was small, her buttocks firm. Her skin reminded him of brown velvet. When she turned and he saw the dark richness of her nipples, his response was immediate.

Before the wine arrived he'd had her again and was feeling completely relaxed. They sipped it together and talked desultorily. There was really nothing much he wanted to say to her, but he liked the soft, musical quality of her voice. She was from Georgia, the daughter of a slave woman and the son of a planter family. Sold in childhood, she had been brought to Virginia where she was purchased by the brothel's owner. Originally she had worked in the kitchens, but three years before, at thirteen, she had been promoted upstairs.

There was nothing unusual about her story, and she told it matter-of-factly. Philip heard her out with only a slight feeling of discomfort. He had known before they went upstairs that she was in all likelihood a slave. If he had owned her himself, he would never have used her sexually. But since he did not, the onus of responsibility was somehow removed. He was free to enjoy her as he would any other whore. By the time she had finished telling him about herself, Philip had revived sufficiently to be aroused again. He indicated that he wanted her to use her mouth, which she did with prompt effectiveness.

Afterward he slept briefly and had a light snack. While he rested Lurraine sent his clothes out to be brushed and pressed. They were returned as he finished eating. She hung them neatly in the wardrobe before joining him on the bed. Afterward he dozed again for an hour and woke to find her curled up at his side deeply asleep. Considering how hard she had worked in the past few hours, he was tolerant of her exhaustion. Leaving a generous tip on the pillow, he dressed and went downstairs to rejoin his father and cousins.

Having spent the night in similar pursuits, they were all relaxed and expansive as they enjoyed a well-prepared breakfast before settling up. The madame herself saw them out with smiles and bows as dawn was beginning to lighten the sky.

Once back at the cousins' house, the men separated to bath and change. Philip lay in the steaming tub, attended by Jacob who stood by to pour in more hot water as it was needed. He had enjoyed Lurraine and thought he might want to see her again, but he didn't imagine that she was a permanent solution to his needs. Despite the pleasure she had given, he found the experience of coupling with a whore—whether black or white—to be vaguely distasteful. Something was missing from such encounters, an element of higher purpose that transformed the carnal and gave it meaning.

He thought of Daphne. Since his welcome-home party the previous summer, he had seen her often, though never alone. Both their families entertained frequently, and there were many occasions for them to be together. The better acquainted they became, the more enchanting he found her. She seemed the very epitome of beauty and gentleness. When she visited Calvert Oaks, carefully chaperoned of course, he was struck by how much she belonged there.

He was still thinking about Daphne as he rose from the tub and allowed Jacob to dry him. Having dismissed the valet, he shaved himself, following the habit ingrained by his father. A slave might perform all manner of intimate duties for his master, but only a fool put a razor in a black man's hands and bared his throat to him.

Dressed in a fresh shirt, trousers and frock coat with his stock neatly tied at his throat, he was ready to go back downstairs. The ladies were at breakfast in the morning room. They greeted him pleasantly and made no comment when he accepted only a cup of dark, chicory-flavored coffee. None of the family lingered at table. Kitty and Louise had another day of shopping with their female cousins. Charles and Philip had plantation business to attend to.

Chapter Nine

RICHMOND'S SLAVE AUCTIONS were held in several locations scattered around the city. More than two dozen slave dealers operated there, and all the more reputable firms were represented. The auction to be held that day had been well advertised in the local papers and with leaflets put up on the major streets. By noon, a good-sized crowd had gathered. Those in attendance were mostly planters, but there were also businessmen from the tobacco and iron factories, merchants looking for help in their stores and ship captains wanting to add to their crews.

Before the auction began, those interested in making purchases—or at least claiming to be—strolled around among the slave pens. They were set out in an open courtyard on which the sun beat relentlessly. The smell of unwashed bodies mingled with the stench from the hard-baked dirt that was the only place for the several dozen men, women and children to relieve themselves. Bluebottle flies droned monotonously in the hot, still air. A few of the children cried softly but most of the blacks were stoically silent. They kept their faces blank and their eyes averted as the white men passed among them.

Philip and Charles, being obviously both serious and prosperous, were accompanied by the dealer himself

who pointed out the particular merits of various slaves.
"If it's a good field worker you're looking for," he
said, "this is the best man I've seen in a long time." He
gestured toward a tall, heavily muscled black man of
perhaps twenty. "Fully mature yet with years of service ahead of him. Obedient, with a placid nature, and
all his own teeth."

Charles was mildly interested but unconvinced.
"Have him take off his shirt."

The slave did as he was told. Standing bare-chested,
he was then instructed to turn around. The marks of
whippings, both old and recent, were clearly visible on
his broad back.

"Placid?" Charles repeated. "He hardly looks it."

"There were problems with his previous owner," the
dealer admitted, "but all he needs is a firm hand. He
won't give you any trouble."

Charles shook his head. "I don't like the whip used
on my property, and I don't like slaves who won't obey
without it. What else do you have?"

Philip's face had tightened at the sight of the whip
marks. He would have preferred to stay away from the
auction but had come at his father's express request.
"However you feel about slavery," Charles had said,
"I believe you will ultimately realize its importance and
should therefore be no stranger to any of its aspects."
Including judging black flesh and getting the best possible price for it.

They moved on to the next pen, where the dealer
pointed out a slightly older man. "Still in his prime,
but with the seasoning a wise buyer wants." Charles
nodded thoughtfully and studied the man. He seemed
healthy enough and was docile under examination.

Several other field slaves were presented for their inspection. The choice was not large—it never was now that the economy was picking up again—but it looked as though there would be enough to fill their immediate needs. Before the auction was due to begin, they took their seats in the hall filled with benches facing a raised platform.

Philip removed his hat and wiped the sweat from his forehead. Beneath his frock coat, his shirt was sticking to him. He closed his eyes for a moment and heard the muted sound of a boat whistle on the river and the jangle of a harness from a wagon passing by outside. Several men were talking quietly among themselves but broke off when the auctioneer appeared and mounted the block.

The sale started off slowly with a few older slaves, male and female, going for small amounts. Though the dealer claimed all manner of useful skills for them, there was little demand. Once a slave passed his prime, he was considered a drain on the plantation's resources.

Philip's mouth tightened as a stooped, white-haired old man whom the auctioneer described as an able gardener was sold to a poorly dressed farmer. The hundred dollars paid for him was clearly all the farmer could afford, but that didn't make the old man's fate any more desirable. He would doubtless be worked to death before very long.

Next on the block was a woman in her mid-twenties. A small child clung to her skirts and she was some six months gone with another. "Here is a true bargain," the dealer extolled. "A proven breeder, as you can see for yourselves. Put her with your young bucks, and you will have a steady stream of little pickaninnies to swell your coffers."

The bidding was prompt. Throughout it the woman kept her eyes averted, one arm around the child. They would be sold together, provided the price went high enough, otherwise they would be separated. Philip was close enough to see the woman sigh in relief when a tobacco planter offered five hundred for them both.

There was a stir in the audience as a young negress was led to the stage next. She was clearly afraid and tried to hang back, but a firm push from the dealer sent her forward. "A rarity in today's market," the dealer began. "Reared by a prominent family in New Orleans. She is familiar with all household duties and is a particularly able seamstress." As he spoke, he winked broadly, which brought appreciative chuckles from some in the audience.

"Of course, she also has other attributes, which you discerning gentlemen will no doubt appreciate." Without further ado he opened the girl's dress at the back and pulled it off. She was naked underneath, her body slender but well formed. Small, budding breasts and the beginnings of hair between her legs indicated that the transition to womanhood had begun, yet there was still much of the child about her.

That was especially evidenced in the way she tried to cover herself, only to be stopped by the dealer. "She needs training yet," he acknowledged, "but her basic nature is tractable. Who will start the bidding at nine hundred?" From there it rose rapidly until the girl was finally sold for almost twice that to a plump middle-aged man who fairly exuded glee at his purchase.

Philip sat stone-faced through the procedure. Were he less sensitive to his father's feelings, he might have expressed his distaste. But the subject of white men making sexual use of their female slaves struck far too close to home. He could feel the stiffness in his father and see the slight flush of his lean cheeks that did not begin to abate until the sale was done and the dealer moved on to the field hands.

The man Charles had taken note of in the slave pens was offered shortly and secured for Calvert Oaks at a cost of nine hundred dollars. Two other likely looking hands were also acquired for about the same amount each.

After the last of the offerings was made, Charles settled up with the dealer and arranged for the slaves to be held until the next day, when they would all be leaving Richmond.

"How I wish we could stay longer," Kitty said as they were boarding the steamer early the following morning. "The shops here are wonderful, and I've barely had a chance to explore them."

"You'll come back," her father promised her. With a grin, he added, "Young Jeremy gives every promise of being a doting husband."

Kitty shrugged. The river breeze was playing with the wide brim of her straw hat. She tied the satin ribbons more securely under her chin as she said, "Why else would I be marrying him?"

Leaning against the railing, Philip laughed. "Don't count on him to be too biddable. He does have a backbone, you know."

"Of course, I wouldn't want him to be any other way." Her manner changed suddenly, becoming wistful. "But you do think he'll let me come back, don't you?"

"Certainly, Jeremy will do anything he can for you." He truly believed that, but he also suspected that Kitty had some surprises ahead of her in marriage.

They reached the dock at Calvert Oaks as evening was falling. Johnson, the overseer, was there to meet them and take charge of the new slaves. Under his critical eye the three men shambled out of the hold, where they had been kept for the journey along with the rest of the baggage. Chained together at the ankles, they moved slowly down the gangplank.

"What do you think of them, Mr. Johnson?" Charles asked.

The dark, squat man shrugged. "Like Ah sed before you left, Mista Calvert, Ah'd have liked to pick 'em out myself. But they're your choice, so Ah guess they'll do."

Philip frowned, not liking the implication that the overseer would have made a better selection. "Do you see anything wrong with them, Mr. Johnson?"

The overseer shifted his attention to the younger man. His small, black eyes set in a square face narrowed. "No, sur, nothin' yet. I just hope they don't take the soft treatment they'll be gettin' as license to do anything stupid."

"Soft? That's hardly accurate, but at any rate it's up to you to see that they don't."

The overseer's face reddened. "I know my job right enough. Get along then," he said, prodding the first man in the line. They stumbled into the wagon that would take them to their quarters.

When they were gone, Philip said, "Johnson has a tendency to overstep himself."

His father nodded as they got into the carriage, where Kitty and Aunt Louise were waiting. "Yes, I know, but he does his job well. So long as we're watchful, I don't think he'll get out of hand.''

Augusta and Rameses were at the door to greet them. Half a dozen other house slaves appeared to unload the carriage. Directly behind them had come another wagon carrying Jacob and the other personal slaves who had made the trip with them. They jumped out to help as Augusta exclaimed, ''Land sakes, Miss Kitty, it done look lahk yo bought out most ahl ob Richmond.''

''Just about,'' the girl said, laughing, ''and I got the most wonderful things. Wait until you see them.'' Philip handed her out of the coach along with Aunt Louise. The women hurried inside to escape the humid night air. The men remained outside for a while on the portico, sipping juleps brought by Rameses and talking over the trip.

''It went well,'' Charles conceded. ''With the new field hands, we'll be able to put even more acreage to the plow. Mackenzie's offer indicated there'll be a definite price increase next year. We'll be in excellent position to benefit from it.''

''Are you sure he's right?'' Philip asked, leaning back in his chair.

''Mackenzie's a shrewd man who does nothing without long and hard consideration. I can't say I like him personally, but I admire his success.''

''He came from around here originally, didn't he?''

Charles nodded. ''From the back country. Apparently he'd had it quite hard though he never mentions it. By the time I met him, he owned the first of his mills in Lowell and was clearly set to acquire more.''

''How does he compare with the other mill owners we do business with?''

"He's smarter and more ruthless, which is saying something since they're all a tough breed. We've been doing business with Mackenzie for some twenty years, and I've never known him to get the short end of a deal. Of course," Charles added with a smile, "I don't make out too badly, either."

Philip laughed and sipped his julep. He knew perfectly well that his father was a shrewd negotiator who invariably came out well in any arrangement.

"There's something I want you to do for me," Charles said. "After Kitty's safely married off, I'd like you to go north. There are business matters that need seeing to and I don't particularly want to make the trip myself."

"Of course," Philip said, doing his best to hide his excitement. He was thrilled that his father proposed to send him in his place. The trip would be his first solo venture on behalf of Calvert Oaks. He was determined to carry it off well.

"But first," Charles added, "we've got that blasted wedding to get through. Do you suppose Kitty left anything behind in Richmond for some other bride to buy?"

"Doubtful," Philip said with a laugh. "It's just as well that she's getting a wealthy husband."

"Let's hope he stays that way. I'd hate to have Daniel Hudson complaining that my daughter had tried to ruin him."

There was little risk of that. Before agreeing to the marriage, Charles had carefully checked out the Hudsons' finances. He was confident that their wealth was secure enough to withstand even a spendthrift bride. Besides, Kitty brought a substantial dowry with her. Not the acreage her soon-to-be father-in-law had hinted would be appropriate, but a sum of money that he had been willing enough to accept instead.

The two men remained on the porch awhile longer, until the urge for sleep overcame them. They retired then and shortly afterward the house was dark. Only a single light still burned in one of the cabins down in the quarters.

Marcus sat at a small wooden table, listening as another man spoke softly and urgently. "Dey be comin' tonight, don' know exactly when. Be three ob dem, if dem ahl gets through."

"We be ready," Marcus said.

His wife, Ginny, sat at the table beside him. She was a slender young woman of about nineteen, her exact age being unknown even to herself. Of medium height with glowing ebony skin, dark eyes and thick black hair cut short around her well-shaped head, she held herself with instinctive strength and grace. Her slim hands moved over the shirt she was stitching as she listened to the men.

"Gotta move dem on fast," the visitor said. "Patrols be in de neighborhood."

"Yas," Marcus agreed, "Ahs know, but wes manage." With a slight smile, he added, "wes always do."

"Wha' 'bout yo'self?" Ginny asked the other man in her softly rhythmic voice. "Can yo get back t'yor place ahl right?"

He nodded. "Ahs got a pass."

"Lemme see dat," Marcus said. The man dug it out of a back pocket of his ragged cutoffs and handed it over. By the light of the lantern, Marcus scrutinized it carefully. "Dis here says yo name Bartholemew an' yo be a house slave. Yo know dat?"

The man shook his head. "Yo knows Ahs can't read. Ahs traded fo' it with a buck bes on de run. He done steal a handful from his massa 'fore he take off."

Marcus sighed and handed the paper back. He knew that some whites had the habit of keeping passes on hand for their household slaves who had to be sent on frequent errands. That saved them the trouble of writing them out as needed. But there was no telling how long ago this particular pass had been stolen. It had probably been reported by now, so that the patrols would be on watch for anyone attempting to use it.

"Dat be dangerous ta show," he told the man. "Even if da slave hunters don' know it's stolen, yo don' match de description on dere. Wha' man goin' ta believe yo a house slave?"

The man shrugged and put the pass back in his pocket. "Ahs knows, but ahs figure it's better t'have somethin' t'show dem dan nothin'."

Marcus didn't argue further. He knew that as useless as the pass might turn out to be, it was a talisman of sorts. No black would willingly venture out without one since to do so invited at best a whipping and at worst death. At least the man had enough sense not to be overly confident. He would stay off the road and do his best to avoid patrols.

When he was gone, Ginny put her sewing in her lap and studied her husband carefully. They had been together for more than a year, but she didn't feel that she knew him. He was a mystery to her, this strong, gentle man who seemed caught somewhere between two opposing worlds. Except for the darkness of his skin, he looked like the whites she loathed. When he chose, he also talked and thought the same as them. But there the resemblance ended. No one had ever been as kind to her as Marcus. He had saved her from a terrible existence, taught her to find pleasure in her life for the first time and given her a sense of self-respect she had never before known.

In return she gave him all her love, in every possible form. There was truly nothing she would not do for Marcus, but that did not prevent her from sometimes feeling that he was wrong. "Des men," she said softly, "dey have to stay here?"

Marcus sighed and ran a hand wearily through his short-cropped hair. After a day in the fields, he was tired in every muscle and sinew. Added to that had been yet another confrontation with Johnson. The overseer made no secret of his hatred for Marcus, whom he regarded as "an uppity nigger who needs to be taught his place." All that prevented Johnson from trying to teach him was the knowledge that Charles Calvert would not take kindly to his mulatto son being harmed. Generally Marcus found little reason to be appreciative of his parentage, but the protection it gave him, and by extension others, was one benefit he could not ignore.

"Everythin' be all right," he reassured Ginny. "Dey be gone in a few days."

"Yo knows wha' happen if dey caught here?"

Marcus nodded. The runaways would be severely punished, as would anyone suspected of helping them. Should he be implicated, not even Charles Calvert would be able to save him. Yet this was a risk he had taken in the past and would take again.

Since the opening of the underground railroad some eight years before, thousands of blacks had made the trek to freedom. In the border states, they were helped by sympathetic abolitionists, but while they were still in the South, they had to depend mainly on strategically placed slaves like himself.

He had lost count of the number of runaways he had hidden in the past few years. They came alone, in groups, sometimes as entire families. For the young men, the journey was difficult enough, but for the women, children and elderly it could often prove fatal. Even if they escaped detection, the desperate march to freedom exacted a heavy toll.

He did what he could to help, providing food and clothing slowly accumulated from the plantation stores so as not to draw attention. Some of the runaways arrived injured, and there Ginny's healing skills had lately proved invaluable. The other slaves at Calvert Oaks were well aware of what was happening, and each of them contributed to the effort in his own way even as they all feared detection. Marcus knew that it was their respect for him, and their trust, that made them take the risk. That was a heavy burden of responsibility to carry. He shouldered it as best he could and tried not to dwell on the possible consequences.

"Best to sleep awhile 'fore dey comes," Ginny suggested. When he nodded absently she stood up and blew out the lamp. Gently she took him by the hand and led him to the narrow pallet they shared. It, the table, two chairs and a chest were the only furnishings in the cabin. Marcus could have lived more comfortably, but he chose to share the circumstances of his fellow slaves, shunning all trappings of the big house where he had grown up.

The mattress was stuffed with straw. They lay down on it together after undressing. As warm as it was, there was no need for any covering. For a long time they lay without speaking or moving, then Ginny turned on her side and gently reached for him.

They made love slowly, drawing out their mutual pleasure. Ginny bit down on her lower lip to still her cries of ecstasy. Before Marcus, sex had been only one more act of violence and cruelty. It had taken him great patience to teach her otherwise, but the results had been more than worthwhile. As she opened to him fully, she hoped that this time he would not pull away at the last. His refusal to get her with child baffled her. She knew it wasn't from any lack he found in her; he had assured her of that repeatedly. The only other possibility she could think of was that he did not want to father a child who would be born in slavery.

As she clasped him to her, her hands stroking his broad back and her hips rising to meet him, she turned her head away so that he would not feel her silent tears.

_____ *Chapter Ten*

LOWELL WAS AT ITS BEST in autumn. The maples, beeches and oaks dressed the town in a cape of scarlet and gold. The smoky scent of wood fires curled through the air. Under a clear blue sky, the river was a winding ribbon of silver and even the mills looked picturesque.

Sarah walked home from school slowly, her books hanging by a leather strap over her shoulder and her boots scuffing in the leaves that littered the road. She knew she should hurry because a guest was expected, but her father had been in such a foul mood lately that the temptation to dawdle was irresistible.

Beside her, Nathan spied two squirrels chasing each other and laughed.

"Look, Sarah," he said, tugging at her hand, "they're playing."

She smiled at him. "I guess they are. Come on now, we have to get home."

He was willing enough, as he was willing to do anything she asked of him. Smaller than most boys of his age, Nathan desperately needed a mother and Sarah was the closest he had to it. He remained with her as much as he could manage despite Gideon's spiteful teasing. That afternoon they were both relieved to be spared his caustic presence since he had stayed late at school where he was being tutored, the extra work required if he hoped to enter prep school the following spring.

Entering the house through the back door, they found the kitchen in a flurry of activity. Mrs. Hobson was at the stove, stirring a thick fish soup she was preparing as the first course in the evening meal. The housemaids were busy peeling vegetables while a special pastry cook hired for the occasion was putting the final touches on the beef *en croûte* that was about to go in the oven.

Nathan slid into a chair at the large wooden table and observed the proceedings wide-eyed. Since his mother's death, there had been few guests in the house and none had merited such activity. He was wondering when he would get to meet the man responsible when Mrs. Hobson said, "There you two are. Your grandmother's been asking for you. She wants you upstairs right away."

The housekeeper's expression was harried and her tone brusque. The task of preparing so elaborate a meal was difficult enough without interference from her employer's mother and sister. So far she had counted six trips to the kitchen by Grandmother Mackenzie and four by Caroline. The next time either of them stuck her nose where it didn't belong, Mrs. Hobson was severely tempted to chop it off and add it to the soup.

"Come on, Nathan," Sarah said. She was resigned to not being able to avoid her grandmother or aunt. They were in the habit of dropping by the house on the slightest excuse under any circumstances; with so interesting a guest on hand, there was no chance they might have stayed away.

Voices from the parlor quickened her step. She heard the deep tones of a man followed by Aunt Caroline's shrill laughter. From the top of the stair landing, Marilee beckoned to them. "The coast is clear," she said with a smile, "if you hurry."

Both girls giggled as Nathan raced ahead. "There's hot water in your room," Marilee called after him.

"I'm not dirty."

"Use it anyway," Sarah instructed, "and put on your Sunday suit."

"I laid out your navy blue dress," Marilee said as they both went into Sarah's room. "Would you like me to fix your hair?"

"If you can do something with it, I'd be grateful. But really, all this fuss for some Southern cotton grower."

"He's the son of a man your father's been doing business with for years. Mr. Mackenzie wants him to feel welcome."

Marilee's gentle reprimand made Sarah shrug. In the little less than a year that the older girl had been living in the house, Sarah had grown accustomed to her devotion to the man she continued to regard as her rescuer. Besides, Marilee had become too good a friend to resent anything she might say.

"You really look pretty," Sarah said as she rapidly unbuttoned her school dress and hung it away in the closet. Mrs. Hobson's good cooking had finally succeeded in adding a few pounds to Marilee's slender frame. Her cheeks and eyes had a healthy glow and her blond hair gleamed. She was simply dressed in a soft pink wool dress that had once belonged to Catherine Mackenzie. It was a little old for her sixteen years, but otherwise looked lovely.

Marilee acknowledged the compliment, then set about getting Sarah ready. The dress she had selected was one she had helped Sarah make. It was still a dress for a young girl, very modestly cut with the hem a few inches above the ankles. But it did not completely flatten the budding swell of her breasts or conceal the slight curve newly come to her hips. Sarah was growing up and in another few months, Marilee intended to broach the subject of a new wardrobe. She was confident that she could win Josiah's approval since he had already proved very amenable to her suggestions.

"I still don't understand how you got my father to agree to let us attend this dinner," Sarah said as she slipped the navy blue dress over her head. "He's never let us eat with guests before unless they were family."

"I simply mentioned that you were getting older," Marilee said as she began to brush Sarah's hair, "and it was time you began practicing the social graces."

"That presumes that I have any to practice."

"Of course, you do."

Sarah frowned in the mirror. She didn't like her hair, which she regarded as limp and uninteresting. But then she wasn't very pleased with her face, either, considering it plain. Her body she preferred not to think of at all since it no longer even seemed to be hers.

"We're going to have to let this dress out soon," Marilee said. "You're getting bigger on top."

"I hate that. Why couldn't I have stayed the way I was?"

Marilee continued to draw the brush through Sarah's hair, gently smoothing out the tangles. "You wouldn't want to be a child forever, would you?"

"No, I suppose not. But the alternative doesn't seem all that wonderful, either."

"You'll feel differently in a few years," Marilee assured her. She stepped back and regarded her handiwork in the mirror. "There, doesn't that look nice?"

She had swept Sarah's hair away from her face and secured it with a blue velvet ribbon, leaving a few loose tendrils to soften her features. The result was simple but effective.

Sarah brightened and turned to give her a hug. "I don't know what I'd do without you, Marilee. You always know how to make things better."

"Thanks, but don't give me too much credit. You're much prettier than you want to admit."

Sarah was openly doubtful about that. To her, pretty meant Marilee's blond hair, delicate features and feminine manners. It had nothing in common with her own awkwardness, much less with the anger she too often felt bubbling just below the surface. Anger made all the worse by the fact that she didn't really understand all that caused it. There were times when she longed to be like Marilee not only in appearance but in the serene acceptance of her nature. If only she could manage to be like that, her life would be so much easier. But instead she rebelled against the restrictions set by her father, the betrayal of her body, the expectations of a world where she seemed fated to never really belong.

"At least this should be interesting," Sarah said as the two girls went down the stairs arm in arm. "I've never met a Southerner before."

"Surely they can't be all that different from us," Marilee ventured.

"Oh, but they are. We're learning all about them in school. They're prideful and indolent, and they make their slaves do everything." Her teacher had made that perfectly clear in a recent lecture about the South.

"Parasites," he had called the plantation owners, "destroying the land they claim to love, living off the blood and sweat of the negroes they hold in bondage and pretending to be good Christians when they are all damned to the fires of eternal hell."

Sarah had shaken her head in dismay along with the rest, but privately she couldn't help but be curious to meet such a creature. She half wondered if Philip Calvert would have horns on his head and a tail.

He did not, but that in no way lessened his impact on Sarah. As she and Marilee entered the parlor, a tall, golden-haired man rose to meet them.

"My daughter, Sarah," Josiah said, "and her companion, Marilee. They are joining us for dinner."

Marilee made a pretty curtsey, but had to nudge Sarah to remind her to do the same. She barely managed it, feeling unbearably self-conscious. Her eyes seemed riveted to the broad chest of their guest; she dared look no higher than his wide shoulders. The mere glimpse she had gotten of his thick, burnished hair, startlingly bright blue eyes and bronzed features had robbed her of breath. Her heart was hammering against her ribs and her stomach felt as it had years before when she fell out of the apple tree and broke her arm.

"How nice to meet you, Mr. Calvert," Marilee said, covering what had been about to become an awkward silence. "I hope your journey wasn't too tiring?"

"He's told us all about that," Grandmother Mackenzie broke in, frowning. She had made no secret of her disapproval of Marilee, believing as she did that her son should never have taken her into his home, much less allowed her to remain there. That she was permitted to live almost as one of the family only made the situation that more intolerable.

Her quelling tone did not disturb Marilee. She merely smiled gently and took a seat opposite their guest. After a moment Sarah remembered that she was still standing and hastily sat down beside her.

"Not too tiring at all," Philip replied, as though his host's mother had not spoken. Though he would never be overtly rude to her, a few minutes' acquaintance had been enough to convince him that Mrs. Mackenzie was a hard, cold woman deserving of no special courtesies. Her simpering daughter seemed little different.

What surprised him was that he hadn't met more women like them since coming north. At Princeton, he had been largely insulated from the female population, his contacts limited to infrequent teas at professors' homes and much more frequent visits to local brothels. This time, he was meeting a much larger selection of northern women and finding them to be not all that different from those he had left at home.

Granted they tended to speak up far more and to show an interest in matters Aunt Louise would have termed unseemly. But they were also hospitable and charming, often going out of their way to make him feel less a stranger.

The present company was not completely an exception. The daughter's companion was a lovely young woman; she reminded him of Kitty. The daughter herself seemed backward and had nothing to say for herself, but there was nothing actually objectionable about her. The same could not be said for the young man Josiah had introduced as his eldest son.

Gideon Mackenzie was a gawky, sullen boy. He had his father's black eyes and hair, but otherwise seemed to resemble him little. Josiah could at least be personable. "It's been a long time since I saw Virginia," he said. "How are things there?"

"I think you'd find that very little has changed," Philip said. He had resumed his seat, one long leg in broadcloth trousers crossed over the other. His black boots gleamed from the polish Jacob had given them that morning. He wore a white shirt with a slight ruffling, an embroidered waistcoat and a gray frock coat. "But then it rarely does."

Josiah did not miss the slight note of regret in the younger man's voice. He was surprised by it. From his perspective, Philip Calvert had the perfect life. Born to wealth and power, he lived surrounded by every luxury both could provide. What then could lie behind the tantalizing hint that he was not quite content?

"You were at Princeton, weren't you? I seem to remember your father mentioning that in one of his letters."

Philip nodded. "I spent four years there."

Josiah's thin smile was barely perceptible. He thought of how differently his own youth had been. To reach his goals, he had denied himself rest, pleasure, all the indulgences men like his guest took as their due. Yet some instinct warned him that he would not be wise to think of Philip as weak simply because he had not been proven in so harsh a school.

He could sense within him the same strength that was in his father, but also something more. Charles Calvert was certainly an honest man in the sense that he adhered to a strict code of honor. Philip, however, seemed to go beyond that to a genuine sense of morality that frankly left Josiah nonplussed. He couldn't decide whether that was a strength or a weakness, and did not like having to wonder.

"Someday," Sarah said without warning, "women will go to college."

There was startled silence, followed quickly by an angry exclamation from her grandmother. "That's quite enough. When your opinion is wanted, you'll be asked for it. In the meantime, hold your tongue."

Ordinarily Sarah would not have been touched by the reprimand, so inured was she to the older woman's harshness. But for reasons she could not begin to fathom, she was acutely embarrassed at being chastised in front of Philip. "I only meant . . ."

"Do as your grandmother says," her father ordered. His face had darkened, and he clenched his hands angrily. It was intolerable to him that Calvert's son might think anyone in his family ill-mannered. He could hear him now once he was home, describing the "boorish" Yankees who dared to get above themselves, so much so that even their girl children didn't know their place.

"You must have missed your home when you were away," Marilee interjected. "Do you have a large family?"

"Not by Southern standards," Philip said, glad of the reprieve. Surprised though he had been by the girl's comment, he had thought it no more than amusing, certainly not deserving of the rebuff she had gotten. The poor thing looked miserable, which stirred his sympathy and made him go out of his way to cooperate with Marilee.

"I have only one sister, Kitty. She was married a few weeks ago."

"Kitty was?" Josiah asked without thinking. "Isn't she very young?"

"Seventeen, certainly old enough to be wed."

"That's one of the differences between your ways and ours," Caroline chimed in. "Here girls wait longer to marry." Archly she added, "And men have the sense to appreciate a more mature bride."

Philip grimaced. If by that she meant herself, a man would have to be beyond all sense. Reconciled to a tedious evening, he followed the others into the dining room, noticing only in passing that the girl—what was her name, Sarah?—hung back. He didn't blame her for wishing she could be somewhere else.

At least the food was expertly prepared, if blander than he liked. Someone had gone to a great deal of trouble, and he tried to appreciate that though it was difficult. No wine was served, nor had he been offered a drink when he arrived. Ordinarily that wouldn't have bothered him but under the circumstances he would have appreciated a relaxant.

"I understand you've increased your acreage," Josiah said as they sat down. "Very wise, given the demand for cotton."

"And the demands placed by cotton," Philip replied. "We can never forget that it exhausts the soil. One of the reasons Calvert Oaks has prospered is because we've always been willing to let a large percentage of our fields rest."

"But there is always more land. The western territories are only beginning to be settled."

"True, but that is not our land. We need to care for what we already have." Philip spoke without much hope of being understood. He had discovered during his years at Princeton that Northerners tended to be so absorbed by the country's exciting future that they gave little thought to caring for it in the present. Yet he had to admit that many Southerners were the same. They seemed to believe that their cherished way of life would go on forever no matter what they did or did not do.

"A laudable sentiment," Josiah said. He swallowed a generous bite of the roast while absently noting that Sarah wasn't eating. She sat with her hands in her lap and her eyes on her plate, whereas Marilee showed every sign of enjoying the occasion. Her eyes sparkled as she looked at Philip.

Josiah frowned. "However, I don't believe it's wise to be too attached to the past. We live in a changing world."

"Of course," Philip agreed. "Change is inevitable."

His host's thick black eyebrows rose almost to the level of his hairline. "That from a Southerner? I thought the mere mention of change was heretical below the Mason-Dixon line."

"There is some truth to that, but there are also some of us who believe that all things must grow or die. Social systems are no exception."

Sarah reluctantly raised her eyes, drawn by the irresistible sound of his voice. Barely breathing, she studied Philip with the intentness previously reserved for unusual bits of wildlife encountered in her too-brief escapes from home and school.

He was not having a good time, that much she was sure of. Yet he was being very polite, far more so than she could ever manage. His good manners seemed bred into him, as intrinsic as the thick pelt of gold hair that brushed past his collar and the deep-set blue eyes that turned suddenly in her direction.

She gulped and looked away. He was replying to some question Aunt Caroline had asked, but she heard neither the query nor the response. Her skin had gone from clammy to flushed, and her stomach still felt queasy. The mere thought of biting into the heavy slab of beef accompanied by fried potatoes and boiled carrots on the plate in front of her made her swallow hastily.

Under cover of the general conversation, Marilee leaned over and touched her arm gently. "Are you all right?"

Sarah nodded but said nothing. She longed for escape, yet again and again she was drawn to look at Philip. Apart from a few servants or tradesmen, the only other man she had ever had a chance to observe at close range was her father. Philip's contrast to him could not have been greater. Where Josiah was brooding darkness, he was golden radiance. The angry tension she felt in her father—and to her dismay sometimes in herself—was absent in the guest. From him she could sense only calm certainty, the aura of a man clear in himself and his place in the world.

It had always amused her that Marilee thought of her father as a knight in shining armor when he was so evidently anything but. Yet something of what the other girl felt made sense to her as she watched Philip. He reminded her irresistibly of the stalwart knights in Malory's *Tales of King Arthur*. How easily she could see him riding to the rescue against a fire-breathing dragon as she, the fair maiden, watched adoringly.

Preoccupied with this romantic vision, she continued blissfully distracted from the conversation until Grandmother Mackenzie asked, "And when is the wedding to be, Mr. Calvert?"

"At Christmas, ma'am. My fiancée is busy assembling her trousseau. In fact," he added with a smile, "I have a list of items I absolutely must not return without."

His eyes softened as he thought of how Daphne had tucked the list into his jacket pocket just as he was preparing to leave on his trip north. She was staying at Calvert Oaks to help plan the wedding and become acquainted with her new home. How he wished he could be there with her but thought it might be as well that he was not. The months until their marriage could not pass quickly enough for Philip, desiring his bride as fiercely as he did.

His decision to marry Daphne had been met by universal approval from friends and family. Uncle James had already announced his intention to gift the young couple with a town house in Richmond. Meanwhile, Charles had arranged for the redecorating of a corner suite at Calvert Oaks so that it would be ready when the newlyweds returned from the bridal trip. He had also taken the unusual step of settling the profits from several hundred acres of land on his son so that for the first time in his life, Philip would have income of his own.

The only bone of contention had been Daphne's plan to bring half a dozen slaves with her from her family home. As her husband, Philip would automatically become their master. He would no longer be simply a beneficiary of the slave system, but an actual owner. When he had tried to explain to her why that did not sit well with him, she had been at first baffled, then tearful. The slaves had been with her since childhood; she could not imagine life without them. Would he be so cruel as to separate her from all that was dear and familiar?

Philip had given in, though he promised himself that in the future he would be firmer. It undoubtedly took time to learn the proper handling of a wife. She wouldn't always be able to win him over with tears and pouts, though he could think of other tactics that might work all too well.

Aware suddenly of the silence around the table, he realized that his mind had wandered. Josiah had asked him a question he hadn't caught. "Pardon me, what was that you said?"

Grandmother Mackenzie motioned with the fingers of one hand, trying to hush her son. He ignored her and repeated his question. "About the mood in Washington. When do you suppose the politicians will stop their jabbering and come to some accord on slavery?"

Philip had to hide a smile. He could well understand why the woman was flustered. Slavery was a touchy subject to raise when both Northerners and Southerners were present. He had noticed that most Yankees were scrupulously careful never to mention it in his presence, and he rather admired Josiah for having the nerve to do otherwise.

Giving no clue to his thoughts, he said, "I fear that won't be any time soon. The differences are too deeply held and fiercely felt."

"Pack of nonsense, if you ask me," his host said. "Personally, I think it's a system that's outlived its usefulness, but the South will come to realize that in its own time. There's no reason to be up in arms over it."

"I wish more Northerners felt as you do," Philip said. "Too many wish to impose their beliefs on us."

"Does that mean you support slavery, sir?" Gideon asked suddenly. He had not spoken since they sat down at the table, and indeed, Philip had all but forgotten the dark, sour-faced boy's presence.

Reminded, he said, "I agree with your father that the system is obsolete. Given time, it can be done away with."

"How much time?" Gideon asked. He was staring at Philip intently, his small eyes flashing and his pale face flushed.

"Why, I don't know...exactly. It depends on what is to be done with the slaves." He smiled at the boy. "As you may know, some believe they should be sent back to Africa while others favor settling them in the Caribbean or South America. There are even a few people who want them to be allowed to stay here after gaining their freedom."

"What's wrong with that?"

"Gideon..." Josiah broke in, "that's quite enough." He did not raise his voice but the effect was quelling all the same. Gideon flinched and looked down at his plate.

"No, it's all right," Philip said. "I don't mind the boy's curiosity. What's wrong is that a large population of freed coloreds would change the nature of this country. They would want to settle land, build towns, send their children to schools, possibly even vote. The purity of our European heritage would be diluted. A new, alien element would be introduced, the consequences of which cannot be imagined."

"What can be done to avoid that?" Marilee asked.

Her courage in entering the conversation surprised Sarah, until she realized that it shouldn't have. Josiah had a tendency to show her far more tolerance and patience than he ever extended to his own children.

"I think the coloreds must eventually have their freedom," Philip said, "and be settled on land of their own, perhaps as a colony or protectorate of the United States. But where that land should be, whether in Africa or somewhere closer, is yet to be determined."

"Then you don't think emancipation is imminent?" she asked.

"By no means. For one thing, there's the question of compensation for the slave owners. No one knows the exact value of all slaves currently held in the South, but it certainly runs into the millions of dollars. Some arrangement must be made to reimburse the former masters of freed slaves."

"You can't just let them go?" Sarah asked. She hadn't meant to speak up, but the idea that it was money that stood between the slaves and freedom had never occurred to her. She had to pursue that.

Philip favored her with an indulgent look. "It would be nice if we could, but that really isn't possible. Some arrangement will have to be made. Don't worry," he added when she frowned, "there are already slaves who are hired out to work and are allowed to keep part of their earnings. Some use that money to buy their freedom."

"I don't understand," Sarah said, "they buy themselves?"

"In a sense. Of course, they can also buy their wives, children, parents and so on. In fact, some freed coloreds have slaves of their own."

"Which only goes to show," Josiah interjected, "that slavery isn't the horror the abolitionists would like everyone to believe. Why if those who have been slaves will own slaves, how bad can it be?''

Only Philip could have answered that but he was not predisposed to do so. Rather he was far more interested in when the interminable dinner might end. He had agreed to spend the night as Josiah's guest, but the next day would see him in Boston on the last leg of his trip. After that he would be only a fortnight from home and Daphne.

Chapter Eleven

WHEN THE MEAL was finally over, he and Josiah adjourned to the library, where the older man at last unbent enough to open a bottle. They sipped brandy before a roaring fire and talked. Philip was very careful about what he said. He fully realized that Josiah was fishing for information about Calvert Oaks's business affairs, and he was loath to give him that.

It was a source of some satisfaction that as the level in the brandy bottle diminished, he was more than able to hold his own. Years of practice at Princeton and at home stood him well when he at last made his way to bed, leaving behind him his host who had fallen asleep. The reverberations of Josiah's snores followed Philip up the darkened stairs as he found the room he had been shown earlier in the day.

Most of his luggage had been left at the station. The bag that held his shaving gear and a change of clothes had been unpacked. A fresh suit hung in the closet and a nightshirt was laid out on the foot of the bed. He stripped off his clothes and remembered to put them away himself. He had sent Jacob on to Boston out of consideration for his host's feelings. There were problems enough in dealing with Northerners without bringing along a visible reminder of what separated the two parts of the country.

Belatedly, he realized Josiah would not have objected, but he still did not regret being on his own. Fending for himself was not really all that difficult. The only difference he could see between servants and the slaves back home was that the former were white and drew a wage, most of which was eaten up in charges for room and board. What little was left no more than equaled the cash gifts a generous master awarded to his slaves on holidays.

Yet he had to admit that there were some distinctions. Lying in bed, his arms crossed behind his head, he thought about how a man like Josiah Mackenzie regarded his servants, and how that contrasted with the attitudes of men like his father toward their slaves.

He did not doubt that Josiah would strike a servant who displeased him, but he would certainly not whip him or use any of the other physical measures slave owners sometimes resorted to. That they were rarely used at Calvert Oaks didn't change the fact that the potential was always there.

The servants he had come into contact with were properly deferential, but they retained a sense of dignity that set them apart from most slaves. The essential distinction seemed to be that they had at least some control of their lives, however slight. They could always leave a position and seek another, though to do so without references might condemn them to brutal poverty.

The brandy he had drunk had made him sleepier than he had realized. Philip blinked slowly and tried to recapture his train of thought. With a start, he recognized the direction in which he had been heading. Not for the first time, he had been trying to convince himself that slavery wasn't all that different from other forms of servitude. His need to believe that was no mystery. Convinced as he was that it would be decades before slavery could end, he had to make some allowances for it.

Which required adroit maneuvering on his part. That wore him out, and he fell asleep before he could become aware of the sound of footsteps creeping past his door.

Sarah had debated whether or not to forgo the meeting on account of the visitor in the house. She had decided finally to go ahead, believing that Philip Calvert's presence only slightly increased the risk of discovery. Nonetheless, when she had passed his room, she breathed a sigh of relief. It was dark on the stairs, Josiah having always refused to leave lamps on unnecessarily. She stumbled and had to catch hold of the banister to keep from falling.

When she had regained her balance, she stood absolutely still for a moment, not even breathing. Only when she was convinced that no one had awakened did she continue. In her dark brown dress with a cloak thrown over her shoulders and her hair covered by a wool scarf, she darted through the hallway and carefully eased herself out the door.

Once on the path leading from the house, she wasted no time. With her skirts in her hands, she ran swiftly to the wrought-iron gate. It creaked ominously as she opened it and passed through, taking care not to close it again behind her. It had rained late in the evening and the cobblestone pavement glinted darkly. Her cloak wrapped securely around her, Sarah hurried along. She barely paused for breath until she had crossed Bridge Street and entered the part of town where the mill girls lived.

Nothing moved except a few stray leaves blown on the brisk autumn wind. Curtains were drawn at the windows, behind which no lights could be seen. In warmer weather, when the windows were left open, the myriad sounds made by hundreds of sleeping women could be heard on the street. But now there was only silence, as there would be until the bell rang before dawn to summon the women back to work.

Sarah turned down an alley and made her way purposefully to the side door of one of the boarding-houses. She knocked three times in rapid succession, paused and knocked three times again. Only then was the door opened, just far enough for the person inside to peer out and determine who she was.

"Come in," the girl said as she stood aside to let Sarah enter. The girl was a few years older than Sarah but looked considerably the elder. Thin and stooped, she wore a plain cotton dress and had her hair tightly pulled back from her pinched features. In one hand she kept a wadded-up handkerchief, which she coughed into at regular intervals.

Four other women were gathered around a rough wooden table in the basement room of the boarding-house. They looked up as Sarah entered and nodded to her. "We weren't sure you were coming," one said.

"I almost didn't. We have a guest in the house, and he stayed up so late talking with Father that I was afraid I wouldn't be able to get away." As she spoke Sarah removed her cloak, hung it on a peg and sat down at the table. There were several stacks of leaflets laid out on it. The women were busy separating them into smaller piles.

"They came," Sarah said. "Do they look all right?"

The oldest of the women nodded. She was thirty-five, a once robust farm girl who had turned pale and gray in twenty years in the mills. Her name was Lucy, and her voice was low and husky from breathing problems. "That Boston printer did a good job. Not that he shouldn't have, considering what he charged us."

"He took a risk printing these," one of her youngest companions said. "If he were caught, the mill owners would put him out of business."

Sarah picked up one of the leaflets. By the dim light of a candle, she read it. "Rise, Sisters, against the Injustices of our Employers. Resist the Callous Disregard for our Welfare that prompts the Lengthening of Work Hours and the Diminishing of Wages. We stand for the Ten-Hour Day, the Restoration of Wage Cuts, and an End to the Speedup. Should our Demands be Ignored, we call for a General Walkout of All Mill Employees at 12:00 noon, Monday next. Signed: The Committee for Justice in Lowell."

"We will post these all over town," Lucy said, "and we will be passing them out inside the mills." She spoke calmly though she, and everyone else at the table, were well aware of the risk they were running. Any woman caught with such inflammatory material would be fortunate to only be fired.

"I have some news for you," Sarah said. In such company, she had learned to speak bluntly and not attempt to soften ill tidings. "The owners are aware that unrest is brewing. They are trying to find out who's behind it."

Pale faces tightened around the table. "But they have no idea yet?" Lucy asked.

"I don't believe so. I heard Father railing about how clever you had all been in not coming forward directly. He is far more concerned about you than about those who are attempting to organize openly."

"As he should be," Lucy said. "Those who speak out in public are so fearful that they won't do more than plead for fairness. We demand it."

"But it remains to be seen if we can enforce that demand with action," one of the others said. Deborah was eighteen, the daughter of the woman who ran the boardinghouse on contract from the mill owners, and she knew that she was risking not only her own future but that of her family. "For each of us who is prepared to lose all, the owners believe there are a dozen others to take our places."

There was silence around the table as each contemplated the possibility that this was true. A strike was their last resort. If it did not work, they and their fellow workers would be condemned to a life of even greater drudgery than anything they had previously endured. With conditions already so harsh, that was all but inconceivable, yet it might well occur.

For almost a year Sarah had been part of the secret effort to improve the lives of the mill girls. She had stumbled into it by accident, after overhearing a conversation between two girls in the hospital she had taken to visiting in her mother's place. When she learned that the mill owners were cutting wages at the same time that they were demanding more work, her half-formed anger at last found a direction.

It had taken months to win the trust of the women enough to be admitted to their inner circle, and even now she did not fool herself that she was completely accepted. They continued to view her with suspicion because of who she was, but she was tolerated for the information she brought and the insights she was able to give them into the thinking of the mill owners.

Her involvement with the strike committee was the only secret she kept from Marilee. The older girl would have been deeply worried had she known and might have been tempted to tell Josiah. Rather than have that happen, Sarah planned her movements carefully.

When she returned to the house, she slipped in through the side door and tiptoed through the pantry. Despite her cloak, she was cold and her fingers were stiff, but she felt a strong sense of satisfaction. Along with two of the women, she had spent the past several hours putting up strike notices on streetlamps, fences, anywhere the mill girls were likely to pass. Come dawn, the town fathers were in for a nasty shock. They would undoubtedly order the notices torn down, but by then word of the strike call would have spread throughout the mills.

She was smiling to herself as she hung her cloak away and climbed the stairs to her room. Slipping inside, she breathed a sigh of relief, until a sudden movement in the darkness made her gasp.

"Wh-who...?"

"You should be more careful," Gideon said as he rose from the chair near her bed. "Anyone might come in here and find you gone." He walked toward her, his narrow shoulders hunched and his mouth twisted in a sneer. In the past year he had shot up several inches and was now considerably taller than she. With his new height had come added strength, as she discovered when his hand lashed out and he grabbed her by the arm. "Where have you been?"

"I don't have to tell you. You have no right..."

"I'll tell Father." He shook her harshly, then let go of her abruptly. She lost her balance and fell to the floor, wincing as her hip struck the hard wood. "He'll beat you for sure. You'll be sorry if you don't tell me."

"I couldn't sleep," Sarah said. "I went for a walk."

"In the cold and rain? Don't treat me like a fool." She ducked as he lifted his hand and brought it down across her face. The blow missed her, and she scrambled to her feet as he came after her.

"Get away from me, Gideon! I'll scream if you don't."

"And how will you explain what you're doing at this hour fully dressed? I'll say I heard you coming back and wondered where you'd been. No one will blame me."

Gasping for breath, Sarah tried desperately to think. Everything he said was true. She couldn't afford to arouse any attention. "All right, I won't scream. What do you want?"

"The truth. Where have you been?"

She couldn't tell him. No matter what he did, the mill girls had to be protected. "I told you, I couldn't sleep." Swiftly she improvised. "What Mr. Calvert said about slavery disturbed me. I kept thinking about it until finally I decided to get up. I went out in the field and sat for a while, but it was too cold so I came back."

Gideon flushed and brought his hand up again. Before she could move, he brought it down across her face. The stinging pain made her cry out, though she managed to mute the sound.

"Liar," he snarled. "I looked in the field. You went to meet someone in town, didn't you?" Before she could respond, he hit her again, knocking her against the side of the bed. She crouched there, holding her cheek and struggling not to scream when he bent down in front of her. Pressing his face close to hers, he said, "It was a boy, wasn't it? You went to meet some mill-hand. What did you let him do to you?"

She stared at him in bewilderment, barely able to comprehend what he was saying. Dimly she was aware that some girls did things with boys and men that they should not, but the thought that she was capable of such folly would have been funny had not her brother been so deadly serious. "Nothing, there was no boy. I don't know what you . . ."

His hand over her mouth silenced her. She could barely breath and was too terrified to move. The foot-board pressing against her head caused pain to radiate down her spine. "You're a slut," Gideon snarled. "I saw how you were looking at Calvert. You thought him handsome."

Desperately Sarah shook her head. The slightest motion increased her suffering but she had to do something to dissuade Gideon. He seemed on the verge of losing all control.

"I don't want you to think that way about anyone," he said. "You must swear you won't."

Despite her helplessness, he seemed almost to be pleading with her. Her fear of him did not lessen though she felt a flash of pity. Gideon sensed the change in her but took it as submission. He removed his hand and stared at the red marks he had left on her pale skin.

"Promise me," he said, his voice low and tortured. "You won't feel that way or let anyone do those things to you. They're dirty and you wouldn't like them."

"I won't," she whispered hoarsely, having no real idea of what she was agreeing to.

"And you'll let me look after you. You won't always try to avoid me."

Sarah hesitated. It was true that she tried to keep her distance from Gideon. He had made her uneasy for years, and now her apprehension seemed justified a hundred times over. Yet she sensed that he would not let her go unless she agreed. "All right, I'll do what you want."

He stood up slowly and held out a hand to her, all the while watching her intently. With difficulty she took it and let him help her up. He did not release her until he was satisfied she would not attempt to pull away.

"Wash your face with cold water before you go to sleep," he said. "You don't want marks to show tomorrow."

His smile made her stomach churn. She had to force herself to stand with downcast eyes until he finally left. Long after the door had closed behind him she remained in the center of the room, staring blindly at the carpet.

——————————— Chapter Twelve

"PULL THE ROPE TIGHTER," Philip yelled. "It must hold the beam." Half a dozen slaves hurried to obey. Three were tugging on the rope while the others worked to steady the long plank of wood, a crossbeam for the new dairy barn. Philip watched a moment, grew impatient and jumped in to help them.

He had been doing that since early morning when the work had begun. Now it was late afternoon and he, like the other men, was covered in grime and sweat. His shirt had long since been abandoned and his bare chest, tanned to a healthy bronze, gleamed in the hot sun. His hat had fallen off somewhere, and his tangled hair clung in damp curls to his head.

"Pull," he yelled again, dragging on the rope. The powerful muscles of his arms and back bunched with his effort. The slaves followed suit. Together, inch by inch, they hoisted the heavy crossbeam into position.

When it was done Philip grinned and slapped Marcus on the back. "Damn good job. Let's take a break."

Marcus nodded and called to the other men to let them know they could rest. He and Philip walked to the water trough and dunked their heads in it, emerging moments later to shake themselves like wet, shaggy dogs as the water ran in glistening streams down their lean bodies.

"Reminds me of when we were kids," Philip said when they had stretched out in the shadow of an old oak tree. "Remember how we used to go all day until we were so hot and tired we could barely see straight, then peel off our clothes and jump in the river?"

"Sure do," Marcus agreed. "Seems to me there were times when we set steam to rising from it."

Philip laughed softly. "Those were good days. Sometimes I think I wouldn't mind going back to them."

Marcus cast him a quick look from beneath half-closed eyes. Those youthful days Philip remembered so brightly hadn't been quite as wonderful for him, but he wouldn't mention that. Philip had enough problems without being reminded of others.

They lay quietly side by side, listening to the drone of mosquitos and occasionally swatting one away. The long hours of grueling work had drained them both but also left them pleasantly relaxed.

In the six months since Philip's marriage to Daphne, he had begun to take on more and more projects around Calvert Oaks. At some point, Marcus wasn't sure exactly when, he had crossed the line from supervising to actually doing. At first, that had raised eyebrows. Neither whites nor blacks were accustomed to seeing the son of the plantation owner sweating and straining along with lesser men. Overseer Johnson was particularly put out by it, muttering about what "fancy pants" was "playin' at." Marcus thought he could have told him, had he been so inclined, but he hoped he was wrong.

"Da' Miss Daphne," Ginny had said only the other night when they were in bed together, "Ahs can'ts help thinkin' dere's somethin' wrong with her."

"Yo hardly ever see her," Marcus had pointed out. Ginny worked in the kitchens under Augusta's supervision, who kept her well protected from her difficult young mistress. While Marcus would not accept a house job for himself, he hadn't hesitated to do so for his wife whom he was determined to spare the grueling work of the fields. "Wha' yo know 'bout her?" he asked gently.

"Not much," Ginny admitted, "but she sure don' seem happy, an' neither does Massa Philip."

Marcus sighed deeply and stretched out more fully beneath the tree. He could tell from Philip's breathing that his half brother had almost fallen asleep and was glad for it. Maybe rest would ease the grim set lately come to his mouth and the shadows beneath his eyes.

When he contrasted his own experience with marriage to Philip's, he couldn't help but feel sorry for him. Which was ridiculous considering their relative positions. Yet so long as he had warm, sweet Ginny in his bed each night—and Philip had only an increasingly strange, bewildering girl child—Marcus had to pity him.

Looking back, it seemed to him that the trouble had started shortly after they returned from their honeymoon, when Daphne miscarried. He wasn't supposed to know about that—Philip had never mentioned it directly—but of course he did know. Secrets like that could never be kept in a house where the slaves talked among themselves simply as a means of survival.

Whatever happened to the white folks might have repercussions for the blacks, and indeed, that had proven to be the case. Daphne had become increasingly short-tempered with the house slaves, to the point where Aunt Louise finally had to take her to task. After that, the younger woman had withdrawn into herself, refusing to have anything further to do with the running of the house, rousing herself only to complain of how bored and unappreciated she was.

Marcus couldn't help but find a certain grim humor in the situation. He wasn't a religious man, but there was something irresistibly fitting about the fact that he, who by man's law was entitled to nothing, possessed a loving wife, while Philip, who in the eyes of man had everything, lacked that which he needed most. Only the deep affection that he could never quite suppress prevented him from finding satisfaction in his brother's plight.

Philip would have been glad to know that; it might even have inspired him to confide in Marcus. He desperately needed to talk to someone but was unable to bring himself to broach the subject. Certainly he could not discuss it with his father. Charles was philosophical about Daphne; he had known other women like her and saw nothing unusual about her nature.

"She'll settle down," he told his son the one time Philip hinted things were not right. "Losing the baby upset her." He winked and added, "Best get her with another quickly."

But Daphne did not want another child growing inside her. She hadn't wanted the first; had, in fact, been horrified when Philip gently broke the news of her condition to her. He had waited several weeks for her to realize for herself what was happening so that she could be the one to tell him. But when she showed no sign of understanding, he had finally felt driven to mention it himself.

"With child?" Daphne had repeated, staring at him blankly. "You mean a baby?"

"That's right," Philip had said. His intense happiness made him even gentler and more patient than he would have been normally. "You're going to be a mother."

"But I'm too young for that."

Her sad bewilderment stunned him. Gently he drew her into his arms. "Daphne, sweetheart, you must have known that when we were married, when we began to live together as man and wife, this would happen."

"You mean the things you do caused this?"

You do? He had imagined they did it together. Certainly, Daphne had not come unwilling to his bed. On their wedding night, she had been shy and a little scared, exactly as he expected. Her trust in him and her amazed delight at the pleasure he gave her made him feel stronger and more powerful than ever. He savored the overcoming of her modesty as she slowly allowed him more and more liberties.

At first he had felt some hesitation about doing to his wife the things he had done with whores, but when he realized the full extent of Daphne's passion, his guilt fled. At her own insistence, he had taught her to please him with as much skill as any courtesan could ever have possessed. Only very occasionally, when she teased and tantalized him, her green eyes aglint with some emotion he could not quite define, had he felt a flash of unease.

A month after they returned home from an extended honeymoon that had taken them to Hot Springs, Charlotte and New Orleans, he had told her the news of her pregnancy. For days she had drifted around the house, snapping at the slaves, refusing to eat and crying without warning. At the end of the week she had slipped away to the stables and taken out her favorite mare. Daphne was a good rider; when she didn't come back after a few hours Philip wasn't worried. But as dusk began to fall, he had become concerned.

Charles and several of the house servants had joined him in the search. Daphne was found some ten miles from Calvert Oaks, walking beside the lathered mare, who had gone lame. Hardly suprising considering how hard she had been pushed.

In the middle of the night, Philip had awakened to Daphne's moans and the realization that their child was lost. Since then he had been reluctant to approach her bed, preferring to sleep in his dressing room. But now, as he lay beside Marcus under the tree, he wondered how long he would be able to maintain that. He had a man's appetite and he wanted a woman, but more than that, he needed his wife.

Unwilling to sink into such thoughts, he called the men back to work. For several hours they hammered and nailed until, by dusk, the dairy barn was more than half completed. It would house a dozen head of cattle Philip had recently decided to purchase, part of his plan to bring new types of farming to Calvert Oaks.

"We should be able to finish up tomorrow," he said to Marcus as they put their tools away. "Then maybe the day after we can get started on the new dock."

"Fine with me," Marcus said. He preferred construction to labor in the fields, especially since it kept him away from Overseer Johnson. The half-dozen men he had handpicked to work with him felt the same way. Their initial suspicion of Philip had faded rapidly, to the extent that Marcus sometimes had to remind them with a quick look when they were getting too close to the line between servility and familiarity. Philip never seemed to notice, he was far too distracted. But that didn't mean he wouldn't have taken offense.

"He means well," Marcus said to Ginny when he returned to their cabin that night. "But he's still white, an' de young massa. Nobody be smart to forget dat."

She nodded silently as she put their food on the table, but inside she was wondering: who was he reminding, her or himself?

Others were also thinking that night of who Philip was and whether or not some reminder of it was needed. When he first began working beside the slaves, Aunt Louise had been appalled. If the habit of tolerance for male whims hadn't been so deeply imbued in her, she would have said something to him about it. As it was, she was finally driven to speak to Charles who, as it turned out, was already aware of the problem.

After dinner he casually suggested to Philip that they have a drink together in the library. It had been a while since they'd had any real opportunity to talk and his son agreed without a second thought. Aunt Louise shot her brother-in-law a meaningful look before taking herself off to bed.

"This is quite a good brandy," Charles said as he poured a snifter for each of them. "It's from a vintner we haven't tried before. I think you'll like it."

Philip took a sip, nodded his appreciation and settled back on the couch. "It feels as though it may rain tomorrow. What do you think?"

"Perhaps." Charles took a seat across from him. They needed rain; it hadn't been a dry spring but a little more moisture would assure an excellent crop. Of course, if it rained too much, the cotton would be ruined. The typical quandary of any planter.

"How is the dairy barn coming along?" Charles asked.

"It's almost finished," Philip said.

"Good, then you can make a trip to Richmond for me."

Philip hesitated. "I was planning to start on the dock next."

"You're not really needed for that. Johnson will take care of it."

"Johnson doesn't know spit about building a dock or much of anything else for that matter."

"No," Charles said quietly, "but he does know when something is happening that shouldn't be. You've got to stop working with the slaves, Philip. It isn't right."

The crack of glass against the table startled them both. Philip had put his snifter down so sharply that the crystal stem almost snapped. "What happened, Father? Did that little weasel come to you complaining about me?"

"Of course not," Charles said stiffly. "You know perfectly well that I would never allow any subordinate to criticize my son. He simply pointed out that you were doing far more physical work than you should be."

"I like the work. It keeps my mind off...other things."

"I understand that," Charles said, so simply that Philip was momentarily taken aback. The look his father shot him suggested that he really did understand, perhaps more than his son wanted him to. "But," Charles went on, "there are other things you can do. Hunting, for example. I've always found that very relaxing. However, if that isn't enough, Devereaux's boy is taking up boxing; he wants to start a gentleman's team. Perhaps you'd like to get involved in that.''

"For God's sake, Father..."

"And then of course there's always Richmond. Which brings me to my initial point. Why don't you plan to visit there more frequently?''

There was silence for a moment, before Philip said quietly, "Is that what you're advising? That I forget about my wife and turn to whores?''

His father did not respond at once. Instead Charles rose, poured himself another stiff brandy and drank it in a single swallow. When he looked again at his son, his face was expressionless. "We haven't always agreed on everything, Philip, but I think you will admit that we have respected one another. Has that ceased?''

"No," Philip said thickly. He regretted his outburst. However they might disagree, his father deserved better.

"Well, then," Charles went on, resuming his seat, "I would like to help. Will you allow me to try?''

Without meeting his eyes, Philip nodded. "I would appreciate it.''

"You and Daphne are having a difficult time. That isn't unusual at the beginning of a marriage. However well you may think you know the woman you wed, she always turns out to be a surprise.''

Despite himself, Philip smiled. His father sounded so rueful and so resigned to what he clearly regarded as an immutable fact of life that he couldn't help but be curious. "Was that how it was with mother?''

"Certainly, and don't misunderstand me, Elizabeth was a wonderful woman. I am not ashamed to say that I adored her. However, within a very short time of our wedding, I realized that I didn't know her at all.''

Philip shook his head, taken aback to hear his own thoughts about Daphne so precisely echoed. "I don't understand. You were second cousins, neighbors, why you had practically grown up together. How could she have held any surprises for you?"

"Simple, my dear boy. To begin with, the fact that we had known each other all our lives, did not mean that we knew each other well, although at the time I presumed it did. Your mother was no more or less guilty than almost every other woman of her class. They are all taught from the cradle to play a role. Shocking though I know the comparison would be, they are almost like actresses on a stage."

"Are you saying that . . . they mislead us?"

"Indeed, and so artfully that they are often misled themselves, fooled into believing that they are what they have been taught to be. Ask yourself this: could any woman truly be the simpering, helpless little fool they pretend to be and still manage to draw breath? Your Aunt Louise, for instance, is the very model of Southern femininity. Yet she manages to run this house single-handedly, supervise dozens of servants and look after hundreds more. Furthermore, she has to do it all without ever appearing to take off her white lace gloves, let alone exuding a drop of sweat. That requires a level of strength few men could ever manage."

"But Daphne, surely she isn't like that . . . ?"

"No," Charles agreed, "Daphne isn't like Louise. But neither is she the shy, gentle creature she wanted you to believe. In her own way, Daphne has a great deal of strength. I'm only concerned that in her case, it will work against her."

"What do you mean?"

Rather than answer directly, Charles said, "I don't wish to be too personal, but does Daphne...enjoy the intimacy of marriage?"

"Yes," Philip said bluntly.

"And does she wish to have children?"

"That...is harder to say. When she learned that she was pregnant, she was dismayed. I put it down to a natural fear of the unknown, but now I'm beginning to wonder if there may not be more involved."

"Then we have been thinking along the same lines. It occurs to me that Daphne does not wish to be a mother, because that would mean she could no longer be a child herself."

"But she isn't—" Philip began, only to break off. Daphne *was* childlike in her refusal to accept anything that did not happen to be what she wanted. Her tears and pouting were the tactics of a three-year-old. All she seemed able to think of were her own desires and pleasures. Even when she appeared to be thinking of him, as when they were in bed together, he wondered if she might not simply be proving to herself that she had the power to make him do whatever she wanted.

"If you are right," he said slowly, "then I have a serious problem. It has never been my intention not to have children."

"I am glad to hear it," his father said. "Now all you have to do is convince Daphne."

Philip flushed slightly. The more he thought about his wife's behavior, the less tolerant he was prepared to be. For weeks he had worked as hard as any slave in order to wear himself out so that he would not be tempted to approach her. Never had she shown him the slightest flicker of gratitude. Under his breath, he muttered, "Why should she? I've been acting like a damn gelding."

"What was that?" Charles asked.

"Nothing. I think I'll go up to bed now."

"You'll consider what I said about working too closely with the slaves?"

"We still disagree about that, but yes, I'll give it some thought."

Charles was satisfied with that, and with the gleam he saw in his son's eyes. Willful, spoiled Daphne was in for a shock. Which was just as well, he thought as he reached for the decanter. It was past time for him to become a grandfather.

_____ *Chapter Thirteen*

DAPHNE WAS ASLEEP when Philip entered the bedroom. She lay on her side with her knees drawn up, her hand under her chin, her lips slightly parted. The windows were wide open, and on the soft evening breeze, he could smell the perfume of his mother's roses.

Looking at Daphne, he thought again of what his father had said about his own relationship with the long-dead Elizabeth. To Philip she had been only the ghost of a memory, someone who walked through the dreams that occurred just before waking or came in a waking dream whenever the scent of roses happened to be particularly strong. She had long since ceased to be a real woman, in the sense that Aunt Louise or Kitty or even the whores he had bedded were real. Daphne had much the same kind of unreality.

Ever since he had first become aware of her at his homecoming party, she had seemed too ethereal, too beautiful, too desirable to be quite real. Yet she was, whether she or he truly wanted to admit it. She was real, physical, mortal, like himself. Putting her on a pedestal had done them both a serious disservice.

No more. He wanted her almost as keenly as he had when she was just beyond the reach of his hand. Instinctively he understood that to desire a woman so much even after she had become a possession was a rare testimony to her attractions. Yet he wanted more than merely a warm body to couple with. Though he only half understood it, he suspected that he wanted a wife who was also a friend. Perhaps even his best friend.

That was so unlikely as to not even bear thinking about. He and Daphne existed in separate worlds. His was the male sphere of action and decision; hers the female realm of duty and obedience. They might reach out and touch across the gulf of their separate existences, but they could never be merged.

Except in the physical sense. Looking down at her, seeing her ebony hair spread out across the damask pillows, her cheeks softly flushed and her thick lashes quivering slightly as she dreamt, he was swiftly becoming aroused.

He had been so damn long without her, ever since the lost baby. Several times it had occurred to him to relieve his needs with a whore or even with one of the female slaves. But he had shied away from doing so, half ashamed of wanting to adhere to vows other men negligently violated. She belonged to him, he had an absolute right to take her. No one, least of all Daphne, could complain at the exercise of his husbandly privileges.

Yet Daphne did complain; when he slipped naked into the bed beside her, she stirred faintly in her sleep. Half awake, she murmured, "What…? No…Philip, I don't want to."

He ignored her. What she wanted at that moment meant singularly little to him. All he could think of was the slight weight of her in his arms, the softness of her curves pressed against him and the hardness of his own arousal.

There was only so much a man could take; he was dangerously close to his limit. The smooth skin of her throat was as satin against his mouth as he bent over her, tasting, savoring, knowing all the while that he was tormenting himself far more than her. Daphne had gone still against him. She wasn't precisely resisting, but he could feel the growing stiffness in her as he slipped her nightgown from her shoulders and over the curve of her breasts.

"So beautiful," he murmured as he bent his head to suckle her. Whatever her feelings, she couldn't contain her physical response. Her nipples hardened and grew darker against the alabaster perfection of her breasts. A tremor raced through her, followed quickly by another.

Philip raised his head. He laughed deep in his throat, not mockingly but with tenderness. "It's been a long time, sweetheart. I understood why you didn't want to, but now..."

"No," she whispered, her eyes wide and dark. "I don't want to."

A dart of impatience flitted through him. "Of course you do. I can feel it." As though to confirm what he knew, he moved a hand down her, pushing the nightgown out of the way, and stroked intimately between her thighs. To his surprise, more correctly his shock, she was dry and tight.

"Daphne..." Sudden pity for her erased his impatience. She really was terrified. Nothing else could account for her contradictory responses. And how could he expect her to be otherwise, after the pain and grief of her miscarriage? Yet surely he would be doing her no favor to let her remain like this.

If she had been a cold wife, a woman who had never enjoyed passion, he might have stopped. But the memory of how it had been between them, of her unbridled ecstasy, washed away his guilt. She was a woman made for lovemaking. It only remained for her to be reminded of that.

"Don't be afraid, Daphne," he murmured. "We'll go slowly. I won't take you before you're ready."

Her hands, small and white with perfectly manicured nails, pushed against him. "It's too soon. I can't."

Shortly after the miscarriage had occurred, Philip had talked with the doctor who attended Daphne. The man had advised him to wait six weeks before resuming intercourse, in order to let her heal fully. Four months had passed. There was no getting around the fact that she was as healed as she ever would be.

Philip lay back against the pillows, watching grimly as Daphne skittered to the far side of the bed. He had a choice: do as she wished or insist that she give in to him. If he gave in to her now, what chance was there that she would feel differently at some later time? If there had been any sign from her, any hope that things would change, he might have waited. But as he stared at her pale, rigid back he realized that to give in to her now would likely mean the end of their intimacy.

He was twenty-two years old, at the peak of his virility and desirous of sons. No twinge of conscience, no sense of pity could change that. She had challenged him too profoundly.

At first she lay stiff and unyielding beneath him, making no sound or movement. He understood the tactic, even respected it. She wanted him to feel like a rapist, and to a certain extent she was succeeding. Except that he knew her too well, remembered too clearly what could drive her to madness.

It became a contest between them. How much could she withstand, how long could he hold out. His hardness was a throbbing torment between his legs as he forced himself to go slowly, caressing her with long, sure strokes. She lay on her back, her arms rigid at her sides, her hands clenched into fists. When he parted her thighs she resisted briefly, until he rose up over her, murmuring, "I'm your husband, Daphne. I have the right."

She turned her head away into the pillows, but not before he saw the gleam of white teeth sinking into her lower lip.

The hair sheltering her womanhood was as dark as midnight and as soft as silk. He tangled his fingers in it lazily, drawing circles on her mound, each one taking him closer to the center of her desire yet never quite reaching there.

Daphne moaned deep in her throat. The jade bright eyes that she had kept tightly closed flew open and she glared at him. "I hate you."

He chuckled softly. "I can see that." Gently his finger eased into her cleft, finding her no longer dry. The rosy lips were slick with pearly drops of fluid. "Fortunately, I like the way you hate."

For long moments more, he tantalized her, enjoying the sense of power it gave him to make her yield, however unwillingly. She had needed to be taught a lesson, about herself as much as about him. He only regretted waiting so long to do it.

But there was no need to wait longer. She was open and ready for him. With a groan, he sank into her, finding her as tight as he remembered but completely able to accept him. Once taken, Daphne could no longer remain still. Her hips arched, and her arms reached up to embrace him fiercely.

Gracious in his victory, he drove into her, bringing them both to a shattering climax before collapsing on top of her. He fell asleep almost immediately, with Daphne still under him, his manhood still within her, confident that his possession was complete.

In the weeks that followed, that conviction began to erode. Oh, Daphne accepted him again in their bed without protest. She joined in their lovemaking with as much passion as any man could wish. It was as though the clock had been rolled back to the early days of their marriage.

And yet something was different. Philip couldn't put his finger on it, but over and over the thought would suddenly occur to him. At odd moments—at a ball, during a hunt, over supper with the family—he would suddenly catch her looking at him with an expression he could only characterize as smug. As though she knew something he didn't, some great joke of which he was the butt. It was a singularly uncomfortable feeling, one he could not completely dismiss no matter how he tried.

Several times he attempted to talk with her, to explain why he had done what he had and give her the chance to admit that he had been right. But Daphne always brushed his explanations aside and went on about her business. She seemed to think that the matter was settled, yet he knew she did not.

With each month he watched for the absence of her flow, only to be disappointed. She would take to her bed like clockwork, demanding a hot brick and laudanum for the pain, and stay there for three or four days, during which he was once again banished to the dressing room.

At least there were other things to think about.

"Fools," Judge Rider exclaimed. "There are fools, damn fools, and then there are Yankees. It's a wonder they have the sense to unbutton their trousers before pissing."

There were no ladies present when he said that, of course, only a few female slaves serving ale and chilled wine to the men after their drilling. The decision had been made to form a local militia, officers to be the leading gentlemen of the district, soldiers to be drawn from among yeoman farmers and other free whites.

By virtue of his experience during the War of 1812, Judge Rider was named commander of the unit. He directed most of his efforts toward designing a glorious uniform comprised of black trousers with a red stripe down the sides, a red tunic emblazoned with gold buttons and a gold sash. Everyone agreed it was most attractive, though Philip privately thought the sash ridiculous. Fortunately it was only required for parades, of which there had yet to be any. For regular drilling the men made do with the trousers, a comfortable shirt and their usual riding boots.

Although Judge Rider was nominally in charge, most of the real responsibility fell to his son, Peter, recently returned from West Point. Peter was a good-natured young man with a keen mind and a genuine love for all things military. He prudently refrained from overdrilling the men, knowing they would rapidly become bored, but resorted instead to a sort of game that in its intent was deadly serious.

Three times each year they took to the fields and hills around Richmond. There under Peter Rider's guidance, they staged mock battles. Their high spirits and innate sense of the dramatic were catered to even as they learned the fundamentals of strategy and tactics. None of the unit's members was ever seriously hurt in these skirmishes, though there were a few minor injuries. Two slaves were crippled when they got caught in a cavalry charge, but given that they were both elderly, no one minded too much, except, presumably, the slaves themselves. Before very long they had become a respectable military force and Philip had even learned to tolerate the uniform.

What he had a great deal more trouble tolerating was Daphne. She continued to baffle him. Drifting through the days, shunning all responsibility more serious than the selection of a new gown—of which she required dozens—she defiantly resisted the inroads of maturity.

His reaction might not have been so critical if he hadn't had the example of his own sister to show what his wife might have been. Kitty had two children, a boy and a girl, in the first two years of marriage. She adored them and was an excellent mother. In addition, she ran her home with seeming ease, creating a warm, welcoming haven of which Jeremy was rightly proud.

Several times Aunt Louise suggested to Philip that she would like to turn over the reins to Daphne but that the younger woman was completely disinterested. She preferred remaining in bed until noon, enjoying a leisurely breakfast, and spending the rest of the day preparing for whatever party they were attending that evening. If there was no party she prowled around the parlor after supper, restless and dissatisfied, and found fault with everything.

In particular, she disliked the slaves who had been at Calvert Oaks before her arrival. They were, in her eyes, poorly trained and spoiled. Augusta in particular provoked her ire, though Rameses came in a close second. She suspected that neither of them approved of her and never lost an opportunity to lash out at them.

Matters finally came to a head one sultry summer evening a year and a half after her marriage when the family was gathered at supper. Aunt Louise had been feeling poorly recently, from what Philip suspected was overwork but which she insisted was merely the effects of the heat. Whatever the cause, she had asked Daphne to see to the week's menus, a charge the younger woman accepted with ill grace.

Augusta entered the dining room carrying a heavy tureen of soup. She had barely begun to ladle it into their bowls when Daphne threw down her napkin and demanded, "What is this slop?"

Startled, the black woman said, "Lobster bisque, missy. Yo've had dis before an' yo lahked it."

"Don't tell me what I like. I specifically instructed you to prepare a leek soup."

Augusta nodded slowly. "Ahs knows, missy, but dem leeks didn't look so good to me, so Ahs thought..."

"Don't tell me what you thought. You have no right to think. All you're supposed to do is what you're told. If you can't carry out a simple instruction..."

"Daphne," Philip interrupted, his tone soft but firm "that's quite enough. Augusta hasn't done anything wrong."

His wife was silent for a long moment, as though she couldn't quite believe that he had taken the slave's side over hers. When the import of his words finally sank in, she jumped to her feet, her face flushed. "All right then, if that's the way you feel, have the damn soup."

Before anyone could make a move to stop her, she seized the tureen out of Augusta's hands and hurled it at the center of the table, where it exploded, showering shards of china and thick glops of bisque over them all. In the subsequent chaos, Daphne smiled coldly and left the room.

His irritation with his wife was so intense that Philip got drunk that night, partly out of a sense that if he failed to incapacitate himself, he would do something irreparable to her. He fell asleep on the leather couch in his father's library, where Augusta found him in the morning.

She set a tray containing a carafe of ice water and another of coffee on the table in front of him and stood back, her hands folded over her stomach, waiting patiently. Long moments passed before he felt able to confront her.

"I'm sorry about what happened, Mammy," he said, holding his head. Small men with sharp hammers were pounding away at his brain. "I'll speak to Daphne this morning. She'll realize she can't do things like that."

Not even the novelty of an apology from a white man could sway Augusta from her chosen course, painfully arrived at in the night. Rameses had argued against it, but she was not to be deterred. That white girl needed to learn a lesson Augusta was happy to teach.

"No need fo' dat, suh," she said softly. "Ahs 'pects missy jus' feelin' bad."

"I don't see why she should be," Philip muttered. He had managed to get his legs over the side of the couch and sat there with his head in his hands, his elbows resting on his knees. Maybe if he just stayed that way for a few hours, the little men would go away.

"Don' make no never mind," Mammy Augusta said. "By de by, Massa Philip, yo happen t'know if missy needs mo' vinegar?"

He looked up at her, puzzled. Was she making some reference to the sourness of Daphne's temperament? If so, he had to agree with her, but she was still seriously out of line for a slave.

Yet Augusta didn't look in the least impertinent. On the contrary, she seemed to have no concern except serving her young mistress. "Dat girl oh hers, Susie, she usually come down once o' twice a week fo' vinegar. Ahs jus' be wonderin' if Ah should take it up instead."

Philip started to shake his head, instantly regretted the action and held it carefully still as he said, "I don't understand; what would my wife be using vinegar for?" She certainly wasn't doing any cooking; he was willing to bet that Daphne barely knew the location of the kitchens. And while she put plenty of stuff on her face, he couldn't imagine her using vinegar for that purpose.

Augusta managed to look both surprised and serenely innocent. "Why Ahs 'sumed yo knew, suh. After de baby was lost, Ahs thought yo must not be wantin' anymore fo' a while."

He stared at her for a long moment, seeing in her coal-black eyes the truth he did not want to recognize.

References he had caught over the years in the various brothels he had patronized surfaced in his mind, along with images of Daphne insisting she had to have her own dressing room, slipping away from his embrace and returning a short time later with a satisfied smile, lying in bed month after month as her flow confirmed that she was not pregnant.

He found the sponges in a drawer in her dresser, under a pile of lacy handkerchiefs. Next to them was a small, stoppered bottle of vinegar. As he stared at the proof of her treachery, something snapped inside him. The groan deep in his throat emerged as a howl of outrage. He seized the drawer and hurled it against the wall where it crashed in splinters.

Daphne had the misfortune to open the door an instant later. She surveyed the scene with disbelief. Having never seen her husband other than completely in control of himself, she could barely recognize the infuriated man confronting her. Nor did she understand at first what was happening when he seized her by the shoulders, flung her to the floor, and snarled, "You goddamn bitch."

Only when she smelled the vinegar from the shattered bottle and saw the sponges scattered over the floor did she realize the trouble she was in. And even then, she did not believe the damage to be irreparable.

"Oh, Philip," she murmured, deliberately widening her eyes and making her voice breathless. "I'm so sorry. I know you must think the worst of me, but I had a good reason, honestly."

"I know what your reason was," he said. "You're too damn selfish to think of anything except yourself."

She started to protest but Philip was beyond listening. The only sound he wanted to hear was that of her silk dress ripping. His throbbing head, the alcohol still in his blood, his black rage at her deception all combined to put him beyond reason. On the floor, without tenderness or compassion, he ravaged her.

In the final moments before his release, he heard her high, keening laughter and a cold finger of horror raced down his spine. Despite his rough handling and his contempt, her passion exceeded his own. She rose to meet him with each thrust, wild for all of him, and finally drained him to the utmost. But when it was over, she would not look at him or touch the tears glistening on his cheeks.

DAPHNE WAS PREGNANT again by autumn. The moment Philip suspected her condition, he set the household servants to watching her constantly. She was not allowed to venture outside without an escort, and the stables were completely off-limits to her. Daphne complained vociferously about the restrictions but there was no real spirit in her. She knew she was trapped and that this time there would be no way out.

The more apparent the child became, the more morose Daphne grew. In her sixth month, as spring began to awaken the land, she took to staying in her room constantly, not even venturing downstairs for meals. Philip, feeling somewhat guilty about her plight, tried to cheer her but with no success. She made it crystal clear that she wanted nothing to do with him.

Early in June, some four weeks before the baby was due, she woke in the middle of the night crying with pain. Her labor lasted three days and at the end of it, everyone, including perhaps Daphne herself, believed that death would be a mercy. She had screamed until she had no voice left, chewed through her lips and clawed at her face until she had to be forcibly restrained, and bled until it seemed impossible that there could be another drop left within her. Neither the doctor brought from Richmond nor the old mammies who had delivered more children than they could count knew what to do.

But nature did, and in the end the child was born, a red, squalling boy who was still half in the birth canal when he began to scream his anger at the world.

Daphne did not hear him. As William Philip Calvert drew his first breath, his mother drew her last.

Part Two

1858-1860

Chapter Fourteen

THE MAN WHO STEPPED OFF the train in Richmond in March of 1858 looked older than his thirty years. Philip Calvert possessed a commanding presence more usually found, if at all, in men considerably his senior. It was a quality for which many envied him, though not any of those few who understood its source.

He had spent the past two weeks in Washington, meeting with various political leaders and others, trying to get a better sense of the course of the country. What he had heard had not reassured him. The positions of both North and South seemed to be hardening. The sense of compromise he had hoped for was not to be found. There was an intransigence on both sides that boded ill.

The few men he had found who like himself still hoped for an accord were vastly outnumbered by the hordes on both sides who did not. The talk, in either camp, was bellicose. Philip had never been in a war, but he sincerely doubted that it could be as glorious as almost everyone else seemed to think. Worse yet, he could not bring himself to agree with those of his fellow Southerners who were convinced they could swiftly and thoroughly trounce the hated Yankees. When he looked north, he saw industrial might, a talent for organization and a degree of ruthlessness that filled him with dread.

Stepping off the train, he was weary and eager to be home. Above all, he missed his little son. William was the light of his life, his reason for accepting without question an existence that was too often burdensome.

Being an intelligent man, he recognized that it was the burden of guilt that weighed most heavily on him. He blamed himself for Daphne's death, and he lacked even the comfort of God's punishment. For divine justice, if that was what it was, had taken as it so often did an indirect route.

Barely two months after his son's wife had been laid in her grave, Charles Calvert had taken his stallion, Satan out for a gallop. Witnesses who saw the accident said the horse balked at a fence, throwing his rider and racing on for a half mile with Charles's leg still caught in the stirrup before he was finally stopped. Philip had personally put the stallion down, but that gave him little comfort in the face of his father's terrible injuries. Charles would never walk again, never enjoy a woman, never even be able to care for himself. He was imprisoned in a helpless body that might take years to die.

Without warning, all the responsibility for Calvert Oaks fell squarely on Philip's shoulders. In the aftermath of Daphne's death, he was ill-prepared to cope with it and for several months he allowed everything to drift, until Marcus asked if he was planning to sell out. The shock of that question, contradicting as it did everything Philip had been raised to believe in, woke him to the reality of his situation. He buckled down to work, finding in it his only relief from guilt and grief.

Rameses was waiting on the platform with several house slaves to collect his baggage. Jacob went with them to the wagon as Philip got into his carriage. He had considered spending the night in Richmond, as he did occasionally, but was not in the mood to linger. There had been an outbreak of trouble recently on several plantations, including an aborted rebellion at Beauterre. While he did not for a moment suspect his slaves of plotting anything similar, he preferred not to be absent any longer than he had to be.

The moment the carriage turned through the wrought-iron gates of Calvert Oaks and started up the half-mile-long gravel drive, a familiar sense of contentment swept over him. For all the anguish of recent years, this was still home, the center of his most cherished hopes and dreams now embodied in the person of his son.

William was racing to meet him before the carriage wheels had come to a stop in front of the house. His short, tanned legs carried him swiftly down the steps and into his father's arms.

"Papa," he chortled, "you're home. Hurrah."

Philip broke into a grin. No matter how burdened he might feel, he had only to look at William to know that everything was worthwhile. "Bring me a toy?" William demanded as he grasped his father's hair in two chubby fists and pulled gleefully.

"Perhaps," Philip said as he carried him inside. "Have you been a good boy?"

"He ben jus' fine, Massa Philip," Augusta assured him as she took the squirming bundle from his arms and set him down gently. "Ben eatin' all his greens and everythin'." She didn't feel compelled to mention that William had also let a lizard out in the parlor, put camphor oil in the gravy and slid down the central staircase banister backward, the last not once but three times.

"Don't you believe her," Aunt Louise said as she came down those same stairs to greet Philip. The recent years had not been kind to her. Her gray hair had turned almost completely white, there were deep lines on her soft face and her once-erect back was slightly stooped. With a fond glance at William that belied her stern words, she said, "This boy is hell on wheels. At least three grown men are needed to control him, and even they have a hard time of it."

Philip laughed. He liked the idea that his son was high spirited, though occasionally he wondered how much of his mother he had in him. Daphne, too, had grabbed at life with both hands.

"Toy," William demanded, pulling at his frock coat. "You promised a toy."

"So I did," Philip agreed as he gestured to Jacob to open the small trunk. The two slaves who had been about to carry it upstairs set it down instead. Jacob searched inside, and with a smile at the small boy avidly watching, he drew out a wide, flat box wrapped in brown paper and tied with string.

William tore it open with glee. Inside was a wooden case that opened to reveal an entire army of toy soldiers, rank upon rank of them lying rigidly at attention. There were even horses for the officers and several miniature cannons.

"You spoil the boy," Aunt Louise said gently after William had run off to play. With him went Esau, son of one of the houseslaves who had been born a few months before William. Esau's mother, a strapping girl born and raised at Calvert Oaks, had nursed them both and ever since then they had been inseparable.

"Who else should I spoil?" Philip asked with a smile. "He's the only son I have." And was ever likely to have, he added silently.

Aunt Louise frowned as though she had read his mind. Several times she had broached the subject of his remarrying, only to be told with absolute firmness that he would never do so. One wife had been more than enough; he could not imagine taking another. Yet lately there had been moments, particularly when he thought of William, when he wondered if his decision wasn't prompted by selfishness. Aunt Louise was the only mother his son had ever known. She did her best with him, but he was rapidly growing beyond her control. Without a true mother, and without brothers or sisters, it wasn't impossible that William might not become the man he should.

"Your father is waiting to see you," Aunt Louise said. "He's very anxious to hear about what went on in Washington."

"I'll go up directly," he assured her. The hours he spent with his father were difficult but rewarding. For all his physical incapacitation, there was nothing wrong with Charles's mind. It was as keen as ever.

"There's trouble brewing," he said after Philip had filled him in on all that he had seen and heard in the capital. "The Yankees will never be content until they force us to live as they see fit."

"I'm afraid you may be right," Philip said. His father had dismissed the male slave who cared for him, and the two men could speak candidly. "Too many among them want to strip us of everything, including pride."

"Hypocrites," Charles snorted. He took a sip of his brandy and sat back in his wheelchair. His legs were covered by a blanket, less for the cold than to hide how thin and twisted they had become. Above the waist, his body remained powerful. Within a few weeks of the accident, he had begun a rigorous program of exercise despite the doctors' stern disapproval. A system of ropes and pulleys controlled weights positioned over his bed. He worked with them twice daily, and boasted of being able to lift as much as he could before he was hurt. Yet no amount of exercise would ever enable him to again lift his own legs or walk an inch.

"Every damn Yankee is a hypocrite," he went on angrily, his proud head tilted. "They're no more interested in freeing the nigras than I am. All they want is to break the Southland's back so that they can impose their will on us."

Philip leaned back in his chair, stretched his legs out in front of him and stifled a sigh. He disagreed with his father about the depth of the Yankees' commitment to emancipation, but he had long since given up trying to convince Charles that at least some of them were genuinely offended by the bondage of other human beings.

"Speaking of nigras," Charles said when he made no comment, "Davies still needs more field hands. Did you bring any back with you?"

Davies was the overseer Philip had hired shortly after his father's accident, after he caught Johnson whipping a female slave who had refused to lie with him. Johnson had been given an hour to get his possessions together and leave Calvert Oaks, but he hadn't gone very far. Frederick Danvers had wasted no time hiring him for Beauterre.

"I didn't stop long enough in Richmond to go to the auctions," he said, knowing full well that his father hadn't really expected him to. Philip bought new slaves only as an absolute last resort; in the six years he had run the plantation he had purchased less than a dozen. That was not to say that the slave population hadn't increased; some forty children had been born of whom thirty-two had survived to their first birthday and beyond. Compared to the mortality rate of slaves on other plantations, that was excellent.

"You won't buy new slaves," his father said, "but you want to put more acreage to seed. How do you figure to manage that?"

"There's a new piece of equipment I've been looking at . . ."

"Machinery, always machinery! A man is better than a machine any day. Haven't you learned that yet?"

"Men can still use some help, Father. Most of the tools we rely on haven't changed in a century or more."

"Because they work, that's why. Why change something that's doing a fine job for you?"

Philip stood up and stretched. He was weary from the long trip and wanted a bath before supper. Gently he put a hand on his father's shoulder. "Let's not argue about this. If my plan doesn't work, that is if I can't bring in the additional crops with the slaves we already have, I'll buy more. All right?"

"I suppose it will have to be," Charles grumbled, though in fact he wasn't displeased. Philip might do things differently than he would have but he got good results, and in the end that was all that counted. "Where's that grandson of mine?"

"Probably waiting to show you his new toy soldiers." Opening the door to his father's room, Philip laughed. William was stretched out patiently on the carpet, maneuvering his tiny army with fierce concentration that dissolved as soon as he saw his father. "Can I come in now?"

"May I," Philip corrected automatically as he ruffled his son's ebony hair. William had inherited his blue eyes and long, straight nose, but otherwise he resembled his mother. In his crib, he had been beautiful. Philip was relieved to see that as he grew older, he became less that than handsome. "Keep Grampa company while I change, all right?"

William nodded eagerly. Between him and his grandfather there was a deep bond of true love and understanding. They had always spent a good deal of time together, far more than Philip was able to give to his son. He was grateful that Charles could do what he could not.

"I'll be back shortly," he said as he left the room, knowing that the other two probably had not heard him. They were already engrossed in the toy soldiers.

Charles came down to supper that evening. He didn't always since, despite his bravado, he was frequently in pain and exhausted. But Philip's return, and the fact that Kitty happened to be visiting with her brood, had buoyed him up. As they sat around the gracious table enjoying the meal Augusta had prepared, he seemed almost like his own self.

"I declare," Aunt Louise said at one point when they had all finally stopped laughing at a story Charles had just told, "I'd forgotten all about those goats and what happened with them. Wasn't that a day?"

"Heaven help us if the children ever hear about it," Kitty said. She laughed softly, her blond curls dancing in the gaslight. A mother five times over, her waist was no longer as slender or her manner as flirtatious as on the day she was wed. But Philip thought that in many ways she was lovelier than ever.

Jeremy clearly agreed with him. He counted himself fortunate to have been able to accompany her on this visit to Calvert Oaks. Since the sudden death of Daniel Hudson the year before, Jeremy had been kept busy managing his considerable inheritance. He welcomed the opportunity to get a few days' rest at the same time that he sought Philip's advice on various matters.

Supper was over and the gentlemen had rejoined the ladies, when Kitty found a private moment with her brother. She drew him to one side of the music room, speaking softly so as not to intrude on the Chopin interlude Aunt Louise was playing.

"Is father truly as well as he is trying to appear?" she asked.

"He is holding his own," Philip assured her. "You know his indomitable spirit. He'll never give in to his injuries."

"I'm only concerned that he may be overdoing."

"Normally he doesn't exert himself this much," Philip said. "But having you here is good for him. Don't worry, Aunt Louise and I will make sure that he rests."

"Aunt Louise should, too. She isn't getting any younger."

Philip smiled lightly. "You know she would take any such suggestion amiss."

"Perhaps, but I'm worried about her, as well." Kitty hesitated a moment. "Philip, you know I've never been the sort of sister who tries to interfere in her brother's life."

"Good heavens, this is beginning to sound ominous."

She shot him a cajoling look reminiscent of the younger Kitty. "Just hear what I have to say, all right? Aunt Louise is a wonderful woman; why she practically raised both of us and look how we turned out."

"I don't think that should be held against her."

"I'm serious! The point is she was much younger then. William is an incredibly active little boy. Why he can even run rings around my Davey, which is astounding. He needs a mother who can keep up with him, and maybe brothers and sisters."

This echo of his own earlier thoughts so threw Philip off stride that several moments passed before he answered. When he did so, his teasing tone was gone and he was completely serious. "I appreciate your concern, Kitty. I know William is a handful."

"He's a wonderful little boy. You have every right to be very proud of him. It's just that as the twig is bent, so grows the tree. Remember how Aunt Louise always told us that?"

Philip nodded. "And you think he may not be getting bent in the right direction?"

"He's...becoming very used to having his own way."

She didn't have to say anything more; Philip understood. In the fullness of time, William would be called upon to assume control not only of thousands of acres of land, but more importantly of hundreds of human lives. The slightest weakness in his character would be magnified that many times over, with potentially tragic results.

They had both seen it happen all too often. A prosperous plantation built up through generations of hard work passed to a son spoiled by power and privilege. Within a very short time, problems arose. Overseers grew arrogant and deceitful. Slaves were abused, supplies were stolen. The land was not properly cared for. Inevitably a slow decline set in that, after a point, became irreversible. It had happened to some of the best families of the Old South, and it would happen to more. But not, Philip was determined, to the Calverts.

"I'll think about what you said," he promised as they rejoined the rest of the family. She was content with that, having known from childhood that his word could always be trusted.

Philip remained in the music room a short time longer before reluctantly excusing himself. As always there was work to be done. Seated in the library behind the mahogany desk his father and his grandfather before him had used, he looked absently at the stack of mail that had accumulated in his absence. On the top was a letter from Josiah Mackenzie. With a sigh, he reached for it.

_____ *Chapter Fifteen*

THE SOUND of carriage wheels rattling along the cobblestones on Broadway woke Sarah. Before she opened her eyes, she smiled. Through the open window she could smell the fresh, tantalizing aromas of spring similar to but not quite the same as what she knew in Boston. New York was different, in all sorts of fascinating ways, and she was eager to begin exploring it again.

Five years before, Josiah Mackenzie had made the decision to move his family out of Lowell. He gave as his reason the fact that the town had become increasingly crowded and dirty, and the influx of immigrant girls, mainly from Ireland, had introduced an element he considered undesirable. Not that he wasn't happy enough to hire workers desperate enough to accept virtually any wage.

Labor unrest continued but no longer worried him. The ragged streams of refugees arriving daily in Boston Harbor were God's assurance that Josiah and the mill owners had been right to take the tough stand they had. No strike had ever succeeded in their mills and none ever would. Josiah had made a particular point of mentioning this to Sarah shortly after the attempted strike of 1852 was crushed. The women and girls she had worked with were fired and forced to leave Lowell.

The grinding helplessness she had felt at that defeat, coupled with the secret shame Gideon caused, had left her numb. Marilee claimed that Josiah had realized that and made the move to Boston in part to give her the benefit of new surroundings and a fresh start. Sarah dismissed that out of hand. Yet she had still come to enjoy the house on Commonwealth Avenue and the broader world of Boston society, or at least as much of it as would admit a mill owner and his family.

If Josiah minded being ignored by the panoply of Cabots, Lodges and their like, he showed no sign of it. The care and feeding of his business kept him too occupied to notice such slights. He was a wealthy man now, richer than he had ever dreamed of being, but he did not take his wealth for granted. He felt for it as another man might have a child and nurtured it with attention he had never given to his other progeny.

Which was just as well with Sarah. She greatly preferred her father's disinterest to those rare times when he took some notice of her. To that end, she did her best to stay out of his way. When he first mentioned his intention to visit New York, she had been delighted, envisioning as she did several weeks of relative freedom. His announcement that she and Marilee were to come along at first dismayed Sarah, particularly when she discovered that Marilee had suggested it. She had some idea that Sarah should get to know her mother's family, still resident in New York but out of touch with Josiah for years.

As it turned out, the Vandenheuvels had been happy to welcome Sarah, though they remained cool to her

father. Catherine's parents were both still alive, very
elderly and unable to get around much, but unexpectedly kind. They made no secret of how delighted they
were with their granddaughter. Sarah wished they
might also have met Nathan, who was away at school,
but she was glad enough that Gideon had stayed in
Boston to oversee the family business. At twenty-four,
he was a precociously dour man whose saturnine
countenance radiated suspicion and secrecy. There were
times when Sarah thought that even her father was
taken aback by Gideon, but had no idea what to do
about him.

Thinking of Gideon would surely spoil her day.
Rather than let that happen, Sarah slipped from the
bed and padded over to the window. Barefoot, wearing a thin white nightgown that hung in voluminous
folds on her slender body, she tossed the thick braid of
her chestnut hair over her shoulder as she studied the
scene on the street below.

The Metropolitan Hotel was one of the best in the
city. When they had arrived the week before, tired and
dusty after the train trip, the manager had personally
escorted them to their rooms, bellboys in red velvet
jackets had hurried to collect their luggage, maids in
lacy caps had unpacked for them and waiters had
appeared almost instantly with refreshments. Sarah
smiled as she remembered it all. With very little effort,
she could get used to such luxury.

A wagon rattled along the street, driven by a grizzled old man with a small boy bouncing beside him. It
turned the corner into an alley that ran behind the hotel, giving her a glimpse of the sign on the side of the
wagon: Carducci Brothers Ice. Seeing it, Sarah smiled
with anticipation. Her father was going to be very busy

all day; she and Marilee already had his permission to go shopping, which meant, at least to Sarah, that they would be at liberty to explore the fascinating, diverse city teeming with people of all races and nationalities. The true capital of the United States, some called it, and Sarah already agreed.

An adjoining door connected her room with Marilee's. She knocked on it lightly and entered when her friend called for her to come in. Marilee was sitting up in bed, wearing a frothy bed jacket of white lace and silk that Sarah had given her on her most recent birthday. Her pale blond hair fell in soft ringlets to her shoulders. Despite the early hour she looked, as she always did, utterly lovely.

On her lap was a tray brought moments before by a maid. She gestured to it as Sarah sat down beside her. "They must have thought I wanted to feed an army. Join me?"

Over coffee laced with cream, French toast with maple syrup and crisp rashers of bacon, they planned their day. Marilee was quite insistent about going to at least a few shops, since that was what they had told Josiah they would be doing. But she also agreed with Sarah's wish to simply wander about.

An hour later they left the hotel and turned north up Broadway. The wide avenue was crowded with businessmen and shoppers. Newsboys hawked copies of the *New York Times*, the *World* and half a dozen other papers. Old women offered apples for sale while younger ones flitted up and down the street selling posies. Drivers of private carriages, cabs, wagons and the horse-drawn trolleys all hollered at each other and pedestrians indiscriminately as they tried to maneuver their way through the tangle of vehicles.

Sarah and Marilee had lived in Boston long enough not to consider themselves country rubes, but they were still dazed by the crowds, the noise and the smells, all of which grew more pervasive as the sun rose higher. With so much traffic, the street was riddled with trampled piles of horse dung, each collecting its own colony of flies.

The young women were forced to step around one particularly large deposit as they crossed the street. They lifted their skirts cautiously, not lowering them again until they had safely reached the other side.

"Perhaps we should have hired a carriage," Marilee ventured. They were standing in front of the handsome five-story iron structure that housed the department store of A.T. Stewart, though not so close to the door as to be trampled by the steady stream of customers heading in and out.

"Oh, no," Sarah protested. "This is much more fun. I've never seen so many different kinds of people in one place." She glanced around as she spoke, noting the Italian organ grinder with his pet monkey, the red-haired shoe-shine boy who looked as though he had just stepped off the boat from Ireland and the Negro in livery carrying parcels for his mistress.

"Neither have I," Marilee admitted, "though I suppose we have them in Boston. Everything here is just so much . . . more."

"Which is why we wanted to come," Sarah reminded her. Before Marilee could reconsider, she added, "Stewart's is having a sale. I read about it in the paper. Let's see what they're offering."

That brightened Marilee up. She loved to shop and would spend hours wandering through stores without ever showing the slightest impatience. Sarah, on the other hand, preferred to be in and out, but she was willing to linger if it would make Marilee happy. Her friend had, after all, done so much for her.

As they entered the store Sarah caught sight of herself in a full-length mirror and a familiar start of surprise raced through her, the same reaction she experienced whenever she unexpectedly saw herself. For the briefest instant, she invariably wondered who she might be looking at. That had been the case ever since shortly after her thirteenth birthday, when Marilee had gently but firmly set about turning her into a lady.

With Josiah's full approval, if dubious expectations, she had schooled a reluctant Sarah in posture, etiquette, conversation, dancing, art, music and fashion, the last being Marilee's special interest. She subscribed to half a dozen magazines that came several times a year directly from Paris and included all the latest creations of the great couturiers.

Marilee had originally paid for the magazines out of the small salary Josiah gave her. But when he saw them, he insisted on taking over the expense himself, as he did with many others over the years. Sarah had long since stopped wondering why it gave her father pleasure to indulge Marilee when he did not care to do the same with his own children.

With information gleaned from the fashion magazines, Marilee had set about dressing Sarah. At first her outfits were simple and modest, as befitted a very young girl. But as she grew older and actually began to take some slight interest in her appearance, Marilee was inspired to go further.

The Second Empire-style ensemble Sarah was wearing that particular day was a testament to her friend's taste and skill, but it depended for its impact on Sarah's attractiveness, which she was so reluctant to acknowledge. Hence her surprise whenever she looked in the mirror and saw a tall, slender young woman whose damask-smooth features were highlighted by large gray eyes remarkable for their clarity and expressiveness. Because she was so fond of being out-of-doors, her cheeks were invariably slightly flushed. Marilee's lemon rinses had turned her once-drab brown hair to a warm shade of chestnut. She would never be the picture book sort of beauty that Marilee was, but she had a kind of loveliness all her own.

Which had certain drawbacks. Men tended to be attracted to her, for reasons she could not divine since she never made any particular effort to be pleasant to them. It was different with Marilee; she was invariably charming but managed to discourage unwanted attentions without ever giving offense. Sarah was more inclined to be blunt. The corners of her mouth turned up as she remembered a particularly pompous young man, the son of one of her father's business associates, who had been immensely put out to discover precisely how unimpressed she was with him.

Her smile faded as she wondered how much longer her coldness would be allowed to discourage would-be suitors. At twenty-two, she was nearing the age when girls were expected to marry. Her only comfort was that Marilee, two years her senior, was at the height of her eligibility. She showed no more interest than Sarah in getting married, but she also had one very great advantage: no one was likely to try to push her into matrimony. Although Josiah had not mentioned it directly, Sarah knew he had always expected her to marry. Not for a moment did she believe he had changed his mind.

"You look so serious," Marilee said as she glanced up from an assortment of ribbons she had been examining. "Is something wrong?"

"No, of course not," Sarah immediately pretended interest in the ribbons long enough for Marilee to be convinced. They bought half a dozen in various shades for Sarah and the same for Marilee. One of the few things Sarah liked about her father was his generosity with Marilee. He had long ago insisted on giving her a generous clothing allowance in addition to her salary, saying that if she was to be his daughter's companion, she couldn't go around looking like a servant.

No one seeing Marilee could take her for such. Her apricot silk day dress trimmed with alençon lace was simple in comparison with the elaborate confections worn by society women, but then Marilee required no great enhancement of her natural beauty. Her hair, parted in the center, fell in ringlets to her shoulders. She wore no jewelry other than the gold studs that had been a Christmas gift from Josiah, and she smelled very faintly of lavender.

As they moved through the store, pausing here and there to buy, they were unfailingly surrounded by attentive male employees. Marilee was hard-pressed to convince several of them that the packages should be sent, rather than personally delivered to their hotel. She rolled her eyes when the disappointed gentlemen finally withdrew.

Sarah joined her laughter, despite the censorious glances of other, less fortunate women. "I thought you might have to adopt that last one, Marilee. He looked at you just like a lost puppy would."

"What about that poor man in the handkerchief department? You made him stutter."

"Me? I thought he'd always done that." It hadn't occurred to Sarah until then that as many men as were taken with Marilee were equally impressed by her. She simply presumed that her friend drew all the attention.

Marilee made a face. "You're so stubborn. Why won't you believe how pretty you are?"

"Perhaps because I was plain for so long that I can't get used to the change," Sarah said. She took her friend's arm and they headed toward the door. "You will simply have to admit that you worked a miracle."

"Nonsense. I did no more than make the most of what nature gave you." Gently she added, "I've seen the miniature of your mother, Sarah. She was a beautiful woman, and you take after her."

For an instant the image of how she had last seen her mother, white and still, bereft of life, flitted through Sarah's mind. She stiffened, but then forced herself to say lightly, "Whether I am pretty or not, Father expects us back in time for dinner, and I still want to explore. Do you feel up to it?"

"Of course, that little bit of shopping could never wear me out."

In fact, they had been in Stewart's some three hours, and even Sarah had to admit that she was tired and hungry. But after lunching at a nearby tearoom, both were sufficiently revived to continue their excursion. They strolled up Broadway past Union Square, pausing to look in the windows of Brentano's News Depot, the great literary rendezvous of New York where writers and book lovers met, and in the windows of Tiffany's, renowned for a different sort of greatness.

Marilee was still extolling the diamond and sapphire necklace on display there when they boarded the stage heading downtown. After dropping their nickel fares in the coin box, they realized that all seats were taken. The driver turned around from his high perch to glare at two men, who promptly rose. Marilee and Sarah kept their eyes averted as they murmured their thanks. It was very daring for them to be riding on a public conveyance, and they were conscious of the need not to attract undue attention.

The ride along the crowded, rutted road was so jarring that they had to hold on to the edges of their seats to keep from being thrown from them. They were glad enough to get off several blocks from the hotel to avoid any chance of being seen. The area was dominated by several hotels besides the Metropolitan, and it was while they were walking past one of them, the New York Hotel, that Sarah suddenly drew up short.

"Marilee," she said, tugging at her friend's arm, "look at that man coming out of the hotel. Doesn't he seem familiar?"

"Which one?"

"The blond gentleman in the gray frock coat. Isn't that Philip Calvert?"

Marilee, who was the tiniest bit nearsighted, squinted slightly. "Who?"

"Philip Calvert. Father buys cotton from him. He came to see us in Lowell, it must have been eight or nine years ago." Actually, she knew perfectly well when he had visited. Her encounter with the handsome young planter was as fresh in her memory as though it had happened only the day before. She wanted to believe that she remembered it so clearly only because it had coincided with that horrible scene with Gideon and with the attempted strike by the mill girls that had ended, as had all the others, so bitterly. But deep inside she suspected there might be another reason why Philip Calvert had made so strong an impression on her.

If the man up ahead of them was Philip Calvert, he had changed a great deal in the intervening years. Not that he was any less attractive, quite the contrary. There was a settled air of strength and purpose about him that had not been present before. He was no less fit though he seemed larger; his shoulders and chest looked broader, as though he had grown into himself. He turned slightly, so that Sarah could see him full in the face, and she realized that her guess had been right; he was Philip Calvert.

At the same moment she confirmed that, his eyes lit on Marilee. He looked startled for an instant before a pleasant smile softened his mouth. "Miss Jamison," he said with a bow. "Forgive me for being so forward, but we've met before. I'm Philip Calvert."

"Of course," she said, returning his smile at the same time she gestured to her friend. "We met at Josiah's house in Lowell. You remember his daughter, Sarah."

Actually, Philip didn't. The child had made only the most shadowy impression on him, nothing at all like the effect of the lovely, rather regal-looking girl who was regarding him steadily. He bowed again to cover his surprise. "Miss Mackenzie, how pleasant to see you again. I was just on my way to the Metropolitan to meet with your father."

"Indeed?" Sarah said, rather surprised that her voice sounded normal. Something about seeing Philip Calvert again had taken her breath away. Aware that Marilee was looking at her curiously, she said, "We're also returning to the hotel."

"Then please allow me to escort you." He graciously offered an arm to each. Marilee took it without hesitation. Sarah followed suit only because she did not want to appear rude. Touching Philip, even through the layers of her glove and his jacket, did nothing for her equilibrium.

She was undoubtedly tired and dazed by all they had seen and done. When she got back to her room, she would lie down for a few minutes and put a cold cloth on her forehead. Whatever business Philip Calvert had with her father would undoubtedly be taken care of swiftly. There was no reason to imagine that she would ever see him again.

Except that her father had invited him to join them for supper both that night and the following. It seemed that the two men had a great deal to talk about.

Chapter Sixteen

"THE NEW MILL I propose to build," Josiah said, "will combine the most advanced machinery with the most efficient means of production. It will employ some two hundred men and women, only a handful of whom will need any real skills to begin with. The rest can be trained. Best of all, it will be close to the source of supply, which will further reduce our costs."

Philip smiled inwardly at the other man's presumption that he would go along with the proposal. He had been careful to give no such indication, at least not yet. What Josiah was offering did interest him, but he was too canny a negotiator to reveal his interest too soon.

"It sounds," he said as he swirled the burgundy in his glass and studied its ruby glow, "as though you have thought this out very carefully."

"Naturally, I'm not a man to make hasty decisions. What surprises me, though, is that more manufacturers haven't thought to build mills in the South before."

"There are a number of reasons for that," Philip said, "among them the opposition of Southerners to industrialization."

Josiah smoothed his mustache and smiled. They had dined very well at Delmonico's and he was feeling expansive, not the least because of the company. Marilee looked lovely as ever in a gown of sapphire velvet that matched her eyes. A glance at his daughter confirmed that in her own way she was as appealing. Something he noticed that had not escaped Philip Calvert's attention.

His smile deepened, and he leaned back in the plush leather chair. "Ah, yes, the famous Southern determination to preserve the past unchanged, as though that were actually possible. I understood you do not suffer from any such delusion."

Philip inclined his head. That was true enough though under the circumstances he saw no reason to stress the point. "This mill you intend to build," he said with studied casualness. "I presume you have a location in mind?"

Josiah drew a piece of paper from his pocket and laid it out on the table. He pointed with a callused finger. "There."

Philip looked up from the map slowly. "I own that land."

"Indeed, your father deeded it to you upon your marriage." If Josiah felt any hesitation about mentioning an event that had ended so tragically, he did not show it.

Sarah flinched inwardly at his tactlessness. She remembered hearing about the death of Philip's wife in childbirth and knew that his father had been seriously injured shortly thereafter, hence his responsibility for all plantation business. If she could have thought of a way to express her sympathy without being overly personal, she would have done so. But he seemed so remote and self-contained that she was glad not to have to.

Marilee caught her eye and looked heavenward. Sarah had to stifle a laugh. She knew her friend was exasperated by the talk of business. The men had apologized perfunctorily in advance when they first sat down to supper. Since then they had spoken of nothing but cotton, mills, prices and so on. Now it seemed they were set to go several hours more. Marilee was understandably bored, but Sarah found the subject fascinating.

Particularly when Philip said bluntly, "Surely you don't expect me to sell you the land?"

"Why not? I'll give you an excellent price."

"I'm not interested. Land is never to be sold."

"There are others who won't feel that way," Josiah pointed out.

"Then deal with them." Philip was growing impatient. He did not like to believe his time had been wasted. The letter from Josiah, suggesting that they meet in New York to discuss a joint business venture, had been interesting enough to prompt him to make a trip he had long been putting off. There were other reasons to bring him to the city: the factor who regularly bought his cotton for export to England, a bank he had recently begun doing business with and so on. But if Josiah seriously believed he would sell him his land, the main purpose of the trip was gone.

He took another sip of his wine and waited to see how the other man would reply.

"It's true that I would like to buy your land," Josiah said at length, "but if you are absolutely set against that, I would consider renting it."

"That," Philip said slowly, "might be possible to arrange." Provided the terms were correct and the lease was written in a way favorable to him. He was not suddenly about to begin trusting Yankees. Which brought him to another point. "Might I ask why you have chosen this particular time to consider a business venture in the South?''

Josiah hesitated. There was a great deal he could say in response to that, but very little of it was personally flattering. He sensed the beginnings of an accord with young Calvert and did not want to shock him with talk of exploiting other men's troubles. ''Let's just say that I am at a point in my life where I can see the wisdom of prudent risk. While it is true that many businessmen are afraid to invest in the South right now because they believe war is coming, I prefer to believe that accord is still possible.''

Since that agreed with Philip's own hopes, if not his actual beliefs, he was willing enough to accept it. Seeing that, Josiah leaned forward slightly, his black eyes intent. ''What I had in mind was that you grant me a leasehold on the land and in return, I grant you partial ownership in the mill.''

''How much ownership?''

''Five percent.''

''Fifty would be fairer.''

''Fifty is out of the question. Fifteen percent is as high as I can go.''

''Thirty,'' Philip said.

''Twenty-five.''

The women, who had been looking from one to the other throughout the rapid-fire exchange, waited. After a moment Philip nodded. ''Twenty-five. Done.''

Josiah reached across the table, and the two men shook hands. As though sensing the moment, a waiter arrived with a tray of brandies and cordials. Sarah and Marilee declined, but with their permission, the men enjoyed a fine cognac and equally good cigars.

It was well past midnight before they left the restaurant. As Josiah hailed a hansom cab he said, "I'll instruct my lawyer to draw up the necessary papers tomorrow."

"Fine," Philip told him. "I will be here a few more days if you would care to send them round to my hotel."

He declined the offer of a lift, saying that he preferred to walk, but did agree to join them at the theater the following evening. Before taking his leave he bowed graciously to both Sarah and Marilee, though it was on the former that his eyes lingered.

Philip waited until the cab drew away before allowing himself to break into a grin. He didn't imagine for a moment that he had gotten more than Josiah had been prepared to give, but neither had he settled for anything less. Twenty-five percent of a new mill was an excellent return on land that would soon have had to be left fallow. His only concern was how his father would react to the news that his son was going into business with a Yankee. Thanks to the brandy, he could laugh about it, but he suspected that when the time actually came to tell him, he would be a good deal more sober.

In the meantime he was surprised to find himself looking forward to another evening in the company of Miss Sarah Mackenzie. She did not at all conform to the usual type of women he found attractive; her friend, Miss Jamison was much more that. Yet he was oddly reassured by that. After Daphne he never again wanted to feel so powerfully drawn to a woman. Sarah Mackenzie, in her cool self-containment, was a far safer proposition.

He fell asleep remembering the intelligence in her gray eyes and, rather disconcertingly, the sound of her laugh.

Sarah was laughing again the next night. They had all gone to see a performance of *The Taming of the Shrew* starring Edwin Booth. The renowned actor played Petruchio as well as he did Hamlet and left the audience at Walleck's Theater enchanted. Even Sarah, who privately sided more with the sharp-tongued Kate than with her beleaguered husband, was delighted.

Afterward, because the night was pleasant, they decided to walk to Philip's hotel, where he had invited them to join him for a late supper. Josiah took Marilee's arm and led her on ahead, leaving the other two to follow.

"I was surprised," Philip said, for want of anything better to say, "that you still have a companion."

Sarah shot him a quick look. "Marilee is my friend."

"Yes, of course. I only meant that she might have married by now."

Sarah made a small, derisive sound. "Why is it that men think marriage should be the goal of every woman? Marilee and I are happy alone."

His eyelids dropped slightly as he gave her a side-long glance. What was she telling him? As quickly as it had come, his suspicion died away. She was too innocent to be involved in anything unnatural, and he was too jaded not to have realized that immediately. Gently he said, "But you are not alone. Your father cares for you."

Sarah started to correct him but thought better of it. If she owed Josiah nothing else, she should at least not criticize him. As quickly as she could, she changed the subject. "It would be fascinating to see the new mill built. I remember when I was a little girl, one of the Lowell mills was renovated. I went every day to watch.''

''Perhaps you can watch this one, too.'' Now where had that come from, Philip wondered, the moment the words were said. There had been no suggestion of her visiting Virginia, though now that he thought about it, she would certainly be welcome.

Startled by the invitation, Sarah said nothing. She wished they could walk faster, to catch up with her father and Marilee, but there was nothing she could do to hurry Philip along. Especially not since he seemed predisposed to linger.

''I've been thinking about that time I visited Lowell nine years ago,'' he said. ''You were how old?''

''Thirteen, Mr. Calvert, though by extension you have just asked how old I am, and surely that is very rude?''

He looked startled for a moment, until he caught her teasing tone. ''Forgive me, I've grown out of the habit of speaking with a beautiful young lady.''

She was reminded again of his dead wife. Awkwardly she said, ''Last evening, when my father mentioned your marriage, I regretted his tactlessness. Losing your wife must have been terrible.''

Philip was silent for a moment. He so rarely spoke of Daphne to anyone that he was hard-pressed to do so now. But at length he said, ''I blame myself.''

Sarah was so surprised that she actually jerked with shock. Never could she imagine that a man would take responsibility for a woman's death. ''She died in childbirth.''

Though it was not quite a question, he nodded. ''With our son, William.'' He didn't add that he had forced her to bear the child. That much of his pain he could not reveal.

"My mother also died trying to give birth."

Something in her voice, a note of old grief never quite resolved, drew him up short. Without thinking he laid his hand over hers where it rested in the crook of his arm. "Many women survive. My sister, Kitty, has had five children and she flourishes."

She sensed that he meant to reassure her and was moved by that, even as she remained unconvinced. "Tell me about Virginia. We hear so much but know so little."

He smiled down at her, making her suddenly aware that she came only to his shoulders. Taller than average for a woman, she was used to looking men in the eye. Having to look up instead was vaguely disconcerting.

"Most Northerners I meet," Philip said, "believe themselves to be experts on the South. They are forever telling me about it."

Beneath the lightness of his words, Sarah sensed a thread of anger. She felt muscles jump in his forearm beneath her hand. "I think no one can know the truth about a place without having lived there."

"Then you are a rarity."

"Don't misunderstand me. Many Southerners seem to believe that they know everything they need to about the North. The misunderstandings are mutual."

It took Philip a moment to realize that he had been gently reprimanded. When he did, his laughter rang out, causing Josiah to pause and glance back at him before returning his attention to Marilee.

"Tell me, Miss Mackenzie, do you have many suitors?"

It was Sarah's turn to be caught unawares "S-suitors? Why no, I . . ."

"You frighten them away?"

Her stomach plummeted as she felt what she imagined to be his disdain. "Yes," she said stiffly, "I suppose I do."

"You don't sound as though you mind."

"I told you, I am happy with my life."

"As I said, you are a rarity. Is there nothing you would change?"

Yes, fear and anger, a sense of never truly belonging, loneliness.

"No, I have everything I could wish."

"Then perhaps," Philip said gently, "your wishes need to be expanded."

She didn't want to think what he meant by that. He was so different from her, so much a part of a world she could not imagine. The only man she knew at all well was her father, and instinct told her that Philip was nothing like him. Yet, she reminded herself, instinct could be wrong. She had always presumed that all men were the same under the skin. However pleasant Philip might seem, he had done nothing to change her mind.

By the time they reached the hotel dining room, Josiah and Marilee were already at the table. Her father looked a bit put out by their tardiness, but he relented quickly enough when Philip began to regale him with talk of his stables. For all his devotion to business, Josiah nurtured a long-held love of good horseflesh. His admiration for the Calverts, indeed his fascination with both father and son, stemmed at least in part from their record of victories on the track.

"That three-year-old of yours, King's Ransom, how's he faring these days?"

"Never better," Philip assured him. He was fond of the horse he called King even though Satan was his grandfather. His dam was a gentle mare named Astreides who had bred a fierce but disciplined son. "He won all over the state last year, and I'm thinking about taking him outside. If there was ever a horse born to race, he's it."

"I'd love to see him run," Josiah said with undisguised longing.

"Perhaps you will. You'll come down when work starts on the mill, won't you?"

"Why yes, I'd planned to."

"Then we'll go around to the meets together."

Josiah could not contain a flush of pleasure. To be introduced to Virginia society by Philip Calvert was an unlooked-for bonus to their business dealings. Too clearly he remembered his boyhood, the grim years spent laboring for other men, never daring to raise his eyes to those who were his betters. Now, at last, he would meet them on equal ground.

"I'll look forward to it," he said. Marilee and Sarah exchanged a glance, which Josiah caught. "And you'll both come along. That is," he looked quickly at their host, "if it's no imposition."

"Of course not," Philip assured him quickly. "These lovely ladies will be a revelation. It's time my fellow Southerners learned there are Yankee belles."

Marilee clapped her hands in delight. "What a wonderful idea. I've heard so much about Southern hospitality, it will be marvelous to experience it."

"What about you?" Philip asked Sarah quietly. "Are you also looking forward to the trip?"

"That depends," she told him with a teasing smile. "When will we be going?"

"In a few months," her father told her. "Perhaps November, early December."

"Perfect. I'm in favor of anything that gets me out of Boston once summer is over."

"You don't like cold weather?" Philip asked.

"She takes after her mother that way," Josiah informed him. "Catherine was never happy once the temperature dropped below sixty."

Sarah's eyes flew to her father. He so rarely mentioned her mother that she didn't know what to make of his doing so now. Nor did she understand the meaning behind the benign smile that he gave to both her and Philip.

Chapter Seventeen

"I'M GLAD TO FIND YOU HOME," Peter Rider said as he dismounted from his bay stallion in front of Calvert Oaks. A slave boy ran forward to take the reins as Peter dropped to the ground. Philip had seen him coming from the window of the library and had gone out to greet him.

The intent set of Peter's features suggested that the visit wasn't for pleasure. His words confirmed that. "There's trouble again at the Danverses' place."

He spoke softly so that the slaves who happened to be around, as some always seemed to be when a visitor arrived, wouldn't overhear him. Philip nodded and led the way inside. When the library door was closed behind them, he said, "When did it start?"

"Yesterday." Peter pulled off his hat and ran a hand through his thick auburn hair. It was a gesture of weariness that went further than any physical exhaustion. "Seems that Danvers senior and Danvers junior got into a little dispute over a slave girl they both wanted to bed. While they were arguing it out, her husband had the gall to object." He grimaced in distaste. "They thought that was funny, and both of them started in on her at the same time, in front of him."

Bile rose in the back of Philip's throat. He walked stiffly to the liquor cabinet and poured them each a jolt of bourbon. Peter took his gratefully, downing it in a single swallow. It gave him the strength to go on. "When he tried to stop them, they slit his throat and hung him up from the hog-butchering tree. Let him bleed to death."

"My God..." Philip's hand tightened around the glass, his knuckles gleaming white.

"I'm afraid God's got nothing to do with this. The other slaves have refused to go into the fields. They're staying in their cabins, so far, but that can't last. Old man Danvers actually had the nerve to send Paul over to our place asking for help. They're afraid the minute they shut their eyes, it'll be their throats getting cut. I've got to say, I hope they're right."

Philip sat down abruptly and stared at Peter. Neither man had to spell out the quandary they were in. They both despised the Danvers, yet if they allowed them to be massacred by their own slaves, they would be inviting trouble on every other plantation, including theirs.

In the final analysis, control of the blacks depended on their certain knowledge that at the first sign of resistance, retribution would be swift and terrible. That was the single, stark reality underlying their way of life. To violate it would be to invite an upheaval the consequences of which could be barely glimpsed.

And yet, when all was said and done, a man had to live with his own conscience.

Slowly Philip said, "I cannot raise my hand to protect scum like the Danvers."

Peter sighed deeply and sat down opposite him. "I feel the same way, but what choice do we have? You know what will happen if we do nothing."

"They'll get what's coming to them."

"And we'll be smack in the middle of a slave rebellion."

Which would have to be crushed by the militia. Have to and would be. There could be no question of that. But before it was over, how many would die? Some whites, perhaps, but it was far more likely that dozens of blacks would perish, some in the immediate fighting, even more in the firestorms of revenge that invariably followed such a crisis.

Philip had a distant memory from his childhood of black bodies hanging from trees, the wailing of women and the terrible stench of fear. He remembered his father, grim-faced but determined, standing with the other men, doing what they believed had to be done. He and Charles had never talked about that scene, though as he grew older Philip realized it must have had to do with Nat Turner's rebellion in 1831, when he was three years old. Numerous plantations had been affected before the uprising was crushed. More than fifty whites had been killed. Many times that number of blacks had died, dozens more had been sold away from their homes and families. It had been a time of almost unimaginable brutality when the thin gloss of Southern civilization was ripped to shreds. Not for anything did he want to see it happen again.

"All right," he said softly, "something has to be done, but not what the Danverses want. If the militia rides onto Beauterre, we'll be saying that every man among us approves of their actions. The nigras will have more reason than ever before to hate us."

"Can you suggest an alternative?"

Philip nodded. "That we go together but not in uniform, and with no show of force. We talk to the Danverses and warn them in no uncertain terms that such brutality must stop." When Peter looked unconvinced, he went on. "You know as well as I do that a silent but very effective condemnation can be brought to bear against people who violate our standards. Neither Frederick nor Paul will want to suffer such ostracism. They'll go along with us once they realize they have no choice."

"All right . . . perhaps we can get them to treat their slaves better, but that won't diffuse the immediate situation. There must be at least a few among the nigras who will want revenge at all costs."

"They'll have to be split up," Philip said. "Separated, there will be far less chance of their doing anything."

"I suppose a dealer might be persuaded to take them," Peter said doubtfully. "Though Danvers won't like selling at a loss."

"That doesn't really matter," Philip said as he rose and reached for his hat. "Either he goes along with us, or he's left to stand alone. That has to be made clear."

It was, though with great difficulty. Frederick Danvers and his son, Paul, at first welcomed the group of planters with open arms; they were surprised they had not come wrapped in the authority of the militia.

"Doesn't matter," Frederick said as he led them inside. There was no sign of any slaves, either in the house or out. They were all either hiding in their cabins or had taken to the woods beyond.

Several days' growth of beard smudged Frederick's thin features. His small eyes were red-rimmed from lack of sleep. He wore a soiled shirt and trousers that were stained with blood. In one hand he grasped an ancient sword that he seemed unable to let go of despite the uncontrollable trembling of his thin arm.

Paul Danvers was far more in control of himself. Though he, too, had gone sleepless for several nights and looked the worse for it, his stance was defiant as he faced the other men. "I presume you're here to help us teach these damn nigras a lesson they won't forget."

The dozen men who had ridden to Beauterre remained silent. Although Peter was nominally their leader, they all automatically looked to Philip to respond. It was he who had conceived the plan and explained it to them, winning their approval through the sheer force of his persuasion. By the time he had gotten finished talking to them, they were all convinced there was no other choice. But they were still uncomfortable with what they had to do and were glad that the burden of it fell on him.

"What we're here for," Philip said, "is to put an end to any trouble that might be brewing. Trouble that you caused." He looked directly at both men as he spoke, making sure that they caught the rage seething behind his words.

"We caused...?" Paul Danvers said. His face flushed and he took a step forward. "What in hell are you talking about? All we did was discipline a buck that got out of hand."

"You killed him," Philip said, "like a hog, because he tried to protect his woman. Why in hell," he deliberately parodied the other man's tone, "didn't you just give your nigras guns and be done with it?"

Paul Danvers had turned a mottled shade of red. His large hands were clenched at his sides. He was clearly about to explode when Peter stepped forward. "You're causing trouble for all of us," he said flatly. "It has to stop. We've come with a plan that we believe can achieve that. If you're calm enough to listen, Philip will explain."

"Damn him if he will," Paul shot back. "He's a nigger lover if there ever was one." With a slashing wave of his arm, he challenged the other men. "What's wrong with the rest of you? Don't you understand what's at stake here? If we don't stand together, the niggers'll be on us in a second."

"We do stand together," Philip said. "That's what this is all about."

"Hear him out," Frederick interjected. He had seen the look in the other men's eyes and thought he knew what was coming. Unlike his son, he was enough of a realist to know it couldn't be stopped.

"The kind of atrocity you committed here," Philip said, "makes trouble for all of us. It has to stop. There are to be no more such...occurrences. In addition, you will sell off any slave you think is liable to cause trouble, no matter how much of a loss you have to take. Some of them, we will buy. The others will have to go to a trader."

"Who won't give us squat," Frederick said. "Why don't you just tell us to cut our veins open?"

Philip gave him a look that made it clear the idea appealed to him. Once again, Peter intervened. "We know this is hard for you, and we'll give you as fair prices as we can on the slaves we take. The only ones you'll have to sell are the real recalcitrants."

"We happen to have more than a few of those," Paul said. He had not made another move toward Philip, but the unholy light in his eyes belied his restraint.

Philip resisted the urge to point out that it was the Danverses' own treatment of their slaves that bred an-

ger and resistance. He sensed that he had pushed both
father and son as far as he could without completely
humiliating them. By the complex, sometimes perverse code of honor, the other men he had brought
with him would not allow him to go further than they
thought was absolutely necessary. If he tried, they
would feel compelled to swallow their distaste and
support the Danverses.

"We'll work something out," Philip said quietly.
"No one wants you to take a loss. All we want is for
this kind of trouble to stop." The other men nodded,
letting him know that he had struck the right note.

The rest of the meeting was given over to bickering.
Frederick and Paul drove a hard bargain. They demanded top dollar for a dozen slaves they admitted
suspecting of wanting to cause trouble but also insisted had it in them to be good workers. For the three
or four that no amount of lying would transform, it
was agreed they'd go in the next cottle of slaves heading south to the cane fields. That amounted to a death
sentence, but no one could suggest any alternative.

Johnson had been called into the meeting when the
time came to decide which slaves had to go. The overseer had not changed much since being fired from
Calvert Oaks. If anything, he had grown meaner and
more vicious away from any controlling influence. He
glared at Philip, whom he instantly knew to be behind
the plan, and barely managed to keep a civil tongue in
his head.

"Don' seem right to me," he said when Frederick
told him what was to be done. "Make a whole lot more
sense to make a 'xample out of some of them bucks.
Lay fifty or so lashes on 'em where the rest can see.
Quiet things down just fine. Always does."

"Not this time," Philip said. When Paul seemed about to speak up in favor of the overseer's suggestion, he added, "Not if you want our continued support."

They did, but only at a price. Before the bargaining was over, the Danverses had cleared what Philip suspected was a tidy profit. It enraged Philip even more to think that they could reap any reward from their viciousness, but by then he was so fed up with the whole business that he simply wanted it ended. Against his better judgment, he agreed to take the wench who had been the source of the trouble in the first place.

"You won' be sorry about that," Johnson said with a leer. "She's high yaller with titties like you never seen..."

"Shut up," Philip snarled. In another moment he was going to wrap his hands around the man's neck and squeeze the life out of him. Given half an ounce of encouragement, he wouldn't stop there.

"Easy now," Frederick said. "No reason to get riled up now. Everything's working out just fine. We'll have each of you gentlemen's purchases sent over to you soon as we can."

"We'll take them now," Peter said.

The old man looked at him narrowly. "You got the money with you?" When Peter nodded curtly, Frederick shrugged. "Suit yourselves then." He didn't offer to help, nor did Paul or Johnson, which was just as well since assistance from them could only have made the task more difficult.

As it was, the slaves were reluctant to emerge from their cabins and other hiding places. More than a few had to be dragged out. Philip, Peter and several of the other men had brought their overseers with them in case of just such an eventuality. They matter-of-factly wielded bull whips and clamped on manacles until the job was done.

The wench, called Sukie, offered no resistance, but her dark brown eyes spat hatred when she looked at the white men. Her ragged calico dress was torn down the front and she was covered with bruises. Shoved into the wagon that would take her to Calvert Oaks, she curled up in a tight ball and made not a sound.

By the time the last of the wagons had pulled away, it was getting on toward dark. Philip was bone tired. He wanted nothing so much as to put Beauterre and all it represented behind him. By the time he reached home, his father and Aunt Louise were asleep, but his valet had waited up to see if he wanted anything to eat.

Philip hadn't thought he was hungry but at the mention of food his stomach growled. He allowed Jacob to bring a plate of cold chicken to him in the library. Like his father before him, it had become his private sanctum. He had long since fallen into the habit of going there whenever he felt the need to be alone.

His solitude, however, was not respected that night. Barely had he finished the chicken when Jacob stuck his head in the door. "Beggin' yo pa'don, massa, but Marcus bes outside an' he say he lahk a word with yo."

For a moment Philip was tempted to refuse. He had a fair idea of what was on Marcus's mind and was not eager to deal with it immediately. But putting it off would do no good and might actually cause some harm. "All right," he said, "show him in."

Marcus waited until the valet withdrew, closing the door behind him, before he said, "Is it true what they're saying in the quarters, that you stopped a rebellion at the Danvers place?"

Philip hoisted his feet off the desk and gestured to Marcus to sit down. "It never fails to amaze me," he said as he reached for the bourbon, "how word gets around so fast."

Philip pushed the decanter in his direction, and after a moment Marcus took it. He poured himself a drink but only sipped it. When they were alone together, he and Philip acted like the brothers they were, but that didn't make him so foolish as to believe that the bond of brotherhood existed outside the closed room.

"The Danverses are idiots," Philip said suddenly. "They damn near brought all hell down on our heads tonight."

"I heard they killed a man."

Grimly Philip nodded. "For trying to protect his wife. That's the girl I ended up buying. She's had a bad time of it. I'd appreciate whatever you can do to help her settle in."

"Ginny's with her now."

Philip stiffened. The words, simple as they were, served to remind him that Marcus's wife had once been on Beauterre and that he, therefore, knew better than most what the Danverses were capable of.

"Some good may come of this," he said. "The other planters—Morgan, Daniels, Carlisle, Rider and so on—stood with me in demanding that the Danverses change their ways. We made it clear that there has to be an end to their barbarism."

"Do you really think they'll heed you?"

"I don't know," Philip admitted. "But if they want to survive, they will. Old man Danvers has spent his life trying to give his family some kind of respectability. He knows now that he's in danger of losing that."

Marcus found it hard to believe that the threat of being denied social acceptability would be enough to deter such animals. But he had long since learned that if the whites could be counted on for anything, it was to think and act strangely.

Still he was cautious. "Danvers is an old man. He can't last much longer. His son will take over soon."

Philip heard the unspoken question. He, too, had his doubts about Paul Danvers, but he knew the younger man well enough to have some confidence that he could keep him in line. "If anything, being accepted by the right kind of people seems to matter even more to the son than it does to the father. Remember, Frederick Danvers survived in far less exalted surroundings for a long time while he was making his way up in the world, whereas Paul has never known anything except our way of life. The threat of being cut off from it should be enough to make him improve his behavior."

"Or simply become more cautious and deceitful."

Philip met his half brother's eyes, so like his own, warily. "What do you want me to say? There are no guarantees that the Danverses won't continue to abuse their slaves. What's important is that the other planters stood together to let them, and each other, know that such behavior is not acceptable. We took a step forward tonight."

Marcus put his glass down and stood up. His features were expressionless but his voice carried the hint of a taunt. "Do you expect us to be grateful?"

"No, damn it," Philip said. "If you ever were, I'd probably fall over dead. Now get out of here and let me get some rest."

Marcus chuckled softly to himself. "You're sounding more like your father every day."

He was at the door before Philip replied. "Has it ever occurred to you that you are, too?"

Marcus turned back, his face in the shadows cast by the single gas lamp that was lit. "What do you mean?"

"You're as stubborn as he ever was and as clever. Tomorrow I'll have to explain to him what happened at Beauterre, and I'll bet he asks me the same questions you just did."

"Will you give him the same answers?"

"They're the only ones I have."

The door shut quietly behind Marcus. Philip leaned his head back against the chair and closed his eyes. He wanted to forget it all, but he could not. His clothes, even his skin, seemed to have become pervaded by the smell of whatever it was that was rotten at Beauterre. He had a sudden fear that no amount of scrubbing could erase it.

With a low groan, he jumped up and strode over to the windows. It was very quiet; he could hear no sounds from the house or from the quarters beyond. But the apparent tranquility did not deceive him. More than ever he understood that it masked a long, silent scream that went on and on without end.

_____ *Chapter Eighteen*

AS IT TURNED OUT, the Mackenzie's planned trip to Calvert Oaks had to be postponed several months because of the death of Grandmother Mackenzie shortly before Thanksgiving, 1858. What with the funeral and the mourning period that followed, they were not able to make the journey until the following spring. Josiah was not pleased to have to put back his plans for the mill, but he had sufficient other matters to absorb his attention.

Principal among them was Gideon. Slowly and with great reluctance he was coming to the realization that his eldest son was not as he would have liked him to be. There was nothing he could precisely put his finger on; Gideon had always been a quiet, withdrawn boy who made no particular effort to extend himself, much less to be pleasant. That was fine with Josiah who considered charm in a man innately distasteful—at the very least he suspected such men of being effeminate; worse yet they might be politicians.

So the fact that his eldest son was by turns dour and surly did not concern him. What mattered was that Gideon was clever, ambitious and unburdened by any excessive sense of ethics. Josiah knew perfectly well that his son chaffed to replace him. He found that more amusing than worrisome, confident as he was that he could keep Gideon in line for many years yet. What did trouble him, so much that he could barely bring himself to think of it, were the strange undercurrents he sensed between Gideon and Sarah.

He had first become aware of them the year before when Gideon returned from Harvard and moved back into the family home. After having lived away for some eight years, first at prep school and then in a dormitory in Cambridge, it was only natural that some adjustments had to be made. What surprised Josiah was how the whole tenor of the household seemed to change.

Sarah, for one, became much more withdrawn, barely speaking at meals Gideon attended and seeming to go out of her way to avoid her brother. When he finally thought about it, Josiah realized that she was simply behaving as she always had whenever Gideon visited. He hoped that would change after she grew used to having her brother home, but months went by and if anything, Sarah's aloofness worsened.

Had his own relationship with his daughter been closer, Josiah might have been able to speak to her about the problem directly. As it was, he knew that the breach between them caused by her mother's death had never truly healed. She was pleasant enough to him, but he never had any sense of warmth from her. For that, he had to depend on Marilee.

It was to her that he eventually took his concerns. She heard him out patiently, sifting through the evasions and euphemisms to get at the heart of what troubled him. Softly she said, "It is best for Gideon and Sarah not to have very much contact."

"Why?" he demanded. They were alone in the drawing room, he pacing up and down in front of the mantel, Marilee seated across from him on the settee, her skirt of blue-washed silk blossoming about her so that she seemed to sit in the center of a giant flower.

"Sarah is afraid of Gideon," she said quietly. "I've been aware of that for some time, though I've never known exactly why she feels as she does. However, I trust her instincts enough to believe that she should never be put in the position of being vulnerable to him."

"She hasn't confided in you . . . ?"

Marilee shook her head. "Not about that. She keeps her own counsel when she wants to."

Josiah sighed heavily and sat down in the chair opposite her. "He . . . watches her. I've seen that."

Marilee flushed delicately. "Yes, so have I." She wondered, for just a moment, if he had forgotten that she was only a few years older than Sarah and every bit as innocent. She put that thought aside as she realized how desperately he needed to confide in a woman he could trust. The idea that he saw her as such banished her modesty and filled her with a rare sense of determination. He had given her so much, and she had for so long yearned to give him something in return. It was past time to begin.

"Mr. Mackenzie . . . Josiah . . . I don't really think there is anything for you to be worried about. After all, Sarah will marry and go to live in her husband's home. Gideon cannot prevent that."

"She shows no interest in marrying."

Marilee nodded slowly. She did not want to betray her friend, but ultimately she felt that she had to do what was best for her. Her hands twisted in her lap, worrying a fragile lace handkerchief. "Sarah believes that she doesn't want a husband, but I think that if she is allowed to make that decision, her life will be very empty."

A moment passed, and another, before Josiah said, "Is that also how you feel?"

Marilee's eyes shot to his, only to instantly fall back. So softly that he had to lean forward to hear her, she said, "Yes, sometimes I do."

Nothing more was said but in the spring, when the Mackenzies went to Virginia, Gideon was left at home to oversee the business and, at Josiah's insistence, both Sarah and Marilee brought entirely new wardrobes with them. "Styles are changing," he announced when they tried to thank him for his generosity. "I won't have anyone saying that my daughter and her companion are not à la mode."

"Imagine," Sarah said with a laugh when she and Marilee were alone. "I never knew that father had any idea of what was stylish, let alone knew an expression like 'à la mode.'"

Marilee looked at her rather strangely. "I think your father probably knows a great deal more than you realize" was all she would say on the matter.

In New York they changed to the Orange and Alexandria Railroad that took them to Washington where they changed again to the Virginia Central which brought them at last to Richmond. To the girls' further amazement, or at least to Sarah's, her father had arranged for a private rail car, which was switched from train to train as they continued along their route. It included sleeping compartments for the three of them, a well-appointed bath, dining and seating areas, and even a place for Josiah to work at the voluminous correspondence he had brought along.

Left largely to their own devices, the girls spent most of the trip staring out the windows, commenting on everything they saw through the haze of coal smoke wafting back from the locomotive. It had been cool in Boston when they left, but by the time they reached Washington, the weather had turned warm. Having to keep the windows closed because of the smoke proved a hardship as they chugged toward Richmond. A smiling black steward finally showed them how to gauge which side of the train the smoke would blow on, so that they could open the windows opposite.

Neither young woman had ever been farther south than New York before. They were fascinated by the changing colors and smells, the differences in buildings and dress, the gradual blurring of speech until, as they stepped out on the Richmond platform, they heard the soft tones of Southern speech and knew that they had arrived.

"Oh, isn't it lovely?" Marilee exclaimed as she gazed in delight at the hanging pots of geraniums and lilies. At the entrance to the station were flowering magnolia trees, their perfume wafting on the sultry air. After the long, drab Boston winter, such an explosion of color and scent was dizzying.

Sarah nodded and smiled. She was no more immune to the languid beauty than anyone else, but she had been thinking what a shame it was that Nathan hadn't been able to come along. Her younger brother would have benefited far more from the warmth and sunshine than from the regimen of his boarding school. Nathan was prone to chest ailments, which worried Sarah greatly. Their father insisted he would grow out of them, but a few months short of his seventeenth birthday, he still showed no sign of doing so.

Philip Calvert had sent a carriage and wagon to meet them. A dignified, white-haired old black man, who introduced himself as Rameses, apologized for his master's absence. "Massa Philip real sorry not t'be here, suh," he said, addressing Josiah. "But one ob de dams in de fields done spring a leak dis mornin'. He hab t'be checkin' on it."

"Of course," Josiah said as he handed Sarah and Marilee into the carriage, noting as he did so how very well appointed it was. Rameses saw to the loading of their luggage into the wagon before clambering onto the seat beside the carriage driver. They were shortly on their way.

Marilee and Sarah had both been silent during their first encounter with the slaves. Neither had seen any before, and in fact had only seen free blacks once or twice. They were uncertain of how to behave and concerned that both their awkwardness and their curiosity might become embarrassingly evident.

Josiah felt no such difficulty. He was remembering the days of his boyhood, when he had watched from a distance as the proud young men of the white aristocracy were attended to by their black slaves. How he had envied them, and how determined he had been to become like them. As he leaned back in the carriage, his eyes on the matched pair of magnificent bays, he basked in the assurance of how far he had come.

Southern hospitality, renowned as it was, looked open-handed only to the uninitiate. Josiah knew perfectly well that it encompassed complex gradations of welcome, everything from a bed for the night in the barn to the most lavish graciousness. That Philip Calvert had sent a fine carriage and two of his best horses, along with what was likely to be his most senior house slave, was a declaration of the regard in which he held his guests.

Though initially put off by his host's absence, Josiah had been immediately reassured. The old black had clearly been given strict instructions to make Philip's apologies in terms that could not help but be accepted. Calvert was not a man to leave any aspect of his plantation to others. If there was trouble, he would be on the scene. Josiah respected that even as he was pleased to know that his respect was clearly returned.

Calvert Oaks lay some two hours southeast of Richmond. By the time they reached it, following a road that ran alongside the meandering James River, all three of the visitors were tired and thirsty. The dust of the road had somewhat dampened their enthusiasm, and they were beginning to feel that the journey might never end when they suddenly passed between two high stone pillars and started up a gravel drive lined by ancient oaks. The coolness of their shade was immediately reviving. They all straightened up and looked eagerly ahead.

"Dis here be de Calvert place," Rameses said proudly as he turned around on the seat. "One ob de oldest plantations on de river and de finest." He waved a proprietary hand toward the horizon, where twin brick chimneys had appeared. Sarah was both amused and touched by the gesture. The old man might have owned the place himself for all the pride he showed, instead of being owned by it.

She had no chance to think about that further before the house itself came into view. A soft exclamation escaped her. In that first instant, as she stared at the three-story Greek Revival house with the unbiased eyes of a stranger, the only words she could think of to describe it were warmth and elegance. That was a combination she had never encountered before; in her experience, elegance was invariably cool while warmth always had a hint of dishevelment. Calvert Oaks possessed a purity of line and purpose that made it appear ideally suited to its surroundings.

The carriage continued to move forward, and she saw the outbuildings beyond the main house, but noted them only distantly. The scent of roses engulfed her as she stepped for the first time on Calvert land. The double doors to the house had been flung open and Philip stood there, a Philip she had never seen before. He was dressed in dark breeches, muddy boots and a loose white shirt left open halfway down his chest. His hair was rumpled and a streak of dirt ran down one lean cheek.

He came forward with a smile, but did not offer her father his hand. "Forgive me, Josiah, but I only this moment returned from the fields and I'm not really fit company." Bowing, he greeted Sarah and Marilee. "Ladies, I'm delighted you are here. You must be tired from the long trip. We'll make you comfortable at once."

Sarah did not see him make the slightest gesture, but instantly half a dozen slaves sprang forward. Within moments they had the wagon unloaded and were hurrying inside with the luggage.

"I must apologize also for my aunt's absence," Philip said as they escorted them inside. "Her cousin in Charlotte was taken ill last week and she has gone there to care for her."

"Your father..." Josiah began as he glanced around at the magnificent two-story hall from the ceiling of which a matched pair of gleaming crystal chandeliers hung.

"Is in the library, awaiting you," Philip said. His father had insisted on being brought downstairs to greet his old business colleague. Philip understood that pride demanded he make light of his infirmities to all but the immediate family, but he hoped Charles would not tire himself too much.

Augusta took the two young ladies upstairs as Philip escorted Josiah into the library. The greeting between the two men who had known each other for so long but had not met for many years was cordial and relaxed. Josiah gave no sign of even noticing that Charles was in a wheelchair, his legs covered by the usual blanket. He treated him exactly as he would any other man he knew and respected.

Seeing that they were well settled, Philip took himself off to bathe. The leak in the dam had been caught before it could become serious, but for several hours he had waded in knee-high mud, checking to make sure that the work crew left nothing undone. Only when he was satisfied that the leak was stopped did he return to the house, barely in time to greet his guests.

Lying back in the tub, he closed his eyes and felt the tension drain out of his body. At this time of year, any flooding of the fields would have been disastrous for the young cotton plants. He had to count himself very fortunate that the leak had been spotted so quickly, but oddly enough, all he could really think about was pretty Miss Sarah Mackenzie. He liked having her in his home to a degree he hadn't expected, and he thought she looked as though she belonged there.

Which was absurd, since she was both a Northerner and a stranger. Their meeting in New York, pleasant though it had been, had hardly been enough for them to become well acquainted. He smiled to himself as he thought that perhaps her present stay would remedy that.

An hour later, clad in trousers, a fresh shirt, waistcoat and frock coat, Philip returned downstairs. His father and Josiah were still in the library; he could hear the low sound of their voices as he passed by. Rather than intrude on them, he went out to the patio, took his favorite seat and settled back to enjoy the cooling breeze off the river.

A houseboy appeared promptly at his side. Philip told him to fetch a bourbon and branch water, and to send word upstairs that the young ladies were welcome to join him.

Sarah received the message from a shy young black girl who had introduced herself as Callie and promptly set about unpacking her bags. Sarah and Marilee shared a maid at home, an Irish girl named Mollie who dealt with them sternly but affectionately. Despite that, Callie's silent flitting about the room made Sarah feel ill at ease. She had the sense that the girl was continually alert to her every move, as she herself might be to a strange animal not yet proven to be harmless.

"I can do that," she said when Callie caught her beginning to unfasten her dress and promptly came over to do it for her.

"Oh, no, missy," the girl said with gentle firmness. "Yo a guest here. Dere no reason fo' yo t'do anythin'."

By the time Sarah had been undressed, bathed and dried, she had to admit that she was feeling a great deal better. The headache caused by the long hours of travel had vanished. She stood patiently while Callie helped her into an evening gown of violet silk worn over the hooped petticoats that had become fashionable a few years before. The dress had short puffed sleeves, a scooped neckline that flirted with the swell of her breasts and a flounced skirt trimmed with ruches. It was a far more extravagant gown than she was used to wearing, but she had to admit as she twirled in front of the mirror, that it brought out her best features in a way she couldn't help but appreciate.

Callie dressed her thick, wavy hair in a chignon at the nape of her neck, then covered it with a caul of gold thread beaded with tiny seed pearls. She had just finished when there was a soft tap at the door. Callie went to answer it and returned smiling. "Massa Philip, missy, he says iffen you an' Miss Marilee lahk t'join him, he bes on de veranda."

That sounded fine to Sarah. She looped her reticule and fan over her wrist, picked up her long white gloves and stepped out of her room at the same time that Marilee left hers. The two girls exchanged a look that spoke volumes and broke into giggles.

"Oh, Lord," Marilee said as they walked toward the stairs, "I think I've died and gone to heaven."

"It is wonderful," Sarah agreed. "I've never seen a more beautiful place."

"And they certainly do everything possible to make you feel welcomed. My little maid, Bessie she said her name is, won't let me lift a finger."

"I suppose we really shouldn't let them fetch and carry for us so much," Sarah ventured, carefully lifting the skirt of her gown.

"Why not?" Marilee asked.

"Because they're...slaves." She and Marilee had talked a great deal about slavery and had agreed that it was an abomination. But that had been in the abstract. The reality of it was proving to be far more confusing. Being waited on hand and foot had a certain seductive quality that was hard to resist.

"Why of course, slavery is bad," Marilee said. "But, we're guests here. It would be terribly rude to mention politics."

Sarah had the feeling that there was something wrong with that, but she couldn't put her finger on it. And she had to admit that she didn't try very hard. Especially not after she stepped through the French doors to the veranda and saw Philip coming to greet her.

Chapter Nineteen

"IF YOU LADIES RIDE," Philip said the next morning at breakfast, "perhaps you would care to join Mr. Mackenzie and myself when we go out to look at the location for the new mill."

Sarah hesitated a moment, long enough for Marilee to step in adroitly. "That's very kind of you, but the truth is I've never learned to be comfortable on the back of a horse. Besides, Augusta promised to show me how to make that delicious poppy seed bread we had at supper last night. However, Sarah rides wonderfully."

"She means I can stay on a horse," Sarah said quickly. Regretfully she added, "I'm afraid that I might hold you up."

"Nonsense," her father said, "we're in no great hurry. If there's one thing these Southerners have all over us it's a willingness to take things slowly. It's much easier to enjoy life that way."

Sarah stared at him in surprise. She would have thought he'd be glad not to be saddled with her company, but instead he seemed to be encouraging her to come along. "All right... if you don't mind waiting a few minutes, I'll go change." She had put on—or more correctly, Callie had put on her—a pretty day dress of white dimity embroidered with small pink rosebuds. It was no more suitable for riding than would be one of her nightgowns. However, the new riding habit she had brought with her was perfect.

At least Philip thought so when he saw her in it. His lean, strong face brightened as she crossed the stable yard. She continually surprised him. The elegant woman of the night before was not the same as the lovely girl who had appeared at breakfast or the tall, regal-looking huntress striding toward him now. The habit was austerely black, relieved only by white lace at the throat and cuffs. With it she wore a black felt hat with a broad brim from which a black veil trailed. He was pleased that she hadn't bothered to pull the veil down, thinking that it would be a shame to hide a face that while not classically beautiful was oddly attractive.

Philip had personally selected a gentle mare named Princess for her. He helped her into the saddle, noting as he did so the slenderness of her waist and the light scent of lemon verbena clinging to her skin. For a brief moment a jolt of sexual hunger engulfed him. He closed his eyes against it, telling himself he was overdue for a visit to Richmond.

They took a fork of the gravel road that branched toward the west and were soon riding along beside the river. Josiah was mounted on a splendid roan that clearly pleased him very much. At fifty-one, he was still fitter than many younger men. His barrel chest, broad shoulders and powerful thighs were the legacy of the long years of backbreaking work he had endured before rising to his present position. Even then he had not ceased riding, swimming and even trying his hand in the boxing ring, finding in such physical activity release from the private demons that too often plagued him.

In the more than ten years since his wife's death, his sense of certainty about the world had eroded. Much of what he had once been sure about now puzzled him, including himself. He did not fully understand why he had never remarried, why he had mellowed somewhat toward his children, why he had begun to yearn for something he could not define. But one need that he had always had remained, and in the verdant land of Calvert Oaks he saw the chance of its fulfillment.

As they dismounted near the fast-running tributary of the James River, where he proposed to build the new mill, Josiah smiled in anticipation. He had remembered the area from his boyhood, but until this moment, standing on it again for the first time in decades, he couldn't be sure that he had selected wisely. Now he was, and already, in a shimmering instant, he could envision all that he would create here.

Hands behind his back, he paced over the land, pausing once or twice to pick up handfuls of it and let the rich, dark soil trickle through his fingers. Philip watched him in puzzlement, surprised by actions that would have been more expected from a man proposing to grow crops on the land. But then, he realized after a time, Josiah was intending to do exactly that.

"The wheelpit will go there," he said when he returned to where Philip and his daughter were standing. "We'll need stone quarried for it and for the mill's foundation. I brought the plans with me and can tell you quantities."

Philip had anticipated that Josiah would want to get started immediately and had arranged for the mason to be present. He was a big, bluff Welshman who had left

the coal mines for a better life in the new world. He and
Josiah understood each other immediately. They went
off to talk as Philip offered to show Sarah around the
plantation.

Curious as she was to see everything, she was most
struck by Philip himself. His pride as he spoke of Calvert Oaks could not have been more evident, yet there
was no hint of the arrogance or smugness she thought
must surely go hand in hand. As Philip dismounted
near a fallow field, which he explained was resting after several seasons of growing cotton, he bent and, in
a gesture reminiscent of what she had seen her father
do, let a handful of the rich soil trickle through his
fingers. For a moment Sarah saw a look of such pensive pleasure on his face that she was riveted by it.

She had heard it said often enough that Southerners
loved their land but not until then did she fully understand how literally that was true. Philip took a sensual
pleasure in the touch of the soil and held it in a way that
was nothing less than cherishing. His eyes, as they
swept out over the gentle swell of the fields, might have
been those of a lover.

Sarah stirred uneasily. She had no personal acquaintance with such emotions and told herself that she
wanted none, yet she could not suppress a dart of envy.
To be loved in such a way was unknown to her.

"What made you decide to rent the land to my father?" she asked when they were mounted again and
riding along the road toward the house. All around
them were fields filled with the soft green shoots of
cotton plants separated by ribbons of brown earth. In
the distance she could see fields of young wheat turning golden in the sun and nearby, the darker green of
broad-leafed tobacco plants.

The many shades of green and brown, too many to count, were set off by the clear blue sky streaked with high, wispy clouds and, at the horizon, by a darker band of gray. At that hour, the hot yellow eye of the sun was beginning to slant toward the west. The air, humid with the promise of coming rain, hummed with the drone of insects, punctuated by the steady clop-clop of their horses' hoofs against the hard-packed ground.

Philip took off his broad-brimmed hat and wiped his brow against the sleeve of his shirt. The gesture strained the fabric tautly over the muscles of his shoulders and back. His blue eyes squinted as he looked out toward the growing band of clouds. "I wanted him to build the mill here."

"But why?" she persisted. "I thought Southerners were opposed to industrializing."

He smiled as he settled his hat in place. From its shadows she could feel his gaze turned on her. "Not all Southerners. In fact, probably not even most. We simply want it to be done in a way that suits us."

"Rather than having Northern ways imposed on you."

"Exactly." There was approval in his voice, but also surprise. He still hadn't gotten used to her intelligence or how little effort she made to hide it.

"Your father." Sarah ventured. "I got the impression he wasn't completely happy with the arrangement." Charles Calvert had been pleasant enough at supper the previous evening, but she had sensed an undercurrent of tension.

"He isn't," Philip said. Her frankness was disconcerting, but at least it enabled him to reply in kind. "If it were strictly up to him, he wouldn't allow the mill to be built. But he respects my judgment enough to tolerate it.''

"And, as you said, you want the mill?''

"And you're wondering why?''

She nodded. "This place seems so…idyllic. If it were mine, I'd be afraid to tamper with it.''

Two things struck him: that she considered Calvert Oaks idyllic, which naturally appealed to his own pride but also reminded him of how deceptive appearances could be; and the fact that she could imagine, to at least some degree, possessing such a place herself. No woman he knew owned property of any kind; the very idea was unthinkable.

"I would never do anything to harm it,'' he said, "but some changes are necessary.''

She cast him a cautious look. "What sort of changes?''

Philip hesitated. The urge to unburden himself was great. He had to remind himself that he barely knew her. "Nothing can remain completely the same. What is suitable at one time isn't at another.''

She frowned briefly, then to his surprise, flashed him a smile. "You'll forgive me it I'm a bit nervous about talking of change with a Southerner. We all know what that's a euphemism for up north.''

The lines around his eyes deepened as he laughed. "Up north? Keep talking like that and you'll be taken for one of us.''

She shook her head, knowing perfectly well that he wasn't serious. No one could ever mistake her for a Southern lady. She was too outspoken, for one thing, and she utterly lacked the magnolia blossom brand of charm and grace. Yet Philip Calvert seemed to like her well enough. She was still thinking of that when they rode back to rejoin her father.

Sarah woke late that night to the sound of rain pelting against her windows. She sat up in the bed, unaware at first of where she was or what was happening. A finger of lightning ripped the sky, bathing the room in stark white light. Hard on it came a long, rolling rumble of thunder. Barely had it subsided than she was out of the bed, hurrying barefoot to the windows.

The wind whipped branches of an ancient oak tree against the panes of glass. It swirled whirlpools of leaves across the broad lawns and sent the clouds skittering wildly across the sky. Sarah eased the window open and felt the rush of cool, wet air molding her nightgown to her body. Lightning ripped again, drawing her eyes to the churning river. It looked like a living thing struggling to break its bonds.

She smiled to herself. Storms were her secret passion. The sight and sound of nature's fury never failed to strike a chord within her. On a practical level, she knew how dangerous they could be. But practicality had very little to do with the sheer, exhilarating pleasure that shattered the safe, staid world.

She paused only long enough to thrust her feet into slippers and pull a wrapper on over her nightgown. Opening her door, she glanced up and down the hallway. The night before she'd had a difficult time convincing Callie that it wasn't necessary for her to sleep on the pallet beside her bed. While she didn't want to be rude, she so disliked the idea of anyone hovering over her that she had felt compelled to insist on privacy. Callie had clearly been baffled but had offered to sleep just outside the door. Sarah was relieved to see that she had managed to convince her that wasn't necessary.

The entry hall was empty as she passed through it, except for the shadows dancing on the walls to hidden music carried on the wind. She opened one of the French doors in the dining room and stepped out onto a covered portico that connected the main house with the kitchen. It was the perfect spot from which to experience the storm.

Sarah wrapped her arms around herself and turned her face to the wind, letting it take her hair. The ivory lace of her wrapper frothed around her ankles. Fingers of air raced over her, finding their way beneath the hem, up the sleeves, down the bodice. Her body was bathed in silken sensation that made her shiver in delight.

She threw her head back and laughed. The wildness of the storm merged with the wildness inside her until she became as much a part of it as the rushing wind and the singing rain. For an endless time she stood like that, the tall, slender line of her body taut with pleasure. All her senses were vividly alive, drinking in the sight, sound and feel of unrestrained nature. Until something—perhaps merely an alien ripple on the edge of her awareness—made her jerk around.

A man was watching her. He stood in the darkness at the far end of the portico. She could see only his silhouette. He was tall and broad-shouldered, dressed in a shirt and trousers. His posture, the way he stood with his feet planted slightly apart, was familiar. When he turned, so that she could see his profile, she relaxed.

"Oh, Philip, it's you. I didn't realize at first. You startled me." She laughed with nervous relief. "I couldn't resist coming out to see the storm."

He took a step toward her, though he remained still in the shadows. Softly he said, "It could be dangerous. You'd be better off inside."

"Nonsense, I love weather like this." Feeling very bold, and not caring, she said, "Watch it with me?"

He didn't answer at once, and she wondered if she had offended him. Proper Southern ladies undoubtedly did not wander around strange houses in their wrappers and invite gentlemen to watch storms with them. But instead of being put out, he laughed gently. "I like storms, too, but this isn't a good night for watching. Besides, you might catch a chill."

"I never get sick. Anyway, why isn't it good?"

Marcus silently cursed himself. He hadn't meant to say that, but coming upon her so suddenly had knocked him off balance. It was bad enough to have such a storm on a night when runaways were due. To also have someone wandering about added immeasurably to his troubles. He had known, of course, about the visitors from Boston and why they had come. The mill sounded like a good idea to him; he was glad Philip had decided to go ahead with it. Now, looking at Sarah, he wondered if there might be more involved than he had guessed.

"You've made a mistake, miss," he said gently. "I'm not Philip." He took another step toward her, but stayed far enough back so that she would hopefully not feel threatened. The last thing he needed was a white woman having hysterics on him.

It was a relief when she merely regarded him with steady scrutiny. "You look quite a lot like Philip, and you sound like him. Are you brothers?"

Marcus's finely drawn mouth twisted wryly. He had little experience with the ignorance of Northerners and was amused by it. "In a sense. At any rate, I think it would be best for you to go back inside, miss."

Instead of doing as he suggested, she continued to study him. "You haven't told me your name."

"I'm called Marcus, miss." As he spoke, a bolt of lightning tore the sky above them and she saw him clearly for the first time.

"You're a slave." The words were blurted out before she could stop them. It was as though she was looking at another version of Philip, the only marked difference being the color of their skins, and even that was by any objective measure subtle. Yet what it must mean...

"That's right, miss," Marcus said patiently. He saw her shock and had no trouble imagining the thoughts going through her mind. Deep inside he flinched at the possibility that she would be horrified or disgusted, but he was used enough to those reactions and had long since steeled himself against them.

What he was not accustomed to was righteous indignation. Southerners, who lived perforce with the reality of slavery, were immune to it. Northerners, however, apparently were not.

"What do you mean you're a slave?" she demanded.

Marcus stifled a sigh. The last thing he needed was a lecture about the injustice of his position. "That's just the way it is, miss," he said as he carefully eased past her and opened the door to the dining room again. "Now if you'd just go back inside..."

Sarah didn't hear him. She was still struggling to comprehend what his presence meant. "I don't understand how Philip could allow such a thing."

"It's not up to him, miss." This was hardly the time to discuss the complexities of manumission and why Charles Calvert would not free his half-breed son. "The storm's getting worse..." Actually, it was beginning to die down, which meant that the men hiding by the river would soon try to make a run for the cabins. From where she was standing she would have a clear view of them. Desperately Marcus said, "Miss, if somebody came out here right now and found us together, I'd be in a whole lot of trouble."

That brought Sarah up short. She had heard all too many stories about the brutal treatment of slaves who dared to forget their place. "Of course, I wasn't thinking." She gathered up the skirt of her wrapper and stepped quickly inside.

The wind smothered Marcus's exhalation of relief, which broke off abruptly when she turned back to him. "Don't worry, I won't say a word about meeting you."

"Fine, miss, I appreciate that."

"But I still think it's wrong..."

"Please, miss, I hear someone coming."

She bit her lip, nodded and moved back far enough to let him shut the door behind her. For a moment more he saw her standing on the other side, her white gown fluttering around her. Then she turned and hurried away.

Marcus slumped against the wall of the house. Despite the coolness brought by the storm, he was damp with sweat. Thank God she had believed him and that she hadn't known enough to question what a slave was doing wandering around at night. Now he could only pray that she would keep her word and not mention having seen him to anyone.

He thought of the men hiding in the bushes, of their desperate fear, and strove to put his own aside. But a part of him longed to be back in his own cabin, in Ginny's arms. He could not give in to that, not only for the sake of the others but also because he recognized the illusion of safety for exactly what it was. For him, and all those like him, freedom was the only true haven.

Someday, he promised himself as he had so many times before, and moved away into the darkness.

———————————— *Chapter Twenty*

SARAH WAS PREOCCUPIED and a bit cool the next morning at breakfast, but Philip barely noticed. He had awakened shortly before dawn and gone to make sure the newly repaired dam was holding. The river had risen enough for him to have some concern, but after checking he was reassured that there wouldn't be a problem.

Josiah was anxious to get back to the mill site. The builder was due in from Richmond, and the final plans would be decided on before the day was over. Philip meant to go with his guest but before he could do so, Rameses hurried in with news that he was wanted outside.

"Slave catchers, massa, wantin' t'have a word with ya."

Philip rose reluctantly and tossed his napkin on the table. He disliked having to speak with such men but knew that realistically he had no choice. There were half a dozen of them, with as many hunting dogs yapping around the legs of their mangy horses. The one in charge, a thin, poorly dressed man with a week's worth of whiskers darkening his chin, tipped his battered hat half an inch when Philip appeared.

"How do, suh. Sorry to bother ya so early in the day, but we got word there's a pair of bucks on the run hereabouts."

"Is that so?" Philip said. He stood on the porch, his hand shading his eyes from the sun, and made no effort to put them at ease. "What makes you think they're anywhere near here?"

"Well, suh, they were seen headin' in this direction, and we thought we'd just check with yuh..."

"Rameses," Philip called, bringing the old man reluctantly from the other side of the open doorway where he had been listening. "Have you heard anything about strange nigras showing up here?"

"Why, no, suh, Ahs sure habn't. No strange nigras in des parts, massa."

"Sorry," Philip said. "I can't help you."

The leader of the slave catchers turned his head slightly and aimed a stream of brown tobacco juice on the ground inches from the steps where Philip stood. "Jus' cause that old nigger says there aren't no runaways around here don't mean nothin' to me."

Rameses ducked his head and scrambled back behind the door, in the process bumping into Sarah who had caught wind of what was happening through the open windows of the dining room and had come to get a closer look.

As she watched, Philip stepped down the stairs from the porch, walked around the clop of spittle lying on the ground and stopped beside the rickity bay the thin man rode. "I don't give a goddamn what you think," he said evenly. "The men you're looking for aren't on my land, so there's no reason for you to be here, either. I'll thank you to be about your business."

The slave catchers looked at one another, moved their horses closer to their leader and waited. The thin man had gone red in the face. He pushed his hat back and glared at Philip. "T'ain't no call fer blaspheming, or fer orderin' us around. We got a right to hunt those niggers."

Responding to his angry tone, the dogs snarled at Philip. He ignored them. "Maybe you didn't hear what I said. I want you off my land."

The thin man sneered, revealing broken teeth widely spaced. "Reckon it's true what some folks say, you nothin' but a nigger lover."

Rameses moaned softly. Sarah turned her head and, in the process, almost missed Philip's response. His right hand lashed out, seizing the thin man by the arm and jerking him from the saddle. The man landed on his back in the dirt. Before his companions could act, Philip flipped him over, bent his arm sharply behind his back and said, "What did you call me?"

Wide-eyed with fear, the thin man looked around for help, only to find that there was none. In the act of getting off their horses, the other men had noticed Overseer Davies and a dozen white jockeys and trainers coming around the corner of the house, each carrying a rifle. Gingerly they settled back into their saddles.

"I asked you," Philip repeated, "what you called me?"

"*Nothin',*" the man cried, "*Ah didn't mean nothin'.*"

"Is there any reason for you to be here?"

"*No, no reason! Lemme go, we'll be on our way.*"

"You won't get confused again and think you ought to come here?"

"No! My arm . . . lemme go!"

As though he had only then noticed the unnatural angle of the man's arm, Philip released it and straightened up. The slave catcher scrambled onto his nag. He glared furiously at Philip, but the sight of the armed men stopped him from doing anything more. Digging his heels into the horse's flanks, he fled with his fellows right behind him.

Philip said a brief word of thanks to Davies and the other men. As he returned to the porch, Josiah slapped him on the back. "I got here just in time to enjoy the show. Wouldn't have missed it for the world."

Philip grimaced. "It shouldn't have gone that far. I lost my temper."

"Seems to me you were provoked."

"Question is," Charles said from the doorway where he sat in his wheelchair, "how many others will see it like that." He looked at his son closely, noting the angry glitter still in his eyes.

"Are you saying I should have let them search the place?" Philip asked.

"No, but you can't blame them for not wanting to take a nigra's word that the runaways weren't here."

"They had my word," Philip said. He wiped his palms on a clean handkerchief and returned it to his pocket. "You know as well as I do the kind of trouble scum like that can cause. They would have gone out of their way to terrorize every one of our slaves."

"I don't disagree with you," Charles said quietly, "but they're doing a job most people think is necessary. Your refusal to cooperate won't be appreciated."

"I'm not going to lose any sleep over that," Philip said. They had returned to the dining room. He held out Sarah's chair for her and nodded pleasantly to

Marilee, who had remained in her place. The rest of the meal passed largely in silence. Before it was over Philip excused himself, saying he had business to attend to. A short time later Sarah glanced out the window to see him walking away from the house, with Marcus at his side.

When Philip returned later that day, there was no sign of the coolness Sarah had shown him earlier. They strolled in the garden together before supper, and she expressed great interest in the roses his mother had planted so many years before. He told her about the background of the house and of his family, including the first Calvert who had come over from England. She, in turn, related something of what it had been like growing up in Lowell and later in Boston, though she judiciously neglected to mention her involvement with the mill girls. They found they had more in common than they had guessed; a love of history, a desire to travel, a tendency to be impatient with stuffiness.

"I'm not saying that everyone in Boston is a hypocrite," Sarah said at one point as she paused to admire a particularly lovely yellow rose. "But there is so much emphasis on form rather than substance. I don't suppose I will ever be able to believe that the precise way one folds the corners of a visiting card is really of any importance."

"It's the same here," Philip said, watching her. The slanting sun warmed her hair to a reddish gold and added a warm flush to her cheeks. She wore a pale yellow silk gown with wide bell sleeves held by tiny pearl buttons at the wrists. By contrast, the neckline was cut low at the throat and shoulders. The boned bodice emphasized the curve of her partially revealed breasts and the slenderness of her waist. As she moved, the wide, flounced skirt floated gracefully around her.

On impulse, he reached out and let his hand cover hers where it rested on the stem of the yellow rose. At her startled look, he smiled reassuringly. "Let me." Before she could protest, he had broken the flower off and gently tucked it into the thick coil of her hair.

"Thank you," she murmured, her eyes averted. The brush of his fingers against her skin had sent a rush of sensation through her. She closed her eyes for an instant. When she opened them again, she discovered Philip bending toward her.

"Sarah . . ." Her eyes fell to his mouth as he said her name. His lower lip was somewhat fuller than the upper. Both were firm and strong. Unconsciously the tip of her tongue darted out to moisten her own lips, gone suddenly dry.

"Don't," he murmured. His hands touched her shoulders. She felt the calluses on his palms and fingertips rough against the smoothness of her skin. They were the hands of a man who did hard physical work despite his station in life, which should have exempted him from it. Distantly she remembered how the muscles of his back and shoulders had bunched under his shirt, how he had looked when he defied the slave catchers, how he had moved with lethal grace to subdue the other man.

Her eyes fluttered shut. She stood, barely breathing, poised between one instant and the next, as slowly his mouth claimed hers.

Sarah had never been kissed before. She had been curious about what it would be like, but had always presumed that she would find it distasteful. On those rare occasions when some boy might have kissed her, the vague shame and guilt inspired by Gideon had kept her from permitting such liberties.

With Philip there was no question of permission. He treated her quite gently, but he gave her no chance to object. His mouth was warm and coaxing on hers, easing her through the first shock of intimacy until she began to relax. Only then did his arms go around her, drawing her into his embrace.

Sarah's hands flattened against his chest, not in an effort to push him away, but out of desperate need to touch him. Through the fine linen of his shirt, she felt for the first time the hardness of a male body so different from her own. Fascination robbed her of the will to resist. With a soft moan, she melted against him.

Philip did not mistake her response for anything other than what it was, the reaction of a complete innocent stunned by her own sensuality. Her lack of experience, in such contrast to his own, made him feel overwhelmingly tender toward her.

Dimly, in the back of his mind, he remembered Daphne and how avidly she had met his caresses. Sarah was different; while she by no means shrank away, neither did she attempt in the least to take the initiative. She was both passive and approving, a combination that allowed him to feel completely in control.

He was smiling when he raised his head, noting as he did so that she was flushed and trembling. With gentle reassurance he stroked her cheek lightly. "We'd better get back inside."

She looked up at him in bewilderment that gave way swiftly to the realization of how complete her involvement had been. As he continued to watch, delighted, she reddened further. "Yes . . . inside."

She was so shyly sweet in her innocent surprise, so utterly pleasing to him, that he was tempted to kiss her again, if only to assure himself that the first time had been no fluke. But he was not so foolish as to overestimate his own self-control. It was already badly strained and could not be tested much further without dire consequences to them both.

They returned to the house in silence, and somehow managed to get through supper, though their eyes kept straying to each other. Their mutual preoccupation did not go unnoticed by either Josiah or Charles, who exchanged a long look, or by Marilee, who smiled to herself.

The following day the pride of Calvert stables, King's Ransom, was running in a race at a meet outside Richmond. Philip and his guests were up early to make the trip. The day was brilliantly clear, the air washed by the storm. Mammy Augusta had packed baskets full of food. Half a dozen slaves in full livery accompanied them. Sarah could barely contain her excitement as Philip handed her into the carriage. She had awakened at dawn and suffered Callie's ministrations with endless patience, determined that no item of her toilette should be neglected. Such concern about her appearance was so foreign to her that she couldn't help but laugh at herself, which only added to her pleasure in the day.

Seated opposite her in the carriage, formally attired in a navy blue frock coat and matching trousers, Philip joined in her merriment. He wasn't precisely sure why he couldn't stop smiling, but that didn't seem to matter. Everything about the day was perfect.

They strolled about the racing course, meeting dozens of people he took pains to introduce them to.

Marilee was at her most charming and Josiah, basking in the acceptance he had always longed for, unbent far enough to be positively gracious. But it was on Sarah and Philip themselves that attention lingered. The undercurrent of excitement running between them could not be mistaken. Assessing eyes followed them everywhere they went.

Philip understood his neighbors' curiosity, but he was also glad that Sarah remained oblivious to it. She twirled her parasol with unconscious ease, laughed at the young men's sallies and so thoroughly enjoyed herself that when King's Ransom won by fifteen lengths the victory was little more than the topping to a perfect day.

That evening they attended a ball in Richmond, at the home of Philip's cousin. By then word had spread of Philip's treatment of the slave catchers, and a few of the gentlemen felt called upon to give him censorious glances. He ignored them, happy to concentrate instead on Sarah.

Once again she had surprised him and, not incidentally, set Richmond on its ear. The gown she wore, of scarlet taffeta trimmed with gold lace, was not the sort of dress considered suitable for a young, unmarried girl. When Marilee had gingerly mentioned that as they were getting ready for the ball, Sarah had blithely reminded her of who had picked out the gown in the first place and added that since most Southern ladies were already wed at her age she could see no harm in dressing as they did.

Neither could Philip. After his initial surprise he admitted to himself that she looked lovely, and he took great pride in keeping her on his arm. The only drawback to her startling attractiveness was the flock of other men who insisted on clustering around her. He was relieved, not to mention amused, to note that she treated them all with forthright friendliness, very different from the flirtatious conduct they were accustomed to, but she also showed no interest in straying from his side.

For Sarah the evening passed in a dream. She had never believed herself to be beautiful, but suddenly she was wondering if even that might not be possible. Certainly, all the limits she had once thought immutable no longer seemed even important. She danced, talked, laughed, always vividly aware of the tall, handsome man at her side. Everyone she met seemed wonderful, the South itself was delightful, life was as near to perfect as she could ever imagine. Even her father had taken to giving her indulgent smiles over Marilee's shoulder as they danced together or stood chatting with the other guests.

When during an interval in the music, Philip placed a hand on her waist and gently guided her outside, she went willingly. When, in the shadows of a willow tree, he tilted her head back and kissed her tenderly, she felt an unexplainable yet perfectly acceptable sense of rightness.

And when he asked her to become his wife, she could think of nothing to say except yes.

_____ *Chapter Twenty-One*

THE SECOND THOUGHTS came later, in the cold light of morning, when Sarah confronted what she had done.

Had she really accepted Philip's proposal without the slightest consideration of what it would mean to her life? Much less of how completely it violated everything she thought she knew of herself? It seemed that she had, and that he meant to hold her to it, although he admitted himself that he was somewhat surprised by his own impetuousness.

For Philip, the decision to ask Sarah to marry him had not come easily, for all that it had apparently come swiftly. Objective, intellectual reasoning was foreign to his nature, though he could do it when he had to. He was far more likely to trust his instincts and his emotions. They told him that he wanted Sarah, and that she was right for him.

After the fact he could list many sensible reasons for them to wed: he had been alone too long, William needed a mother, Calvert Oaks needed a mistress. All that he said as they sat in the parlor after returning from Richmond. It was the day following the ball. Josiah and Marilee had tactfully taken themselves off. Though they hadn't been informed of what had happened, they both seemed to sense it and to be willing to give the couple time to come to their own decisions.

For that Philip was grateful, though for his part he was determined to allow Sarah very little opportunity for doubts. She was concerned enough about the differences in their backgrounds, afraid that the gulf might be too wide.

What he did not say, even as he reassured her, was that it was precisely because she was a Northerner that he felt safe in making her his wife. There was nothing about her to remind him of Daphne. Unknowingly, he characterized the two groups of women—Northern and Southern—in the same way that men had been doing for generations and believed all the generalities about them both.

Daphne had been a fiery, self-indulgent, capricious, seductive child. She had cajoled, enraged and ultimately defeated him. By comparison, Sarah seemed all sweet reason; she was predictable, rational, controllable. With her, there would be no surprises. She would share his bed, run his house and care for his son—and whatever other children they had—with the same capableness she brought to everything else. He neither wanted nor asked for anything more.

Nothing was quite so simple for Sarah. There was so much she couldn't say to him, if only because she had never come to terms with it herself. In the light of his determination, her fears seemed so nebulous. Granted her mother had died in childbed, and the experience had scarred her, but why had she decided she never wanted to marry? Confronted with the reality of her desire for him, that seemed absurd.

Yet it was over that same desire that she stumbled when she thought of what marriage to Philip would truly mean. The shadow of Gideon haunted her. What could she say: that he had frightened her when she was a child, that he looked at her in ways that made her ashamed, that she suspected him of unclean thoughts? She was too innocent to more than barely understand the implications of all that, yet she shied away from confronting them. Gideon, and all he represented, was a prison she longed to be free of.

Philip seemed to hold the key. For every doubt she raised, he had a gentle, well-reasoned response. Of course she was surprised by the suddenness of it; so was he. Certainly there were differences between them, but they also had a great deal in common. It was only natural that she be concerned, but really there was no reason. He would do nothing to harm her.

This last part was what Sarah could not deny, even in her own mind. There was no refuting the fact that she truly could not imagine Philip ever causing her any ill. If she had loved him, rather than simply liked and desired him, she would have feared the terrible vulnerability that could come with that state. As it was, she felt almost unnaturally safe.

In her experience, admittedly very narrow, love was one of the two explanations given by women who had fallen into self-destructive circumstances. The other was necessity, because they believed they had no option but marriage to a man who ultimately abused them. To her great relief, neither was true of her. She knew that Philip would not hold her to her impulsive promise if she said she could not go through with it. Yet why couldn't she? The thought grew more tempting as the morning passed, and he patiently eroded each of her doubts.

When her father and Marilee returned from their walk, Philip took Josiah aside in the library. Over port and cigars, he formally asked for Sarah's hand. Josiah did not agree immediately. The request came as no surprise; he had hardly been blind to the attraction between his daughter and his host. But now, confronted with the inevitable result of it, he had some qualms.

First among them was the fact that there was going to be a war. He was quite certain of that no matter what he claimed to Philip. The differences between North and South would never, in his opinion, be settled peacefully. For that reason, more than any other, he wanted to have a mill operating below the Mason-Dixon line that could continue to produce profits for him after the South was cut off as a source of both supplies and markets.

Despite what he knew Sarah believed, he wasn't unfeeling toward her. He would never have agreed to place her in a position where she might encounter genuine tragedy and horror. But the war he envisioned would be brief; he guessed it could last no more than a few months before both sides came to their senses. There was no reason to believe that she would be in any way distressed by it.

That consideration settled within himself to his own satisfaction, he had questions about the financial condition of Calvert Oaks, about Philip's own expectations and about the standard of living his daughter could expect. When his concerns were answered as he wished, he asked to see Sarah privately.

They met in the music room, where she had paced nervously during his discussion with Philip. When she heard his step, she sat down quickly on a petit-point chair and folded her hands in her lap, hoping to look properly decorous. Josiah was not fooled. He saw the color in her cheeks, the tremor of her shoulders and rightly judged that her emotions were high.

The silence stretched out between them as he selected another of Philip's excellent cigars and carefully lit it. Not until the first smoke ring rose toward the ceiling did he turn his attention to his daughter. "Philip has asked for your hand in marriage."

Sarah had a sudden, perverse desire to ask if he didn't want the rest of her, as well, but managed to restrain herself. The gravity of the situation demanded a full measure of propriety. "What did you tell him?"

"That I had no objection, provided you were in agreement."

Once again, Josiah had managed to surprise her. She had not expected him to give any thought to her wishes. "It would be a good marriage from your point of view, wouldn't it?"

"Yes," he acknowledged, "but we both know that is not any reason for you to agree to it." Implicit between them was the awareness that, if anything, Sarah would be more disposed to act against her father's interests.

"I...have a very high regard for Philip," she said at length.

"I'm glad to hear it. He speaks very highly of you."

The conversation was rapidly taking on aspects of a farce. There was a glint of amusement in her father's eyes that Sarah was not accustomed to seeing. "I really can't think why he wants to marry me."

"All the usual reasons, I would think. Why do you want to marry him?"

"I haven't said that I do."

Josiah rubbed his chin thoughtfully. "It was my understanding that you had accepted his proposal."

"Well, yes...that's true. But it was at the ball last night. I was...not quite myself."

"Who were you then?"

"What? Why... no one. I mean, there isn't anyone else I could be, but I wasn't acting... normally."

"You seemed," Josiah said, "to be having a very good time."

"That's just it. I'm not usually like that. Being here, being with Philip, has had a strange effect on me."

"It happens like that sometimes."

Sarah did not ask him how he could possibly know such a thing, at least not out loud, but her eyes posed the question for her.

Josiah took a long draw on his cigar before responding. "I never told you this, and I don't imagine your mother did, either, but before she met me, there was a young man she cared for very much."

Surprise kept Sarah silent. She waited anxiously for him to continue.

"They met in the course of some charity work she was involved with in New York, and they very quickly became good friends. That was all there was to it at first, although I believe she thought that if they could have remained together, it might have ripened into something more. At any rate, he was penniless, with no real prospects, and her parents put a stop to her seeing him. A few months later I began doing business with the family and one thing eventually led to another."

"You say she didn't love him..."

"No, as I told you, they were friends. Is the same true of you and Philip?"

Slowly Sarah nodded. "I like him very much, and I have a great deal of respect for him." She didn't mention that both had been tested when she encountered Marcus and realized that Philip's own half brother was kept a slave. But what she had seen and heard since had made her believe there was more to the story than they wanted anyone to know, and that restored her faith.

"How would you feel," Josiah asked, "if he married someone else?"

Sarah's head shot up. She regarded his father intently. "There is no reason to think he would do so, is there?"

Josiah shrugged. "As Paul says in First Corinthians, it is better to marry than to burn."

Sarah looked away. Her father's brand of religious faith, tempered though it had become over the years, still made her uncomfortable. For too long it had been the substitute for true kindness and affection. Remembering that provoked her to say what she had wondered about for many years but never dared to question. "Yet you never married again after mother died, though everyone expected you would."

"To everything there is a time." He stood up before she could respond, the tightness of her lips telling him how much the retreat into scripture distressed her. He didn't know himself why he did it, except that it was easier than revealing his own thoughts. "Is this your time, Sarah? Do you want to marry Philip?"

She looked up at him defiantly, seeing the patriarch of her childhood, the man she still in her heart held responsible for her mother's death. Seeing her future down through the many years to come, unless she chose another road. "Yes," she said firmly, "I want to marry Philip."

MARILEE WAS DELIGHTED when she heard the news. Sarah truly believed that she couldn't have been happier had she herself been the bride. Certainly she threw herself into the preparations with a skill and determination of which Sarah was then quite incapable.

Word was quickly sent to Aunt Louise, who rushed back from Charleston. Philip had announced that he wished the wedding to take place in three weeks, which his aunt informed him was impossible. When he merely smiled she rolled her eyes to heaven and her sleeves to her elbows. "We'll do it," she told Marilee, in whom she had quickly recognized a kindred soul, "but only because Sarah wants it, too."

To Sarah, Aunt Louise exhibited genuine delight. If she privately thought that Marilee was better suited to take over the running of a great house, she gave no hint of it. Philip had chosen Sarah, nothing else mattered. Not the askance looks of her friends who could not imagine a Northerner as mistress of Calvert Oaks, and certainly not the murmurings of the slaves who were deeply concerned about the great change coming in their lives.

On that score, at least, Marcus could reassure them. "She all right," he said over and over, though he refused to explain how he knew.

"How come yo trust dat white lady?" Ginny asked one night as they lay in bed together. "She no better dan de rest ob dem."

Marcus stared up at the rough wood ceiling. He could hardly tell Ginny the truth, that he trusted Sarah because she hadn't betrayed him the night of the storm. Knowing that would only reassure his wife very briefly. All too soon she would realize the implications. Sarah had also been present when the slave catchers came. Everything he sensed about her told him that she was smart enough to connect the two events. She couldn't know for sure, but she must strongly suspect that he was involved with runaways. Which meant that his life was, quite literally, in her hands.

"She a Yankee," he said at length. "Dey on our side."

Ginny scoffed at that. "Ain't no white person on our side. Dems dat want us free wants to ship us back to Africa. Yo ever been to Africa, Marcus?"

He laughed wryly and drew her closer. "No, an' Ahs gots no desire to go, same as yo. But dis here a big country. Gotta be some place fo' us."

Someday, someplace. An elusive wish perched on top of a vague dream. Yet the hunger gnawing at him was real enough. He could feel freedom inside him, a living presence only waiting to get out. How many times he had thought of running. With his "white" speech and his literacy, he had a far better chance than most of making it north. Passes could be forged, for both him and Ginny, the coins under their mattress could be used to smooth the way. He doubted very much that his father would ever send the slave catchers after him, and he knew for sure that Philip would not. They could make it, get all the way to Canada, start a new life in freedom.

He let Ginny believe that he refused to do so because he knew he was unusually well placed to help other blacks on the run. That was true, but there was also another reason he had never confided to her. He was Charles Calvert's eldest son. In another, fairer world, he would have been the heir to Calvert Oaks instead of Philip. As much as he hated slavery, equally did he love the land. It held him far more securely than any chains or ropes ever could.

The futility of that love did not escape him. Calvert Oaks would never be his. He could spend his life there and never possess so much as a single particle of its soil. Yet whenever he thought of leaving, it was as though he contemplated ripping out his own heart.

Ginny stirred in his arms. He stroked a hand down her back, soothing her. Beneath his fingers, he felt the ridges of welts he knew as well as the features of his own face. The result of beatings years before when she was on Beauterre. Those scars would never heal, but the scars on her soul might. Someday, someplace. In freedom.

Sarah was also thinking about freedom, and how much of it she was about to give up. Like Marcus, she had few illusions about her true status, though she had hitherto managed not to contemplate it too closely. Legally she had no more rights than a slave. She could not vote, own property, have a bank account, sign a contract, decide where she wanted to live or do any number of things men took for granted.

Theoretically at least, a freed black man had far more rights than she ever would. When she married she would pass from the control of her father to that of her husband. Should she be widowed, some male relative would take charge of her. At no point would the law or society recognize her right to control her own destiny.

Yet she was determined to do exactly that. In Philip, she sensed an ally in her search for freedom. Unclouded by romantic love, their expectations were quite clear. He wanted a wife who would be a true helpmate, not one more burden in a life already loaded with responsibility. She wanted a husband who would understand that she needed to think for herself and act on those thoughts. He would manage the plantation; she would manage the household. In their separate areas, they would have autonomy.

They had discussed it all the night before their engagement party. "I don't wish to sound presumptuous," Sarah had said, "but I have a good mind and the need to use it. Had I been a boy, there would have been no question but that I would go into the family business. That would have suited me very well. As it is, I need to find some other area to use my abilities."

Though Philip was amused by her seriousness, he answered gravely enough. "As mistress of this plantation, I don't think you'll lack for challenges. Aunt Louise will fill you in on all the details; I confess I don't know a fraction of what she does, except that she's always very busy."

Sarah had already noticed that. She presumed that a great deal of the activity around her had to do with the wedding, but there were other things that seemed to be simply a normal part of running the plantation. Only the previous morning she had come downstairs to find Aunt Louise out behind the house, bent over a bubbling vat of animal fat, into which she was dipping candle molds. When Sarah had asked her why she didn't turn the job over to a slave, Aunt Louise had explained, somewhat wearily, that they were all occupied elsewhere, and besides, candle dipping was really too complex to be trusted to anyone else.

With some coaxing Sarah had convinced her to show her how it was done. She quickly learned that Aunt Louise was right; it was extremely difficult to do correctly. After several hours' work she had less than a dozen usable candles to show for her labor. Far more notable was the backache that resulted from it and which had only begun to fade by the following day.

"Surely," she had ventured, "candles could be purchased?"

Aunt Louise had looked at her in surprise. "We never buy anything we can make ourselves."

"But if the labor is so great . . ."

"That doesn't matter. We strive to be as self-sufficient as possible. Nothing is wasted, especially not money."

When she mentioned the incident to Philip, he saw nothing amiss about it. "Each December we butcher several thousand weight of hogs and the fat from them is used to make wax. With a bit more practice, I'm sure you'll become adept at it."

Sarah was less certain, but she was willing enough to try. The realization that she would actually have a necessary role to play excited her. For the first time in her life she would truly be needed. Not only by Calvert Oaks and by her husband, but also by the small boy who was to be her stepson.

William had been somewhat hesitant when his father explained that he was to have a new mother. He had never known his real mother and had long ago accepted his aunt "Luisey" in that role. The thought that she was to be replaced by a stranger distressed him. Two fat tears rolled down his tanned cheeks as he shook his head stubbornly. "No, Papa, don' want a new momma."

Standing beside Philip, Sarah felt her throat tighten. She hadn't expected the child to love her immediately, but neither had she thought he would reject her so completely. On impulse she knelt beside him and gently touched his ebony hair. "I know this is a big surprise for you, sweetheart. But we'll have lots of time to get to know each other. You don't have to think of me as your mother right away, if you don't want to. Let's just concentrate on being friends, all right?"

He looked at her doubtfully but made no attempt to pull away. She went on talking to him, her voice low and soft, until the stiffness eased from his small body and he actually smiled at her.

"Friends?" Sarah asked gently.

William nodded and returned her smile with one of his own that fairly took her breath away. When he had run off to play with Esau, she turned to find Philip watching her with a look in his eyes she hadn't seen before.

"You're very good with children," he said, an odd huskiness in his voice.

"I haven't had much experience."

"No, but you seem able to make up for it." God help him, he was wondering if she would prove as skillful in other areas where she also lacked experience. The closer they came to their wedding, the more eagerly he found himself anticipating their wedding night.

At first he tried to believe that was simply because he hadn't been with a woman in a while. But the better he got to know Sarah, the more he realized that it was she herself he wanted. Innocent, proud, prickly, kind Sarah. Not only did he want her, but he wanted her to want him. Which worried him, because never again did he intend to become trapped in the kind of relationship he'd had with Daphne.

Desire could be a treacherous weapon in the hands of an unscrupulous woman. Much as he told himself that Sarah wasn't like that, he found himself dreading that he might be wrong.

Chapter Twenty-Two

THREE SEAMSTRESSES from Richmond had labored without pause for a fortnight to create Sarah's wedding gown. She had lost count of the yards of satin, silk, lace and ribbon that had gone into the making of it, not to mention the vast quantities of seed pearls used in the intricate embroidering. All she knew was that it was impossibly elaborate, ridiculously impractical and breathtakingly beautiful.

As she stood in front of the full-length mirror, she saw what might have been a fairy-tale princess from the pages of one of the picture books she had cherished as a child. The gown was a confection of pleated flounces and lace-trimmed ruffles that only a tall, slender woman could have worn. A smaller woman would have been overwhelmed, but Sarah merely looked utterly feminine. With a wry smile, she had to admit that she felt the same way.

Beneath the gown were three petticoats of the purest silk worn over the de rigueur hoops. Take those away and she would be left in lacy pantaloons, a camisole so delicate as to be all but transparent and a corselette trimmed with rose buds and laced up the front to both raise her breasts and narrow her waist.

For an hour she had soaked in water scented with rose blossoms, then rubbed cream fragrant with the same perfume over every inch of her skin. Callie had washed her hair, rinsed it in lemon juice and toweled it dry before rubbing it briskly with a length of silk. She had sipped a cup of chamomile tea and nibbled on a few biscuits brought to her by Augusta while her finger and toenails were buffed.

When her underclothes were in place, except for the petticoats and hoops, she sat down at the dressing table. A lotion of oatmeal and lemon juice was used to clean her face, which was then soothed with cucumber cream and dusted with rice powder. Her hair was dressed in twin braided chignons, exposing the lobes of her ears from which dangled the pearl-and-diamond earrings that were Philip's gift to her.

Now, as she stood in front of the mirror, Marilee carefully set the transparent lace veil on her head before adding the coronet of tiny white roses. Her friend stepped back and gazed at her wide-eyed. "You look absolutely radiant, Sarah. There's never been a lovelier bride."

"Ain't dat de truth," Callie murmured, smiling broadly at the vision in the mirror. "Massa Philip gonna be de happiest man on dis here earth when he see yo."

Like all the female slaves, she was dressed in a new calico dress. The men had received new trousers and shirts. For the field hands, there was a day of rest. The house slaves had to make do without that, but for them there was the consolation of silver coins given in appreciation of their extra work.

Since early morning the noise from downstairs had grown gradually louder as more and more guests arrived. When Sarah had first seen the list of those to be invited, she had jokingly asked if anyone in Virginia was being left out. Aunt Louise had sighed deeply and said, "Oh, Lord, I hope not. At least not anyone who is anyone."

Two hundred were expected, though it was likely the number would actually be higher as guests brought friends who had suddenly stopped by. The drawing room was filled to bursting with their gifts. Sarah had never guessed there might be so much crystal and silver in the world.

Not to be outdone, her father had presented to her and Philip a matched pair of magnificent stallions to accompany a carriage emblazoned with the Calvert coat of arms. Sarah had been astonished to see this evidence of nobility, but when she questioned Philip about it he merely laughed and said there were some things best taken at face value.

To Sarah herself, her father gave a string of pink pearls brought all the way from the Japan Sea and a cameo that had belonged to her mother. The latter had been sent at his instruction by courier from Boston. With it had come a letter from Gideon, in response to Josiah's telegram informing him that they would not be returning as planned and why.

Sarah did not know what was in the letter, but something had caused her father to scowl fiercely he tossed it into the fire. For much of the rest of the evening, he had been unusually silent, his eyes frequently going to her with a brooding intensity she found hard to bear. Only Marilee had eventually been able to lighten his mood, though how she had managed it Sarah did not know.

There had also been a letter from Nathan for Sarah. In it he had expressed some concern about the suddenness of her decision but had also said that he wished her all the best and looked forward to meeting Philip soon. Sarah had cried when she read it, but was comforted when Philip promised that Nathan would always be welcomed at Calvert Oaks.

With so few members of her family present at her wedding, she was all the more dependent on those who were there. Marilee put a reassuring arm around her shoulders and, mindful to not wrinkle the dress, gave her a quick hug just as Josiah knocked on the bedroom door.

Like the other men in the wedding party, he was dressed with the utmost formality in black satin knee breeches, an embroidered white satin waistcoat over a silk shirt and a cutaway jacket. His hair, still black except at the temples where it had turned silver, was carefully slicked back from his high forehead. His mustache was trimmed and his sideburns fluffed. He smelled of bay rum with a hint of whiskey, no doubt taken for medicinal purposes.

He appeared stiffly uncomfortable until Marilee exclaimed, "Oh, Josiah, you look so handsome." At that he flushed, almost as much as Marilee herself did. She had spoken without thinking and was taken aback to have said something so personal. Sarah was less struck by that than the fact that her friend clearly meant what she had said. She really did believe Josiah was handsome, a possibility his daughter had never considered. Nor did she have a chance to more than admit it might be true before it was time to leave.

To the strains of Mendelssohn's "Wedding March" played on an organ brought from Richmond specially for the occasion, Sarah walked between the rows of guests seated on chairs on the lawn. Ahead of her walked Kitty and Marilee trodding on the rose petals scattered by Kitty's little daughter. Behind Sarah one of Kitty's sons held on to her train and tried very hard not to trip. At the end of the improvised aisle, Philip waited. She was only dimly aware of Peter Rider standing at his side as best man or of the Reverend Charles Donnelly, the kindly, gray-haired minister who would perform the ceremony. All her attention was concentrated on Philip himself.

In some part of her mind, she was aware of acting exactly like the typical bride, all aflutter at the sight of her groom. Yet she couldn't seem to help herself. He was ... not handsome. That was too weak a word and besides, Marilee had already taken it. In his proud features and the erect carriage of his powerful body, she saw strength and certainty. He was a man who knew precisely what he wanted and had acted to get it. And when he turned to her, seeing her, and his face lit with pleasure, she knew an instant's bright joy that it was she who had inspired his happiness. Hard on that came the prayer that she was not then and never would be a disappointment to him.

The holy words were said over them, vows exchanged, a ring given and received. The gold was chilled against her skin, but the warmth of Philip's fingers holding hers more than made up for it. He raised her veil slowly, savoring the moment, and smiled at her gently before he bent to kiss her. The touch of his mouth, light, tender, in keeping with the time and place, nonetheless made her tremble. Because this time, for the first time, she had a sense of all the rest that was to come. As they walked arm in arm past the smiling guests, she stole a glance toward the west and caught herself wondering how soon the sun would set.

Time has a capriciousness about it matched only by the whims of fate. Looking at a clock, or a calendar, it might appear that time marches to an orderly beat. But in fact everyone knows that it really passes in fits and starts, now slowly, now quickly, now stopped.

In the bright light of that spring day, beneath a cloudless sky, floating on air scented by ten thousand magnolia blossoms, it seemed to Sarah that time had turned the season upside down and frozen in place.

She danced, talked, laughed, all with only the dimmest awareness of what she was doing and why. Only when Philip took her in his arms and they moved as one to the haunting strains of a waltz did she have any sense of reality. Only this was real. Nothing else, not the other people or anything they did and said, had any meaning. She and Philip might as well have been alone, so utterly engrossed were they in each other.

The guests saw that and were amused, but their indulgent smiles went unnoticed by the man and woman at whom they were directed. Sarah could see only Philip, he filled her vision. Golden in the sunlight, his voice low and caressing, his smile brilliant, he was all the world to her.

And that frightened her. Because time for all its caprice would someday have to start up again. The sun would resume its journey across the day. Night would come. They would be alone.

How she longed for that, and dreaded it. What they had right then—the light and music and the sheer, heady pleasure of being together—did not bear to give way to disappointment. But it was her duty; she repeated that as she sipped another glass of champagne and laughed at something Judge Rider was saying. If she was honest, she would admit that she wanted it. If only to have the waiting end, the mystery be revealed, so that she could come to terms with it and get on with the rest of her life.

Finally, with maddening slowness, the day drew to a close. The horizon turned pale orange and red as a full moon rose over the river. Sarah danced once more with Philip, who had loosened his stock and was flushed and laughing. When she returned to her seat, Marilee tugged lightly at her sleeve. "It's time to go upstairs," she murmured.

Sarah rose a bit unsteadily. For a moment her hands gripped the edge of the table. She saw Philip looking at her and slowly let go.

CALLIE WAS WAITING for her in the bedroom she would henceforth share with Philip. Sarah had never been in there before, except to stick her head in one day when curiosity overcame her. It was an essentially masculine room with a large four-poster bed, a mahogany bureau and a desk. Some of her belongings had been moved in already. Her clothes hung beside Philip's in the armoire, her hairbrushes nestled beside his on the dressing table. Her nightgown was laid out on the bed beside his nightshirt.

Callie giggled as she undid the long row of buttons down the back of Sarah's gown. She had enjoyed her share of the wine and rum passed out to the slaves in honor of the day and was feeling a bit more loose tongued than she otherwise would have. Her dark eyes rolled toward the frothy lace and silk confection as she said, "Dat sure is a pretty thing, missy, but Ahs guess yo won' be needin' it fo' long."

Sarah murmured noncommittally. For every step she had walked up the stairs, her mood had turned downward. It was as though anticipation had buoyed her and kept her fears at bay. Now that the reality was almost upon her, she felt quite differently. Too soon Philip would come, to find her in that nightgown, in his bed, waiting for... what?

Rebellion flared through her. She was hardly a lamb to be led to the slaughter. "That's enough," she said sharply once the girl had removed her dress and detached the heavy hoops. "I can do the rest for myself."

"But missy, Ahs gots ta do fo' yo."

"No, you do not. I want to be alone." Seeing the girl's stricken face, she softened somewhat. "It's all right, Callie, you haven't done anything wrong. I just need some time to... calm down. All right?"

A look of purely female understanding replaced Callie's dismay. Softly she said, "Ahs un'erstands, missy. Ain't nothin' to be scared of. Massa Philip, he a good man."

"I know," Sarah murmured, half-ashamed of her outburst. "It's just so... different."

"Course it is. Why Ahs 'members de first time me an' Benny—" She broke off. "Neber mind 'bout dat. De point is yo got no call to be worried, but seein' as how yo is...dere's maybe a lit'le somethin' could make yo feel better."

"What something?" Sarah asked.

"Jus' a lit'le tonic is all. Augusta tol' me iffen yo was anxious to give yo some ob it." She giggled again, puttin' her hand to her mouth. "Natur'ly, Ahs nots give my missy anythin' Ahs not suhr 'bout, so Ahs has a lit'le taste myself. Taste real fine."

Sarah couldn't help but laugh. Whatever the mysterious tonic was, it clearly agreed with Callie. She seemed to be positively blooming. But, of course, she couldn't drink anything like that. Or could she? Perhaps it wasn't fair to Philip to let him find her so strained and nervous. It was, after all, his wedding night as well as hers. Just a few drops of whatever Mammy Augusta had concocted couldn't possibly hurt her, could they?

"All right," she said, "I'll try a little of it. But not a word to anyone about this, Callie. It's our secret."

Looking very important, Callie bustled out to find the small bottle she had hidden under a pile of sheets in the linen closet. She returned and shut the door firmly behind her before, with due seriousness, pouring a half inch or so of the brown liquid into a glass. "Now drink all dat up, missy. Make yo feel right fine."

Sarah sipped it gingerly. The liquid was the color and consistency of tea, but was otherwise nothing like it. It tasted slightly bitter, though as soon as it had settled on the tongue, it was sweet. After a moment Sarah recognized the flavors of cinnamon and cloves mingling with brown sugar. She caught a hint of rum and something else that she couldn't identify and that she therefore presumed to be the most critical ingredient. "How is it supposed to make me feel?" she asked a bit nervously after she had drunk it down.

"Jus' relaxed, is all," Callie said as she hurriedly slipped Sarah out of the rest of her clothes, then dropped the nightgown over her. Her mistress was still staring into the bottom of the glass when Callie guided her over to the dressing table, sat her down and pulled the pins from her thick brown hair.

As she felt her hair fall about her, Sarah tipped her head back and smiled. "Hmm, I think it's working." She really did feel quite a bit better. Her anxiousness was fading, and she was actually looking forward to Philip's arrival.

"Dat real good, missy. Now jus' sit still fo' a lit'le minute whiles Ahs brush out yo hair. Such pretty hair," Callie crooned softly as Sarah's eyes closed. "Massa Philip gonna lahk it so much. Lahk silk it is."

Sarah was barely aware when Callie at last put down the hairbrush and gently urged her to her feet. She smiled at the black girl as she guided her across the room and sat her down on the edge of the bed. "Yo git under de covers now, missy. Don' wan' yo catchin' no chill."

But how could she when it was so warm in the room? So very delightfully warm. And the bed was so soft, the feather pillows fairly melting under her head. The sheets smelled of lavender and were satiny smooth. They caressed every inch of her body as she stretched out and sighed languorously.

"Ahs be goin' now, missy," Callie murmured. "Massa Philip, he be comin'."

"Tell him to hurry, Callie."

The black girl stifled a laugh. "Yas'm, missy, Ahs do dat."

Carrying Sarah's discarded bridal raiment, she retreated from the room, moments before Philip entered. He had slipped away from the other guests, denying them the opportunity to escort him to his bride by the simple expedient of having Peter Rider lie about where he was going. When he didn't return from the necessary, they would realize how he'd tricked them, but he trusted that no one would really mind. They were far too occupied in having a good time, an example he intended to promptly follow.

The curtains were drawn in the room and only a single candle was lit. By its glow, he could see Sarah lying in his bed. He took a step toward her, stopped and stared.

Surprises; she was always handing them to him. When he had seen her go upstairs, he had been concerned that she looked somewhat apprehensive. That was only natural and he had resolved to treat her with utmost gentleness no matter how difficult it might be for him, but the glorious creature in the bed banished any such thoughts.

"Sarah," he murmured, "are you all right?"

She gave him a dazzling smile. "Of course."

He approached the bed cautiously. She continued to smile at him. As she did so, she sat up. The covers fell back to reveal her breasts, barely concealed by the diaphanous gown. They were full and high, crested with dark nipples that pressed against the thin fabric.

Philip found that he was suddenly having difficulty breathing. His hands trembled as he stripped off his jacket and tossed it carelessly on a nearby chair. "I was concerned that you might be nervous," he said.

"Oh, I am..."

"You don't look nervous."

"That's because..." She hesitated, wondering how much she should say to him, then decided that he was her husband and honesty was the best policy. "I drank something."

"You mean the champagne?"

"No...something Augusta made for me. A kind of...tonic."

Philip stopped in the midst of unbuttoning his shirt and stared at her. "Brown stuff with a taste of cinnamon and rum?"

"That's right." Her gray eyes widened. "Did you drink some, too?"

With great effort, he stifled a laugh. "No, sweetheart, but you did and it stopped you from being afraid?"

She nodded slowly, her gaze fastened on his half-bared chest. Unconsciously she moistened her lips. "I'm not scared at all now."

He turned away from her with suppressed amusement and matter-of-factly went about the business of removing the rest of his clothes. Trust Augusta to come through for him. She'd been peddling that tonic to every nervous bride, both black and white, for more than a quarter century, and it never failed to work. Never mind that it's "secret ingredient" was a dash of nothing more arousing than cayenne pepper.

More happy wedding nights were probably owed to Augusta than anyone would ever know. He grinned as he turned back to the bed, thinking that he and Sarah were about to add another to the tally.

Chapter Twenty-Three

"WELL," SARAH SAID as she lay back against the pillows and waited for her breathing to return to normal.

"Well, well," Philip murmured beside her.

"That was really very...nice."

"It wasn't bad at all," he agreed.

"Is it always so...vigorous?"

"Sometimes...other times its slow and languorous."

"Oh, really?" she said, trying not to sound too interested.

He smiled in the darkness. "I'll show you, after a while."

Silence crackled between them, until he laughed deep in his throat and turned over, pinning her beneath him. She gasped but made no attempt to throw him off, as she had when he had first taken her. Then pain had cut through the dazzling haze of pleasure, and she had bucked like an angry mare resisting the bridle.

He had waited, utterly still within her, until the pain eased and she stopped struggling. Only then had he raised himself enough to see the bright glitter of her eyes and the silver sheen of tears on pale cheeks. The soft curse that broke from him was followed quickly by the gentle lapping of his tongue as he drank away each drop of grief. By the time he finished, she was gasping and twisting beneath him, driven by anguish of a far different sort.

"Sweet," he murmured, and began to move inside her, easing his weight so that she could move with him. At first she didn't know how, but soon she caught the rhythm. When she did, his control broke and he thrust heavily to his release.

How different she was from Daphne. His first wife had stunned him with her ability to climax almost as swiftly as a man, which had led him to believe that she had long since found the path for herself. Sarah, on the other hand, had no idea of what she had missed, and he had no certainty that he could show her.

Like most men, he prescribed to the theory that women were not necessarily capable of experiencing sexual pleasure. He had never considered that particularly unfortunate. But then he had never wanted a woman to respond to him as he did Sarah.

Looking down at her, he saw a faintly mutinous glint in her gray eyes and was provoked by it. Seizing both her hands in one of his, he stretched them above her head, smiling at her protest. "Are you sore?"

She blushed fiercely and refused to answer him, until his very masculine chuckle drove her to respond. "No."

"You're sure."

"I'm fine. Augusta's tonic..."

"Is a fake."

"Wh-what..." Sarah stammered. She couldn't have heard him correctly.

"There's nothing in it except a few spices, some rum and a dash of sugar. But don't feel badly, sweetheart. You're hardly the first bride who's believed in it. More than a few grooms have, too."

"I don't understand. How could it have made me feel like that if it wasn't..."

"Like what?" he asked.

She shut her mouth firmly, only to open it again when his free hand slipped down over her breasts. "Warm and...needing," she gasped.

"Hmm, an excellent description." He bent his head, rough silk hair brushing her nipples as he nuzzled her gently. "What you felt came from inside you, not from the tonic."

"It couldn't have..." she protested, only to break off as a low gasp escaped her. "Philip, don't..."

He raised his head reluctantly. "Don't what?"

"Touch me like that."

"Like how?"

"Like you were."

"I forget. Tell me."

She looked at him in disbelief. Surely he didn't expect her to... "I can't."

He moved against her, languidly. "Yes, you can." He moved again. "You will."

Tremors wracked her. She could no more control the movement of her body than she could stop herself from saying, "Your mouth on my breasts...don't."

"Why not?"

"You shouldn't."

"You liked it before," he reminded her relentlessly.

"That was different...the tonic...I thought..."

"You had an excuse."

Harsh, but true. The tonic, and what she had believed of it, had freed her of responsibility. She could give into the urgings of her body without really believing that she was to blame for them. Now she had no such excuse to hide behind. Philip was making even the simplest denial impossible for her.

"You want me," he said, his hand roaming down between her thighs still wet with his seed. "And I want you. There's nothing wrong with that." Yet he liked the fact that she had to be coaxed. He wanted to be the one in charge, the one to decide what they did and how. Never again did he intend to feel in thrall to a woman. But it was perfectly all right if she felt that way about him.

Lessons learned in the brothels of Richmond and Princeton served him well. He understood her body better than she herself did and knew exactly how to bring her to a sustained peak of pleasure that dissolved all restraint. Sarah cried out beneath him. Shame burned away.

Her eyes opened wide, reflecting the taut features of her husband above her. There was no softness in him, no yielding. He was all hard muscle and sinew, driving into her, demanding something she could not name but felt nonetheless welling up within her.

A flower opened slowly, inexorably, reaching for the hidden sun. She smelled the perfume of her own arousal mingling with his and cried out again. Then there was only darkness and the explosive scattering of seeds blown on an ancient wind.

WHEN SHE WOKE she was alone in the bed. Philip had left some time before; the side where he had rested was cool. She lay for a few moments, her head turned toward his pillow, her eyes focused inward. A slow blush spread across her cheeks.

She left the bed, noticing only after the fact that she was naked. The nightgown she had briefly worn lay in a tangle of lace on the floor. Rather than bother with such scant protection, she pulled a silk wrap from the wardrobe and hastily donned it.

She was still tying the belt when Callie entered, a broad smile on her round face. She carried a tray that she set with some ceremony on the table near the window. "Mornin', missy, looks lahk another real fine day." A soft giggle and a sidelong glance followed.

Sarah kept her eyes lowered as she sat down at the table. "Yes, Callie, it does." A sudden thought occurred to her. "What time is it?"

"'Bout noon."

"I shouldn't have slept so late." Her first day as mistress of Calvert Oaks and she had spent half of it in bed. What must Aunt Louise and the others think of her? Worse yet, did they have any real idea of why she had been so exhausted?

Callie clearly did. She giggled again, then busied herself pouring hot water into the china basin and laying out a fresh towel. "Don' bother yo'self none, missy. Nobody 'pect a bride ta be up early. Massa Philip, he say let yo sleep long as yo lahk."

"Where is he, Callie?"

"Massa? He out in de fields, missy. Be back round sundown."

There had been no talk of a honeymoon; Sarah had instinctively understood that Philip didn't want to repeat experiences he'd had with his first wife. But she had thought he wouldn't immediately return to work. Apparently it was to be business as usual right from the start.

"Get my pink dress ready for me, Callie," she said abruptly. "I'm not going to sit around all day."

"But, missy..."

"No buts. I have a great deal to learn, and the sooner I get to it, the better."

Half an hour later she was downstairs, confronting a surprised Aunt Louise. "Why, dear, I didn't think to see you so early."

Sarah smiled gently. "It's afternoon, about time I was up and around. What do you have planned for today?"

"Me?" The older woman looked a bit flustered. "Why, there's still some cleaning up to do from the party. China and crystal to be washed, linen to be boiled, that sort of thing. Nothing for you to be concerned about."

Sarah hesitated, not sure how firmly to stake her ground. Louise had been mistress of Calvert Oaks for more than twenty years; it might be that she was not eager to yield that position. Sarah didn't want to do anything that would make her feel threatened, but neither did she intend to remain a guest in her husband's home. "I'd really like to help," she said.

Aunt Louise looked at her uncertainly. Having never married herself, she shied away from imagining what her new young niece had experienced the night before. But whatever it had been, it certainly didn't seem to have done her any harm. Unlike some brides she had seen, Sarah showed no sign of being in the least horrified or frightened. On the contrary, she had the self-assurance of someone who has successfully triumphed over a great challenge.

"All right," Aunt Louise said, "if you truly don't mind, I certainly would appreciate your help. You know, dear," she added as they reached the yard, "I don't want you to ever feel that too much is being put on you, but whatever you wish to learn, I'll be happy to teach you.''

So began Sarah's tutelage in her new life. By night she lay in Philip's arms, discovering a part of her nature she had never before suspected. In the darkness, restraint dissolved and she became a creature of pleasure, never quite easily or without lingering reservation, but always eventually driven mindless by the things he did to her and taught her to do to him.

By day she worked at Aunt Louise's side, discovering that everything she'd thought she knew about the Southern woman was ludicrously inaccurate. As was her idea of what constituted hard work. As she quickly discovered, the men—led by Philip—were responsible for growing the cash crops and getting them to market. The women were responsible for everything else. Everything.

Fabric had to be woven and clothing made for each of the three hundred individuals who lived at Calvert Oaks. Even their shoes—one pair each year to each slave—were made on the premises. Milk, pork and corn had to be doled out in regular rations, accompanied whenever possible by fresh fruit and vegetables. Whenever slaves had accidents, felt ill or gave birth, they had to be properly cared for.

There was no respite from the constant work. If Sarah wasn't seeing to the care of the vegetable fields or the making of butter or the knitting of socks, she was rushing about trying to get carpets cleaned, geese plucked, preserves put up or any number of other tasks. Nor was it a question of merely supervising the household slaves; she did a fair measure of the work herself, enough so that by the end of each day she could barely remember its beginning.

Which was not to say that she was unhappy. After the initial shock she quickly became accustomed to the relentless pace of activity, though as the early months of her marriage passed, there were times when she would pause in the midst of whatever she happened to be doing and wryly remember her expectations of what life would be like in the "lazy" South. Perhaps somewhere there was a plantation whose mistress sat about all day without lifting a lily-white hand, but she knew of none such.

When early on she marveled to Kitty about how wrong the popular conception was, her sister-in-law laughed ruefully and explained that Northerners weren't the only ones to make that mistake. "It's something of a secret here, as well," she said. "Hardly anyone ever speaks of it, as though that means it doesn't happen." She looked away, out the window they were sitting beside while stitching baby clothes. Kitty was expecting again, her sixth, but that hadn't prevented her from coming over to Calvert Oaks to see how everything was going.

"Surely you knew," Sarah ventured, "before you were married?"

"Not really," Kitty smiled, showing her dimples. "I was a belle. My head was full of nothing except gowns, parties, beaux. The most work I did was having dresses fitted."

"Do you mean that Aunt Louise didn't teach you how to run a household?" Sarah asked, more surprised than critical.

"Not at all. It simply isn't done, any more than the young men are taught to run a plantation. Philip was the exception to that, thank heavens. But for me there were a few years of sheer self-indulgence which I truly wouldn't have wanted to miss, considering what comes after.''

Sarah was puzzled. Kitty didn't seem to dislike her life, she appeared to be genuinely fond of her husband who doted on her and of her children who were adorable. Yet there was a note of regret in her voice, as though she wished things were somehow different.

"There is always so much to be done..." Sarah said.

"Oh, I don't mind that. It's good to have a sense of purpose, and I like being needed. Not, of course, that there aren't times when I think I absolutely can't cope with another thing.''

"What do you do then?''

"I have a good stiff jolt of bourbon." At Sarah's startled look, Kitty laughed. "Men aren't the only ones who need that. Besides, it's better than laudanum. I know far too many women who can't quite get through the day without their 'drops.'''

Having grown up in her father's puritanical household, Sarah had only recently learned to drink wine. The thought of anything stronger made her stomach churn, yet she couldn't condemn Kitty. Happy though she was at Calvert Oaks, she was not oblivious to the disadvantages of such a way of life. More than anything else, the isolation chaffed at her. She hadn't expected to feel so completely cut off from everything she had once known. But then she had presumed that Marilee would be staying with her.

"Have you heard anything from Boston recently?'' Kitty asked, returning to her stitching.

"I had a letter from Nathan last week. He's considering applying to the divinity school at Yale.'' She had been surprised by that, having never considered that Nathan might have a calling to the ministry. But when she thought about it, she realized that his gentle, kindly nature predisposed him in that direction.

"Is everyone else well?"

"Father had a bad case of the flu this fall, but he's recovering. Marilee is . . . fine."

Kitty shot her a sympathetic look. "It was a shock to you, wasn't it?"

Sarah shrugged. "I should have realized how they felt about each other long ago."

"It's always hard to see that people are different from the way we expect them to be," Kitty said.

Sarah put down her sewing and stared off into the middle distance, her forehead wrinkling. "I always knew that Marilee cared a great deal for father, I just never thought that . . ."

"He might return the feeling?"

"Or that it could become what it did."

All too clearly she remembered the afternoon a week after her marriage when Marilee had sought her out in the pantry where she was taking inventory. It was the first time she had done that, and she was concentrating hard in her effort not to make any mistakes, when her friend appeared round the door.

"Do you have a moment, Sarah?"

"Wh-what . . . ? Oh, Marilee, come in. Perhaps you can read this label for me. Does it say 'cucumber' or 'cauliflower'?"

"'Cucumber,' I think. You're very busy, aren't you?"

Sarah laughed and brushed a stray wisp of hair from her forehead, heedless of the dusty streak she left in its place. "I think I may be busy for the rest of my life, there's so much to be done. Aunt Louise is wonderful about teaching me."

"Yes . . . your father and I were talking about that. You seem to be settling in so well." Marilee suddenly clasped her hands together and looked at Sarah intently. "Are you happy, truly?"

"Why, yes . . . I think I am. It's hard to say exactly since everything is still so new. But Philip is . . . a good man." She felt herself blushing and looked away. That was such an inadequate description for her husband, and perhaps not even accurate. She thought she knew some things about him but wasn't really sure of anything. The calm, capable, pleasant man she saw at meals had little in common with the voracious lover who claimed her each night, nor did he bear any resemblance to the stern-faced ruler she occasionally glimpsed.

"Sarah . . . there's something I have to tell you."

"What's that?" she asked absently, her thoughts still on Philip.

"I'm going back to Boston with your father."

"You're . . . but why? Why would you want to return to Boston?" The possibility that Marilee might not stay with her hadn't even occurred to Sarah.

"It's been my home for a long time."

"Yes, but surely you must realize that if you stay in the house with father and Gideon, now that I'm gone . . . people will talk." She hated to put it that way, but the truth had to be faced. Their neighbors knew that Marilee was not, strictly speaking, a member of their family. Nor was she considered a servant. Her indistinct status made it impossible for her to remain in a house with two men without arousing scurrilous gossip.

"Sarah . . . your father and I . . . we've decided . . . that is, he asked me . . ."

Marilee's manner, more than her words, brought a glimmer of understanding to Sarah. She froze, her hand outstretched to examine another jar, before turning slowly. "You . . . and my father?"

Meeting her eyes, her own dark with worry, Marilee nodded. "We really do care for each other, and now that you're settled, we thought . . ."

"I don't believe it."

"It's true. Please don't be angry."

"But you're barely half his age," Sarah exclaimed, "and you're beautiful. You could have anyone."

Marilee smiled gently. "I don't want anyone, except Josiah. Don't you realize, it's been that way for me from the first day he brought me home."

"You were a child."

"But old enough to know what I wanted. Sarah, I realize how difficult your relationship with your father has been. But I see him in a different light. He is everything to me."

"Everything?" Sarah echoed, her throat tight. "What about our friendship, all that we have shared together?"

"Why, of course, I value that. Don't think otherwise for a moment. You have been a sister to me."

"But my father has not been as a father." Sarah laughed bitterly.

Marilee drew herself upright and regarded her steadily. "Why should he have been? He was never my father, nor did I wish him to be. I have waited a long time for him to come to terms with his feelings. Now we can begin to live . . . together."

"Sarah?" Kitty said softly, recalling her to the present. "Are you all right?"

"I'm sorry...I was just thinking. Really, I'm glad for father and Marilee. It just takes some time to get used to."

"Change always does." Kitty leaned across the space separating them and patted Sarah gently on the arm. "Though I must say, you're one change I heartily approve of. Calvert Oaks is a much happier place since you came."

"Thank you, but there are times when I think I will never be able to manage as I should."

"You seem to be doing well enough, but if you do run into difficulty, remember I'll be happy to help." Kitty patted her rounded stomach ruefully. "Though I can't guarantee how much use I might be."

Sarah noted her sister-in-law's pensive smile as she contemplated the child growing within her. She couldn't help but contrast that with her own monthly concern. Each time her flow occurred she didn't know whether to be relieved or disappointed. Philip had made no secret of his desire for more children, but her own fears made her less than eager to comply. Not that she had any choice in the matter; nature would have its way. If they went on as they were, and there was no reason to believe they wouldn't, surely pregnancy was inevitable.

And with it, what? Kitty had survived five internments and did not seem to be dreading her sixth. Numerous other women had done the same. She had no reason to dread childbirth. Yet that did not prevent her from hearing the screams that, after more than a decade, still echoed in her memory.

Chapter Twenty-Four

"I HAVE NEVER," Sarah murmured, "been so tired in my life."

"December is a trying month," Aunt Louise agreed with a wan smile. "I often think how wonderful it must be to associate it only with Christmas."

"Instead of hog butchering."

The women looked at each other, and despite their great fatigue, they laughed. They were seated at a rough wooden table in the kitchen, where Augusta was attempting to revive them with hearty bowls of soup they were too weary to eat. For a week—no, for ten days—the usual life of the big house had been put aside as all efforts were devoted to the killing, butchering and preserving of the hogs. Never, thought Sarah, would she be able to look at a piece of bacon as she once had. Or at a ham, a sausage, a bit of lard, a bristle, any number of useful items would henceforth remind her of the experience.

Not that she needed to be reminded. Aunt Louise had assured her that it was an annual event. She could look forward to it every December from now on.

"Why," Sarah said as she slumped in her chair, heedless of any effort to maintain a ladylike posture, which was quite beyond her, "are there so many hogs in the first place and why do we have to kill them?"

"You've been asking that for days now, dear," Aunt Louise said gently. She took a sip of her tea, holding the cup between hands that trembled from weariness and recited as though from memory. "The hog is a highly useful animal. He provides food, hides, fat for soup and wax, and any number of other products. It is no exaggeration to say that after regular sun and rain, he is the planter's best friend. My dear father told me that, I forget how many years ago. Of course," she added with a most uncharacteristic scowl, "he never had to actually deal with one of the slippery, squealing beasts."

"I feel as though I now know more than a few of them intimately," Sarah said. She stretched her arms above her head, trying to relieve the kinks in her neck and back. How many hogs had been butchered? Fifty? Seventy-five? She had lost count. After the first shock of seeing the slaves hit the shrieking animals over the head to stun them, then slit their throats before hoisting them over stout oak limbs, she had become immune. A blessed numbness set in that could not be penetrated by the noise, stench or general chaos.

Ruefully she looked down at her hands. They were red and chapped from the salting barrels and looked as though they belonged to a woman many times her age. A frown creased her forehead. "When is the first Christmas ball?" she asked.

"Next week," Aunt Louise said with a heavy sigh.

"Then I have that much time to transform myself once again into the vision of a proper Southern lady."

The older woman laughed. "If it's any consolation, dear, so do we all."

Yet they managed somehow. Before the season's round of entertainment began, all trace of their labors had been carefully erased. For a joyous fortnight they forgot their burdens and gave themselves up to celebration, culminating with the great New Year's ball to be hosted that year by the Carlisles.

As the carriage she shared with her husband and Aunt Louise drew up in front of their hosts' river-front mansion, Sarah quieted a tremor of nervousness and told herself there was no reason to be concerned about meeting so many of Philip's friends. After all, most of them had been at the wedding so in a sense they weren't really strangers.

Except that she remembered very little of that day, such a daze she had been in, and since then there had been almost no opportunity to give or accept hospitality. The traditional period of dispensation from social obligations offered to a newly married couple had given way to a season of constant work on the plantations, which was only interrupted by the Christmas festivities. Most of these people she was effectively meeting for the first time, and she worried how they would receive her.

Philip sensed her unease. He smiled reassuringly and touched his lips lightly to her cheek as he helped her down from the carriage. "Relax, my sweet, you look exquisite."

She laughed nervously. "Actually, I'm having a little trouble breathing." Callie had laced her corset so tightly that she could only draw air into the upper part of her lungs. The fashion for small waists was growing more absurd by the year. A great battle was waging between the women who insisted on being laced even during pregnancy and the doctors who claimed this damaged their babies. Even little girls were being put into whalebone corsets at increasingly tender ages.

Yet when Sarah had looked at herself in the mirror after Callie was finished with her, she was struck by the heightened extent of her own femininity. She appeared almost impossibly delicate, yet also undeniably sensual. Her breasts, pushed up by the corset, swelled above the edge of her gown. The tight laces forced her to move slowly, with small steps that did not overtax her punished lungs. Meanwhile, the huge hoops beneath her many petticoats completely hid her lower body, leaving to the imagination what delights it might contain. She was a ripe female tethered in such a way as to make escape impossible.

The image both disturbed and excited her. She had turned away from the mirror gladly and done her best not to understand the light in Philip's eyes when he saw her.

On his arm, with Aunt Louise on the other, she entered the reception hall. A black majordomo waited to relieve them of their cloaks. That done, they stood in line to greet their hosts. The Carlisles—John; his wife of two years, Mary; and his widowed mother—exchanged a few words of welcome with each guest.

"How nice to see you again, Mrs. Calvert," Mary Carlisle said in her soft whisper of a voice. "I had planned to call, but we've been so busy..."

"Yes, I know," Sarah said with a wry smile. "Was it hogs here, too?"

Mary looked momentarily taken aback, then broke into laughter. "It was, indeed. How I hate the loathsome creatures. But I take it you survived all right?"

The men exchanged a slightly puzzled look. They knew, of course, that the women took care of getting the hogs butchered, but none of them had any real idea of what that entailed. Mary and Sarah's amusement, in which Aunt Louise and the Widow Carlisle joined, surprised them.

"Come along, sugar," Philip said with his hand on Sarah's elbow, "there are a lot of people here I want you to meet."

She went with him willingly enough, reassured by Mary's understanding. It was almost as though some sort of secret communion flowed among the women. They shared an existence in which men, with all their domineering, sometimes childish ways, were allowed to penetrate only to the periphery. The rest, the vast bulk of their lives, was kept separate and apart. A glance, a smile, a single word were enough to acknowledge this sisterhood, and to welcome Sarah into it.

For that she was grateful, even as she began to realize that there were some women in the group, and more than a few men, who were not so comfortable with her.

"From Boston, you say," a matron sumptuously gowned in black velvet and lace said. "How interesting. I don't believe I've ever met a female Yankee before." She tittered slightly, as though she had come in contact with some lumbering beast that faintly shocked her.

"I don't imagine we're really very different," Sarah said. She was momentarily without Aunt Louise's support, the older woman having retired to the room upstairs set aside for ladies to refresh themselves. Philip stood within a circle of men busy debating the merits of horseflesh. He flashed her a quick smile but hardly looked disposed to come to her aid.

"For that matter," she added impulsively, "I don't imagine there are really all that many differences between North and South. At least nothing that couldn't be settled by a little common sense."

The women, about half a dozen, who surrounded her looked askance. Only the fact that no man was immediately present kept them from turning aside from any hint of politics. As it was, it was left to the lady in black, widow of a prosperous Richmond business-man, to pursue the matter. Plump despite lacing that could only be described as remorseless, she drew her-self to her full height—a shade over five feet—and pitched her voice somewhere between censure and rep-rimand. "Common sense? I would say rather that it would all be settled if the Yankees would confine themselves to their own affairs and not try to interfere in ours."

"It's not that simple," Sarah said, wishing that it were. "We are, after all, one nation."

"At the moment," the widow said. She smirked, and her friends with her.

Sarah dismissed that without thought. "North and South cannot divide; apart we would be weak while together we can be even stronger than we are today."

The women shrugged, their bare shoulders gleam-ing white in the candlelight. "The South has strengths no Yankee can understand," said the widow. "We can only benefit from separation."

A cold finger of anger moved down Sarah's spine. What she was hearing was absurd. Surely these women could not possibly represent any general belief? It must only be her bad fortune to have come upon a coven of fanatics.

"If you would excuse me," she said, "I see my hus-band beckoning."

Philip was blatantly doing no such thing, but she took her leave shamelessly and left the whispering circle behind her as she crossed the ballroom to his side. He greeted her with a smile, placed a hand on her shrunken waist and went on listening to what John Carlisle was saying.

"Douglas is a fool. If the Democrats nominate him, the Republicans will sweep the South."

"With what candidate?" Louis Devereaux demanded. "There's talk that they will nominate the rail-splitter."

"No one takes that seriously," John countered. "Can you imagine such a bumpkin in the White House?"

Sarah, who rather liked what she had read about Illinois's Lincoln, was hard-pressed to keep still. Only the dawning realization that she was in a hostile gathering made her do so. With hindsight, she realized that she shouldn't be surprised. Abolitionist John Brown had been hanged early in the month, just as hog-butchering season was getting underway. She had been too busy to take more than the barest note of his death, but she had felt then, and continued to feel, that it was a mistake. The South had branded him a traitor for the uprising he had led at Harper's Ferry, but to the North he was a hero. And now a martyr.

"The fact remains," Philip was saying, "that Douglas, Lincoln, Seward and Davis are the moderates. We could do far worse."

"If you had to pick among them," John said, "which would you choose?"

Philip thought a moment. "Douglas. He is the strongest for state's rights, the one who would leave it to us to decide our own way."

The men around him had stiffened with surprise. "What about Davis?" one demanded. "Surely Jefferson has first claim on your allegiance."

Philip was tempted to ask why that should be so, simply because the senator hailed from Mississippi, but he stopped himself. Instead he said simply, "Mr. Davis believes that the North must—and eventually will—accept the fact of slavery as immutable and eternal. That it will never do. The best we can hope for is a man like Douglas, who will let us work out our problems for ourselves. Failing him, we may be inflicted with Lincoln, who though he would set no timetable for the destruction of slavery, wants us to at least admit that it is wrong."

"Lincoln," Paul Danvers muttered. Alone among the group of lifelong friends, he was still waiting for his patrimony, and while he waited, he drank. The results showed in his spreading gut, his reddened nose and in the touch of the poet he affected. "That gaunt specter of a man already haunts us. I was in New York, you know, during his speaking tour last year. I went to one of his talks. He is gruff-voiced and awkward in presence, but he uses words well."

"Which will avail him nothing," Louis insisted as he motioned impatiently to a liveried slave. His empty glass was quickly replaced by a full one. "Let Lincoln spout all the words he likes. In the meantime, we sharpen our swords."

The other men nodded, except for Philip. He had gone very still. "Is that what you want, Louis? War?"

"Why not? It will settle the matter once and for all."

"But in whose favor?"

"You're joking," John said. "We can crush the damn Yankees and be home in time for spring planting."

"Perhaps," a voice from the edge of the group replied. Peter Rider smiled as he joined the discussion. "But it would be foolish to underestimate them. They have more than a few capable officers among them."

"Are you saying," John demanded, "that they are a match for men like yourself?"

"No," Peter replied mildly. "I am far too arrogant to say such a thing. If we could fight a short war, we would undoubtedly win. Our leaders, our men, our will are all superior. However," he went on before they could comment, "should we fail to achieve a quick victory, then it will be a different matter."

"Then there is nothing to be concerned about," Louis said. "We will teach the Yankees a salutary lesson and that will be the end of the matter."

"I pray you are right," Peter answered as he and Philip exchanged a look. "But I caution you against unwarranted optimism. Nothing else so guarantees an army's defeat."

Sarah could see that the very idea of defeat was so alien to these men that what Peter had said was meaningless. They shrugged it off, even as the women had her own comments, and went on to talk of other things, principally horse racing. King's Ransom had just concluded a banner year of unbroken victories, and Philip was being pressed to put him out to stud.

"I have a mare," John said, "newly arrived from England, that I would like to put to him. You have only to say the price."

Philip smiled, but shook his head. "You understand that once he is bred, he will become far more difficult to handle. I would prefer to race him another year.''

The men tried to convince him otherwise, but eventually gave up. In the ebb and flow of the party, they were drawn off in different directions. Philip and Sarah found themselves alone with Peter. She wondered briefly if that was a coincidence, since they had all three expressed unpopular opinions.

Peter touched a hand lightly to Philip's sleeve. ''About the horse. I'd breed him, if I were you.''

Surprised, Philip said, ''I never knew you took much of an interest in such things.''

''I don't, ordinarily, but you are a friend, and I would hate to see you disappointed.'' He glanced around the room, as though confirming that they were out of earshot. ''After this year we are about to begin, there will be little opportunity for horse breeding.''

Philip looked at him curiously. Much passed in silence between the two men who knew each other well. ''You are serious?''

''Regretfully so. There is nothing I can say that will convince the firebrands, but the horizon looks very dark to me.''

''Surely, if it comes to that, we can achieve the swift victory you advised?''

''Do you hear yourself?'' Peter asked. ''You phrase that as a question, and rightly so, for the South has never been truly tested.''

''Neither has the North,'' Sarah broke in. Her palms were suddenly damp, and she was regretting the wine she had drunk. It made her queasy.

Peter bowed over her hand. ''Dear lady, how I regret to disagree with you. But perhaps because you come from there, you do not see it clearly. The North is a great arena, where the mettle of men is constantly tested. Only the strongest survive. They look south like hungry wolves."

For a brief terrifying instant she had an image of Gideon, his eyes narrowed and feral. "No, there are men of goodwill on both sides. They will keep the peace."

Peter shot her a quick, apologetic look. "I have upset you, and I beg your pardon for it. Pay no attention. The holidays, joyful though they are, have a dour effect on some, myself included."

He took his leave then, and Sarah did her best to forget all he had said. But the memory lingered as she danced with Philip and they chatted with other guests about safe things.

And at midnight, when in the shadows of the veranda he took her in his arms to kiss her, she knew an unexplained shiver of dread. The tolling bell seemed strangely at odds with the cheering crowd welcoming the new year. She closed her eyes, felt the warmth of her husband's lips on her own and tried to find a fragment of happiness within herself.

There was none, only coldness and the undeniable conviction that Peter Rider was right. Search the horizon of her mind though she did, then and in the months to come, she saw only darkness.

Part Three

1861-1863

Chapter Twenty-Five

"IS THERE AN ANSWER, ma'am?" The weary messenger shifted from one foot to the other as he stood on the bottom step leading to the veranda. Behind him, his swaybacked horse looked round for forage and, failing to find any, closed its red-rimmed eyes.

"What?" Sarah looked up from the letter she had been scanning. It took her a moment to realize what the young man had asked. "No, no answer. Here, this is for your trouble." She fished in the pocket of her cotton day dress to find the silver dollar she had scooped out of Philip's desk when she saw the messenger coming. She knew he would have been paid before setting out, but he looked so tired and worried that she wanted to reward him.

"Thank you, ma'am," he said, a smile creasing his face for the first time. "If that's all then, I'll be on my way."

"You're welcome to stay for a bite to eat."

"I sure appreciate that, but I've got another half-dozen messages I promised to deliver 'fore nightfall, so I'd best be going."

Sarah nodded. The letter fluttered in her hand as she watched the boy mount and ride away. Only when he had disappeared around the bend of the road did she read the paper again.

"My dearest," Philip had written, "I regret that business will keep me in Richmond for a few more days. In my absence, I trust that you are well and are carrying out all my instructions. Your loving husband."

Brief though the letter was, it told her more than he had perhaps intended. His handwriting was ragged, exhaustion evident in every line. The bottom of the paper was crumbled, as though he had grasped it in frustration. And the reference to his instructions—that alone was enough to fill her with dread.

Philip had been in Richmond for four weeks, since the end of February. He had gone in a last-ditch effort to stem the talk of war that had come hard on the heels of Abraham Lincoln's election and inauguration. Though he had claimed to be hopeful that peace might yet be preserved, before he left he had given instructions for the stockpiling of food and other necessities. To Sarah's surprise, he had even allocated the spending of precious cash to purchase seed, leather, machine parts, coal, cooking oil, flour and other goods, as though he expected them to be in short supply.

Yet how could that be? As she turned back into the house, the letter safely in her pocket, she told herself for the uncounted time that even if war did come, it would be brief. There was no need for such elaborate preparations, yet as Philip's wife, she felt compelled to do as he said.

No, that wasn't honest. She stopped in the hallway, listening to the door close behind her and mentally corrected herself. She was doing what he said because a part of her, unwanted and largely unrecognized, thought that he might be right.

It had taken her a long time to come to terms with the fact that there could be a war. Not until the two major parties nominated men who were, to some degree, committed to an end to slavery, did she begin to consider that the fire breathers of both North and South might get their way. Even then she had smothered her own instinctive preference enough to hope that Stephen Douglas would win; he at least would support gradual change. When Abraham Lincoln carried the day, she had begun to fear the worst.

And yet, the tall, gaunt rail-splitter was really asking for so little. All he wanted was for the South to commit itself to the ultimate abolition of slavery, which many Southerners believed was inevitable in any case. Certainly, Philip did, though he believed the process had to be slow and reasoned. He had gone to Richmond to argue just that; the tone of his letter suggested he was having no success.

In his absence, Sarah had taken to using the big desk in the library to sort through her receipts and bills, as well as the lists of what still had to be done. It was a convenient place to work, and it allowed her to feel a little closer to him.

She was surprised by how much she missed Philip. Lying alone in their bed at night, she was hard-pressed to sleep. During the day, she tried to keep thoughts of him at bay, but they intruded more often than not. No matter how busy she was, she would catch herself listening for the sound of his step or his voice, for the touch of his hand, for his warm breath on her.

Almost two years since their marriage, he still kept her on edge. She had expected that after the novelty of being a wife wore off she would feel a certain complacency, yet she did not. Perhaps because she had yet to take her married state for granted. She still felt very much a stranger in a strange land.

Resting her elbow on the desk, she stared off into space and sighed. It was warm for late March. The windows were wide open, and through them she could hear the voices of the house slaves as they went about their duties. She had become accustomed to having them around and even managed to forget more often than not that they were any different from the servants she had known in Lowell and Boston. Only occasionally was the reality of slavery brought home to her.

Even then she knew that she only sensed a tiny fraction of what it truly meant to either be or possess human chattel. The lives of the field hands, who made up the majority of the slaves on Calvert Oaks, were largely hidden from her. She saw them only when they needed doctoring or when there were rations of food and clothing to pass out. She had tried, more than once, to talk with Philip about the slaves, but he had steadfastly brushed off her inquiries. She understood that he did not want her to be touched by the problem that dogged his own life, yet she couldn't help but think that his efforts to protect her would turn out to be futile.

Determined to distract herself, she turned to another letter spread out on the desk. Marilee's neat handwriting filled several pages. She had written to say that they were all well. Nathan was happy at the seminary, Gideon continued to work for his father, all of Josiah's many businesses were progressing satisfactorily. He was particularly pleased with the profit from the new mill that, under Philip's management, had flourished.

Sarah was relieved by the cheerful tone of the letter; six months before Marilee had suffered a miscarriage and for some time thereafter had been badly depressed. Sarah had thought of going north to stay with her, but Josiah had taken matters into his own hands and taken his young wife to Paris. They had only recently returned.

"There is much talk among the French," Marilee wrote, "of the troubles here, yet no one seems to believe they will come to anything. *'Beaucoup de bruit mais pas d'action'* was how one gentleman described it to me. I pray he is right and that there will continue to be only noise rather than action."

So did Sarah, though she feared that prayers would avail them little. Action was invariably more dependable. Rising, she carefully folded both Marilee's and Philip's letters and put them inside the journal she had recently begun to keep. When the leather-bound book was locked away in the desk, she steeled herself to return to work.

It was late in the day and the last of a newly arrived shipment of brandy, wine and cordials had been locked in the pantry, when Sarah decided to take a walk through the quarters to see if anything needed to be done there. When she mentioned where she was going, Augusta looked up from the sauce she was stirring and frowned.

"Wha' yo want t'go down dere fo', missy? 'Specially dis late in de day?"

"There's still an hour or two of daylight left," Sarah said, "and I think I may need to order more whitewash. I won't be long."

"Massa Davies, he could see t'dat."

Sarah hesitated, her hand on the latch of the kitchen door. "He has enough to do. I don't want to bother him." Actually, she felt awkward speaking to the overseer, who persisted in treating her as though she was some very delicate, volatile substance which might suddenly erupt in his face.

Augusta opened her mouth to protest further but before she could do so, Sarah slipped out the door. She was amused by the old slave's efforts to discourage her. Winning the allegiance of Augusta and the other house slaves was a long, hard battle. They accepted her gingerly, and for the most part followed her instructions, unless they happened to really believe she was wrong.

Truth be told, Augusta and several of the others had saved her more than once from costly or at least embarrassing mistakes. Even with Aunt Louise's guidance, she had often felt at a loss to deal with all the many demands of the big house. Only recently had she begun to gain some confidence, which was just as well since Aunt Louise was less and less able to help her. Arthritis had begun to cripple her hands, and her eyesight was not what it had been. Though she tried valiantly, there were days when she was content to sit on the veranda, keeping Charles company.

Sarah was thinking of her father-in-law as she stepped around a corner of the house and took the path leading to the quarters. Off to one side, she could see the stables and beyond them the horse pastures. King's Ransom was there, his black mane rippling in the sunshine.

Charles had objected the year before when Philip told him he wanted to put the stallion to stud without delay. Sarah didn't know the content of their discussions, but she was aware that the older man believed

Philip was worried unnecessarily about the future. What impressed her was that much as he disagreed with his son, he had in the end gone along with him. She couldn't imagine her own father doing the same with Gideon, but then her brother and her husband were nothing at all alike, for which she was heartily grateful.

To date, King's Ransom had sired some twenty colts with several more coming. Mares from as far away as the Gulf states were brought to be serviced by him. The cash he earned for Calvert Oaks had gone into the purchase of several sturdy workhorses, half a dozen mules and the equipment for a brewery under construction not far from the main house. All part of Philip's plan to make the plantation even more self-sufficient than it had been before.

There was even a new clinic for the slaves, larger than the one it had replaced and better equipped. Sarah paused there to have a few words with a young slave girl who had given birth the day before. It was her first delivery and the labor had been long and hard. Sarah was relieved to find her looking as well as she did.

After promising to see to it that cow's milk was sent to the nursery to augment the girl's own milk, which was proving inadequate, Sarah went on her way. She found some satisfaction in the knowledge that of the twelve children born since she came to Calvert Oaks, only two had died. Even more importantly to her, no mothers had perished. In some small way, that made up for her own continued failure to conceive.

At this time of year, when there was so much to be done, the quarters were largely deserted. The field slaves, their drivers and the overseer would not be back until twilight. In their absence, only the very oldest and youngest slaves were on hand. Sarah stopped to catch the ball of a grimy toddler who smiled at her enchantingly. The old woman who cared for him and a dozen other children laughed through toothless gums as Sarah gently loped the ball back to the little boy. He seized it gleefully, being bolder than the rest who peered at her shyly.

An old man, who had been at Calvert Oaks so long that when he spoke of the "massa" he meant Charles Calvert's father, dozed in the sun. His brittle bones were only lightly covered by gnarled brown skin. Each time Sarah saw him, he seemed to grow more ethereal. She thought she would not be at all surprised to hear some day that he had simply disappeared.

Thinking of slaves disappearing made her frown. In recent months there had been an epidemic of runaways throughout the country and beyond. Despite the best efforts to keep them in ignorance, the slaves knew of the trouble that seemed to be coming. They feared that war would mean the complete closure of the borders with the North and an end to the underground railroad that had meant freedom for so many of them. Those who had only been thinking about running were driven to seize the chance before it vanished, perhaps forever.

Shortly before Philip left, there had been a problem with the girl, Sukie, whom he had purchased from Beauterre after the aborted rebellion there. For a time she had worked in the kitchens with Ginny, but neither Aunt Louise nor Sarah had felt comfortable with her. Even Augusta had complained about her slowness and her insolence. She had been sent to work in the fields, where she proved little more cooperative.

Sarah knew few of the details, but she thought that late in January, Sukie had simply walked away from a work party. She got as far as the nearest rail junction, where she was apprehended by a suspicious ticket agent. Philip had gone to fetch her back. When he returned with her, his face was marked by deep scratches, as though he had been clawed. From Rameses, who had accompanied him, word spread that Sukie had attacked him in front of a group of whites. That had sealed her fate.

For the first time since Sarah had come to the plantation, a slave had been whipped. Tied to a stake in the center of the quarters, Sukie was given fifteen lashes, wielded by Overseer Davies with Philip looking grimly on. Afterward she had convalesced in the clinic for several days during which Sarah had forced herself to tend to her. Not once did the black girl say a word, but the eyes that had followed Sarah as she moved around the room had made her so anxious that she breathed a sigh of relief when Sukie healed enough to be sent to the fields.

She was looking carefully at the outer walls of one of the cabins, trying to determine whether or not it needed to be rechinked and whitewashed, when through a narrow opening between the planks of wood, a movement caught her eye. For a moment she thought she had imagined it. The cabin was one of several that were presently empty. But even if it had been occupied, at that hour of the day, there was no reason for anyone to be inside. Yet someone was definitely there. As she watched she caught sight of a man's arm, reaching for a plate of food beside a pallet.

Sarah backed away from the cabin. Her hands were trembling. She clasped them tightly together and continued staring at the wall. A runaway. There was no other possible explanation. A slave was hiding on Calvert Oaks and was being helped by at least some of the slaves there.

She swallowed hastily against the sour taste of fear. Since the night of the storm, she had presumed that Marcus continued to be involved with runaways, but gradually over time, as nothing happened to remind her, she had managed to push it out of her thoughts. Now it was back, with a vengeance.

Afraid that someone might have seen her looking into the cabin, she glanced around quickly. There was no one in sight, but that did little to reassure her. Picking up her skirts, she hurried back to the main house, not stopping until she was once again in the kitchen.

Augusta and Rameses had their heads together when she entered. They broke apart and looked at her. "Yo ahl right, missy?" Augusta asked.

Aware that she must appear flushed and out of breath, Sarah managed a tight smile. "I'm finc, except that I seem to be more tired than I thought. I'll check on the cabins some other time."

Augusta and Rameses exchanged a quick glance. It might have been her imagination but she thought they relaxed slightly. "Dat a good idea, missy," Rameses said. "Why don' yo go sit on de veranda an' let ol' Rameses bring yo a nice cool drink?"

Tempted though she was to agree, Sarah shook her head. She needed to be alone and unobserved for a while, long enough to work out what she should do. Yet after sitting in her room for several hours, looking through the window at the fields bronzed by the setting sun and the long rows of slaves wending their way back to the quarters, she decided that the best thing would be to do nothing at all. Surely the man would be quickly gone. She could forget what she had seen.

Except that she would have to find some way to warn Marcus to be more careful. The odds were slim that some other white might happen to walk through the quarters and glance in that particular cabin, but with life and death hanging in the balance, it hardly paid to take such risks. In Philip's absence, she could not summon Marcus to the house, but she could send him a message she was certain he would understand.

Returning to the kitchen, she assured Augusta that she was feeling refreshed, then puttered around a bit, looking in various pots and commenting on how good everything smelled. Ginny had returned from the root cellar. She worked quietly at a table, peeling potatoes. Sarah sat down across from her. Ginny cast her a wary glance that was quickly masked.

"I suppose," Sarah said to the room in general, "that we should think about doing something with those empty cabins."

As one, the half-dozen women busy in the kitchen paused in their labors. Only Ginny's hands continued to move. She kept her eyes on the potatoes, but Sarah had the feeling that all the young woman's senses were straining for her next words.

"After all, we can't know when they might be needed and I happened to notice today that some of them aren't in as good repair as they ought to be. There are chinks in the walls that you can see right through."

"Yo' right, missy," Augusta said. "Somethin' needs bes done 'bout dat."

Sarah nodded. "Ginny, perhaps you could mention it to Marcus. He's good at construction and will know what to do about it."

The younger woman looked up, meeting her eyes for the first time. In a clear, steady voice, she said, "Ahs tells him tonight, missy. He takes care of it right away."

Chapter Twenty-Six

"WE GOTS TO RUN," Ginny said. "Be crazy to stay here now."

A single candle burned on the rough-hewed table where she and Marcus both sat. They had been talking for several hours, in whispers that grew increasingly tense. Ginny pleaded with him to get out while they still could. Marcus insisted that the time wasn't right. "Yo knows dere be mo' runaways headin' here right now. Wha' yo suppose happen if dey git here an' we be gone?"

"Ahs don't know," Ginny admitted, "an' tell yo de truth, Ahs don't much care, not when it be yor life at stake." She leaned closer to him, straining with the urgency of her fears. "How many yo saved jus' since Ahs knows yo? Hun'red? Two hun'red? When it gonna be enough?"

He shook his head, knowing he wouldn't be able to make her understand but driven to try nonetheless. "Neber be enough, Ginny, not till dey ahls be free."

"Dat neber happen."

"Oh, yeah, it will. Ahs cans almost smell it comin'. Freedom on de air." He smiled in the darkness. "Dem Yankees, dey might hab other reasons fo' fightin' dat got nothin' to do with us, but dat ain't gonna matter in de end." He put his hand over hers. "We free soon, sugar. Ahl ob us."

The light burning in his eyes made her hesitate to disagree with him. He wanted so much to believe in what he was telling her, and she couldn't blame him for that. Once, when she was a child, she had seen a man fall out of a boat on the river and start to drown. He had struggled for long, desperate minutes, thrashing in the water and screaming for help before someone threw him a rope. The look on his face at the moment his hands made contact with the rope and he knew he was going to live was the look she saw on Marcus now.

For the first time in his life, he had hope. Not only for himself, but for all the other people that, incalculably to her, he felt a genuine sense of kinship with. Ginny herself felt no such sense. To care for a great many other, largely anonymous people was a luxury she had never known. She hadn't even valued her own life until Marcus had taught her to, and she was fiercely devoted to protecting his. Beyond that she could not see. But he could, and she desperately feared what that would do to him.

"Yo gots to u'nerstand," she whispered. "Missy Sarah knows. She ain't stupid, wha'eber anyone wants to say 'bout white ladies. She figure out he a runaway an' yo helpin' him."

"So wha' she do 'bout it? She say anythin' to Massa Charles? No, she gib yo a message fo' me. Dats wha' it was, honey. She git yo to tell me dat she know, an' dat dere be danger somebody else maybe find ou'." When Ginny continued to look doubtful, he went on. "Don' yo see? She protectin' me."

"Why she do dat?"

"'Cause she a Yankee. She don' lahk slavery."

Ginny made a soft sound, somewhere between a snort and a laugh. "She sure don' seem to mind habin' slaves. Works us hard enough, dat no lie."

"Works pretty hard herself, an' she neber be nasty to any ob yos, is she?"

"No," Ginny admitted, "Ahs guess she not so bad, but Ahs still don' see why yo trust her lahk yo do."

Marcus hesitated. He had never told Ginny about what had happened the night of the storm, but now he felt that he had to. Quietly he described the incident when he was certain Sarah had realized that he was helping runaways.

"She keeps de secret dat long?" Ginny said. "Since 'fore she an' Massa Philip gits married?"

"Dat right, so yo see why Ahs don' think she say anythin' now."

Ginny nodded slowly. "Ahs 'pect yo right. Be mighty hard to 'plain to Massa Philip how come she didn't speak up before."

Her interpretation of Sarah's motives didn't agree with Marcus's but he let it go, recognizing the futility of trying to change her set view of all whites as inherently evil. It was enough that he had managed to calm her immediate fears. There was no further talk of escape as they settled down to rest for the few hours remaining until dawn.

SHORTLY AFTER first light, Sarah was out in the vegetable garden behind the house. She was trying to decide whether it was worth the lingering risk of a frost to begin the spring planting. If she could get even a few of the cucumber and tomato seedlings in, there would be that much less to do later. An old slave walked beside her, leaning on a stout wooden cane. In his stooped back and gnarled hands was more knowledge of how to coax new life from the soil than she would ever possess if she lived centuries.

"What do you think, Jebediah?" she asked. "Should we give it a try?"

He smiled toothlessly. "Yes'erday, Ahs sees a flock ob snow geese passin' by, missy."

Not too long ago, such a pronouncement would have baffled her, but she had learned enough to understand that few blacks ever said anything directly to whites. They were more comfortable with the protection of parable and metaphor. "So the geese believe the winter is over?"

" 'Pears dat way to me, missy. 'Course, ol' Mother Nature, she always keeps a few surprises up her sleeve."

"Let's hope that this year she'll be generous. Today we'll weed what's left of the stubble. Once that's done, we'll begin to plant."

"Yassum." Jebediah said nothing more, but he gave her a smile signifying his approval before shuffling off to round up the half-dozen youngsters who helped him.

Sarah went inside assured that the job was in good hands. Which was just as well as there were numerous others to claim her attention. Since the day promised to be warm and dry, she had decided to have the carpets aired. That required the assistance of a dozen house slaves as the carpets were moved out from under the heavy furniture, rolled up and carted outside, where they were strung over heavy ropes. Slave children would beat the dust from them with long-handled mesh paddles. To them it was a game, to Sarah it was anything but.

She was feeling sore, tired and thirsty by the time the last of the carpets was hung in place, but there was no opportunity to rest. From the earliest days of her marriage, she had set aside the midday hour to be with her stepson. No matter what else had to be done, that time was for William.

She found him in the stables with Esau, currying the Connemara pony that had been his father's gift to William the year before on his eighth birthday. The pony, one of half a dozen brought from western Ireland, were being crossed with several of Calvert Oaks's thoroughbreds in the hope that the agility and hardiness of the smaller horse would breed true. The boys were debating the merits of the effort, their strong, young voices echoing in the vast reaches of the stable.

Sarah stood for a moment looking at them. Both were tall for their age and strongly built from a lifetime of healthful activity. They moved around the horse with confidence, sharing their pleasure in him. Dust motes danced in the sunlight steamy with the aromas of straw, manure and leather. Against that golden radiance, they had a kind of timelessness that unexpectedly comforted her. She did not want to interrupt them, but the combination of habit and a genuine need for William's company drove her to do so.

When she called to him, he smiled ruefully. "I forgot, didn't I? It's dinnertime?"

"That's right. Come and wash up now."

He said a quick word to Esau and handed him the currying comb, then hurried to join her. As they emerged from the shadows of the stable Sarah glanced at him. Each day William seemed to grow more like his father. Though their coloring was different, their features and expressions were identical. William had lately even begun to walk like Philip, his long legs eating up the ground so that she had to hurry to keep up with him.

They lunched on the veranda at a table set for two, waited upon by Rameses and a young house slave he was grooming to eventually take his place. As always, William fidgeted for a few minutes after they sat down. His energy was such that it was difficult for him to stay in one place very long. But he quieted after a while and obligingly told Sarah about his day.

"Esau and me, we went down to..."

"Esau and I," she corrected gently.

"Sorry. Esau and I went down to the river. Saw three barges going by, heading for Richmond, I figure. Bet they had guns on them."

Sarah stopped in the midst of buttering a roll. "Why do you say that?"

"'Cause there's going to be a war, of course." He smiled broadly, relishing the thought, only to abruptly remember to whom he was speaking. With one of those flashes of sensitivity she was beginning to see in him more and more, he said, "I guess it must be pretty hard to be a Northerner living in the South right now."

"There are certain problems," she admitted. "But I'm hoping everything will calm down soon."

"You don't think there'll be any war?"

He looked so disappointed that she was tempted to laugh, except that the implications of his eagerness had not escaped her. Were he only a few years older, he could easily be caught up in any fighting that might occur. The mere thought of that filled her with such dread that she put her fork down and looked at him earnestly.

"William, I pray there won't be. It would be terrible for everyone, both North and South. Many good men would die."

"I suppose there would be a chance of that, but it wouldn't last long, and then we could all be friends again."

"Is that what your father has told you?"

William frowned. He shook his head slowly. "No, Father's said very little, but I suppose he wouldn't be in Richmond right now if he didn't care about what was happening."

"Of course he cares. He's doing his best to help find a peaceful solution."

"Then I suppose there won't be a war." William's absolute faith in his father clashed briefly with his hunger for excitement. Reluctantly he put aside his imagined scenes of glory. "Father is right, of course. War would disrupt the planting."

"And do a great deal more besides." Sarah hesitated, not sure how much to say to him but knowing that she could not leave him with the impression that everything was settled. Finally she said, "There are other men like your father—planters, merchants, politicians—who are trying to bring about some sort of compromise. The problem is that they may not succeed."

The thought that his father might fail had clearly never occurred to William. He stared at her in astonishment. "You mean there may be a war after all?"

"Yes...I think there may be. That's why we've been so busy here the past few weeks stockpiling supplies. Not," she added quickly, "that I think they'll really be needed."

He was mulling that over, in between bites of chicken and gravy, when Sarah suddenly stiffened. Far off, down the long road that ran to the main gates of Calvert Oaks, a dust cloud was moving. Riders.

She jumped to her feet, William with her. "Father," he said eagerly, starting down the veranda.

"Wait." She held out a hand to stop him, without knowing exactly why. Except that Philip's letter had made it clear he wouldn't be home for several days yet. These visitors, whoever they were, were unexpected.

And unwelcomed. That much was certain as soon as they came close enough to be recognized. The thin, grimy man in the lead was familiar to Sarah; she had seen him only once before but his identity was burned on her brain. As was that of the men who rode with him. Slave catchers.

She turned to Rameses. "Go into the house. Tell Massa Charles who's come."

Glad enough to get away, he trotted for the door. Sarah had turned toward the riders. She heard William's gasp before she realized what had prompted it. Behind the horses, strung out on ropes tied to several of the saddles, was a long, dust-covered bundle. She was wondering what anyone would choose to transport so carelessly when the reality of what she was looking at roared through her mind.

"Oh, my God..."

"Get back," William said, in a voice she had never heard him use before. Deeper and more assured. So much like his father's that it sent a tremor through her. Before she could respond he had stepped in front of her. "What do you want?" he demanded as the slave catchers drew rein beside the veranda. The dark bundle did not move.

"Where's your daddy, boy?" their leader demanded. "We got business with him."

Sarah was about to blurt out that he wasn't there when the press of William's hand on her arm stopped her. "He'll be here. I asked you what you want."

"An' I told you. We got business here. Slave-catchin' business."

"We have no missing slaves."

The man leaned forward in his saddle, grinning around blackened teeth. "Pretty sure 'bout that, ain't you, boy?" As he spoke he gestured to the other riders, several of whom dismounted and went toward the bundle. They kicked it over.

Sarah moaned deep in her throat and clutched hold of William as she fought the urge to vomit. The young black man had died in agony, that much was clear. His body was covered with welts deep enough to show the white glint of bone. His eyes had been gouged out, and he had been castrated.

William recovered first, at least enough to speak. *"How dare you bring that thing here? Get the hell off our land before we..."*

"You what, boy?" the man demanded, idly fondling the rifle that had appeared in his hand. Similar weapons were held by the others. This time at least, they were not going to be taken by surprise.

"What's the meaning of this?" Charles Calvert demanded. He had been wheeled to the door in his chair, where he sat glaring at the men. Despite the incapacity of his body, he still radiated a fierce sense of power and outrage that should have sent them scurrying. And would have, if they hadn't been so certain of their purpose.

"This here nigger," their leader said, gesturing to the dead man, "before he went to his reward, he done some talking. Seems he was here last night, in a cabin in your slave quarters. Your slaves sheltered him, like they be doing many another. We knowed for a long time that somebody in these parts was helping runaways, an' now we finally found out who." He paused for a moment to assure that he had everyone's full attention, then said, "Give us the buck called Marcus an' we be on our way."

"No!" Ginny slapped a hand to her mouth too late to stop her hoarse cry. She had come out of the kitchen to see what was happening and had been frozen in place by the sight of the dead slave whom, despite his terrible injuries, she recognized as the man they had sheltered the night before. The mention of her husband, and the brutal intent written clearly on the faces of the slave catchers, galvanized her into action. Before anyone could make a move to stop her, she picked up her skirts and raced toward the fields where she knew Marcus was working.

"After her," the leader shouted. "She gonna warn that buck an' he'll run for it." The men spurred their horses and galloped off, the obscene bundle dragging behind them.

"You have no right," Charles yelled, trying in vain to raise from his chair. The effort left him shaking and breathless, his face ashen and his hands clenched futilely. Sarah was about to go to him when she was distracted by William. He was running toward the stables.

"Go after him," Charles gasped. "Don't let him see this."

But by the time Sarah reached the stables, William had already shot past her. She had to wait through seemingly endless minutes while a slave saddled her own mount. Even as she started after William, calling his name, she knew she would not reach him in time.

Halfway to the fields, she passed Ginny lying in the dirt. Her face was bruised and she was crying brokenly. Sarah paused, torn between the need to go on and the desire to stop and offer what comfort she could. As she hesitated, Ginny looked up. Their eyes met for a moment. On impulse, Sarah held out her arm. "Come on."

Ginny staggered to her feet, grasped the offered hand and pulled herself into the saddle. Her arms around Sarah's waist, they galloped off.

With the fields so large and so spread out, they had no way of knowing exactly where Marcus was. But they found him by following the swirling clouds of dust, the angry shouts and the fearful cries of the other slaves huddled together, staring in terror at the slave catchers.

Overseer Davies, his face red, stood confronting the mounted men. William was beside him. Neither was armed, except for the pistol Davies carried, which held only a single round.

"What the hell you mean coming here an' telling me to give you a slave?" Davies was demanding as Sarah and Ginny rode up. "This here is Calvert property. You've got no call to touch any of it."

"We do this time," the leader said, "an' there ain't nothin' on earth gonna stop us. That buck—" he pointed a bony finger at Marcus "—been helping runaways. We caught him dead to rights an' we gonna see justice done."

Ginny slid from the horse and ran to her husband. His stoic control broke when he saw her, but he regained it quickly as he put an arm around her shaking shoulders and drew her close, trying vainly to comfort her.

Sarah remained in the saddle, not trusting her legs to hold her. A sickening sense of dread knotted her stomach. Several of the other slaves found their courage and stepped closer to Marcus, only to be gestured back by him.

"This true?" Davies demanded, turning to him.

Before he could answer, William spoke up. "Whether it is or not, these men have no right to take him. At the very least, they must wait until my father returns and says what he wants done."

"Ain't but one thing he could want," the slave catcher said. "Nigger been helpin' runaways, he dies. No question 'bout that."

"You can't do this," Sarah said, finding her voice at last. "Guilty or not, he has a right to a trial."

The men, slave catchers and overseer alike, stared at her blankly. "Best go back to the house, Miz Calvert," Davies said quietly.

"No, I won't do it. You can't let this happen..."

Several of the slave catchers were dismounting while the others kept their guns trained on the slaves. They grabbed hold of Marcus roughly and dragged him toward the horses.

Ginny screamed and threw herself at them, only to be knocked to the ground. A rope was looped around Marcus's wrists and pulled taut. "You goin' for a ride, boy," one of the men said. The other end of the rope was handed to the leader, who tied it to his saddle pommel.

William tried to seize hold of it but was pulled back by Davies. "Ain't nothin' you can do, son," he said quietly. "They gonna take him."

Marcus cast a last anguished look at Ginny who had gotten to her feet. Something passed between them, silent, powerful, intimately their own. She straightened her shoulders and stood dry-eyed. One of the other slaves, a woman, went to her and put an arm around her.

The slave catcher lifted his hand, brought it down hard. His horse leaped forward. The rope strung out taut. Marcus managed to stay upright for several minutes by running, until he stumbled on the rough ground and went down on his face, to be dragged alongside the dead man.

Ginny moaned and swayed against the woman holding her. William stood frozen in anguished disbelief. Only Sarah moved. She turned her horse around and dug her heels into its side. The mare took her head, nostrils flaring widely, and raced for the road. Away from Calvert Oaks.

Chapter Twenty-Seven

THE WOMAN WHO RODE into Richmond little more than an hour later bore scant resemblance to anyone's idea of a proper Southern lady. Hatless and dust covered, her skirt in tatters and both shoes lost, Sarah dismounted in front of the hotel where she knew Philip was staying. She was amazed that she had managed to stay in the saddle throughout the wild ride and did not want to think about how she was going to feel in a few hours. Ignoring the startled glances of passersby, she tied her exhausted horse's reins to the railing and hurried inside.

The lobby was crowded with an unusual number of excited-looking men in intense conversation. Sarah plunged through them toward the desk, where the clerk took one look at her, blinked in disbelief and dropped his pen. "We don't . . . that is, you can't . . ." Recovering himself somewhat, he said stiffly, "This is a proper hotel."

"I'm glad to hear it," Sarah said, "since my husband is a guest. His name is Philip Calvert. I must see him at once."

"Your husband . . . ? But . . . ?"

"Are you hard-of-hearing? I said at once. This is an emergency and I assure you, he won't thank you for keeping me waiting."

Her autocratic manner, at odds with her ragamuffin appearance, so bewildered the man that he seemed incapable of any response at all. With a snort of impatience, Sarah grabbed hold of the registration book, flipped it around and quickly scanned the pages.

"P. Calvert," she murmured as she traced the familiar handwriting over to the next column. "Room 32."

"You can't go up there," the man protested, finally recovering himself. "How do I know you are who you say? This is a proper hotel..."

He spoke to Sarah's back. She ran up the stairs without pause, reaching the third floor out of breath. From the landing, twin corridors stretched out in either direction, with dozens of doorways at regular intervals.

"Twenty-seven..." she gasped as she hurried past, "twenty-eight..." Room 32 was at the end of the hall, on the side of the hall that looked out toward the river. She banged frantically on the door. *"Philip, it's me. Oh, God, please be here."*

The door was flung open by her startled husband, wearing a dressing gown and with his hair still damp from a bath.

"Sarah... what on earth...?"

She pushed past him into the room and stumbled against a heavy oak chair. Instantly Philip took hold of her. She was shaking so hard that he feared that she was on the verge of collapse. "Sarah, what's wrong? Tell me!"

"It's Marcus," she gasped, between tortured breaths. "The slave catchers came... they found out about him helping runaways... they took him away." Her composure, what little of it was left, broke and she cried out piteously. "Oh, Philip, we couldn't stop them! They're going to kill him. You must do something."

Grim-faced, he lowered her into the chair. "Stay there. I'll be right back." She heard him moving around in the dressing room, throwing on clothes. Moments later he returned. "Don't leave this room, Sarah, until I send someone for you."

"I'm coming with you," she insisted, pushing herself to her feet.

"No, you're not. It's bad enough that you're involved this much. I won't have you go any further."

She would have argued, but he stopped her peremptorily. "There's no time to discuss it. You'll do as I say. I'll try to send someone before nightfall."

Then he was gone, the door slamming shut behind him. She was left in the suddenly quiet room with only her frantic heartbeat to drown out her tormented thoughts.

Sarah stayed in the room for half an hour, until her breathing returned to normal and she felt able to stand without falling. Even so, she rose from the chair carefully, as an invalid might, and crossed to the door with one hand bracing herself against the wall.

The desk clerk paled when he saw her approaching again. "I'm very sorry about the misunderstanding, Miz Calvert. Your husband said . . ."

"Never mind. My horse, she needs looking after."

"Already taken care of, ma'am." He eyed her cautiously. "If I might suggest a nice cold drink and a bath . . ."

"I need to rent a carriage." Determined though she was, she was also realistic enough to know that she couldn't make the trip again on horseback. "You can put the charge on my husband's bill."

"He didn't indicate anything about . . ."

"Please." She managed a faintly apologetic smile. "I know this must all seem terribly strange to you, but if you'll just be kind enough to assist me in this little matter, I'll be on my way. Otherwise . . ." She left that dangling, deliberately giving him the impression that she was prepared to remain in the lobby, in her disreputable state, until he saw the light.

"Of course," he said, "I'll take care of it right away. Will you require a driver?" Normally Sarah knew he would never have asked. No lady could be expected to drive a carriage herself. But he was apparently beyond being surprised by anything she might choose to do.

"No, I can manage fine." The fewer people who knew what was happening at Calvert Oaks, the better. She wished she didn't have to know herself. The reality of it was only beginning to set in, and with it a terrible rage beyond any she had known in all the years since her mother's death.

NO SLAVES WERE IN SIGHT as Philip rode up to Calvert Oaks, and nothing moved in the quarters or beyond. He swung off his lathered horse and looked around quickly. "Davies, William, where the hell is everyone?"

"Here, Father." His son looked out from an upstairs window. "You'd best come up."

"I can't. There's no time."

"It's Grandfather."

Philip took the stairs two at a time. He found his father stretched out on the bed, Augusta and Rameses at his side. Charles Calvert's face was ashen, his features seemed to have collapsed in on themselves. Only his wide, unblinking eyes still held a spark of life.

"Somethin' happen to him, suh," Rameses said softly, "when Mistah Davies come to say dos men done take Marcus. Massa Charles cry out an' grab hol' ob hiz head, lahk him habin' a terrible pain. Then he jus' keel over lahk. Hasn't moved o' said a word since."

Philip knelt beside his father and took his hand in his. The skin was cold, as though he already touched a corpse. "F-Father..."

"Ain't nothin' yo can do fo' him, massah," Augusta said softly. "Up to de good Lord now."

But there was something Philip could do, and he saw in his father's eyes the will that he act. Getting to his feet, he laid the older man's hand gently back on the mattress. "William, stay with him."

"I want to go with you."

"No!" Not for anything would he let the boy witness this. To soften the order, he added, "Someone has to take charge of things here."

Somewhat mollified, though by no means entirely, William nodded. Philip gave him a quick, reassuring smile that he was far from truly feeling before he hurried from the room.

The unnatural quiet of the quarters extended to the stables, where the jockeys and trainers had gone to ground. With some difficulty Philip flushed them out and got them armed and mounted. They were clearly reluctant to ride with him, until he spoke to them in blunt terms he was certain they could understand.

"There is a matter of justice involved here. Whatever Marcus has done, I cannot permit white trash to come onto my land and take my property. It's as simple as that. Why if we let this go by, next thing we know they'll be saying they have a right to steal our horses.''

That got to the men, as nothing else could. They straightened in their saddles, the scent of battle egging them on. The slave catchers had left a trail of broken branches and flattened earth. Philip and the other men followed it in silence, each knowing full well what he was liable to encounter at the end. The last hundred yards or so, they were spurred on by the rhythmic sound of a whip striking flesh and the cheers of drunken voices.

Philip pulled his rifle from his saddle and cocked it. ''We go in firing, two rounds at the sky. But if any of them moves, blow his head off.''

There were a dozen men in the clearing. They were passing around a keg of moonshine and taking turns with the whip. At the sight of the armed riders and the bursts of gunfire, they froze in place, only dimly understanding what was happening.

Philip didn't want to look at what was tied to the tree. He took a deep breath before forcing himself to. Marcus had been stripped to the waist, his arms stretched out above him and looped to a high branch. Another rope had been secured around his neck, and that one was tied to the trunk. Each time he tried to jerk away from the whip, he came close to strangling.

And the whip had fallen many times. It was impossible to estimate how many lashes he had taken. The flesh hung from his back in tattered ribbons. Blood soaked the ground at his feet. Philip swallowed against the bile burning his throat. He slid out of the saddle and crossed the small distance. His hand trembled as he cut Marcus down, catching him in his arms as he fell.

Mercifully, he was unconscious. Settling him to the ground, Philip looked up at the men gathered around in various attitudes of surprise and bewilderment. His eyes fell on the leader of the slave catchers who swayed as he stared back belligerently. Moonshine ran from his mouth. He wiped it away with a bloodstained hand. "Wha' t'hell you think you're doing, interruptin' us?"

Philip got to his feet. He gestured to one of his men to throw a blanket over Marcus. Slowly he advanced on the slave catcher who, with the false courage of the drunkard, did not have the sense to run.

"Goddamn you," Philip said. "You and all the scum like you."

"You ain't got no call to..."

"I could kill you, happily. Do you understand that? I could kill you with my bare hands."

For the first time the man had the sense to look alarmed. He began to back away. "I got friends here..."

Philip's hand lashed out, seizing him by the throat. He lifted him off his feet, where he dangled in the air, croaking frantically. "You're the worst part of us," he said to his uncomprehending foe. "What's led us to the very gates of hell." His hand tightened.

His own men looked at each other nervously. They had come to see justice done, but they didn't hold with killing a white man because he had whipped a slave. Gingerly one of them took a step forward. "Suh..."

Philip didn't hear him. All his attention was concentrated on the man he gripped relentlessly. The slave catcher's eyes were opened so wide that they threatened to pop out of his head. His mouth was agape in a silent scream. As Philip watched, his skin began to turn blue.

Abruptly he let go of him. The man fell to the ground moaning even as Philip's own men breathed a collective sigh of relief. "Why should you be spared what's coming?" Philip whispered hoarsely. "None of us will be." He stared down at the cringing man, then up at the others watching mutely as dumb animals. "Get away from here. Put as much distance between yourselves and Calvert Oaks as you possibly can. If I ever see any of you around here again or even catch a whiff of your rancid scents, I'll hunt you down like the filth you are and leave your carcasses to rot."

Without looking to see if they obeyed, he bent and lifted Marcus gently in his arms. The other man's weight was equal to his own, but he carried his burden alone, refusing all offers of help. And he continued to hold his brother throughout the long ride back to the house, his tears mingling with the long rivulets of blood that stained them both.

Sarah was waiting when he returned. She stood in front of the house with Ginny at her side. William had told her the news about her father-in-law. She had been up to see him briefly before taking up her vigil on the veranda. As the riders neared, the two women went to meet them.

Ginny didn't make a sound as Marcus was lifted from the saddle into the arms of two waiting men, who carried him carefully into the house. She bit her lower lip and twisted her apron so tightly that it almost ripped away, but otherwise there was no outward sign of her horror.

Philip wasn't fooled by that. He reached out a hand to her but let it drop when she shied away, staring at him with hatred so profound that he could not bring himself to meet her eyes for longer than an instant. Yet that was long enough to see her thoughts. To her, he wasn't the man who had saved her husband, if indeed rescue had come in time. He was simply another white, whom she now had more reason than ever to loath.

"He'll have the best care, Ginny," Philip said gently.

She took a deep breath and said what she instinctively knew would hurt him most. A cold, mocking light shone in her eyes. "Yassuh, massa."

Never had the words been meant as more of an insult, and Philip knew it. He shook himself, as though to cast off pain beyond bearing. "Damn it, it wasn't my fault..."

"Yassuh, massa."

"If I had been here, I would have stopped them."

"Yassuh, massa."

"God damn you! He betrayed me! I trusted him and all this time he was making a fool of me!"

About to reach out to him, Sarah froze. What was he saying? "Philip, you knew..."

He turned on her, welcoming any outlet for his anger. "About the runaways? No, I didn't." Half-remembered words echoed in his mind, like the sound of a key turning in a lock. "But you did. At the hotel, you said they'd found out about him. You weren't the least bit surprised." His hands shot out, seizing her by the shoulders. "When did you find out, Sarah? How long have you known?"

"I don't understand," she said as he shook her. "You must have known." She couldn't be hearing this. She had fallen in love with him, had married him, because she believed he was an honorable man fighting the best way he could against a terrible system. Had it all been a terrible mistake?

"I would have stopped him if I'd known," Philip said. "This would never have happened."

"Yo couldn't hab stopped him." Ginny's voice rang clear in the gathering dusk. Nothing else could have jarred Philip and Sarah from their private anguish. They stood stock-still, looking at her. "Ain't no man could stop him, no woman neither. Ahs tried. Freedom eb'rythin' to Marcus. Only way to stop him was kill him." Her voice fell, low and somber as the grave. "Maybe somebody done dat fo' yo.'"

Philip's hands slowly dropped away from his wife. Anger drained from him. In its place was nothing but a great emptiness. He had seen the look in Sarah's eyes when she realized he hadn't known what Marcus was doing. Though he didn't fully understand what that meant to her, he suspected enough to understand that something had changed radically between them. For his part, too, because he could not reconcile what he had thought he knew of her with the fact that she had kept such a secret from him.

The very earth seemed to be cracking open beneath his feet. The foundation of his life, all the principles and beliefs by which he had lived, were being buffeted by a great force no man could understand or control. He felt a yawning maw before him and knew that he was about to fall into it.

Without looking at either woman, he walked up the steps into the house and disappeared into the library.

Sarah found him there an hour later, when she came down from helping care for Marcus. In addition to the injuries from the whipping, which were bad enough to have killed most men, he had numerous bruises and cuts from being dragged behind the horses. Two ribs were broken and she thought that he might have a concussion. But more serious than any of that was the possibility of damage to vital organs aggravated by infection. Ginny had informed her that it was not uncommon for a man who had been whipped so severely to die from kidney failure or any of numerous other causes. Only time would tell whether or not Marcus was to escape that fate.

Meanwhile, there was Philip to deal with. Like it or not, she couldn't simply leave things as they were between them. He was, after all, her husband, and he had some right to be upset by her failure to confide in him. She was prepared to tell him that she was sorry, but the words died in her throat as she stepped into the library and found him going through his desk, tossing things into a satchel.

"What are you doing?" she asked.

He didn't stop or look up. "Packing."

"Why?"

"I have to go back to Richmond tonight."

She shook her head. "You said you'd only be there a few more days. Why do you need those things?" He was taking his journal, a leather box holding pen and ink, writing paper and a small locket she recognized as holding a miniature of his mother and another of herself, added a few months after they were married.

He stopped at last and snapped the case shut. The sorrow in his eyes almost overwhelmed her. She thought at first that it was for Marcus, only to realize when he spoke that his anguish for his brother was only a part of a far larger sorrow.

"Fort Sumter was attacked today. The war has begun."

Chapter Twenty-Eight

IN THE LOBBY of the Richmond Hotel, men in frock coats and deerskins, in the elaborate uniforms of private regiments and in the rough homespun of simple farmers jostled one another indiscriminately. They stood in clusters of two or three, sometimes more, talking so loudly that no one could be heard above a shout. Messenger boys hurried among them, delivering notes of undoubted importance that were perused gravely before being shared with the assembled company. A constant stream of new arrivals crowded around the reception desk, beseeching the harried clerk to find room for them.

Philip stopped inside the entrance, knocking the dust of the road from his hat, and glanced around. The hustle and bustle, the nonstop excitement, the constant air of momentous events occurring should have been intoxicating. He found them merely wearying and looked forward to nothing more ambitious than a hot bath and a long drink.

He had been traveling for some two months, since shortly after his abrupt departure from Calvert Oaks. Barely had he returned to the city than he had been asked by Judge Rider, acting at the personal behest of President Jefferson Davis, to undertake a survey of the South's military stores. He suspected the judge himself of engineering the request; word of what had happened at Calvert Oaks had spread quickly and the older man undoubtedly thought it wise to remove him from a delicate, dangerous situation. Philip had been tempted to refuse, but in the end could not bring himself to do so, if only because he believed the job really did need to be done and that he would do it fairly.

At the time, he had not guessed how difficult the task would prove. Now he knew, and he was not looking forward to the report he would shortly have to make. Thoughts of the bath and the drink spurred him toward the desk. He was girding himself to work through the crowd when a hand reached out to grasp his arm.

"Philip, you're back," Peter Rider exclaimed. Resplendent in a gray uniform with captain's bars on his shoulders, he looked fit, eager and determined. A sharp contrast to Philip's road-stained civilian attire and air of weariness. "You're just in time. There's a meeting you should be at." He grasped his friend's arm and started toward the door.

"Hold up," Philip said, not moving. "I've already got plans for this evening, and they don't include sitting around a smoke-filled room listening to more talk of how easily we're winning the war. Besides," he added more gently, "I've got a report to prepare."

Peter stopped and looked at him more closely. What he saw gave him pause. Harsh lines were etched into Philip's face, his blue eyes had a harshness not seen before and his weariness seemed to come from somewhere so deep inside him that it had to touch his soul.

"Was it a bad trip?" Peter asked quietly.

Philip sighed. "Let's just say that I suspect myself of being more the odd man out now than ever. You know I didn't want this war in the first place, and after having seen what we actually have to work with, I'm even less enthused."

"Is that what you will tell Davis?"

"I must. To give him other than my most truthful judgment would be to fail in my commission." His one meeting with the Confederate president, in Montgomery, Alabama, during the time when the capital was in the process of being moved to Richmond, had been very brief. But Davis had left the clear impression that he wanted Philip to help evaluate the South's stock of war material precisely because he knew he was not rabidly prowar and therefore could be trusted to give an objective appraisal. Nonetheless, Philip didn't fool himself about what reception his report would get. With war fever running higher than ever, his somber assessment was not likely to be welcome.

"The meeting isn't really all that important," Peter said. "Besides, all we seem to do these days is talk. What do you say to some supper instead?"

That was far more appealing to Philip, particularly because he had not been looking forward to being left alone with his own thoughts. Since setting out on his trip for Davis, he had done his best to keep from dwelling on the events at Calvert Oaks. They were an unhealed wound that needed only the slightest probing to become exquisitely painful.

Before his departure he had sent a stiffly worded letter to Sarah giving instructions for what he expected to be done in his absence. It was the sort of letter he might have written to a business factor or possibly a servant. There was nothing in the least personal about it, no trace of emotion be it anger or hurt, forgiveness or understanding. Since then they had corresponded several times, her letters catching up with him as he moved from city to city. They were as devoid of feeling as his own.

Peter studied his friend with some concern when they were seated at a table in a corner, as far from the bar as they could get. The rowdy crowd gathered there to drink, sing war songs and retell for the thousandth time the details of the victory at Fort Sumter did not appeal to either of them. Both were silent until after the waiter had taken their orders and returned with a bottle of bourbon and two glasses.

Pouring for them both, Peter said, "It must have been difficult for you to be away from home just now."

Philip downed half his drink in a single swallow before deciding that it was foolish to try to deny what must be well-known. "I have to return there soon, to try to settle matters."

"Have you decided what you will do?"

"I'm not going to hang him, if that's what you mean. Marcus has already been punished for what he did." Sarah's letters had indicated that his brother was recovering, though slowly. That he lived at all was miraculous.

"There is some sympathy for your position," Peter said slowly. At Philip's surprised look, he went on. "The slave catchers took too much on themselves when they acted without your approval. Also no one knows for sure how many runaways Marcus helped. Some want to blame him for every slave lost going back twenty years, but they are in the minority. Most prefer to believe he was caught the first time he tried it. Given all that and the fact of your father's stroke, you might get away with simply selling him."

Philip finished his drink and reached for the bottle. "I'm not going to do that, either." At Peter's start of surprise, he said, "What good does it do me to sell him at a loss so that he can die in some damn cane field? He's of far better use right where he is."

Plates of mutton and potatoes were put in front of them, along with a wooden tray holding a yellow round of cheese and a fresh baked loaf of bread. Both men fell to eating with scant attention to the food.

"You realize," Peter said, "that you are plowing a hard road for yourself. Between the trouble with Marcus and the report you intend giving to Davis..."

"What does one have to do with the other?" Philip asked, though he had a clear enough idea.

"Nothing directly, except that both set you apart from the general way of doing and looking at things. It is unheard of to keep a slave who has committed such a serious crime, and it is—to say the least—unfashionable to believe that the South will not trounce the North within a matter of months."

Philip took another drink, noting that his throat had become pleasantly numb to the raw bourbon. He was tempted to keep drinking until that insensibility spread through his body and mind. Only the knowledge that the relief would be temporary kept him from immediately ordering another bottle. "As to Marcus, can you tell me honestly that were you in my position, you would condemn him to death?"

Peter hesitated. He knew perfectly well the relationship between Philip and the slave; no one who had ever seen the two of them could be ignorant of it. But such things were not discussed openly. "I don't know," he admitted at length. "Pray God I am never faced with such a problem."

"But if you were?" Philip persisted. He knew he was treading on dangerous ground, but the impetus was too great to stop. "Mulattos, quadroons, octoroons, there are more of each every year. The mathematics of ancestry has become the hand of fate. Do you know what I ask myself these days? What if I had been born Marcus and he had been born me? Would I have simply accepted my lot in life, or would I have found some way to fight against it?"

"You can't put yourself in the position of a slave," Peter insisted, startled by the very notion. "The gulf between us is too great."

"Is it? Marcus is a man, like me. He laughs, cries, desires, loves...hates." Philip's eyes darkened with remembered pain. "I can certainly testify to the fact that he bleeds, and that the color of that blood is no different from the color of my own."

"Don't talk like this. It's one thing to have some doubts about slavery. Who among us hasn't at one time or another? But to even suggest that blacks and whites are the same..."

"I'm not saying that. Of course there are differences between us, but I wonder how many are truly inherent and how many are the result of the different ways we live."

The bourbon was beginning to go to his head, or was it to his tongue? He pushed aside the half-empty plate and leaned his elbows on the table. "Let me tell you something. One summer, when I was about twelve and Marcus was fourteen, we ran away from Calvert Oaks. It was an adventure, a lark. We stowed away on a barge that had stopped to load cotton. The point is, we were both so tanned and the sun had streaked Marcus's hair, that we looked more alike than ever. We talked the same, and I guess we had a certain air of confidence about us. Anyway, we pretended that we really were nothing other than brothers, and no one questioned that. We got as far as Williamsburg before father caught up with us. He found us in a tavern there where we'd gotten work tending the horses. When he realized what had been going on—that Marcus had been passing for white—he took him aside. I'll never forget what he said to him.''

He paused, long enough to swallow another shot of bourbon. "He asked him if he wanted to keep going. There were ships out of Norfolk that would have taken him north. Father offered to give him enough money to get started in a new life.''

"Why didn't he take it?''

"He was tempted to, no doubt about that. I've never seen a man struggle with such temptation as Marcus did then. But finally he told father that he couldn't do it.''

"Why not?''

"Because it was too easy.''

Peter frowned and reached for the bottle, as though it might contain a glimmer of comprehension. "I don't understand.''

"Neither did I, at first, but father did. He didn't say another word all the way home. A week later, when Marcus said he wanted to move out of the house into the quarters, father let him go. I was crushed; I couldn't figure out why he wanted to be one of 'them' instead of one of 'us.' ''

"Why did he?''

"I figured it out finally, when I found him hanging from that damn tree. It was because he felt a sense of obligation, of responsibility, to help those who, unlike him, had no escape from slavery. He couldn't simply turn his back on them and walk away. We talk about loyalty and honor being the cornerstones of our lives. Marcus has both in ample measure."

Which was the crux of his problem. How could he kill a man whom he aspired to be like? How, more to the point, could he end the life of one who, twisted though it seemed, he envied? Marcus believed in something, enough to risk even his dreams for it. Philip desperately wanted that same kind of faith to strengthen him against the darkness he saw coming. But he did not have it, and he felt its absence keenly.

"I must go home," he said quietly. "I must see Sarah, try to resolve this with her."

"What has Sarah to do with it?"

"Nothing. She is only my wife."

Peter did not understand him, but he had the sense to recognize that such a rueful acknowledgment of the self-evident should not be pursued. Instead, he and Philip finished the bottle, along with the meal, then went for a walk to clear their heads. They passed a brothel and briefly considered going in, but decided against it. Only, they told each other, because they had to be up early the following morning.

Lying in perfect accord, as only good friends can, they made their way back to the hotel, where the crowd round the bar was whipping up for yet another rendition of "Dixie." Philip fell asleep with the defiant words echoing in his mind: "In Dixie land I'll take my stand, to lib an' die in Dixie."

His head hurt only moderately the next morning as he delivered his report to Jefferson Davis. He was surprised to see the president himself, having expected to be shunted aside to a lesser being, but Davis apparently liked to deal with certain matters himself rather than risk having them misinterpreted for him.

The man chosen to lead the Confederacy was something of an enigma to Philip. Reserved in manner, severe in outlook, Davis lacked the exuberant, virile excesses of much of the planter class. He was slightly built, almost blind in one eye, and known to be prone to severe bouts of neuralgia. Hardly the stuff of a great warrior, yet in his square jaw and firm mouth Philip saw a stubbornness he hoped would not prove insurmountable.

"Let me see if I understand you," Davis said after Philip had finished summing up his findings. "You believe the Southland is vulnerable on every level of military preparedness, from grain for our horses to bullets for our guns. You believe we lack the might for an extended war and that if we are still fighting a year from now, we will be in extremely grave straits. Is that accurate?"

"Yes, sir," Philip said. He shifted uneasily in his chair. It was unfortunate that they were not meeting alone. The other men gathered around the table looked by turns skeptical and derisive. Only a very few seemed to be giving any serious consideration to what he had said.

"Need I remind you," Davis said, "that we captured Fort Sumter without difficulty and that we will shortly be marching on Washington? The Army of the Potomac is in disarray. Lincoln's call for volunteers has burdened him with a force of untried, untrained amateurs. His cabinet is divided against him, even his most fervent supporters question his strategy, presuming that he even has one. Nothing, absolutely nothing indicates that the South will have any difficulty winning."

"Nothing, sir," Philip said, "except the possibility that the North will be able to hold out long enough to organize itself and turn its might against us."

"Then, sir, we shall have to make sure that doesn't happen," said a smiling, bearded man seated near the head of the table. Philip did not know Robert E. Lee personally, but he did know that he was highly spoken of and that his loyalty to the South, particularly to his native Virginia, had come as a great relief to those who feared that he might accept command of the Union Army. It was well-known that he had been offered it in April immediately before his departure from Washington. Had he accepted, not a few were certain that the South would have lost an unusually able officer and gained a deadly foe.

"Tell me," Lee said, "if you had to cite what you regard as our greatest need, what would it be?"

"Guns, sir," Philip said without hesitation. "Guns and ammunition. We can tighten our belts, live on short rations, even kill our breeding stock if we must. But we cannot win this war without sufficient weaponry, and the fact is that we produce very little of it. All the major armaments factories are in the North or in Europe."

"And how," Davis continued, leaning forward in his high-backed chair, "should we arm ourselves?"

"Europe needs cotton. We can trade it for rifles, pistols, cannon and shot. At the same time, we will be starving the Northern mills, and give the Yankees all the more reason to make peace."

"Not a bad idea," Davis agreed, "but there are those of us who feel our cotton can be better used by withholding it from all markets."

"I don't follow you, sir..."

Davis frowned; he did not like to be contradicted, even by the suggestion that what he said wasn't immediately clear. "It isn't very complicated. We want Britain and France to put pressure on the North to settle quickly. What better way than to deny them the cotton they need?"

Philip shook his head. He wasn't sure that he had heard correctly. "Not sell our cotton . . . ?"

"Precisely. It is the best weapon we have, and it would be a shame to squander it."

"But Britain and France will not support us unless they believe we can win."

"Of that," Davis said conclusively, "we will shortly assure them."

Peter put a hand on Philip's arm. The meeting was at an end. Outside in the corridor, Philip shook off his friend's restraining touch. He was angry and upset, and in no mood to listen to reason. "They're crazy! We have a chance, right now, to make ourselves strong enough to win. But they're going to throw it away."

"Easy," Peter said as he steered him toward the stairs. The corridor outside Davis's office was crowded with people hoping to see him. They were receiving far too many curious stares. "This has been very carefully thought out. You'll see, it will work."

"You can't really believe that," Philip insisted. "You're a soldier, you must see the value of being well armed."

"Of course, but as a soldier, I know that there are other ways to get guns besides buying them. Once we begin to meet the Yankee in battle, we will have a ready supply of all the armaments we can carry."

"By robbing their dead?"

Peter flushed. "From time immemorial, the victor has taken the weapons of the defeated. They would do the same to us without hesitation."

Philip looked at him for a long moment, his face grim. "Then pray that they do not, my friend. We have both very little to lose and far too much."

"We won't," Peter said gently. They were out on the street again, surrounded by the noise, heat and smell of the war capital. Wagons carrying eager new recruits rumbled by. Men on horseback shouted the latest news to each other. Ladies in bonnets and hoop skirts, their black maids in tow, clustered on the corners to cheer the warriors on. Lovely young belles, giggling excitedly, were shepherded along by eagle-eyed chaperons.

Philip took a deep breath. He wanted so badly to be part of it all, to feel the heady confidence and excitement, to know that victory—and vindication—were within grasp. But he could not. Too clearly he remembered all that he had seen and heard in his recent travels.

The Southland was not the mighty bastion these people imagined. It was a pastoral land built on fertile earth and plentiful labor, most of it slave, and it wanted nothing so much as to remain that way. In a world in which men spoke glibly of spanning continents with rail and wire, taming the mysterious forces of nature and bending them to their will, it was an anachronism.

Yet one that he loved and yearned to protect. He was tired in body and soul. No amount of rest would ease his weariness. He needed the comfort of home, the peace of the dearly familiar. Except that it, too, was changing. As he turned his horse toward Calvert Oaks, he had no idea of what he would find.

Chapter Twenty-Nine

SARAH STEPPED OUT of the dairy barn, glanced up at the sun and, seeing that it was barely afternoon, stifled a sigh. It was wrong of her to want time to pass more quickly, especially with everything there was that needed to be done, yet she couldn't help herself. Every moment dragged by on leaden feet, and had done since Philip had left.

She thought of him far too much, and far too kindly. By rights, she should be fiercely angry, and for a while she had been. But the specious comfort offered by that emotion had worn off quickly enough, and she had been left with only desolation.

How she missed him! Her longing for him when he first went to Richmond was nothing compared to what she felt now. She needed him in every possible way, not only at night when the large bed mocked her solitude, but during the day when the problems she faced threatened to overwhelm her.

There were times when her very longing for him made her resent him deeply, especially when she reread his cold, impersonal letters. Then she would swear to steel herself against him, to never again let herself be so foolishly vulnerable as to care for any man, but especially for the arrogant stranger of a husband who had abandoned her.

Abandoned. Such an inappropriate word. He had done nothing of the sort. He had simply gone off to do his duty as he saw it. But what about his duty to her? She pushed the thought aside. Whatever she wanted, it wasn't that. To hold him through some twisted sense of obligation would be to make a mockery of all they had, however briefly, shared.

She stood absently rubbing the soreness at the small of her back and stared off toward the road. The temptation to gallop down it haunted her dreams. She thought of herself sometimes, as she had been two years before on the day she arrived at Calvert Oaks. Such innocence could not possibly have survived, but she wished her idealism had. In its place she had only the uneasy sense that nothing was as simple as she had thought, not marriage or loyalty, and certainly not love.

Briskly she drew herself up and set off toward the laundry shed, where she meant to speak to the woman who did the sheets. Lately they had been showing an unusual amount of wear. She suspected them of being pounded too hard, but she also knew that they might simply be getting old.

In her stores were several dozen complete sets of sheets that had never been used. She was reluctant to pull them out because she knew that they could not readily be replaced. That they could, in a pinch, be used for bandages was something she did not want to think of at all.

By the time she had finished that chore, it was her time to sit with Charles. She looked upon their periods together as a rare interlude of peacefulness in an otherwise hectic day. Though he could say only a few words, he was always eager to hear what she had to tell him. She suspected he knew that she censored her remarks, relating only those that were cheerful, but he showed no sign of minding. On the contrary, a spirit of understanding had grown between them that she found oddly comforting.

But when she entered the room where the shutters were drawn to protect eyes lately become painfully sensitive to light, she discovered that Charles was unusually agitated. His wasted body, the upper part now conforming to the enfeebled lower, was twisted in an unnatural position. His covers were pulled out and his hair, turned snow white in the past few months, was mussed.

"Solomon," she said sternly to the large black man who served him, "what is the meaning of this?"

"Ah, sorry, missy," the man murmured, "but Massa Charles, he not feelin' so good today. Don' know what's wrong, just can't get him to stay still."

"Has he eaten anything?"

The slave shook his head. "No, missy. Wouldn't let me feed him. Wouldn't take his nap, either. But maybe seein' yo will settle him down."

Sarah lowered herself onto the edge of the bed and took her father-in-law's hand in hers. His skin was warm and dry to the touch, the bones underneath thin and fragile. He had lost a great deal of weight in the past few months, despite their efforts to keep it on him. His features were honed to their essence, giving him the look of a weary hawk who has finished his final flight. For a moment he didn't seem to recognize her. Then his gaze cleared somewhat and he managed a faint smile.

"Sa-rah."

"That's right. How are you feeling, Father?"

He shook his head, but otherwise did not answer her.

"Do you hurt somewhere?" She fought to keep the anxiousness from her voice even as she wondered what she would do if he suddenly took a turn for the worse.

Again the shake of his head and the plaintive look that demanded she guess the words he was struggling to form. "You don't hurt . . . do you want to go outside? No? Shall I read to you? Yes, a book? No . . . what then?" Realization came, and with it a frown. "Philip's letters? Again? Isn't there something you'd rather . . . ?"

There wasn't. Resigned, she rose to fetch the letters, telling Solomon as she did so that he might as well give Ginny a hand while she was occupied. Marcus was getting around some now, but it was still hard for him to do many things and she knew that he was far too proud to ask for help. Ginny was, too, but between her and Sarah the understanding born of shared suffering made for common ground. Solomon went off with a smile as she settled down to read the words that she could in fact have recited from memory.

How Charles could find them comforting was beyond her; she certainly did not. The dry litany of which fields to put to seed, which to leave fallow, which fences to repair, which dams to check and so on left her untouched, except by annoyance. Yet the man in the bed seemed reassured by them, as though they told him that the son who was absent physically was still with them in spirit.

Halfway through the letters, Sarah thought he had fallen asleep. But when she stopped and rose quietly to go, he opened his eyes and looked at her with a rare flash of complete lucidity. "Mar-cus?"

She did not pretend to misunderstand him. How could she when that was the same question he asked each day? The name of his mulatto son was one of the few words he could consistently utter. "He's better."

Charles's eyes brightened slightly. "See him?"

"Soon. Perhaps tomorrow."

"Truth?"

She swallowed against the tightness in her chest and put her hand over his. "Yes, it's the truth. He really is better, though it's still hard for him to get around. I'd have Solomon put him in your chair to bring him here except I think Marcus would resent it. Does that make sense to you?"

Charles nodded, following her every word with concentration she knew had to exhaust him.

"Ginny stays with him, almost all the time. She sleeps on a pallet beside his bed. She helped look after you, too, you know. I think it was her way of saying that . . . she didn't blame you."

His eyes clouded over with tears he no longer had the strength to repress. "My fault."

"No! It wasn't. You tried to protect him."

"Old . . . weak . . ." His voice cracked.

"Don't say that, Father. You did everything you could. Let's just be grateful that Philip was here to stop them." At the mention of her husband's name, she broke off. All the painful longing of the last few months swept over her. She lowered her eyes, not wanting Charles to see the agony in them.

He was silent for a moment, then said softly, "Love him."

"Wh-what . . . ?"

"You . . . love . . . him."

"No, that is, I'm his wife. Love has nothing to do with it."

Charles looked at her sadly. "Everything."

"I don't understand."

"Love . . . everything."

"Love is everything? Do you really believe that?"

He nodded, his face grave. "Loved Elizabeth . . . Philip's mother."

"Yes," Sarah said gently, "I know you did. Everyone says she was wonderful."

"But before . . . loved Lacey."

"Lacey?" Sarah frowned. "Who was she?"

"Marcus's . . . mother."

Her eyes opened wide, reflecting her shock. "You loved her? A slave?"

Charles's large head jerked back and forth in a wobbly nod. "Wrong . . . know . . . but couldn't help . . ."

This was something she had not expected, that Charles might actually have cared for the mother of his eldest son. And yet it made a kind of sense, since she knew that he had violated the rules of his society when he had refused to sell Marcus away, choosing instead to keep him with him.

"What happened to her?" she asked.

"Died . . . Marcus six months old . . . typhoid . . ."

So simple, yet the lingering grief was still so poignant. She wondered if there had been anyone, free or slave, to give him a word of sympathy. Doubtful. Both sides would have looked on his feeling for Lacey as a threat and would have been just as glad to see her go.

How had Lacey herself felt? Sarah had no way of finding out. She could hardly ask Charles, even presuming that he could have told her. Yet in her heart she could imagine the terrible conflict the other woman must have felt, not wanting to love a member of the race that kept her people in bondage, yet perhaps not able to help herself.

"Punished..." Charles rasped faintly.

"What?"

"Pun-ished. Lacey said... we would be..."

"For loving each other?"

He nodded, his hands gripping the sheets. "Not fair... she suffer. My fault."

"No one ever understands why these things happen. It couldn't have really been anyone's fault."

Charles was unconvinced. "Now...I pay. All right. But not Marcus."

"Is that what you think, that he's paying for your sin of loving Lacey?" When he nodded, she seized his hand, forcibly wresting it from the sheets and held it firmly within her own. "I don't believe that. It can't ever be wrong to love, and no child conceived in love should ever have to pay for it. You..." She couldn't help herself, it had to be said. "You might have let him go."

"Tr-tried."

"He wouldn't do it?"

"Said...too easy." He made a harsh sound, that might have been a rasping laugh. "Thought he meant for me. Now...not sure."

"Too easy for himself?" That made no sense to her. What could have kept him in bondage when freedom beckoned?

"You know," Charles said.

"Me? No, I don't. I can't see why he stayed."

"You stay."

"But...that's different." What could he be getting at? "I'm Philip's wife. This is where I belong."

"True?"

"I...I don't know."

"But you stay."

She lowered her eyes, uncomfortable suddenly with the perception in his. He was making a point she didn't care to recognize but could not deny. Both she and Marcus were bound to Calvert Oaks by law and custom. He was tied by the chains of his color and status as a slave; her tether was her sex and the society that saw her as a chattel of her husband. Yet they could both have escaped.

Marcus could have taken his father's offer of freedom; Sarah could have gone in Philip's absence. Both would have found a welcome in the North, if not wholehearted, at least enough to begin anew. But that wasn't enough for either of them. It was an immutable fact of life that no matter how long or how far you ran, you could never flee from yourself. Marcus loved a land he could never call his own, yet which held him in thrall. Sarah loved a man she couldn't even say she really knew yet from whom she could never walk away.

She didn't want to love, had fought against it with all the strength of her stalwart nature, had denied it long after it should be been self-evident. All the while it had been growing, taking over her very being, changing the shape of the world as she saw it. She could no longer be satisfied with the safety and the sense of purpose that she had believed were all she wanted. She needed— no, she demanded—far more. And her father-in-law knew it.

He was smiling at her gently. "Sa-rǝh...don't cry."

"I'm not." She raised a hand, brushing away the tears that inexplicably had gathered on her cheeks. A shaky laugh broke from her. "There I go again, trying to fool myself."

"We all do."

She rubbed briskly at her face. "Well, it will have to stop. I've no time for this."

His eyes twinkled. "Good Sa-rah."

"Good, indeed. I'd say I'm more trouble than I'm worth, except that you'd feel called upon to defend me, and you really should rest instead." She bent, kissing him gently. "Thank you, Father."

"Small thing . . . to do."

"No, big. Very big. Sleep now?"

He nodded, his lids drooping. She waited until the hand holding hers eased its grip, then she slipped away to sit on the veranda and rock awhile.

PHILIP STOPPED on the hill above Calvert Oaks, the same hill where he had paused so many years before when he came home from school. He sat there, looking at the blessedly familiar scene before him, trying to convince himself that it was still the same. Yet it wasn't, and sooner or later he must come to terms with that.

Calvert Oaks had changed, as he had himself. Years of evasion, of ignoring half-heard whispers and turning aside from the sound of his own conscience, haunted him. He had known. Deep inside, in the place he didn't want to look at too carefully. Marcus had never really lied to him, and certainly there had been no question of betrayal. Where was it written that one man could keep faith with another by being a willing or at least complacent slave? Only in a book of fools, concocted for the mad.

It was a fantasy in an age of increasingly relentless reality. Which made him think of Richmond and the dream being woven there. Nothing was impossible, he told himself as he put his spurs to the horse and started down the hill. Not even his own dreams.

Sarah was sitting in the swing on the veranda, rocking in the twilight, a glass of lemonade beside her and sewing in her lap. He dismounted and handed the reins to the boy who had appeared beside him. She hadn't moved. He didn't think she even blinked as he mounted the steps and came toward her.

"Nice evening," he said.

She nodded. "Cooler than yesterday."

"It's hot in Richmond."

"I thought it would be."

Rameses stuck his head around the door, broke into a smile when he saw Philip. Sarah gestured to her glass. "Another lemonade, Rameses, for both of us."

He sat down beside her, not so close as to be touching but near enough to smell the perfume of her skin. Lemons and lilac, sugar, butter and woman. He eased his shoulders back and smiled. "You've been busy."

It wasn't a question, but she answered it anyway. "Not as much as at hog season."

Philip laughed, a deep, joyful sound that made Rameses start as he hurried back with the lemonade. "Don't you spill that," Philip warned. "I've been thinking about Augusta's lemonade for the past ten miles."

"Yassuh, anythin' else yo want, Massa Philip? Somethin' to eat, maybe?"

"No, this is fine." He took a long sip of the drink and smiled his appreciation. "Still the best."

"Yassuh, Ahs tells Augusta."

When they were alone again, Philip studied his wife's profile. She sat wrapped in quietude, except for the anxious flutter of a pulse in her slender throat. Her hair was caught up in a bun at the nape of her neck. Wisps had escaped to trail around her forehead and ears. She wore a simple cotton dress without hoops, suitable to the hard work she had been doing. He thought she looked beautiful, but tired. A stab of guilt darted through him.

"How is Father?"

"Better. His speech is clearing, and he has more words. He can move his head and arms, though not easily."

"What does the doctor say?"

"That there is nothing to be done, except to make him as comfortable as possible."

He stood up and walked over to the railing, where he stood looking out sightlessly over the rolling lawns. "I should have come back sooner."

She privately agreed, but not for anything would she add to his pain by saying so. "You had a job to do."

"It was wasted. They don't agree with anything I've told them."

"Mr. Davis and the rest?"

He nodded and turned back to her. "They're convinced the war will be won in a matter of months, if not less."

"Pray God they are right."

"You surprise me." He came to stand in front of her, then went down on his haunches so that they were eye to eye. "I should think you would want the North to triumph."

Sarah flinched but did not look away. "This is my home now. I must give it my loyalty."

"It?"

"All right, you."

He sighed deeply and reached for both her hands, catching them in his. Her fingers were reddened, and he could feel traces of calluses on the palms. Knowing that, she tried to pull away but was stopped by his firm grasp. "Badges of honor," he said. "Every Southern woman should be proud of them."

He bent his head, golden in the setting sun, and gently kissed each of her hands. When he looked up again, her gray eyes had gone dark. "I cherish your loyalty, Sarah, though I question how much I deserve it. Yet at the same time, I want more."

"So do I."

The words hung between them as the cicadas trilled, and hidden in the rose bushes, a nightlark sang. Philip stood up, drawing Sarah with him. Her sewing fell at her feet, unheeded. His arm around her shoulders, they went inside and climbed the stairs to their room.

Chapter Thirty

THE PAIN WAS WORSE than she had expected. Not all the anticipation of the past six months, since she had finally come to terms with her condition, had prepared her for it. Not until the reality of the twisting, grinding agony struck did she fully comprehend what was happening to her. Worse yet, it was insidious, having begun the day before as no more than a dull pain in the small of her back, moving gradually to her bulging front, finally taking over her entire body.

Beyond the pain was fear. She did not want to die. Life, for all its present uncertainty, was sweet. When she thought of never seeing Philip again, she cried out in protest.

"Push," a voice commanded. "Yos gots to push, missy."

"Do as she says," another urged. "It will be over soon, Sarah. *Push.*"

They were lying, it would never be over. This was her fate, as she had sensed it from the day of her own mother's death. This was the hideous thing always lurking on the edge of her vision, waiting for her. She could almost see it.

Sarah screamed again and fought to escape. Hands held her down, voices murmured. The air stank of blood and sweat. She was trapped, a victim of her sex, her body, of stark realities over which she had no control. Only one thought kept her tethered to sanity. The baby. The unknown yet familiar and loved being moved within her these many months. Part of her in a way that no one else, not even Philip, could ever be. Her secret companion, her fellow conspirator in nature's great mystery. Baby.

"Push."

She obeyed, straining with all her might, not even daring to hope that it might be enough. The last of her strength was gone. Nothing was left except desperation.

"Push."

Aunt Louise's face floated in front of her, gray with worry, strained by the long night of waiting. Sarah reached out a hand, grasping the older woman's. She stared at their fingers intertwined.

"Jus' one more, missy." Augusta crouched at the foot of the bed, between her legs. Ginny was beside her, her face grim.

"Push."

She wanted to tell them that she couldn't, but the words would not come. She drew breath, thinking distantly that it might be her last, and expelled it with long, aching force.

A high, thin scream rent the air. Sarah stiffened, her eyes flying wide open, reflecting the porcelain light of a spring morning. Another scream—angry, indignant, full of remarkable self-importance.

Baby.

She struggled to sit up, supported by arms that trembled. "Let me see." Was that her voice? So weak and dazed?

Gnarled black hands with pale palms held something out to her. Red and wrinkled, wet and slick, with a small mouth open and wailing. "Yos got a beautiful lit'le girl, missy," Augusta said.

Sarah reached out, took the messy thing into her arms, held it close. The cord with the twisted spiral of the vein protruding prominently was still attached. She held both, wonderingly, overcome by the completeness of her own achievement.

"A daughter."

"Dat's right, missy. Now give her here. She got to be cleaned up an' so do you."

Sarah gave the baby up reluctantly. Her eyes followed every movement as the cord was cut, and her daughter was taken to a nearby table, where Ginny quickly began to wash her. "Bear down, missy," Augusta directed. "Wes almost done."

She was hardly aware of the afterbirth passing or of the women attending to her, washing away the blood and mucous, changing the sheets, putting her into a fresh nightshirt. She was so sore and so tired, but she barely felt either. She saw only her daughter, now clean and comfortable in her swaddling clothes.

"What yo gonna name her, missy?" Augusta asked as she laid the child at her mother's breast. Aunt Louise stood nearby, smiling through her tears.

"Elizabeth," Sarah said, staring down at bright blue eyes and a fuzz of golden hair. "Elizabeth Catherine." She and Philip had agreed on the name before he left. He had somehow been certain that the baby would be female. She was fiercely glad to have given him what he had hoped for.

"Mighty big name for such a lit'le thing," Augusta said with a laugh, "but she grow into it."

Sarah's eyelids drooped. She wanted so much to stay awake, to study the remarkable thing she had done. But her body had other ideas. Softly Aunt Louise took the baby from her and laid her in the cradle beside the bed. "Sleep now, child. You need your rest."

Sarah tried to say something to her, about watching over the baby, but the words wouldn't come and she knew they weren't really necessary. She drifted off, her mind full of Philip, wishing that he could have been there with her at the end as he had been at the beginning.

She had known exactly when she at last became pregnant. It was the night of Philip's return from Richmond. They had lain in each other's arms until dawn, recapturing the passion they had known together but with an added depth neither had experienced before.

He was by turns demanding and gentle, alternately taking the lead and allowing her to be the aggressor. Sarah had no idea which she preferred and was glad she didn't have to choose. She loved him with a passion she could no longer deny, and she wanted to express that love in every possible way.

Once, as he lay between silken thighs damp with his seed, she stared up into his glittering eyes and smiled weakly. "Are we making up for lost time?"

"Yes," he said, "past and future. Nothing exists except now."

She started to ask what he meant, especially about the future, but the question turned to a gasp when he bent his head and drew her breast into his mouth. All of it, not only the nipple engorged with need. He sucked her voraciously, his teeth marring the smoothness of her flesh, as though he truly wanted to devour her.

She reached down between them, guiding him back to where he had so lately been. With a low groan, he moved inside her. Her hips rose, taking him deeper. He lifted his head, face taut with the effort at control, teeth gleaming white in the darkness.

"I love you, Sarah."

"And I you, Philip."

Silence then, except for their soft cries mingling in the predawn light. When she felt him throb within her, felt the hot outpouring of his seed, she gripped him tightly. He was hers, this man, as she was his. For now, as he had said, without thought of past or future. Except that she was a woman and as such, she was more firmly knitted to the continuity of things.

Even as he slipped away from her, she kept a part of him within her. And when, after three months of her flow failing, she at last accepted what that meant, she wept with the sheer triumph of it.

"Yo DOING FINE, MISSY," Augusta said. "Jus' makes shur yo hold her lit'le head up 'cause she can't do dat fo herself yet."

Elizabeth Catherine was ensconced in a large china washing bowl filled with tepid water. She gurgled up at her mother who was trying for the first time to bath her. Gingerly Sarah slipped a hand under her head, replacing Augusta's.

"Dat's the way, missy. Now jus' take the soap an' wash her. It ain't hard."

Sarah was tempted to cast the old black woman a dubious look, but was afraid to take her eyes off her daughter for even an instant. At five days of age, Elizabeth no longer looked quite as wrinkled and scrawny as she had at birth. Her skin tone had faded to a soft pink. Her rosebud mouth moved almost constantly, making small sucking motions or breaking into a wide grin to display her toothless gums.

She was an active baby but also—so Aunt Louise assured Sarah—a good one, crying only when she was hungry or wet. Of course, she seemed to be one or the other most of the time. Sarah was nursing her herself, ignoring the tentative suggestions that she find a healthy slave girl to take over the duty. Privately she had to admit that might change soon, at least at night. She was getting very little sleep and that slowed up her recovery from the birth.

There were other concerns as well that kept her from regaining her strength as quickly as she would have liked. Philip had managed to get three letters through to her since he joined his regiment in Richmond. The capital was on full alert for the attack that was believed imminent. The Yankees had landed at Fort Monroe on the Chesapeake the month before. Since then, they had been attempting, under the guidance of the charismatic General McClellan, a three-pronged attack on Richmond, up the James and York Rivers and overland.

They had made very little progress, thanks to the admittedly theatrical but nonetheless effective efforts of the South's own General "Prince John" Magruder. In charge of the garrison at Yorktown, he had ordered his bands to play at night, his men to march in relays within sight of the Yankees and his artillery to fire constantly. Rumor had it that the unfortunate General McClellan—who liked to hear himself referred to as the "Young Napoleon"—believed the Southern forces

outnumbered his own by at least two to one. That was
thanks not only to Prince John's efforts but to the in-
advertent assistance of a certain Mr. Pinkerton, hired
by the Yankees to gather information, who had proved
remarkably gullible so far as the blandishments of
talkative Southerners went. A good chunk of northern Virginia knew he was being lied to, but the Yankees—bless their arrogant hearts—remained in blissful
ignorance.

Sarah shook herself. She had no business drifting off
to thoughts of the military situation when she had
Elizabeth to care for. Lifting the baby carefully, she
dried her off as Augusta stood by to supervise, then
laid her in her cradle. The task done, she allowed herself to relax a bit. "You're right. That wasn't so hard."

The black woman beamed at her. "Ahs tol' yo,
missy. Yo doin' just fine. Why yo a natural mother."

Sarah was hard-pressed to believe her. She had never
looked after a baby before. Nathan had been born
when she was five, and by the time he was old enough
to draw her attention, he had been toddling around and
doing things for himself. Elizabeth was quite the opposite; she was utterly dependent. It shocked Sarah to
discover exactly how helpless a baby was. Although, as
days passed she began to wonder if that was correct.
Her daughter might not be able to do anything for
herself, but she was remarkably adept at getting others to do for her.

In a household weighed down by the danger of war,
she was a spot of brightness no one could resist. They
all vied for her attention; her mother, Aunt Louise,
William, her grandfather, even Augusta who had cared
for more children than she could remember and Ginny,

who tended to shy away from babies because they reminded her too much of what she herself did not have.

Between the two of them—Sarah and Ginny—understanding ripened. They had first come together when Marcus was hurt and they discovered their mutual horror at that atrocity. Since then their budding friendship had been at first tentative, then cautious. Black, white, slave, free—nothing could change the reality of their contrary lives. Yet they still had a great deal in common.

When Sarah found Ginny one day alone, bending over Elizabeth Catherine's cradle, she wasn't surprised, or concerned. The stories whispered to her by other white women of the terrible perfidy of slaves who took out their hidden resentment on helpless infants didn't even occur to her. She knew exactly what she was seeing in the delicate touch of Ginny's hand on the baby's head.

"I had almost given up hope," she said, walking across the room to join the other woman.

Ginny looked up, her eyes damp, too. Surprised by the admission so close to her most private pain, she spoke without thinking. "Had you?"

Sarah smiled in the same instant that Ginny realized what she had betrayed. "When did you learn to talk white?" Sarah asked.

Ginny sighed and stood up. The burden of her deceit was heavy; she was glad enough to put it down, if only for a little while. "It was hearing Marcus talk that did it, I suppose. I picked it up bit by bit."

"I've thought since I came here that it was very strange how blacks and whites spoke differently. It didn't make any sense to me."

"But we different people. That is . . . we are different people."

Sarah smiled down at her daughter, who was awake and regarding them both solemnly. "I suppose. Still, you'd think that people who live in such close contact would inevitably come to speak the same way."

"Most of us never talk to a white person," Ginny said. She had backed away from the cradle. Her hands were folded over her apron. "Most of us work in the fields and never see any whites except for the overseer. All you got to say to him is 'yassuh.' "

The bitterness in her voice poured over them both. Sarah didn't try to ignore it, "Someday things will change."

Ginny laughed. "That's what Marcus said."

"Said?"

"He don't—doesn't—say much now."

Sarah had noticed that herself. Though he was physically recovered from the savage beating, he remained withdrawn, saying little to anyone and keeping his own counsel. Before he left to take up his post in Richmond, Philip had convinced Marcus to continue living and working in the house, rather than returning to the quarters and the fields. He had done so by playing blatantly on his brother's ill-starred love of Calvert Oaks, telling him that in his absence he needed someone who would keep a close eye on things. Their father was incapable and Overseer Davies, well-meaning though he was, had neither the education nor the understanding.

Marcus had agreed, though reluctantly. He knew well enough that illusions were treacherous, yet they could also be too seductive to resist. That was the case with him. Unwillingly yet inevitably he had slipped into the routine of advising Sarah on what needed to be done. She in turn relayed the instructions to Davies as though they came directly from her, a pretense that fooled no one but left the revered barriers intact, if somewhat askew. It worked out well and in the last months of her pregnancy she became increasingly dependent on Marcus. Now, as she recovered from Elizabeth's birth, it reassured her to know that he was on hand.

Sarah needed all the reassurance she could get. Besides her worries over whether or not she would be a good mother, there were dangers pressing on her that she could hardly bear to think about. The threat to Richmond was extreme; the Union Army—for all that it had been fooled by Magruder—was large and well equipped. It was led by a man of vaunting ambitions who saw the opportunity to make his career. Pitted against McClellan was a force fiercely determined never to surrender. If a battle occurred between the two, it would be brutal. And Philip would be caught in the midst of it. Not only that, but so would Calvert Oaks, because the plantation lay directly on the route the Yankees were following to the capital.

"Please look after Elizabeth for me," Sarah said. "I need to talk to Marcus."

Ginny nodded. She no longer believed that Sarah's courtesy was merely a smoke screen for the cruelty and deceit she had experienced from other whites. Slowly she had come to accept that it was genuine, as was the trust that enabled her to leave the child in her care. As Ginny bent over the cradle, she couldn't help but smile. Babies did that to her, despite the sorrow she felt at having none of her own.

She lifted Elizabeth and held her close, finding some comfort from the warm little bundle, and tried not to think about what Sarah had to say to her husband.

Marcus was standing on the earthen parapet overlooking the river. He had Philip's brass spyglass in his hand and was looking out toward the east.

"Do you see anything?" Sarah asked as she climbed up the mound beside him.

He turned and shook his head. "There was some movement about half an hour ago, wagons, I think, and horsemen. But there's been nothing since."

"They won't stop coming."

"No," he agreed. "But so long as they stay on the other side of the river, we've got nothing to worry about."

Sarah prayed he was right and that the Union Army advancing on Richmond would not come near to the plantation. Already there were stories circulating of farms burned and property looted as the Yankees marched up the Peninsula. They had been delayed at Yorktown, where the Confederates held out for weeks, blocking the Union advance. The night before the Yankees were to finally get their big guns in place and begin bombarding the town, the Confederates slipped away under cover of darkness, leaving a frustrated McClellan to follow as quickly as he could manage.

His advance was proving to be all too rapid. Sarah squinted slightly as she looked away down the river. "I'd like to have men watching tonight."

"Good idea," Marcus said. He was looking through the spyglass again, studying every tree and hillock for what it might conceal. He stood straight, the scars on his back concealed by a white linen shirt tucked into trousers that had been made for Philip but never worn.

He had found the clothes in his room one day when he came back from checking on the fields. Ginny had said only that she got them from Sarah, and when he had objected to wearing them, she had simply shrugged and said it was that or nothing. His old clothes, the ragged cutoffs and shirts he had worn before, had vanished.

His new appearance troubled Marcus, not in the least because of how comfortable he felt with it. He wasn't a white man; he wasn't free; he wasn't some wealthy planter surveying his domain with a fancy brass spyglass.

"I'd better get back to the house."

"Are you feeling all right?" Sarah asked.

"I'm fine." He wanted to walk away, but he couldn't just leave her standing there. Not knowing as he did all she had to bear; husband gone, new baby to look after, danger coming. Damn Philip for leaving. Not that he'd had any choice. But damn him for the responsibility he had laid on Marcus before he went.

"I know you don't want this," Philip had said, "but there's no one else I can turn to. Someone has to look after things while I'm away. Someone I can trust. Will you agree?"

"What makes you think you can trust me?"

"You're my brother."

They had stared at each other for what seemed like a long time. Marcus had wanted to say that he was crazy, that he had no business thinking of him that way. He was a black man, a slave. If Philip had any doubt about that, all he had to do was look at his back.

"I'm sorry," Philip said, reading what was in his eyes. "I'd have done almost anything to prevent what happened."

"Almost?"

"I wouldn't risk Sarah or the baby. But beyond that . . ."

"Don't make promises, *brother*."

"All right. But I still need your help."

And Marcus hadn't been able to deny it, not when it called to everything he was and everything he dreamed of being. To walk over the land and think of it as his, to give free rein to the need to protect and nurture the rich soil, to know with pride that he was doing a job no one else could, all that was balm to him. It completed his healing even as it brought him face-to-face with the essential conflict of his life: he was neither black nor white. The contrasting colors of his heritage canceled each other out. He was a man, pure and simple.

And Sarah was a woman, who needed his help. "Don't worry," he said, "there'll be someone on duty all night. If anything happens, you'll know. But for now, you should get some rest."

When she hesitated he held out his hand. She took it, and together they walked to the house.

—————————— *Chapter Thirty-One*

THE YANKEES CAME shortly after dawn. Not from the river, as Sarah had feared, but by land. They rode up in neat columns three abreast, a major in the lead. He doffed his hat and regarded her gravely as she stood on the veranda.

"Ma'am, we'd just as soon not have any trouble here, but my men need food and water, and we have several wounded. If you're predisposed to help us, we'd be grateful. If not, we'll take what we need."

Sarah stared at the tall young man and considered her options. Choosing her words carefully, she said, "Major, my husband is in Richmond with the militia."

His lean face pale with the fatigue of battle stiffened with resignation, only to give way to surprise as he realized all that he had just heard. "You're a Northerner."

In the past few years, Sarah's speech had blurred slightly as she picked up the softer cadences of the people she lived among. But for the major's benefit, she had spoken with a pure New England drawl. "That's right. From Massachusetts."

He glanced at his men, then back to her. "You have us at a disadvantage, ma'am. This is the Massachusetts Fifth."

"I thought I recognized the flag."

"Perhaps we'd best be on our way..." He began to turn his horse that, weary as its master, resisted.

"Wait." Sarah held out a hand. She was no more certain of what she was about to do than the major himself. All she knew was that she couldn't watch these men who reminded her so much of her brother, Nathan, ride away and live with herself afterward. "You said you had wounded."

He looked at her carefully. "Three. They were injured at Williamsburg, where we fought the Rebels. We should have stopped before now but there's been no chance."

"Bring them into the house."

"Ma'am?"

"The house. Bring them inside. We can tend to them better in here."

The young major hesitated. "You don't have to do this, ma'am."

Sarah tilted her head proudly and met his gaze. "You're wrong, sir. I do."

"Your husband won't be pleased," Major Jeremy Blackston said an hour or so later when he and his men had ate and drunk their fill. Ginny and several of the other women had cared for the wounded. One was not likely to survive, but the other two were well enough to travel. "We'll be on our way before noon, so perhaps he won't find out about this."

Seated across from him in the parlor, Sarah smiled faintly. The major was about thirty, with light brown hair and hazel eyes. His manner was gentle but firm. She suspected he was a good leader and had earned his rank through merit. "You don't know much about plantation life, Major. It's impossible to keep any secrets here. When Philip returns, I'll tell him myself.''

"You're confident of the outcome then?''

"No, I'm not confident of anything.'' That was the truth; she had rarely felt less certain. Nothing was as she had imagined it would be. The Yankees should have come with guns blazing, instead of quietly and in need. They should have been brash, rude and hateful. Not solemnly courteous and so grateful for everything they were given.

They were only boys. That thought more than any struck her most forcibly. Major Blackston was the eldest of the lot. The rest were in their early twenties or their teens. She suspected a few of them had lied about their age and were really no more than children.

It was the same in Richmond. Philip had written her about that. Young men and boys were fighting this war. Fighting and dying. "Major...do you think it will be over soon?''

"I don't know, ma'am, but I surely hope so.'' He had told her, reluctantly but needing to talk about it, that he had a wife and a young son at home. He had joined the army because he felt it was his duty to do so, and he had risen to the rank of major so quickly because he had been at West Point.

"I know someone who went there,'' Sarah said before she thought to stop herself. "Peter Rider, he...''

"I know him.'' One look at her face was enough to tell Jeremy where Peter Rider was and what he was doing. "Oh, Lord, that's what I hate most about this horrible thing.'' The moment the words were out, he regretted them. "I'm sorry, I...''

"Never mind. We all hate it.''

"You must especially, caught in between the way you are."

"I have to be honest with you. I don't feel caught. Philip is my husband; I love him and I'll do whatever I can to help him."

"And he supports the South."

"He doesn't have much choice," Sarah said, "being a Southerner. But he doesn't necessarily approve of everything that happens here."

"How do you feel about it?" Jeremy asked. He liked what she said about loving her husband because he felt the same way about his wife. He also missed Katie terribly. He was used to talking to her about all sorts of things and didn't like having to keep his thoughts to himself. With Sarah, he sensed that he didn't have to.

"I don't approve of slavery," Sarah said, "if that's what you're asking. I think it's an abomination. But I've also lived here long enough to understand that changing the situation isn't going to be as easy as some people think."

"You mean the abolitionists? They're convinced that all that needs to be done is to declare the slaves free and that will be an end to it."

"Do you believe that?"

He shrugged broad shoulders covered by blue broadcloth. "I guess I haven't thought about it much. Seems to me slavery ought to end, but what's more important is holding the Union together."

"It was slavery that split the Union, wasn't it?"

He shook his head. "In my opinion, ma'am, it was more a matter of business. The North wants high import tariffs to protect its products and the South doesn't. The South wants to sell what it grows to the highest bidder, the North wants first claim on it. That's why we've come to blows.''

"You think that's right?" Sarah asked. She sat with her hands folded in her lap, the picture of serenity. But she was feeling anything but. Inside was terrible sadness, for young Major Jeremy Blackston, for Philip, for herself, for all of them caught in a conflict they had not wanted and could barely understand.

"No," he said softly, "it isn't right, but it is the way things are. I figure some compromise should have been reached and would have been if it hadn't been for slavery. That's the rub. We couldn't come to terms so we fight. What counts now is that the Union be saved.''

"Perhaps there will be some sort of compromise.''

He shook his head. "I don't think so, ma'am.''

"If the South wins..."

"They can't, ma'am. They might do all right at first, but we can outlast them. Eventually they'll have to give up."

Sarah remembered that several weeks later when Philip came home. Richmond had held against all odds. The Yankees had been turned back just upriver from Calvert Oaks, at Drewry's Bluff, where Confederate guns had stopped them cold. They had been forced to withdraw, leaving many of their dead behind them. The Richmond *Examiner*—still being read in Washington thanks to the blockade runners—had printed a list of the casualties on both sides, among them a Yankee major named Blackston.

"He was young and sincere," Sarah said as she lay beside Philip in their bed. His arms were around her. They had made love earlier, with mingled tenderness and passion made all the greater by the abstinence of the past few months. Now they were talking. Or at least she was; he was listening. "And he had a wife, and a little son. It seems so unfair."

"Yes, it is." His arms tightened around her. Life was brutally unfair. He was more convinced of that than ever. Good men died, bad ones lived. Bullets did not discriminate. He had thought about that earlier as he held his daughter for the first time and savored the precious continuity of life.

"Do you think I was wrong, to let him and his men rest here?" Sarah asked.

"Wrong? No, after all, he would have done what he had to with or without your agreement."

"I didn't do it for that reason. At least . . . I don't think I did."

"It doesn't matter." He supposed that it should; the Yankees were, after all, the enemy. But he couldn't begrudge the man the few hours of comfort he'd had. Any more than he could pretend not to understand the conflict within his wife.

"It's all right to feel sympathy for both sides," he said. "You have to expect that."

"I didn't. I thought I'd made my choices."

He turned over, drawing her under him and propped himself up on his elbows. "It's not simple for any of us. My loyalties are firm, but I still have doubts about the rightness of what we're doing."

"I know you hoped so much for peace."

"It isn't just that," he said. "It's the killing. We were lucky at Richmond, to have the Yankees turned back when they were. But I had plenty of time to listen to the men who had been at Bull Run and Ball's Bluff. It's a terrible business watching a man die and knowing you're the cause of it."

"Don't think about it. It will be over soon and then..."

"Yes, I have to believe that." He bent over her, his mouth warm and persuasive, and she forgot about killing and about death. Instead she gave herself up to life, and the moment, however fleeting.

Philip was gone a few weeks later. The Army of Northern Virginia under General Robert E. Lee was rumored to be massing for an assault on Washington. The hope was that they would be able to take the Union capital before the end of the year and write finis to the war.

Sarah prayed that would happen. The longer the war went on, the more she feared the outcome. A letter had reached her from Marilee, written several months before and telling her that Nathan had joined the army. He could easily have avoided it, Josiah being more than willing to buy substitutes for both him and Gideon, but Nathan had felt it was his duty to go. He still hoped to become a minister, but in the meantime he would serve his country as best he could.

She had wept when she read the news. She thought of her little brother, whom she had not seen in so long, and cried for what was happening to them all. Aunt Louise tried to comfort her. "He'll be a while yet in training, dear, and then waiting for an assignment. Why we all know how confused the Yankees are. They may just forget about him altogether."

"I hope you're right," Sarah said between her tears. "Nathan doesn't belong in battle."

"I'm sure he doesn't." Aunt Louise sighed and looked out the window at the fields ripening in the sun. "But then none of them do. They should all be at home with their families."

"I thought you believed in the cause," Sarah said.

"I believe men are sometimes fools."

Such wisdom, coming from an elderly maiden, surprised Sarah. She smiled and immediately felt better. The rest of the day passed busily as she cared for Elizabeth, spent time with William and talked over several problems with Marcus. By evening she was happy to soak in a hot tub before crawling into bed. She lay awake for a few minutes, wondering if she needed to update the map she was keeping that showed the positions of the two armies, at least so far as the newspapers disclosed them. Lee's forces were reported in Western Maryland near a town called Sharpsberg. There was a creek there that they had to cross, the Antietam. She fell asleep thinking that they might already be on the other side, on the way to Washington.

In fact they were not. The Army of Northern Virginia had taken up position on a ridge overlooking Antietam Creek. That was not the original battle plan, but rumors were sweeping the ranks that Lee had been forced to change strategics when details of his original intentions fell into McClellan's hands. Despite that setback, they had succeeded in crossing the Potomac two days before, where they were joined by the brigade led by Stonewall Jackson, who had just taken the garrison at Harpers Ferry. None of them could understand why McClellan had delayed giving battle, allowing Jackson time to unite his forces with theirs. But neither were they anxious to question it.

"We'll be fighting soon enough," Peter Rider said. He and Philip, along with the other men of the cavalry brigade to which they were attached, had found a night's shelter in a barn. They shared a dreary meal of cold beans and hardtack, knowing better than to light a fire that could give away their position. At least they were out of the fog and drizzle, which had worsened steadily over the past few hours.

As they spoke they kept their voices low. Not long before their General, Jeb Stuart, on a night's reconnaissance, had stopped by to warn them that the Yankees were camped only a few hundred yards away in a cornfield. He didn't suggest that they move—dry ground was too precious to be so easily surrendered—but he did advise caution.

Philip leaned back in a pile of hay, folded his arms behind his head and did his best not to think of the men sleeping nearby—or at least trying to—whom he would be called upon to kill the following day. Unlike Peter, who had fought at Williamsburg, he as yet had no combat experience. A lack he understood was to be speedily remedied.

"I've been thinking," he said quietly. "About tomorrow..."

"That's a good idea," Peter said.

"What is?"

"Doing your thinking now. Once it starts, there won't be any time for it."

"Is that what you found?"

"Absolutely. They warned us about it at the Point, and it turned out to be true. Don't worry," Peter added quietly, "you'll do fine."

Philip grimaced in the darkness. "I'll be satisfied not to disgrace myself."

"What's this, a Southern gentleman suggesting that he isn't the greatest hero God ever put upon earth?"

"I'm afraid so, which, to be honest, isn't all I'm afraid of."

"You think you'll run?"

"Of course not."

"Then don't worry," Peter advised.

"There has to be more to winning a battle than not running."

"Not really. For all the fancy talk of military tacticians, the fact is whichever side holds its line the longest wins. Provided, of course, that it isn't massacred in the process."

Philip sighed and tried to find a more comfortable position without much success. "They say we're badly outnumbered."

"Probably true, but we have a few advantages. The cream of the officer corps pledged for the South. We've got the best leaders this country has ever bred. Tomorrow we'll prove that."

Philip remembered that the next morning. It was very quiet in the clearing where they were assembled. A few horses nickered anxiously, but the men themselves were silent. There was nothing more to be said. They had their orders, and they knew what had to be done. Through the ribbons of swirling fog, he could see the light gradually creeping up. Beneath his gray tunic, his skin was damp. He shifted in the saddle and gripped the hilt of his sword more securely.

A sudden thud shook the silence, followed immediately by another. The heavy batteries were firing. King's Ransom shied under him. He soothed the horse with a murmur. A cry rang out. As one, they moved forward, slowly at first, then more rapidly as the direction of battle swept them on.

They came and they came and they came, the green Union boys and their rabid-eyed commanders intent on revenging the humiliation of Fort Sumter, Bull Run, Yorktown. There was no stopping them, not the fury of Rebel cannon that tore men apart, not the murderous cross fire that trapped them in valleys of death, not the relentless drive of the men in gray who surged forward over the bodies of their own dead to wreak devastation before it could be wreaked on them.

Philip rapidly discovered that nothing in his training had prepared him for the reality of battle. It was chaos in which there was no time to think, no chance to plan, only action and reaction. The first man he killed was no more than a boy, run through by his saber, who stared at him in surprise before slumping onto the blood-soaked ground. The second was an older, grizzled man very intent on killing before he could be killed. He raised his rifle to fire point-blank into Philip's face, only to be knocked off balance by King's Ransom's flailing hooves. The horse, bred to a different kind of contest, was near to panicking, but Philip had no thought to spare for him. He was caught within the flow of battle, part of the surging mass of men in gray and blue fighting under a leaden sky.

"Your left," Peter cried. Philip wheeled, seeing the Union officer coming at him in scant time to raise his saber to block the other man's blow. He feinted, blocked another, parried. Steel glinted in the cold light, grunts and moans and the terrified cries of the horses filled the air. Philip's sword arm ached but he had no awareness of the pain. He pulled hard on the reins, wheeling suddenly, and drove his blade into flesh.

There was no time to savor his survival. Peter was under attack from three sides. Philip tightened his thighs around the horse, murmured a command in his ear and raced forward. He rose up in the saddle, swinging the sword above his head, a guttural sound bursting from him like an ancient war cry.

Distantly he was aware of men falling before him, of he and Peter riding side by side, cutting a swath through the opposing force. He knew they had crossed the main road leading through Sharpsberg and were fighting in open fields. Behind him he could see a church that had been pointed out to them on maps the night before; ahead were several neat farmhouses. Dimly he understood what he was doing; those were people being pounded into pulp beneath his horse's hooves, lives being snuffed out at the point of his sword. But he fought on without hesitation, knowing only that they were the enemy and they had to be stopped.

His tunic and trousers were stained with blood, red all but obscuring the gray. He had a flesh wound to the left thigh and another across his back between the shoulder blades. His teeth ached from clenching his reins in them as he wielded his sword with one hand and fired his pistol with the other.

King's Ransom had fallen twice in the damp earth, each time rising to his feet with greater difficulty. He went down again with a desperate whinny. Philip cursed under his breath. He could spare no pity for the proud animal, knowing as he did that his own life depended on him.

"Get up boy!" he rasped in a voice that was almost gone. "For the love of God, get up!"

The horse struggled to obey, his giant body trembling. Intent on urging him, Philip barely felt the burning pain in his left shoulder until he realized that his arm had fallen limply to his side. He stared at it in bewilderment, unable to understand why there was suddenly a jagged hole in his sleeve big enough to stick his fist into.

With a tremendous heave, King's Ransom regained his feet. Philip hung on blindly. He could hear men screaming all around him, but the sounds were growing too faint to disturb him. Ahead of him a cluster of Rebel infantry, their officer down, milled uncertainly. He galloped into their midst, unaware of their startled stares. "Come on, we've got them on the run. Forward!"

Without waiting to see if they would obey, he spurred King's Ransom ahead. The line of blue was a scant hundred yards away. Bullets whistled past him. The acrid stench of gunpowder filled his lungs, warring with the iron tang of blood. Closer...closer... enough now to see the faces of individual men, set and grim, filled with dismay and something else...fear.

"Forward." Splotches of gray whirled around him, mingling with the blue. He registered distantly that the men had followed, were fighting beside him. His sword slashed again and again, relentless, unstoppable. On and on he urged King's Ransom, over green fields, through smashed fences, following the blue line.

Until there was nothing more to follow. Only the gray blurs moving around him, voices lifted not in screams but in cheers. He swayed in the saddle, struggling to understand what was happening. A rush of sound, like the pounding of waves, filled his ears. The mist thickened and embraced him. He fell a great distance into darkness.

Chapter Thirty-Two

"ASHES TO ASHES, dust to dust, in the sure and certain knowledge of the Resurrection to come."

Loose dirt fell on the pine coffin lying in the freshly dug grave. Sarah stared down at the raw wood, thinking that it should have been oak, properly aged and polished, gleaming with its own strength and endurance. Once it would have been, but coffins were in such short supply these days that they were lucky to have gotten what they did. The only alternative would have been to cut down one of the plantation's own trees, and that would have desecrated the land for which so much blood had been spilled.

Beside her Philip breathed in sharply. She knew that he was in pain, but that it would be futile to offer him any assistance. For more than eight months, since he had been brought home from Antietam near death, he had refused to accept other than the most minimal help from her. Even when he had been only semiconscious and racked by fever, he had said little and asked for nothing.

His father's death, merciful as it was, was one more blow from which he would somehow have to recover. If he could. While his physical recuperation had been remarkable, all things considered, emotionally he was numb. It was as though a key part of his mind and heart had simply ceased to exist.

She could hardly blame him. The compounding of grief on top of grief was enough to undo even the strongest man. For weeks after he had finally regained consciousness she had managed to keep from him the news that Antietam had not been a clear-cut victory for the South but merely a draw. He had found out finally not from her but from Marcus who reluctantly gave him the information he demanded.

The two armies had met, battled and achieved in essence nothing except the deaths of more than twenty thousand men, most of whom lay buried in common, unmarked graves in the same ground they had died for. Others had been found and brought home to lie in family graveyards, Louis Devereaux and William Morgan among them. The bloodiest day in the nation's history could be redeemed only through peace, and that seemed more elusive than ever.

Nor had the anguish stopped at Antietam. The legion of the dead had grown greatly at Fredericksburg and most recently at Chancellorsville, about which reports were still coming in, to be received with shock and despair. As though it weren't enough for the South to lose so many of her fine young men, Stonewall Jackson was reported dead, a cruel twist of fate that could hardly be believed by a populace that expected increasingly brutal fighting throughout the coming summer.

Sarah could only thank God that Philip was out of it, though she knew he felt no such gratitude. The fact that he had emerged from Antietam a hero did nothing to soothe his increasing frustration with himself and everything about him. He despised what had happened to his body, hated his weakness, and—she greatly feared—resented her. Only little Elizabeth seemed able to ease his anger and sorrow. While holding his daughter, he could look almost content. At all other times he was aloof and withdrawn.

None of which made it any easier to bear Charles's passing. The love she had never been able to give to her father had been cherished and fully returned by the man now gone to his final rest. Much as she tried to be glad that his suffering was ended, she knew she would miss him terribly. All the more so because she could not share her grief, or anything else, with Philip. He refused to let her.

At last it was finished. Kitty, who had wept quietly throughout the service, took Sarah's arm and together they left the churchyard. Philip followed with Marcus. The house slaves brought up the rear, many of them crying. It had been of necessity a small service. So many of their neighbors were away fighting. Others were afraid to stray off their own land, scared of encountering marauding Yankees who had been raiding up the James since spring.

Even those who might have traveled were reluctant to do so, not knowing what they would find when they returned home. Hard on the heels of Antietam, a proclamation had come out of Washington declaring all slaves in the seceded states to be free. On the surface it was meaningless since it could not be enforced, but it made the old fear of a slave uprising more real than ever.

"It's so warm today," Kitty murmured when they at last reached the veranda. Her heavy black dress trailed behind her. "So very warm."

"Sit down and rest," Sarah urged. "I'm just going to check on Aunt Louise." The older woman had been unable to attend the service, having been stricken with severe chest pains shortly after her brother-in-law's death. The doctor who attended her had privately told Sarah and Philip that she could yet recover provided she had absolute rest. Getting her to go along with that might have been difficult, except that all her spirit and vitality seemed to have drained away.

Sarah found her sleeping, with Ginny in attendance. They exchanged a few whispered words before Sarah returned downstairs. She was surprised to hear raised voices and even more startled to realize that Kitty and Philip were arguing.

"I don't care what you think about it," he was saying. "Marcus is mentioned in father's will. Therefore, he must be there when it is read."

"How can you insist on such a thing?" his sister demanded. She had risen in agitation and stood with her hands clasped tightly in front of her, a posture at once stubborn and pleading. "It is simply never done. If father left some small bequests to a few of the slaves, then they can be told that privately. But to have one of them at the reading as though he were a member of the—"

She broke off, her face flushed. Philip did not help her. He merely held her eyes until she looked away. Sarah went to her quickly, shooting her husband an angry glance as she put an arm around her sister-in-law and urged her back into her chair. Kitty had insisted on coming to the funeral despite the fact that she was pregnant again, apparently the result of a brief leave Jeremy had been granted in December after Fredericksburg. She was desperately afraid that she might lose both him and the unborn child.

"You must rest," Sarah said. She beckoned to Rameses. "Pour us all a cool lemonade, and then we'll see about something to eat."

"I couldn't," Kitty murmured.

Sarah patted her hand gently. "Please try. You have the baby to think of."

"I'm sorry, Kitty," Philip said. He took a chair beside her and managed a faint smile. "It's been a hard day for all of us."

"Then you won't..."

His smile faded, replaced by the closed look they had all become so familiar with. "My mind is made up."

"Let's not discuss it any more right now," Sarah said. She gestured to Rameses, urging him forward with the tray he carried. In a deliberate bid to change the subject, she turned to Kitty and asked, "Have you heard from Jeremy lately?"

Her sister-in-law sniffed and nodded. "I had a letter three days ago. He can't say much, of course, but he claims to be well."

"Then I'm sure he is."

"I don't know... In Richmond they're saying that the army doesn't have enough food or medicine. Some of the men don't even have boots anymore. They have to... take what they can from the dead." Her voice cracked.

Philip leaned forward and took her hand in his. Such a gesture had become unusual for him. Sarah saw the struggle he was waging against his gentler emotions and silently prayed that he would yield to them, if only a little. At length, he said, "Don't think about it. Jeremy's a strong man. He'll be all right."

They all knew that his comfort was specious—no one could say for sure who, if anyone, was immune from the devastation. But Kitty wanted to believe him so badly that she let herself seem to. "He hopes to be home when the baby comes, if he can get leave again. At least he thinks there's a chance."

"Perhaps there is," Philip said. At the women's quizzical looks, he elaborated. "Lee can't go on forever trying to break through to Washington without success. If he doesn't manage it soon, the impetus will have to move elsewhere and perhaps then the Virginians will be given a bit of rest."

"He must break through," Kitty insisted, some of her old spirit returning. "This can't possibly go on much longer. Why everyone knows that we should already have won, and would have if it hadn't been for that treachery at Antietam."

Philip sighed and let go of her hand. He didn't want to talk about Antietam, didn't want to even think about it, but he had gradually schooled himself to respond as an impersonal observer, as though considering events in which he had had no part. "Lee knew his battle plan had been stolen. He changed it before we engaged the enemy, so they didn't actually have advance warning of what we were going to do."

"But the first plan was better," Kitty said. "Everyone says so."

"Maybe it was. That hardly matters now."

His weariness and his impatience finally reached her. She subsided with a tired sigh as silence fell. Kitty was wrapped up in her own thoughts, Philip was staring out over the broad lawns to the fields beyond. Sarah could guess what was going through his mind; the same question that had haunted him for weeks.

Would the ripening crops ever be harvested? So far no slaves had run away from Calvert Oaks, but it would take only one solid foray by the Yankees to tempt them. If they could bring the crops in, would the wheat, cotton and other produce reach the government buyers who had contracted for them—with Confederate dollars, of course, and for far less than would have been gotten a few years before on the open market? Could the mill be kept operational, turning out fabric for the gray uniforms that were in such short supply?

All those questions and more plagued him. Despite the doctor's orders, he was working from before dawn until long after dark, not coming to bed until exhaustion racked him and even then often falling asleep on the couch in the library. Sarah had given up trying to convince him to go easier on himself. Understanding as she did what drove him, she could only stand back and pray that no lasting damage would be done. Or at least no more than had already occurred.

Insects droned in the rosebushes growing beside the veranda. It was uncomfortably warm even in the shade. The heavy black clothes were scratchy. Philip's hand went absently to his left arm. Sarah's throat tightened as she saw him freeze, then jerk away from the empty sleeve of his jacket.

"I, CHARLES EDWARD CALVERT, being of sound mind do hereby declare this to be my last will and testament." The lawyer's voice was deep and measured, as required by such a somber occasion. He was an elderly, white-haired man who had come down from Richmond the previous day and now held the place of honor at the desk in the library.

The rest of them—Philip, Sarah, Kitty, Aunt Louise and Marcus were ranked opposite him with all except Marcus sitting stiffly. He stood, near the door, as though not fully committed to being present.

"To my son, Philip Charles Calvert, I bequeath the plantation known as Calvert Oaks, including all property and possession associated with it, except for those items I shall henceforth specify. In addition I bequeath to him the shares owned in the Alexandria and Virginia Railroad, the Richmond Iron Works and sundry other companies to comprise all of such stock certificates to be found in the safe box held under the name of myself and the aforesaid Philip Charles Calvert in the Bank of Richmond. I also leave to him all monetary sums held in that bank or any other or owed to Calvert Oaks."

"To my daughter, Katherine Helen Calvert Hudson, I leave the sum of ten thousand dollars deposited for her in the Bank of Richmond. In addition, she is to have the Louis XV escritoire given to her mother on the occasion of our first wedding anniversary, as well as the diamond-and-sapphire necklace given upon the birth of said Katherine Helen Calvert Hudson."

Kitty cried softly into her handkerchief. Her father had been very generous with her dowry, and she really had not expected a great deal more. Welcome though the money was, the fact that he remembered how much she loved both the escritoire and the necklace touched her more.

Various other bequests followed to old friends, to the local church and to several slaves, including Augusta and Rameses, whom he did not free but did provide with ample funds to purchase their own freedom if they chose and live comfortably afterward.

When those were concluded the lawyer cleared his throat and glanced around the room. Not until Philip nodded at him impatiently did he continue.

"To my son, Marcus, I leave the attached writs of manumission as well as the attached deed to the property known as Santa Vista in the territory of New Mexico. In addition, I bequeath to him the sum of ten thousand dollars. It is my most cherished hope that Marcus will use this bequest to begin a new life for himself in which the scars of the past will at last be healed."

With obvious reluctance the lawyer detached from the will four pieces of paper that he slid across the table to Marcus. "I don't suppose you can read them," the man said, "so I'll tell you that they are writs of manumission for yourself, the slave known as Ginny and any unnamed children the two of you may have had. In addition you have the deed to the New Mexico property, which is apparently a good-sized ranch well situated on the Rio Grande."

Marcus barely heard him. He was staring at the papers as though unable to believe they were real. Still holding them, he turned and looked at his brother.

Philip rose and went to his side. "Father wanted you to have this. He felt it was only right."

"And what do you feel about it?"

"Honestly?" At Marcus's quick nod, he went on. "I'm not looking forward to losing you right now. In fact, I'm hoping to convince you that it's safer and smarter to stay here until the fighting dies down. But then you'd be crazy not to take this chance and make everything of it that you can."

"Freedom..." Marcus glanced down again at the papers, at the neat black lettering that spelled out all he had ever hoped for. "I can hardly believe it."

"You know you could have had it before."

"Yes, but not in the same way." He rifled the pages, coming to the deed. "Not this way, with land and a real chance." Suddenly he smiled, his eyes alight. "New Mexico. My God, I don't know anything at all about it, but it sounds wonderful!"

"Father bought the land five years ago. He checked it out carefully. There are two thousand acres, most of them well watered by the Rio Grande. It's prime cattle country, but you also shouldn't have any trouble raising horses."

"I can hardly believe it. And Ginny, wait until I tell her."

His enthusiasm was infectious. For the first time in a very long time, Philip's laughter was unfeigned. "Go ahead. She shouldn't be kept waiting."

"No," Marcus agreed. "She's waited long enough."

He started toward the door, then stopped and turned back to his brother. "You knew about this?"

Philip nodded. "Father talked it over with me."

"And you don't object?"

Instead of answering directly, Philip asked, "Do you really think I would regard this as wrong?"

"You've fought and almost died to maintain a way of life that doesn't allow for this kind of thing."

Sarah held her breath. She looked from one to the other of the two men, so much alike and yet so different. Brothers, separated by a gulf few had ever managed to cross. Fate had placed them on opposite sides, but they had never really given in to that. She prayed they wouldn't do so now.

Philip shook his head slowly. "I fought for the good; it does exist though I know you don't think so. But I've always known there was much that needed to be changed. All I wanted was for us to be able to do it ourselves rather than have it imposed on us."

Marcus looked unconvinced. "The South will never change, unless it's forced to."

"But it already is," Philip said. "Too many men have died, too many others have had the arrogance knocked out of them, for anything to stay the same. Win or lose, the old South is gone."

Marcus raised the hand that grasped the papers and gestured suddenly at the empty sleeve. "Is that the price of change?"

Philip flinched but did not look away, "Nothing so noble. Merely bad luck."

"Really? Since when has it been bad luck to still be among the living?"

He turned away then and left the room, going quickly to find Ginny. In his wake he left silence.

_____ *Chapter Thirty-Three*

MARCUS STAYED; Overseer Davies left. It was an arrangement that suited everyone. The crops were brought in, and most of them did reach the government warehouses from which they were distributed to the troops. Philip tried to find satisfaction in helping to feed and clothe the army he could no longer fight with.

It seemed little enough to do. In July of that year, a scant few days after Charles's death, the South was defeated at Gettysburg and almost simultaneously, at Vicksburg. The tide had been turned. Philip knew it, so did a few others, but no one wanted to speak of it.

In Richmond, where Philip went in August to help coordinate the increasingly scarce supplies of ammunition and other war matériels, he found the mood stubbornly defiant. They had suffered setbacks, but they would recover. To suggest otherwise was treason.

He said it anyway. "This is the time to sue for peace. Both South and North are weary of the fighting. A compromise can be reached."

He was not heard, not even by as good a friend as Peter Rider, on leave from the army and looking a decade older than his true age. They shared a bottle at the Richmond Hotel and talked of better times, until Philip tried to steer the conversation to thoughts of peace.

"There can't be any," Peter said flatly, "not until the dead are avenged. How could you imagine otherwise?"

"Easily. I've seen the dead—not as often as you have, granted—but I remember clearly enough what they look like. If there is any truth to life it is that the dead are beyond all thought of us, all grief, all comfort and certainly all vengeance. They are gone, Peter. Nothing we do can change for one moment the finality of their deaths. What counts now is those who are still living."

He leaned back in his chair, glancing around the half-empty room. It was very late and most everyone had staggered off to bed. Only a few other men remained at scattered tables or leaning against the bar. He wondered how many of them were like him and Peter, seeking a refuge from nightmares.

"I have a brother-in-law fighting for the North," he said. "A young man named Nathan I've never even met. We get word of him occasionally. Sarah cries when she reads the letters. But then, she cries so rarely that she can hardly be blamed."

"I am sorry for that," Peter said as he refilled their glasses. "There is nothing worse than a family divided by this conflict, though it has happened often enough. At any rate, I better understand now your desire for peace."

"I would feel the same way if I had no brother-in-law at all. We are destroying ourselves with this insanity. It must stop."

"Insane or not," Peter said, "it will go on. Nothing you say or do can alter that." He rubbed a hand over his face pale with exhaustion and dark with the foreshadows of doom. "Go home, Philip. Look to the future and salvage what you can for it."

"You can do the same. We all can."

"No, for most of us the chance is past and will not come again."

"I can't accept that..."

"Then don't, but know that I do." Peter stared into his glass, swirling the bourbon absently. "I can't explain it exactly, but it's as though the world of peace and security that we all once knew no longer exists. There is no reality except the battlefield and the fighting. Even this—" he gestured around the room "—doesn't have any meaning. The struggle has become everything; it has absorbed us as surely as the ground absorbs the blood of the dead. Whatever it has taken—perhaps our souls themselves—we cannot get them back."

"Don't say that," Philip exclaimed. "It sounds as though you think you're already..."

"Dead? Sometimes I do. I've lain among bodies, slept among them, crawled over them, talked to them. The dead are no strangers to me. It's no exaggeration to say that they are among my dearest friends, very few of whom still remain among the living." Abruptly, he asked, "Did you know John Carlisle died at Vicksburg?"

Philip nodded. "I had heard that. As you said, so few are left."

Peter reached for the bottle. "Well, we mustn't get morbid. Have another drink."

They had several and fell asleep at the table. When Philip woke the next morning, he was alone.

SARAH FINISHED changing Elizabeth—Bethie as she had come to be called—and laid her gently in her crib. She protested, screwing up her small face and wiggling her chubby arms and legs, but her mother persevered. She knew through experience that Bethie would be asleep within minutes. She'd had a busy morning playing with William and visiting with Augusta and Ginny in the kitchen. Sarah smiled to herself. Tired though her daughter was, in an hour or so she would be fully recovered and ready to start over.

Which was more than she could say for herself. The August heat seemed more draining than in previous years. She tried to blame the heavy black dresses she wore out of respect for Charles, but she suspected her weariness had more to do with other factors.

She slipped out of the nursery quietly, thinking that she might steal a few minutes to herself away from the continual demands of the big house. Not that her own company was so appealing. She found her thoughts, and her fears, increasingly difficult to deal with and had become adept at avoiding both. A condition that, she knew, could not be allowed to continue.

It was not in her nature to hide from trouble, much as she would have liked to. Whatever was wrong she was determined to face it squarely and try to find some solution. In the back of her mind, it occurred to her that she was behaving much as her father would in a similar situation. Josiah had always had a talent for confronting unpleasant realities head-on. She had resented that for a long time, thinking it meant that he didn't care. Lately she had begun to wonder if she might have been wrong.

Despite Philip's and her own precautions, shortages were beginning to be felt at Calvert Oaks. Whereas once all the vegetables and dairy products produced there had been earmarked for use on the plantation, now many of them went to the army stores. About half the cattle had been butchered to help feed the troops and more would inevitably follow. Many of the horses were gone, a sacrifice she knew Philip especially regretted. Much of Calvert Oaks's finest breeding stock had perished on the battlefield.

Even if they had been able to hold on to the horses, there would be little enough to do with them. Racing meets were no longer held, along with balls, hunts and theater parties. Sarah hadn't realized how much she had enjoyed the social life of the South until it ceased. Isolated on the plantation, without recourse to the friendship of other women, she felt increasingly like a woman at the center of a storm. Which, to be fair, was exactly what she was.

A very lonely woman. She missed Philip dreadfully. Even knowing as she did that she was far more fortunate than most women to at least have her husband home, she couldn't help but feel that he was in every essential way absent.

His latest visit to Richmond had come almost as a relief. At least for a few days she could drop the pretense of being unaffected by his coldness. She could admit, if only to herself, how worried she was, all the more so because she had no idea how to deal with it.

Not that she hadn't tried. Walking through the gardens where she had gone for refuge, she stopped beside a rosebush ripe with pink blossoms and stared at them unseeingly. Her fingers curled around a rose, tracing the curve of drooping petals. Since Philip's return she had tried everything she could think of to help him recover, both physically and emotionally. Considering how close he had been to death and how strong he was now, she had succeeded at the former. But as for the latter...

Tears misted her eyes but she refused to let them fall. Her back straightened. She let go of the rose and looked toward the house, drowsing in the hot afternoon sun. Had there ever been a place lovelier or more gracious? Easy though it was to say that the beauty was a facade, hiding a terrible ugliness, she knew that wasn't really so. The house, and the way of life it represented, had much to recommend them: honor, decency, courage, reverence for the land and the need to keep faith with both past and future. Philip had believed that so much good could overcome the bad. He had been convinced that the South could not only exist without slavery but would also benefit from its end. But he had wanted to be the master of his own destiny, as well, and for that she could hardly blame him. Not sharing as she did the same need.

Beyond the house, linked to it by the covered portico, she could see Augusta through one of the kitchen windows. The old black woman was busy with preparations for supper. As Sarah watched she spoke to someone out of sight, then laughed energetically.

A wry smile played on Sarah's lips. She had a nerve moping around in the garden feeling sorry for herself when an aged slave who had never known anything but endless work could find something to joke about. If she had come out there with any idea of reaching a decision, it had not happened. She was no more certain than she had been before about what she should do. And that in itself told her something. She was waiting, like a swimmer floating in still water, for the current to catch her and take her in one direction or the other.

THAT NIGHT a storm blew up out of the west. It brought lashing rain and a high wind. Sarah had not really been asleep when it began. She left her bed and went into the nursery to check on Bethie. The baby was a little fretful, to the concern of the young slave girl who stayed in there at night to keep an eye on her. Sarah murmured for her to lie down again and soothed her daughter herself. Soon enough Bethie quieted, drifting into sleep with one small fist tucked against her mouth.

When Sarah returned to her room, she stood for a while at the tall window looking out at the storm, and remembering another night when she had done the same. She had changed a great deal from the young woman who had first come to Calvert Oaks. Experiences, both good and bad, had left their mark on her. There were things that she regretted: the brutality unleashed on Marcus; Charles's slow, anguishing death; the savage war neither side seemed able to end. But she did not, and she would not, regret anything to do with Philip. Not even his own suffering.

She shivered at that and wrapped her arms around herself. It seemed harsh not to pity him for the loss of his arm. Even now, when time should have dimmed the memory, she could hardly bear to remember those agonizing weeks after he had been brought home. Until he regained consciousness and realized his condition, she had helped to care for him and had seen for herself the results of the amputation performed in the field hospital by a harried surgeon fighting desperately against the tidal wave of wounded and dying. The saw he used to cut through the shattered flesh and bone had left a jagged, pitted stump. Lacking any anesthetic, Philip had not unexpectedly been overcome by shock, followed quickly by infection. By the time he had reached Calvert Oaks, he was close to death. In fact, Sarah might have given him up if she hadn't been so fiercely determined that no one should suffer so and not live.

And so he had, though increasingly she wondered if he blamed her for it.

The storm was growing worse, which suited Sarah. She needed some outlet for the emotions kept so tightly reined within her for so many months. The sudden need to feel cool rain on her face drove her to open the window and lean out. It was then that she heard the noises: a clatter of hooves on gravel, the jangle of bits and spurs, the low voices of two men, one white, the other black.

"Ahs takes care ob him, massa."

"Fine, Willy. Good night."

Philip. Without thinking Sarah grabbed up her wrap and headed for the door, thrusting her arms into it willy-nilly. She hurried down the curving stairs in time to see him go into the library. When she reached there, pausing at the door, he was standing in the shadows beside the empty fireplace. His back was to her, but she saw that his broad shoulders were slumped and his head bent.

"Philip." He did not hear her at first, but remained where he was unmoving until several seconds had passed. Only then did the sound reach him and he turned.

"I thought you'd be asleep."

"Not with the storm." She took a step toward him, stopped and looked at him closely. For all that he was clearly tired and travel-stained, he was still the most handsome and masculine man she knew. There was an air about him of strength combined with gentleness that seeped through her pores and touched her at the very center of her being.

No lamps were lit in the room, but the sky was the eerie silver gray that happens during such storms; it seemed to catch up and radiate the light from the distant sea. Off in the distance thunder rumbled. "How could I have forgotten," Philip said, "how much you enjoy storms."

His eyes were warm on her, and she knew what he was remembering. A night not so long after their marriage when, during another such storm, the last barriers of her modesty had dissolved and she had made passionate love to him. The memory was painful; he looked away.

"How is it in Richmond?" she asked, walking over to his desk and needlessly straightening the piles of papers set out there.

"The same. I saw Peter, by the way."

"He's all right?"

"He's...tired, I guess." He ran his hand through his damp hair, wondering as he did if she had any idea how beautiful she looked. The white lace nightgown and wrapper she wore seemed little more than a veil over her body. A body that he knew all too well had fully recovered from the demands of childbearing and remained as lovely as ever.

Lovely, and whole.

"You should go to bed," he said, more harshly than he intended.

Sarah bit her lip. A week before, even a day before, she would have taken the blow of his words and gone away. But standing out in the garden something had happened to her. Perhaps it was the scent of Elizabeth Calvert's roses reminding her of how beauty could endure even after death.

"Yes, I suppose I should, but before I do, will you tell me something?"

He looked wary, but nodded. "If I can."

"When do you intend to stop feeling sorry for yourself?"

He stared at her for a long moment, his face growing hard and taut. "I wasn't aware that I did."

"Then how else do you explain your behavior?" She really didn't mean to go on, but the reins held so firmly for so long had slipped and, given her head, she could not stop. "You lost an arm; that's very sad. But you still have your life, your home, your family. You're not lying in cold ground in an unmarked grave or dying slowly in a Northern prison camp. You're not like Peter Rider, trapped in one battle after another, never knowing when it will end, or if it ever will."

He stared at her, trying to frame his thoughts into words that would have meaning to them both. But all he could say was, "You're a woman; you know nothing about what it's like to be in battle, what it does to men."

His words had a terrible ring of finality, as though he was saying that the gulf between them could never be crossed. Her shoulders slumped slightly as she turned to go.

He hesitated a moment, then held out his hand to stop her. "Sarah . . . why . . . ?"

"Why what?"

"Nothing. You should go to bed."

"Tell me." She reached up and caught his face between her hands, taking him by surprise so that he was compelled to look at her. *"Tell me."*

"I woke up one day . . . I don't know exactly when, perhaps a few weeks after they brought me home . . . and I saw you looking at me. Or more correctly at what had been done to me. Your face was . . . twisted with disgust. You looked as though you were about to be ill."

"Is that why you . . . insisted I stop caring for you?"

"What else could I do? You were clearly sickened by the way I looked."

"No, it was nothing like that."

Wearily he shook his head. "Sarah, there's no reason to pretend with me. I don't blame you for how you feel."

"How very generous of you, especially considering that you have absolutely no sense of my feelings. In fact, I'll go further and say that you have no sense at all."

She whirled around and started for the door, only to be stopped by his hand on her arm.

"Sarah . . . wait. If I misjudged the situation, I'm sorry." He was also a good many other things: surprised, taken aback and—for the first time in a long time—hopeful.

"Sorry? That's all you can say, you're sorry? My God, when I think of all the nights I've lain awake..."

"No blasphemy, Sarah. It doesn't suit you."

She forced herself to take a deep breath, then she spoke in a rush. "If you thought that I could turn away from my husband simply because he was injured, you must have a very poor opinion of my character. So much so that I wonder why you ever married me."

"I married you," he said quietly, "to have a mother for William, a wife to bear more children for me and a mistress for my home."

"I see..."

"And then I fell in love with you. As, I believe, I have told you."

"Not," she said distantly, "in a very long time."

"Because I was afraid that you no longer loved me." When she would have protested, he went on. "I know I am not the man you married, or came to love. I have changed in more ways than simply losing my arm. So much of what I believed in has been proven false. Not only that, but what I cherished most, the ability to care for and protect all that I love, is now in serious doubt."

The words to refute what he had said were on her tongue, but she could not voice them. Not when she knew that he was right. Everything dear to them both was at risk and growing more so by the day. For the moment the tide of war had swept westward, but that would inevitably change. The South would fall like a great tree crashing in a storm, and as she did she would bring down many with her.

But not, Sarah was resolved, the Calverts. What their family was—the pride, the honor and yes, the love—that would survive. There would be changes, certainly, and hardships, but there would never be defeat. Not for Philip, and not for her. Whatever came, they would face it together, and in the sharing of pain and joy, find their ultimate victory.

She took his hand from her arm, touched it gently to her lips and went into his embrace.

Outside, the storm raged. Within, love and courage prevailed.

**An intriguing story
of a love that defies the boundaries of time.**

BEVERLY SOMMERS

Time and Again

Knocked unconscious by a violent earthquake, Lauren, a computer operator, wakes up to find that she is no longer in her familiar world of the 1980s, but back in 1906. She not only falls into another era but also into love, a love she had only known in her dreams. Funny...heartbreaking...always entertaining.

 WORLDWIDE LIBRARY

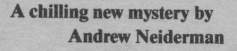